YOURS FOREVERMORE, DARCY

◈

KARALYNNE MACKRORY

Quills & Quartos
PUBLISHING

Copyright © 2019 by KaraLynne Mackrory

All rights reserved.

This is a work of fiction. Names, characters, businesses, places, events, locales, and incidents are either the products of the author's imagination or used in a fictitious manner. Any resemblance to actual persons, living or dead, or actual events is purely coincidental.

No part of this book may be reproduced in any form or by any electronic or mechanical means, including information storage and retrieval systems, without written permission from the author, except for the use of brief quotations in a book review.

Edited by Christina Boyd and Ellen Pickels

Cover Design by Ellen J Pickels

Sir Humphry Davy, Bt by Thomas Phillips © National Portrait Gallery, London

ISBN

Ebook 978-1-951033-13-2

Paperback 978-1-951033-14-9

Andy, you drew me with your smile, you wooed me with your love notes, and captured me with your heart. I am yours forevermore.

TABLE OF CONTENTS

Prologue	1
Chapter 1	3
Chapter 2	13
Chapter 3	23
Chapter 4	31
Chapter 5	42
Chapter 6	54
Chapter 7	64
Chapter 8	75
Chapter 9	87
Chapter 10	95
Chapter 11	103
Chapter 12	110
Chapter 13	125
Chapter 14	133
Chapter 15	146
Chapter 16	158
Chapter 17	171
Chapter 18	179
Chapter 19	189
Chapter 20	198
Chapter 21	206
Chapter 22	216
Epilogue	226
Acknowledgments	231
About the Author	233
Also by KaraLynne Mackrory	235

PROLOGUE

Darcy rubbed his face while he waited for the ink to dry. Groaning, he folded the missive then addressed and sealed it. It was to her—always her. Miss Elizabeth Bennet. Unfortunately, he was never to send her this letter or any others he had written her. It had begun as a cathartic activity for him to write to her. Whenever he had felt overwhelmed by his feelings, he would pull out a fresh sheet, address it to her, and write them down. Then, just like all the others, to finish it off, he would write her direction and seal it. Knowing that she would not receive it did not deter him. And now it had become a compulsion of sorts.

Looking at the letter sitting upon his desk, he laughed humourlessly for being so ridiculous. It was one thing to write to her. It was quite another to complete the process by preparing it to post. But in his mind, those final steps made him feel he was sealing his feelings away. The Darcy crest stamped into the hot wax was an ultimate statement that he had purged those feelings within him. Standing, Darcy went to his bookshelf, removed a large tome, and brought it to his desk. The volume had been hollowed out long before he assumed ownership of it from his father, who had used it as a secret hiding spot for important documents. But Darcy had since installed locks on his desk, so for years the tome had no purpose—until some many months before when he first met one Elizabeth Bennet of Longbourn and began to write. Now it held all his letters to her. Despite their innocuous nature, he was loath to part with any of them.

Tenderly, Darcy placed the latest letter on top of the others, closed the book, and replaced it at the corner of his desk instead of returning it to the shelf. He ought to have done so, but he was not yet ready to put that much distance, even an extra few feet, between himself and this connexion he held with Elizabeth. Drawing a deep breath, Darcy drew his estate book in front of him to look at the agenda for the day. He had a meeting scheduled soon with his solicitor, and it would not do to be so distracted. Glancing down at the date, he stilled. *Has it really been two months since Hunsford?* Nearly undone again, Darcy allowed his head to drop to the desk. He was still tortured by that day, his terrible words, and the hateful fire in her eyes, haunting him. Worst was the indelible fact that she was lost to him forevermore. He had written her then the only letter he had actually given her. Suddenly, the parting appellation in his most recent letter came back to his mind in full poignancy. His heart might forever be hers but she would never be his. He had accepted these terms, convincing himself that he ought to remember her in love and allow her rebuke to make him a better man.

Darcy stopped himself from reaching for another piece of paper. If he wrote to her every time his heart broke, he would be inundated with letters, their words surrounding him like a cage. Somehow, he must conquer this torment and be master again under good regulation. Determined, he began his preparation for the meeting with his solicitor, forcing himself to think of other things.

CHAPTER 1

Two Months Previous

The carriage door shut, and Colonel Richard Fitzwilliam turned to him with a smile on his face. "Well, I cannot say that I have ever enjoyed a visit to our Aunt Catherine more. What a difference a pretty face makes!"

While Richard laughed, Darcy winced and made some inconsequential sound of acknowledgement. Quickly, he schooled his expression. A pretty face, indeed—one that lit with brilliant fire when angry, as he well knew. *Blast! How could she be so stunning while uttering such heated words?*—words that consumed his every hope and wish. Darcy shook his head swiftly to knock the thought from his mind and studied his cousin.

Colonel Fitzwilliam had relaxed into the plush velvet of Darcy's carriage, ready for the journey back to London. His head was turned, and it dipped slightly to look out the window as the carriage passed through the grounds of Rosings Park. The smile still touching the edges of his mouth caused Darcy to clench his jaw with some emotion. *Jealousy? Probably.* And likely a mixture of all he felt since leaving the parsonage the day before: anger, disbelief, and ultimately despair. Looking at his cousin then, Fitzwilliam Darcy knew for the first time in his life what it was to covet. He coveted his cousin's serene countenance, his life's contentment, and the fact that *he* had not been rejected by the lady with whom he had hoped to spend the rest of his days. It mattered little that Richard had naught to do with Miss Elizabeth Bennet—Darcy winced again as the name passed through his mind—what mattered was that his life had purpose while Darcy's was consumed with this…this…nagging and infernal discontent.

A slow burn built in his breast as he remembered the day before. How could she so cruelly and thoroughly reject him? He was Fitzwilliam Darcy, for heaven's sake! Some said he was the most eligible and sought after bachelor in all of England. While he cared little for that appellation, he cared much for its removal. At least, he cared had a short four and twenty hours ago. Fury was a safe feeling to have, growing stronger in his spirit. It helped scorch the torn edges of his heart and pulled him back from the brink of another more vile emotion: desolation. She would not be his.

Darcy rolled his head to the side and also watched the gardens of Rosings pass as he tried to will his mind away from that avenue. Spring had come to Kent. In the short time he had been there, the gardens and landscape had been reborn into brilliant hues of greens and gold. He usually cared very little for the way his aunt liked her gardens. He had a biased preference for Pemberley, of course, where natural beauty had been so little counteracted by an awkward taste. Lady Catherine de Bourgh preferred ridged lines and sharply manicured hedges. Yet at present—in the chaos of his mind—he found the controlled, organised view of his aunt's gardens acutely reassuring. It firmed his resolve—and his jaw—to at once drag his wayward and battered heart back into severe control. It helped to dull away the unfathomable emptiness inside and put his poor judgement and past regrets aside. He could not have her, and he must—*by all that is holy!*—learn to live with it.

"The feelings, which you tell me have long prevented the acknowledgment of your regard, can have little difficulty in overcoming it."

She had said it the day before, and he hoped fervently that her words would prove true. He did not want to endure much more of this. The sooner he was in London, in the protection of his home and with his sister, the sooner he could forget this humiliation and his love for Miss Elizabeth Bennet of Longbourn.

As the carriage came within view of the parsonage, Darcy turned his head away from the window, unable to behold the structure that paid end to his future plans and levelled his life into rubble.

"Ah—and there is the good parson to wish us well on our journey," Richard said with a chuckle as he gave Mr Collins an animated wave. He turned his merry eyes back to Darcy and laughed again. "He was a ridiculous fellow, was he not?" Darcy could not agree more but remained silent as his cousin turned again towards the window, describing the enthusiasm with which his aunt's parson heralded their departure.

"I just wish I could have paid my farewells to the delightful Miss Bennet before we left," Richard said with true regret.

That startled Darcy and his averted gaze snapped back to his cousin. "Did she not return before you left this afternoon?"

"She did not, much to my disappointment." Richard's half smile bothered Darcy more than he wanted to admit.

"But you returned long after I did."

Richard shrugged as he twisted in his seat, presumably to catch the last sight of Hunsford Parsonage. "I stayed well beyond what was polite though Mrs Collins was kind enough to pretend otherwise. And still Miss Bennet remained out on her walk."

"Then she did not speak to you," Darcy said more to himself.

Richard frowned slightly at his cousin. "No, she did not."

Darcy's thoughts flew promptly to his letter and their encounter that morning. He had not slept all night for composing it, her accusations weighing heavily on his mind. In regards to his actions towards her sister and his friend, he could not but defend himself. He had acted as he thought a friend must. But with respect to that other weighty accusation of having injured Wickham—Darcy forced himself to draw in a deep breath to control the sudden fury he felt—he had no choice but to lay before her the whole of Wickham's connexion with the Darcy family. He had not realised until that moment how much he depended on her speaking to Richard to exonerate himself. If she had not returned from her walk, had never spoken to his cousin to verify Darcy's letter, then he had no assurance that she had read it. And still less hope that, if she did, she would believe him—so great was her dislike for him that he dared not think she would have trusted his word alone.

That uncertainty added yet another burden to his shoulders as he thought about how very much it pained him to think she was somewhere in the world and thinking ill of him. He hoped that letter might…with time…make her think better of him. That she, on reading it, might give credit to its contents. Darcy chastised himself for caring about what she thought. Had he not resolved moments ago to forget her and move on from such folly? Forget her he would, he vowed.

It was moments before Darcy began to be aware of the minute scrutiny directed at him from Richard.

"Out with it," Darcy huffed. "I am in no mood for your philosophizing gaze."

Colonel Fitzwilliam simply lifted his brows. "You look a right mess, Cousin."

Darcy groaned and looked away. It would have been better for him to ignore his cousin. He would have been sensible to pull out a book to read or, better yet, his writing desk. His hands twitched at the thought. He would certainly *not* tell Richard the reason for his mood.

"I am merely eager to return to London. I have much business, and our delays in leaving Kent have now caught up with me."

"*Our* delays?" Richard said with a smirk. "Forgive me if I do not lay claim to any responsibility in that quarter. I am at *your* disposal as you well know."

Darcy shook his head. "In any case, I need to return."

"I had thought"—Richard hedged with a smile—"that *our* delays had something to do with—"

"Miss Bennet was, as you stated earlier, a pretty face. One that I will admit detracted from the usual drear of Rosings. However, my decision to extend our stay—"

"—twice," Richard injected with a wry smile.

"Twice"—he allowed with a begrudging nod—"had everything to do with Aunt Catherine's estate business. All of which, I might remind you, fell at my feet while you traipsed around the countryside paying visits to pretty faces."

Darcy bitterly swallowed that falsehood and hoped his cousin would as well. He was relieved to see Richard acknowledge his word with a nod and say nothing further, though Darcy was uneasy with the gleam in his cousin's eye.

∽

Elizabeth remained by the window long after the dust from the carriage wheels settled. She had returned from her walk to have Charlotte inform her that both the gentlemen from Rosings had come to pay their farewells. Mr Darcy had stayed a short time but his cousin had waited quite a while for her return before he was obliged to return to his aunt's house and prepare for his departure. Darcy's letter was still in her hand, tucked between her fingers, its contents swirling in her head. She had watched silently from her bedchamber window as Mr Darcy's carriage drove by the parsonage. From above, she observed her cousin's absurd bowing and scraping as he waved animatedly at the passing equipage. One might think, with his vigorous salute, that he was glad to see them go rather than honouring them. Elizabeth could not help the blush that crept into her cheeks as she watched her cousin's display. Nor could she help feeling embarrassment to see Colonel Fitzwilliam lean out the window and return the gesture with equal enthusiasm, an act that thrilled Mr Collins into stunned immobility. Unfortunately, the paralysis was indeed momentary for he soon awakened from his awed stupor to redouble his ridiculous flapping adieus.

Of the other gentleman, she saw nothing.

It neither surprised nor upset her. He could be gone forever for all she cared for the man. When she recalled his proposal of marriage—*was it only yesterday?*—she shuddered, and righteous indignation coiled in her breast. His declaration of admiration and love was toppled by his pronouncement of familial and societal disapproval of the match. And though his eyes had pierced her with their gaze, emotion stirring mightily within them, she could not be moved by his ardency when presented with the evidence of his disapprobation for her connexions, wealth, and status. She was not insensible to the great compliment that she had garnered the affections of such an eligible and rich suitor, but she could not ignore the insults being handed out to her along with his hand.

Elizabeth turned from the window and padded back to her bed. Sitting against the headboard, she brought her hands together and absently turned the folded paper between her slim fingers. The letter, her first from any gentleman and one she ought not to have accepted considering the risks, was nearly as unsettling as the events of the evening past. Where she had felt confident in her fervent defence of both Jane and Mr Wickham last evening, now turning and tumbling through her fingers was an insignificant piece of parchment—covered fully by a strong, masculine script—that in the span of a few short hours had knocked loose the foundation of her argument.

Here was this explanation of his actions towards both. And what a contrariety of emotion they excited! Her feelings, as she read, were scarcely to be defined. Concerning her sister, she felt her emotions flux like the winds. When she considered the suffering her dear sister experienced at Mr Darcy's contrivance, her anger took flight with all the might of a great bird of prey. And that arrogant, presumptuous, and meddlesome *friend* of Mr Bingley was its target. How insufficient were his excuses upon her first reading. Jane was not indifferent but merely shy!

His words—one could scarcely conceive how they tortured her. His description of her family—their impropriety stabbed her with painful recollections, and she must concede his misgivings in that quarter.

When next she read his narrative about Mr Wickham, fully believing his excuses proved insufficient, her powers of cognition failed her. Astonishment, apprehension, and even horror oppressed her. How wrongly she had judged the whole affair—Mr Wickham, the perpetrator, and Mr Darcy, the acquitted! Never could she have conceived that Mr Darcy had the means to exonerate himself of Mr Wickham's charges, yet with perfect acuity, he did and with total absolution.

Elizabeth drew the heels of her hands up and pressed them into her eyes as they had become traitorously wet with the recollection of her folly regarding the two gentlemen. How staunchly she had vilified one while defending the other—and all because her pride had been hurt by one unintended moment of disregard. Sliding down the counterpane, she lay flat and stared blankly up at the ceiling as silent tears rolled down her cheeks to the pillow.

She recalled with a biting pain that, whilst in the grove after discovering how blind and partial were her prejudices favouring Mr Wickham, she returned to Darcy's explanation regarding her sister and Mr Bingley.

A second perusal with less strength to protest allowed for a broader understanding. When he confided his belief in Jane's indifference, she at once remembered Charlotte's warning of Jane's earlier reticence. Elizabeth could then give credence to his views of the matter though it was some time, she confessed, before she was reasonable enough to allow their justice.

A knock at her door brought Elizabeth out of her tumult of emotions. After quickly tucking Darcy's letter in her pocket, she wiped her eyes of the evidence that anything was amiss and opened the door to Charlotte.

"Mr Collins has gone off to console Lady Catherine on the loss of her nephews. I thought perhaps you might like to walk with me into the village."

Elizabeth smiled and, though it did not reach her eyes, was grateful for the distraction. "I will be down directly. I have a letter to post that I must ready."

Charlotte smiled and went on to collect her sister Maria as well.

Elizabeth quickly turned to her travelling trunk, and reaching deep into the back, tucked Mr Darcy's letter in a pocket. She then hurried to finish a note to her father, affirming their plans for departure within a se'nnight. Her quill paused just above her signature as she thought of her return home. How glad she suddenly felt to soon be reunited with Jane. After a brief visit in London at her Aunt and Uncle Gardiner's, they both would be travelling on to Longbourn.

How exceedingly glad was she that the remaining time in Kent would be free of a certain gentleman. Considering the variety of emotions with which she was burdened—not to mention the discord of their recent meeting—if she never saw Mr Fitzwilliam Darcy again, it would be too soon.

～

Not an hour into the journey, Darcy decided to pull out his writing desk. He hoped it would give him the needed distraction and keep his cousin from wishing to converse. He was in no mood for civility. Though he longed for the relief writing a certain letter might bring, he rigidly kept himself to dealing only with correspondence of non-clandestine origins.

It would not do to indulge in the temporary relief he had found in that secret habit—and certainly not in full view of Richard. Though writing letters to Elizabeth helped him manage his thoughts and dispatch them, it was a crutch and, considering the disastrous four and twenty hours, a habit he ought to break. Still, his hand paused over a fresh sheet of parchment, his fingers tapping a slow rhythm as he fought the temptation.

Darcy slid his nimble hand along the underside of a cubby drawer in his travelling desk, tripping a hidden lever. Silently, a secret compartment opened, and a letter was exposed. Being careful to keep it from his cousin, Darcy fingered the folded missive, his thumb running over her name in his script. *Miss Elizabeth Bennet*: such a beautiful name to precede these words of burden. Perhaps he ought to have chosen better and burned the letters as soon as they were created. Maybe it would do his battered heart good to let go of her—any connexion to her, even the ones he created himself.

Mutely, he touched the edges of the hidden letter. He had written it while in Kent. When he returned to London, he would transfer it to join the others in the tome in his study. They were secret relicts of his heart, protected from the eyes of their intended recipient.

The details of the letter he gave her that morning poured over him with an acute mixture of pain and pleasure. What bitter irony that the one letter he had written and given to her would be filled with the pains of his misdeeds and past misery. Recalling that letter, its providence, and the happenstance that provoked its creation pulled the emptiness from his eyes as he gazed on the other. Instead, his brown eyes were filled with anger again as he fought the great demon of despair once more.

With jerking movements, Darcy shoved the letter back into its hiding place and closed the compartment. When he returned to London, he would destroy it along with the others in the volume. He did not need any reminders of his ill judgments. He did not need further proof of his foolishness.

Luckily, he had secured the letter before a sudden lurch of the carriage sent his writing desk flying and tumbling across the squabs next to his cousin. Their eyes met as they braced themselves against the sides of the carriage, which groaned and lumbered in sudden jolts then stopped at an odd angle.

Darcy could hear his grooms shouting to one another and then calling out to him and his cousin to ascertain they were unharmed. He felt the movement as his men jumped from the carriage to the ground.

"What the blast has happened?" Colonel Fitzwilliam exclaimed, holding himself upright while his side of the carriage dipped unnaturally.

"I intend to find out." Darcy opened the carriage door and jumped out.

His cousin quickly followed, and together they walked to the front of the equipage to survey the damage. One of his grooms was bent low to look under the carriage, and another was out of sight. His voice carried his discoveries from the other side of the carriage. "She busted near through over 'ere."

Darcy addressed his head groom. "John, what has happened?"

The man crouched in front of him sprang up and, tugging at his forelock, replaced his livery hat. "We 'it a ridge aboot 'alf a mile back—"

"Yes, I felt the bump," Darcy answered, urging his groom on as he bent himself to look at the undercarriage himself.

"Affer I 'eard the creakin' but thought naught of it, seein' as the roads were soft. I figure it were just the conditions." He squatted down near his master and pointed to the front axle spring as it ran across the length of the carriage. There Darcy could easily see the substantial crack running deep through the fore carriage. He groaned and rubbed a hand across his face.

His driver apologised profusely for his poor judgement, to which Darcy immediately assured the man it was of no consequence though he knew that was not the case. A break of such magnitude would require many days to fix, and he wanted—nay, needed—to be as far from Kent as he possibly could. He turned to his driver as he stood and dusted off his trousers.

"Can it be driven, do you think?" Darcy asked with little hope.

His cousin laughed as he stood up after making his own inspection. "I very much doubt even you could command this carriage to move, Darcy."

Darcy ignored his cousin's jest, turning to his groom instead.

The man shook his head and, pulling his hat once again from his head, ran a leathery hand through his hair. "She's as good as done, sir." He then added that they might be able to hire a carriage in the village about a mile back. They would have to unload this one and wrap the broken axel tightly with rope to add enough support for it to get to a coaching inn.

"Very well. Send James off for the carriage, and we will wait here," Darcy said with reluctance. Alarm then began to creep into his chest that he might not have such an easy escape to London.

After he and Colonel Fitzwilliam watched his groom ride one of the carriage horses bareback down the road back to the town, Darcy surveyed the area around them. He was familiar with the journey to and from his aunt's house, and the recognition of their location plunged his spirits. They were not far from Rosings, no more than an hour. How futile had his efforts been to escape, he thought with a humourless laugh.

"There, there Darcy." Richard laughed, patting his cousin abruptly on the back. "It is only a carriage. You look as if you have lost something far more precious!"

Darcy's eye twitched at his cousin's words, but he remained stoic in his expression. "Do you not see, Richard, what a delay this will cause in our return to London? I have serious doubts it can be accomplished by the evening!"

Darcy watched Richard shrug without a care. "Then we do not get to London tonight."

Darcy walked away before his temper, which had almost nothing to do with his cousin, caused him to say something he knew would be intemperate. Thinking of intemperance, Darcy instead directed his feet back to the carriage where he reached into the drawer beneath the seat, pulled out a decanter, and filled one of the two crystal glasses held within its velvet folds. He quickly downed the burning liquid, relishing the warmth spreading immediately through him.

"Ah, now you have hit on an excellent idea." Richard took the decanter from his hands and filled his own glass, leaning nonchalantly against the dipping carriage to savour his drink. Darcy did the same, and the two were silent for a time.

Eventually, the colonel spoke. His voice was quiet and devoid of his usual flippancy. "Do you want to tell me what great burden you are struggling under presently?"

Darcy turned flat and hollow eyes lazily towards his cousin, who did not look at him but remained acutely interested in the contents of his glass.

Sighing, Darcy rested his head back against the carriage and looked up into the darkening sky. *How long have we been waiting for the groom to return? Never mind.* Darcy shook away the thought. It was only a distraction from his cousin's inquiry anyway. Though Darcy trusted his cousin implicitly, the wounds were so fresh from the day before that he could not utter any words for a time.

"You are correct in your assessment of my current mood, Richard, but I cannot give you the satisfaction of a complete answer at present. Words defy me as my mind has yet to comprehend it."

That small confession caused Richard to frown as he met his cousin's eyes. He could not determine what he saw there but knew that Darcy was telling the truth. Whatever oppressed him was too great to sort through easily. Little did Richard like to see his cousin burdened in such a way, yet he knew that, if Darcy could make no sense of the issue, he likewise would be of no help to him.

Within the hour, hoof beats reached their ears, and they both turned to see Darcy's groom returning. The town had one livery stable—*thank the heavens at least for that!*—no inn, and only a donkey cart to hire. The groom had managed to engage two plough nags from a nearby farmer for the gentlemen to ride. Reluctantly, Darcy agreed that the easiest course would be to load the trunks onto the donkey cart and ride the dilapidated beasts back to Rosings. If he were lucky, from there he would borrow one of his aunt's carriages, and damned if he would not leave for London the next day. He was nearly certain his heart could not handle seeing Elizabeth again, not after all it had suffered. His own carriage could take all the time in the world to be repaired as long as *he* escaped from Kent.

CHAPTER 2

◆◆◆

Never in my life..." Darcy's voice drifted away appalled.

Colonel Fitzwilliam grunted in matching disgust as he eyed the sorry excuses for horseflesh before them. The nags, brought by Darcy's groom to carry them back to Rosings that evening, might as well be dead for all the life they looked to have in them. His gaze shifted at the sound of protest from one of the animals as the groom prompted the horses closer for the gentlemen to mount.

Laughter rumbled up through Darcy's chest, surprising him as the volume grew. He could not think of a more fitting end to the worst four and twenty hours of his life. His cousin, naturally bent towards humour, soon joined him as they walked hesitantly towards the horses. Man and beast eyed each other with equal apprehension.

His voice laced with mischief, Richard said, "Care to place a wager, Cousin?"

Darcy did not answer at first; instead, his eyes widened with alarm at the unsettling sound emitted by his mount after he settled into the saddle. He looked over at his cousin, lips pursed in apprehension and humour still dancing in his eyes.

Remembering his cousin's challenge, Darcy answered, "You know, Richard, if this were Salazar, I would not hesitate to race you. Salazar would and has many times bested your Moros soundly in the past. However"—Darcy paused as he looked down upon the half-alive beast he now sat upon—"I cannot think a race the most prudent of choices with these glue pots."

Colonel Fitzwilliam laughed. "I must concur, my dear man. Mine looks more like to fall over if the wind picks up than he is to win any derby."

Darcy smiled in response. Anticipating the long ride back to Rosings, he cursed himself for sending his and Richard's mounts on ahead of the carriage though that was his custom.

"No, what I propose is that, should we be lucky enough to make it back to Rosings"—Richard clasped his hands together and gestured in pious supplication to the ever-darkening heavens above them, prompting a good laugh from his cousin—"the gentleman who arrives last must bear the esteemed privilege of an audience with our aunt to inform her of our return."

Darcy grimaced at the thought. His aunt was likely to expound on a wide range of topics: from the imprudence of travelling in a broken carriage to the providence of such an event occurring. She would likely see it as another opportunity to ensnare from him that coveted proposal to her daughter Anne. Darcy's eyes darkened suddenly as he thought upon the proposal he *had* bestowed during that visit to Rosings and the callous way in which it was rejected by its recipient. The pain slashed through him again, erasing from his features all the hard-won joviality that the banter with his cousin over the nags had produced. Despite Richard's observant nature, Darcy was grateful to have him nearby. He provided much needed relief from such oppressing thoughts. Attempting to laugh or smile with Richard helped Darcy learn to mask the darkness dwelling in his heart. With a shake of his head, he wasted little more thought on the subject before accepting his cousin's bet and adding, "And the loser must also secure from Aunt Catherine the use of her carriage for tomorrow."

Colonel Fitzwilliam laughed darkly, shaking his head as he contemplated such an unpleasant task. Lady Catherine would likely do anything or give anything to Darcy should he ask, as he was her favourite. However, she would not be as amenable to *him*. Furthermore, asking any favour of his aunt always came with some cost, even for Darcy. His eyes blazed as he smiled in acknowledgement.

"Good luck, my dear cousin. But I must warn you, I am not afraid of you."

Darcy laughed, though the smile did not reach his eyes, as the two gingerly directed their mounts towards Rosings. They exchanged scowls as the horses made their first halting steps and began plodding along at an even, pitiful pace. After nearly an hour, they were just reaching the outskirts of the back farms of Rosings. Darcy groaned as he contemplated that, even with his prime stallion given his head, the remaining journey would take more than twenty minutes to reach the stable yard of his aunt's home. He shifted and twisted as he stretched his back to try to alleviate the tense muscles there as he had felt every step of the dilapidated horse's gait over the past hour. He was rubbing his neck when his cousin spoke, a challenge in his voice.

"I will give you the advantage of the choice. Here we might split ways and make this wager more interesting. You may choose to keep to the road or take the shortcut through the back fields."

Darcy thought on the advantages of each before choosing the road. It might be slightly longer, but he was certain it would be easier on his mount. He did not relish the idea of being stranded far from the manor house and left to walk the rest of the way because his barely ambulatory horse came up lame. Darcy hid a smile that tugged at his lips when he informed his cousin of his choice. Let Richard, reckless risk-taker that he was, follow through the fields. He would stick to the steady, predictable, and safe road. He had once chosen recklessly, and little did it gain him, he thought bitterly.

~

Mr Collins arrived back at the parsonage in particularly high spirits as he expounded repeatedly on the great benefit he was to his dear patroness. Elizabeth rolled her eyes as she heard him once again describe how fortunate it was that he was in a position to give comfort to the great lady so soon upon the loss of her nephews. The ladies had withstood the loss of his company earlier in the afternoon by enjoying a pleasant walk to the village. When a note later arrived from the great house, informing them that Mr Collins had been asked to stay to continue administering to Lady Catherine through supper, the ladies of Hunsford Parsonage bore their abandonment with great composure. Upon his return, just as the skies were beginning to darken, he spoke of nothing but Rosings, Lady Catherine, and his meal there.

For Elizabeth, it had been a great pleasure to dine with Charlotte and Maria without her cousin. She enjoyed the bond of friendship—and it successfully distracted her mind from a particular letter from a certain gentleman—without the interruption of Mr Collins.

"I daresay Lady Catherine was quite displeased to have them leave so quickly. I do not doubt that my kind words brought solace to her."

"I believe, dear, that Mr Darcy and Colonel Fitzwilliam did not depart as you say, 'quickly.' It was my understanding that they delayed their original departure twice," Charlotte said with a glance at Elizabeth for confirmation.

Elizabeth could not meet her friend's eyes and instead studiously kept their attention on the piece of stitching she held in her hands. She could not like that Charlotte assumed Elizabeth might have such intimate knowledge of the gentlemen's plans. Nor did she wish to contemplate the reasons Mr Darcy might have delayed his departure.

"And so they should have, my dear Charlotte! For their aunt is the very expression of congeniality, and she desires, above all, their presence. It is only natural, and I might add the Christian way, that they should extend their stay to please their aunt. I only question whether they might not have arranged to stay longer—but here I ought to stop, for I do not like to criticise any relation of my esteemed patroness even if they display a lack of consideration."

Mr Collins moved on graciously, in his mind, to the topic of the great pleasure he experienced and the generous condescension of Lady Catherine with regards to the menu at Rosings that evening. With much forbearance, the ladies of the house withstood the description of each remove. When the maid came with tea, Elizabeth sighed in relief, for after the tea was finished, she could seek her bed without suspicion.

~

Darcy thought he was making excellent time as he found that, though the horse protested meekly, he could persuade it to a faster pace than he had previously thought the beast was capable. Though still no better than a walk, at least his movement was quicker than it had been aside his cousin before they parted ways. Darcy was confident that more than made up for any slight advantage of distance his cousin held, and with the regularity of the road, he believed the wager was as good as won. He relished the fantasy of sinking into the plush leather armchair in his aunt's library with a relaxing glass of brandy after his long ride. He would savour the taste of the drink with a satisfied smirk as he listened to the voluminous strains of his aunt's voice as she admonished Richard and manipulated him to do her bidding in return for the borrowed carriage.

It would seem he remained in his dream-state longer than he thought for, when he came to the present, he realised he was quite close to Rosings. He rounded the familiar bend with the attitude of a confirmed winner only to pull up short at the sight of the parsonage before him.

How could he have forgotten that, by taking the path of the roads, he would pass right by where *she* was? A great well of emotion then choked him as he felt the full weight of her loss. Looking at the glow from the window as it spread out upon the ground below it, Darcy experienced a magnificent searing through his heart.

A shadow passed near enough to the window for him to recognise her through the wispy window coverings. Though he could not see her in detail, he knew her form as well as he knew his heart. And that heart, though broken, still traitorously beat for her.

Swiftly, Darcy turned away, urged his horse on, and refused to look towards the parsonage again. He encouraged the anger back into his heart. How grateful he was that he never would have to bear the pain and pleasure of seeing her lovely face again.

The feeling her words engendered echoed through the gaping hole he felt in his chest for the duration of the ride to Rosings. *"You could not have made me the offer of your hand in any possible way that would have tempted me to accept it."*

∼

Darcy could not remember a time when he had been so pleased to arrive at Rosings than when his hired horse's steady clopping ended in front of the home of his aunt and he saw the liveried groom approach to receive his mount.

Immediately, he asked, "Has my cousin arrived yet?"

The young man responded with a bow. "Welcome back to Rosings, sir. I have not seen the colonel arrive, sir."

Satisfied, Darcy motioned to his valise and writing desk, strapped to the sides of the horse, and asked that they be brought to his suite as soon as possible. Darcy then took the stairs to the house two at a time, the thrill of having won the wager effectively erasing the last of his morose thoughts. When he entered his aunt's home, he was greeted by the surprised butler, who was nevertheless quick to order a footman to retrieve his coat and hat.

"Our carriage axle broke outside of Dunton Green, Gibbons. We shall stay only the night and use my aunt's carriage to convey us to London tomorrow."

"Very good, sir. Welcome back to Rosings."

Darcy stopped on his way towards the stairs, and with a laugh, he turned back to the butler. "When my cousin arrives, show him to my aunt and inform him that I shall be in the library should he need me after his interview with her."

"It shall be done, sir."

The butler waited to see whether Mr Darcy had any other requests before walking with purpose towards the parlour where her ladyship remained after her parson had departed and her daughter had retired for the evening.

It was with great pleasure that Lady Catherine's butler was able to inform his mistress of the news of her nephew's arrival.

Once assured of their wellbeing after the carriage break, Lady Catherine exclaimed, "A carriage accident! Indeed, that is most alarming. But you say, Gibbons, that my nephew plans to depart again on the morrow?"

The long-time servant, oddly loyal where most were not, could see the disappointment in his mistress's eyes at the news that the gentlemen were to leave so soon.

Gibbons turned, and under the guise of checking the mantel for dust with a swipe of his perfectly white glove, he said, "Mr Darcy mentioned the use of your carriage to convey them to London tomorrow. I only wish I had known that this misfortune would befall your dear nephew, my lady."

Lady Catherine, catching the glint in her butler's eye and having always entrusted him with her most personal orders asked, "Why is that, Gibbons? Out with it. I must hear why you say that!"

"It is nothing, your ladyship. I shall simply send word to the coach maker that his services will not be needed for…at the very least…a few days and not until your carriage can safely return from transporting your nephews to London."

The edges of Lady Catherine's mouth began to pull up in a slow smile as she understood her butler's suggestion. She had ordered the velvet seat coverings to be replaced, and though they did not need immediate attention and could be delayed any number of days, it served a purpose. At that moment, Lady Catherine had her doubts that the coach maker had even been hired for the job.

"You will do no such thing, Gibbons. My character has ever been celebrated for its austerity and nobility, and in such a moment as this, I shall certainly not depart from it. I cannot fathom the neglect of a family carriage in such days as these. No, the squabs must be replaced. My nephews will simply have to stay until they are ready. I will not be moved on this."

The butler withheld a knowing smile as he bowed and prepared to exit the room just as the arrival of Colonel Fitzwilliam was heard in the vestibule.

"Gibbons!" Lady Catherine barked. "Have the grooms remove the squabs this evening. I shall not have any time wasted."

"Yes, your ladyship." With another bow as he left his mistress with a smirk on her face, Gibbons went to see to Colonel Fitzwilliam's arrival. He could hear some commotion at the door that sped his steps until he came to an abrupt stop, struck with disbelief at the sight of the usually impeccable military man.

With only the slightest hesitation, Gibbons lifted his nose and went forward to greet his mistress's nephew. Years as butler guaranteed his face gave away none of the disgust he felt—neither at the stench coming off the colonel nor at the puddle of questionable substance pooling around his feet on the polished floors. He did not even blink when his ears caught the many curses coming from the black-smeared face of Colonel Fitzwilliam.

"Blast! Careful, my good man!" Colonel Fitzwilliam cursed as the footman attempted to remove his jacket, jarring his tender shoulder. He had made a serious miscalculation in strategy by allowing Darcy to choose the road instead of the shortcut through the fields. He knew Darcy would choose the predictable path and had hoped that would be the case. Not a mile into the journey, the horse met with a pasture of clover and refused to go another step. Dismounting, Colonel Fitzwilliam had tried to urge the horse onward to no avail. The horse puffed disinterestedly at him and bent his large, grey nose back to the ground for another mouthful. Disgruntled, but by no means in a mood to forfeit, the colonel had untied his belongings and hauled them himself in the direction of Rosings.

Fearing he would lose the wager to Darcy, Colonel Fitzwilliam quickened his pace as he traipsed through the farmland. He was a trained professional and no stranger to long, arduous physical activity. But, in the dark, he was still no better prepared to encounter the sudden loss of earth beneath his feet as he stumbled unexpectedly upon a small ravine. Sliding the short distance down its muddied slope initially caused no injury to him physically, but his pride smarted at the stench of livestock that adhered to his backside as he came to a halt most unluckily in a pile of—

"Shall I call for your bath, sir," Gibbons asked with a pinched sniff of the air.

"Please, but first: Has my cousin arrived yet?" Richard held his breath, ever hopeful.

"Mr Darcy is arrived and awaiting you in the library, sir." The butler paused, allowing a stoic eye to pass over the colonel's appearance. "He said you are to find him there after your interview with her ladyship."

Colonel Fitzwilliam was in no mood for his aunt's imperious butler, whose tone of voice just then indicated his disapproval of such an interview in his current state. He groaned, both in frustration for having lost the wager—thus having to see to his aunt—and at the thought of approaching her in such a state. Never would he present himself in similar disadvantage to any foe, and when facing his aunt, the greatest of foes, he needed every advantage.

"I shall clean up and see to my aunt presently. Thank you, Gibbons," Colonel Fitzwilliam said with steel in his voice.

He and his muddy attire slopped their way up the stairs to his chambers, ignoring the distinct sound of disapproval from the butler as he went. He could hear the sound of the donkey cart on the gravel drive and snorted at the luck of it all. He could have ridden with the trunks and arrived safely without the indignity he was even now experiencing.

～

Darcy choked on the sip of brandy he had just swallowed when he saw his cousin walk into the library, an expression on his face so savage that it led Darcy to understand immediately how Richard had swiftly climbed the ranks of His Majesty's army at such a young age. Darcy could not imagine a more fearsome creature than his cousin was at that moment.

He watched silently as the colonel strode with determined steps to the sidebar, poured himself a substantial amount of brandy, and downed the liquid with impressive vigour. Darcy swallowed a teasing retort, waiting for his cousin's temper to cool. He had heard some commotion when Richard arrived and much later the sound of his cousin addressing his aunt in muffled tones. Darcy smiled as he pictured the torture of such a conversation.

Finally, Colonel Fitzwilliam settled himself into the opposing armchair and glared at the fireplace. When he lifted his glass to drink from it, Darcy noticed him wince.

"What did you do to your shoulder?"

Colonel Fitzwilliam glared. The seriousness, contrasting so astoundingly with his usual jovial countenance, caused Darcy to smile at the incongruence.

"A setback upon climbing out of a ravine."

Darcy's lips twitched. "And you were in the aforementioned troublesome ravine because…?"

Darcy waited as Richard's lips twitched as well, his usual high spirits returning again at the memory, perhaps smarting a little less.

"I did not foresee the troublesome ravine before I was upon it—or rather, sliding down it."

Darcy laughed then, imagining the indignity of it all. With a sniff of the air, he began to detect something more, and said, with humour in his expression, "Did the troublesome ravine perhaps hold the ordure of—"

"Blast!" Richard interrupted with a laugh, sniffing himself. "I thought I had rid myself of it in my bath."

Darcy pulled a handkerchief from his pocket and made to cover his nose in exaggeration. "I hope the horse fared better than you, Cousin."

Richard chuckled and stood to return his glass to the sideboard. "He fared much better. While I landed in…something foul, he landed in clover."

Colonel Fitzwilliam was pleased to see a lessening of the dark shadows that had previously been so obvious in Darcy's eyes. He did not know what had put them there, and caring as he did for Darcy, he did not wish their return. He worried they *would* return, however, after he relayed the sum of his interview with his aunt.

Expecting to be further entertained by his cousin's interview with Aunt Catherine, Darcy sobered, observing the concern on Richard's face. "Your interview with Aunt Catherine was rather short."

Richard looked up at this, turning from his examination of his sleeve. "It was rather painless actually."

"What did you have to promise in return for the use of her carriage?"

"She asked nothing, which is all the more troubling, I fear."

Surprised, Darcy sat back and rubbed his chin. "You must have misunderstood her. Are you certain she made no subtle hints at…?"

"She made no requests, Darcy, and her explanation is far less complicated or devious than you might think."

Darcy lifted a brow at that, and a foreboding began to lurk at the back of his neck, running ominous fingers of dread up his spine.

"And?" Darcy asked carefully.

"We cannot borrow her carriage—"

"She would not allow it?" Darcy sat forward, appalled at the selfishness of his aunt—extreme even for her, he thought. He stood, prepared to use his power over her on the matter when Richard spoke again, preventing his departure.

"Her carriages are not available, Darcy. She has ordered the seats reupholstered. Currently, they—none of them—have any seat coverings."

"Impossible! All of them, you say?" Darcy sputtered in disbelief at his unquestionable misfortune. Refusing to allow his mind to contemplate staying any longer in Kent—*near her*—he questioned further. "She has four of them. How is she to go anywhere herself if she has no transport?"

"I asked, and she said that she had no previous engagements and, as her character was celebrated for its economy, had all readied at once."

Darcy, suddenly feeling utterly defeated, slipped heavily into the nearest chair and ran his hands through his hair as his head hung dejectedly. When his eyes began to sting with the threat of disgracing him, he covered his face with his hands and breathed in great heaping breaths to rein in his emotions.

Richard thought it best not to question his cousin's state of distress over the news and give the man his dignity. "So…we must delay our return a few days at least. Your carriage ought to be fixed in a couple of days, or if you really must return, we can go by post."

Darcy thought it an excellent alternative and was tempted beyond reason, despite the conditions of such travel, to book his way with haste.

What stopped him, however, was the thought that Elizabeth was to travel by post. Though he knew her plans were to quit Kent in a se'nnight, might she have altered them after their disastrous encounter the previous evening? No, Darcy could not risk it. Painful as it was, there was no reason he had to leave the grounds of Rosings or even the manor house itself. He did not have to encounter her.

"You will excuse me, Richard. It has been a long day." Darcy stood to leave again, intending on reaching his chambers—perhaps purging the gulf of emotion by means of a letter and drinking himself into a stupor despite his usually conservative habits. He longed for oblivion and knew of no other way to reach it.

"Darcy, shall I book us tickets on tomorrow's post?"

Darcy stopped at the door, his hand lifted, ready to push it open. Without turning, he answered, "We shall wait for my carriage to be repaired."

"Very well then, get some sleep, and I shall see you in the morning."

Colonel Fitzwilliam frowned as his cousin nodded silently and slipped from the room, his shoulders looking to have borne the weight of the world. The colonel's attention was then drawn to the window as a crack of thunder vibrated through the glass. A tempest had rolled in, and he could see the blanket of oppressive rain pound at the ground when another flash of lightning lit the sky. He turned and looked at the library door his cousin had exited. A dark storm had certainly arrived.

CHAPTER 3

◆◆◆

HAD THERE NOT BEEN A SERMON TO WRITE FOR THE UPCOMING SABBATH, MR Collins might have been in a pitiable state. From the day of the gentlemen's departure to the day five days hence, there was such a succession of rain as prevented his walking to Rosings even once. No Lady Catherine, no efficacious compliments, and no tea at the great house could be sought. Even Elizabeth might have found some trial of her patience in weather that totally suspended her daily walks around the grounds had she not had the distracting company of Charlotte. However, despite her friend, she was often left to her own thoughts that—much to her dismay—frequently turned towards one gentleman. Unjustly, when Mr Darcy left, he had not taken with him her thoughts of him. Had she known that the object of her troubled musings was once again in residence at Rosings Park, she might have found her rain incarceration a blessing. His letter and the explanation contained within kept her emotions in such a flux of contrary states as to make it entirely beyond her to fix on one determined opinion of the man.

Despite all that, when Elizabeth awoke on the morning five days after receiving Mr Darcy's letter and saw dappled sunlight streaking through the lace curtains of her room, her spirits lifted, and she quickly readied herself to walk out.

Stepping across the threshold at the back of the parsonage, Elizabeth's upturned face met the early morning sun and breathed in its warmth with pleasure. She remained thus only a minute before securing her bonnet in place and, with a smile touching the edges of her lips, set out briskly through the small garden to the gate leading to the grove. She let the environment choose her path as she enjoyed the verdant landscape and nature's symphony. Birds sang their unique praise while woodland creatures scurried across branches and down trunks in search of food. It seemed to Elizabeth that all of God's creatures were also pleased with the cessation of rain.

Refreshed from her exercise, Elizabeth slowed her steps as she allowed her musings to return to the topic most frequented during the recent poor weather. Expending some energy allowed her thoughts to clear. Mr Darcy had been wrong in his addresses to her. He had been uncivil and arrogant in his assumption. The sting of his words still smarted as she remembered his decided description of her deficiencies in status, wealth, and connexions. His sense of her inferiority, of its being a degradation, and of the family obstacles that judgement had always opposed to inclination were dwelt on with warmth. He had spoken of anxiety and apprehension, but she remembered the line of his jaw and the calmness of his countenance that exposed the real security he believed in his suit.

His security ought to have infuriated her, and at the time of his proposal, it had. As unfathomable as it was, that security now brought her offended sensibilities around to another feeling—something more compassionate in nature, less defensive of her own wounded pride, and strangely like concern for the immense disappointment one might feel when receiving an answer contrary to expectations. Mr Darcy had certainly thought she would accept his hand, and while his objections, apprehensions, and struggles will have been some comfort for him during the past few days, still her answer must have bought him *some* pain.

She allowed that his justification regarding Bingley and Jane, though insufficient, had allowed her to see his perspective. And his account of his history with Mr Wickham went a long way towards softening his great dark shadow in her mind. Still, his manners in society, aside from both these matters, were always reprehensible. No matter how much concern or compassion Elizabeth might have towards any disappointment Mr Darcy might feel, nothing could change her opinion of his character in that area. Mr Darcy was Mr Darcy still: arrogant, presumptuous, and above his peers.

A frown marred Elizabeth's sun-kissed face as she realised her footsteps had led her directly to the principal gate into the formal gardens of Rosings. During the entirety of her stay in Kent, she had preferred the more natural, sprawling landscape of the grounds beyond. The rigid pathways, manicured lawns, and chiselled topiaries of the formal gardens had never appealed to her. Though they were lush with a painter's touch and colourful blooms bursting everywhere, Elizabeth had not taken any of her walks in their direction.

She looked to the great house, still some distance from where she stood, and as her eyes rested on the dark grey stone of Rosings, her mind dwelt on her time in Kent once again. Elizabeth could not look at its broad edifice without recollecting that, had she chosen it, she might have been presented to Lady Catherine by that time as her future niece. Nor could she think without a smile of what her ladyship's indignation would have been. The humour at that thought clear on her expression, Elizabeth lifted the latch of the gate and ventured in.

She wandered only a few minutes along the gravel path when she heard footsteps behind her. Her heart suddenly beating in her throat and a blush warming her cheeks, she spun around in surprise when her name was called. "Cousin Elizabeth, I am pleased to see you chose Lady Catherine's gardens for your walk this morning."

Her hand rested on her chest, calming the beating organ beneath. She might have laughed if it were not for the immense relief she felt encountering her cousin before her. Mr Collins was dressed nearly as fine as if he were attending an evening at Rosings rather than a morning call. She chastised herself for her panicked reaction to his approach. She refused to consider why she supposed it might have been Mr Darcy walking in his aunt's gardens. The man was well safe in London by then.

"The blooms are lovely, sir." Elizabeth could hardly manage more when she considered the curious disappointment that was slinking up her back and wrapping her heart.

Mr Collins replied with his delight in the change of weather, which allowed him once again to ascertain the health and happiness of his most beloved benefactor. Grateful that a reply was unnecessary and most likely unheard, she remained silent until such time as Mr Collins finished his speech and bid her a hurried adieu. She watched him turn along the path towards the house, wiping his brow as he went. Elizabeth halted among the shrubbery, stunned that she should have almost wished for Mr Darcy to be the one to encounter her.

Shaken by the disquieting realisation, Elizabeth firmly turned in the opposite direction from the house and walked deeper into the gardens. When the path took her around a bend where she might have once again had a view of the stone edifice, Elizabeth purposely took the next bend that kept her back to it. Rosings now represented that gentleman, and if she could keep herself from looking upon it, she might be able to return her thoughts to safe indifference.

When she entered the maze, she laughed half-heartedly at herself as she considered her jumbled thoughts resembling a maze of sorts. At least now, the tall hedge of the maze kept her from seeing much more than the buttresses of Rosings. That thought drew forth a laugh as she remembered her cousin expounding once on their expense.

Her boots came to an immediate stop, grey pebbles from the path skipping ahead. Elizabeth's last turn led her to a dead end. It was the entrance to a lovely alcove, complete with a small stone fountain. Tiny pink and white flowers grew up a vine adhered to the hedge, bringing a springtime blush to the green walls. The sun filtered through, leaving half of the natural room in cool shadow. Delighted, Elizabeth brought her hand up to the rim of her bonnet while her eyes adjusted to discover a lovely bench that now was visible in the shadowed portion of the alcove. The angle of the sun made looking in that direction difficult as the rays were just filtering across the top of the hedge above it.

Elizabeth stepped towards the inviting bench, and she soon was embraced by the shadow of the hedge before her. The bench had a lovely stone box of flowers next to it, and she bent to inhale their sweet aroma. While natural landscaping was her preference, Elizabeth found the serenity and lush beauty of that bloom-filled chamber enchanting. She sat on the bench, immediately chilled from the cold stone. Relaxing against the seat, Elizabeth tilted her head up, admiring the way the flowers grew in a seemingly random pattern along the hedge and around the corner, and she esteemed the meticulous skill and strident work of her ladyship's gardeners that coaxed the vine into its current path.

Elizabeth rested quietly, her hands clasped together on her lap as she listened to the songbirds and the pleasant sound of buzzing as bees harvested nectar from the flowers around her. For the first time, Elizabeth considered her response to Darcy's proposal at the parsonage. And like a pebble dropped in a pond, once introduced, the thought rippled, expanding until she could think of nothing else. She was troubled by her intemperate words. Although justifiably offended by *his*, she still could not like how her temper had provoked her to such a fiery response.

Elizabeth closed her eyes, intending only to alleviate the sting of tears that lapped at their edges. The restless sleep she endured over the past couple of days kept her eyes closed. Her thoughts returned to the letter and the man who wrote it as she considered his strong, masculine, yet elegant hand that seemed to fit him perfectly. The peace of the garden chamber, the warmth of the sun, and the buzzing of the bees that drowned out all other sound seduced Elizabeth, lulling her with its song into a quiet sleep.

∽

Darcy was restless. He had not wanted to return to Rosings. Yet luck had been against him from the beginning of his journey—nay, from the beginning of his ill-advised admiration of Elizabeth Bennet. Even now, he struggled again, as he had in London, with thoughts of why he was so unfortunate as to fall for a penniless, inconsequential...beguiling and bewitching lady. Yet now those thoughts were darker, blanketed with soot from her scorching words as he now had the distinction of knowing he could not have her should he choose it.

He had sought her only a few days before. He had sought her, and he was denied. The rain over the past few days received daily praise from Darcy. It prevented any communication between the parsonage and Rosings—and better yet, any possible visitors. He did not think his heart was capable of encountering her again. He wanted to hate her, to let his disappointment soak into that part of his heart that she still occupied, and evict her. But he still filled with warmth, and that heart, wounded yet still traitorous, beat with a rapid tattoo at the perfect image of her in his mind. Even her eyes, brilliant in their anger, brought such a troublesome consequence.

Darcy moved to the window, his very stature displaying the strain he felt. He had avoided his cousins and aunt during this prolonged stay, explaining he had some business to attend. Colonel Fitzwilliam, he knew, did not believe him, but whether his aunt did or not, it was of little importance. He had spent most of his days alone, thinking about *her*.

Returning to his desk, Darcy looked at the sheet of parchment before him. His eyes scanned the words etched in ink. Each swipe of the quill had been a beat of his heart. It was foolishness on his part but a habit he began to fear he could not afford to break yet. While his soul still yearned for Elizabeth, his hand would still write to her.

Even still, God bless you,
Fitzwilliam Darcy

His eyes slowed and stopped at the closing words he wrote only moments ago. He had purged himself again of his thoughts and feelings in another letter to her. This one had raged at the extreme injustice she had dealt him and of his desire to make her repent her hasty refusal. His anger had burned hot on the page as he wrote his pain in ink. He had wanted so desperately to express his contempt for her. And for a few black lines, he had almost accomplished it. Not until his hand stilled to dip his quill again did the dam of fury break and he along with it.

He laid his head down upon the desk and nearly wept. *Hatred* was a blind, and as his head pressed against the hard wood, he knew that he was only fooling himself. He did not hate her. He could only love her still. He lifted his head and poured out once again upon the page a confession—a plea of mercy. *Release me of your hold!*

With numb fingers, Darcy folded the letter. Absentmindedly, he lifted the candle below his sealing wax and watched red drops drip upon the seam of the letter. Like an observer to his actions, he pressed his seal into the wax, blew it cool, and addressed it to her.

Miss Elizabeth Bennet
Longbourn, Hertfordshire

Drained of all emotion, Darcy slipped his finger along the underside of his writing desk, popping the lever to reveal the secret compartment. It brimmed with his secret thoughts.

Not wishing to dwell on such proof of his weakness for her, Darcy placed the new letter with the other and closed the compartment with firmness. He stood again and returned to the window, his jaw flexing painfully. Suddenly, he longed for the outdoors and wished again for his horse that was already in London. He considered the park, but she would likely be walking those avenues, and even if she was not, they held too many memories.

A movement below him in the formal garden drew his attention. He saw Mr Collins reach the portico directly below his window. The thought of possibly being summoned by his aunt to take tea with Elizabeth's odious cousin was too tiresome. Not only would the company be tedious, there was a possibility that *she* would be mentioned.

Turning abruptly, Darcy slid into his coat and left his chambers. Upon reaching the stairs, he headed towards a side door and exited the house into the formal gardens.

His swift steps took him deeply into the garden as he weaved around rose bushes and manicured topiaries. A gardener ahead of him saw his approach and stood with head bowed until he passed before resuming his work. Darcy's steps did not slow until he was far from the house and beyond his aunt's summoning. He looked over his shoulder at the great edifice behind him, his eyes scanning the windows until they found his own. He noted the curtains to Fitzwilliam's rooms were still drawn. Darcy turned again from the house and walked leisurely around the early blooms of spring.

His hand touched the delicate silk of a pale yellow rose within reach. Gently, he drew a finger along its curved bell shape before dropping his hands to his side and, with a sigh, lifting his head to the sky. He knew he must look the part of a man defeated, teetering between despair and listlessness.

Darcy resumed his walk and resolutely fixed his mind on subjects other than the one his heart longed for. He reviewed the meeting with his solicitor in London and made a list of items about which he wished to consult the man. Then he turned his mind to Georgiana and was heartened to think of his reunion with her. She would provide comfort even without knowing his need for it.

After a time, Darcy became aware of his surroundings and saw that he had entered the maze without having remembered doing so. He fondly recalled his childhood pleasures when every wonderment and desire could be fulfilled with a run through a maze. The direction of his thoughts naturally led to a time not many days past when his every desire was at the cusp of his fingertips as he had walked eagerly to Hunsford parsonage. Alone in the garden, Darcy allowed himself to be engulfed again in the memories of that ill-conceived proposal. He leaned against the wall of the hedge and dropped his head. A single tear escaped his eye and fell unheeded to land on the toe of his boot. The moisture darkened the leather not unlike the way the pain seemed to stain his heart.

His nostalgic surroundings brought to mind the loss of his mother many years before. He and his father, along with little Georgiana, came to Rosings for a visit. Lady Catherine had witnessed him running around these very gardens with Georgiana. He remembered making her small body double over in childlike abandon as laughter rang through the garden. He made to capture her around a rose bush, feigning left as she went right. He remembered Georgiana running off before he pursued her again, securing her four-year-old frame in his arms and swinging her in a great arch into the air. Her delight and laughter filled his heart with peace like nothing had since his mother's death. Georgiana had missed their mother too, and seeing her eyes alight with happiness again encouraged Darcy to want to provoke more laughter.

Lady Catherine had interrupted them then with a stern rebuke for his impropriety. Immediately, he had placed Georgiana down beside him, and they both stood silently as she unleashed her displeasure at his display. He remembered how she had accused him of a disgraceful lack of mourning for his mother. Georgiana had withdrawn again, hiding partially behind his leg, his hand in her soft curls. When his aunt had withdrawn with an indignant rustle of skirts, he leaned down and kissed Georgiana's head before passing her off to the maid that stood nearby. Then he had walked, quickly and resolutely, to the very maze he stood in now.

Darcy began walking to ascertain his whereabouts within the maze. He wanted to find the small alcove with the fountain—the one he had found long ago to sit in and conquer his fury towards his aunt, his remorse for the loss of his mother, and the agony that engulfed him and mirrored the pain he felt now. After a few wrong turns, Darcy recognised his location and confidently started on the path that he knew would take him to that chamber.

He remembered his father had found him there an hour later and sat with him quietly. As it often is between men, nothing needed to be said. They both mourned a great loss. After a while, his father had turned to him with a hand upon his shoulder and said, "You are a good boy, William." He then patted his knee and stood to leave Darcy again with his thoughts.

With one more turn, Darcy saw, at the end of the green corridor before him, the entrance to the chamber. He could hear the soft gurgle of water from the fountain and could see glimpses of the flowered walls. Reverently, Darcy made his way towards the archway into the garden room.

CHAPTER 4

※

A CALM SETTLED IN HIS BREAST AS HIS EYES IMMEDIATELY WENT TO THE fountain, the gurgling water bringing a contented smile to his face. He contemplated for a moment how a place from one's childhood could look so different yet the same. He might not have been exactly a child at the time, but he noticed that the cool stone of the fountain had aged, the rock darkening with time. A dusting of moss had begun to grow around the edges, but the crystal-like reflection of the sun pouring down upon the water looked just as magical as it had so many years ago.

Darcy stepped slowly towards the edge, the quiet crunch of his boots soon silenced by the soft grass surrounding the fountain. He dipped his fingers briefly in the sparkling water, surprised at how cold it was. Straightening, he shook the droplets free and slowly looked around the garden room, wanting to discover the differences, the sameness.

The sun blinded him as he looked towards the bench, and his head bent instinctively even as his eyes closed. He lifted his hand to his brow and moved towards the shadowed seat.

His feet, along with his heart, lurched to a stop upon seeing her sitting there peacefully, eyes closed. His throat constricted and choked upon so pronounced an emotion that he could not have been able, if pressed, to describe it. His surprise was so marked that, before he could realise it was not his mind calling her name, his voice strangled through the utterance, "Elizabeth."

Immediately, Elizabeth's eyes snapped open in astonishment, and with a great cry of surprise, she stood swiftly. Her legs bumped into the bench and then the flower box as she sought greater distance from him. Her startled movements came to an end when she pressed herself against the hedge behind her, a hand coming to rest upon her chest. The rapid rise and fall of it drew Darcy's eye fleetingly before they once again settled on her beautiful face.

His heart sank to see her act in fear of him, and although his mind reasoned that she was but startled, it was an apt reaction to the way he felt right then. Neither had power over themselves enough to speak. Her surprise could hardly be any greater than *his* was at encountering her in that alcove of all places. He had not expected to see her again in this lifetime and had hoped he would not have to endure that pain—yet the pleasure of it before him made him wish for the moment to never end.

She found her words before he did. "Mr Darcy!" Her shaky hands smoothed down the folds of her skirt, and finally, one hand came to rest upon her stomach, fingers splayed as she drew in a deep breath.

"I startled you. I apologize," he said tenuously, intending to leave her then. However, his intentions were thwarted by the disobedience of his feet.

Elizabeth observed his lowered brow, firm jaw, and fisted hands, and she could see at once that he wished to be far from that place. She could hardly account for her own feelings. She had been more than startled to see him in the garden today and not just because she had been awoken suddenly. *What is he doing here?* And to be awoken so suddenly by the sound of her name? Her heart beat faster as she realised he had used her Christian name! How utterly shocked he must have been to discover her.

Her breathing slowed as she forced herself to breathe deeply. "Please, do not trouble yourself, sir." Looking up through lowered lashes, she saw his gaze fixed upon her in a startlingly focused way. *I must go!* "I am afraid you have been long desiring my absence. I will leave you now, sir. Good day."

She attempted to curtsey just as Darcy's lips opened to protest. Her head being bowed missed the disappointment in his eyes.

To her mortification as she made to leave, she found she could not curtsey as her straw bonnet was caught in the climbing blooms behind her. She reached up to disentangle her bonnet but found that, as soon as she would nearly release it, the straw would be caught by another thorn from the flowered vine.

As she struggled, Darcy was half charmed by her blush and half wishing to step forward to offer his help. His feet remained firmly in place with the fear of coming closer to her—of touching her. He was certain the feel would be burned into his memory, and he did not desire that. Then, he spied a small hive of bees buzzing agitatedly just above Elizabeth's head as her hands struggled in their attempt to free herself.

He stepped forward, his arms stretched in entreaty. "Still yourself, Miss Bennet." His calm but serious tone drew her eyes to his, and her hands stopped. "You are decidedly close to a hive."

Elizabeth stilled as he cautiously stepped closer to her, his eyes darting from hers to a spot above her head. She could hear the bees buzzing loudly now, and her heart sped at the sound. At least that is what she reasoned, as it surely could not be the decreasing distance to the gentleman before her. And certainly not the slight scent of lemon and sandalwood she detected as his broad shoulders now eclipsed any of the garden behind him.

Darcy looked down at her face, a tiny bit of the blackness in his heart chipped away at the fearful countenance. He spoke softly since he did not wish to startle her further and his breath seemed to be caught in the constriction of his chest. "Please allow me."

He could see her stiffen as he stepped abreast of her, mere inches away, and raised his arms to her bonnet. Elizabeth thought she might faint from the unexpected closeness and held her breath, determined to block the sensations engulfing her as his arms came around her. Her eyes were level with his jaw. From that distance, she could see the tiny black dots of his clean-shaven jaw. A thought came to her that, if she but lifted only slightly on the balls of her feet and angled her head a little, she could place a kiss on the edge thereof. Her eyes went wide at the unexpected thought and then squeezed shut tightly, amazed at her own absurdity.

She expected to feel his fingers at the top of her head, releasing the tangles of her bonnet with the thorns. Her breath hitched when she felt his warm fingers brush the underside of her jaw to untie the ribbons at her throat. She felt the slight pull of the ribbon, heard the nearly inaudible hiss of fabric against fabric as his fingers pulled on the ends of the bow in slow motion. The cool air then kissed her exposed neck at the same time that his warm breath brushed across her face in barely a whisper.

"You are free, Miss Bennet."

Elizabeth's wits came rushing back to her, and she dipped below one of his arms where they held onto the edges of her bonnet and stepped out of his embrace. Taking several hasty steps backwards, she felt the backs of her legs encounter the fountain where she sank heavily to seat herself on its edge.

Darcy remained with his back to her as he tried to carefully disentangle her bonnet without further upsetting the hive above. Despite the agitated bees, he found himself prolonging the task because he was not equal to meeting her face to face. So jumbled were his emotions that he had yet to gain mastery of himself. Her beauty eclipsed any and all other females of his acquaintance, and holding her—in the loosest of definitions—in his arms was torture of the sweetest kind. He allowed himself the pleasure of reflecting on it as he released a part of the bonnet from the hedge, pricking his fingertip against a thorn.

With a murmur, he pulled the hand back and then immediately brought the finger to his mouth. He heard Elizabeth come closer behind him.

"Take care, sir," she said softly, a hint of embarrassment in her tone.

Darcy closed his eyes briefly. Her tender concern brought only pain with it as he remembered how lost she was to him. How very apropos it was with the rest of his ill luck to encounter her here in the garden. He had not expected to see her, and he hoped and reasoned that she would be in the greater woods without. But that would require luck Darcy did not possess. Of course she would be in the garden he dared to enter. Of course she would be in the one chamber—and he believed there were four—that he had sought. Certainly, he would have hoped to encounter her one day, if he was to encounter her at all, with composure and indifference—not this riotous swell of emotion. And, of course, he would find himself under her power every bit as much as he was on the night he proposed.

How miserable he now felt as he worked to release the last tangled bit of lace on her bonnet. He felt utterly pathetic. Even now, he was prolonging the job because he knew with certainty that, once the bonnet was returned, she would swiftly leave this private place. Was it so wrong to want, even for a moment longer, to keep her with him?

Without much more delay, he managed to release the bonnet just as one of the angered bees landed squarely on the back of his hand and stung him. Another painful hiss escaped his lips as he hastily stepped away from the hedge line. His injured hand pressed against him, and he held her bonnet limply in the other.

Elizabeth saw the bee sting and immediately rushed forward with concern as he stepped back. She took his hand in hers to examine it, pulling it away from its protected space near his chest.

"Mr Darcy, you are injured. Come…" She pulled him absently towards the fountain and, with her small hands, gently pressed his shoulders down, indicating he should sit.

Stunned by her touch, Darcy mutely sat. The bee sting was entirely forgotten in the sensation of her fingers once again taking up his hand in both of hers. He watched disbelievingly as she held his hand in hers, her thumbs brushing the skin on the back of his hand this way and that as she bent her head to look closer at the injury.

He took in the sight of her chocolate curls, highlighted in the sun as it fell upon them, and bit his lip. The struggle with her bonnet had dislodged some of her careful coiffure. He wanted nothing more at that moment than to reach for the dislodged curl and feel its texture between his fingers. Still, she twisted and tilted his hand in the light as she examined it, and Darcy felt that he might expire from the intimacy.

"Mary is frightfully sensitive to bee stings, and I have learned it is crucial to remove the stinger." He half smiled at her nervous rambling. "I do not see the stinger, sir. Do you feel it? Do you think it is still in you?"

Elizabeth looked up at him, and before he could stop himself, he had pulled his hand free of hers and engulfed her delicate face with both of his, her bonnet floating to the ground as he discarded it to hold a more beautiful object. His eyes bored into hers, watching them grow drowsy at his touch. It was all the encouragement he needed, and he bent his head swiftly down to hers, pressing his lips to hers.

Oh, what lightning then flooded his veins! With every beat of his heart, he soared higher and higher as—

"Mr Darcy? Sir, do you believe the stinger is still there? I cannot see it."

Darcy blinked and opened his eyes. Elizabeth sat before him, his hand still in hers, with a look of concern on her face. His gaze fell to their hands and then shifted to see that his other hand still held her bonnet and rested on his leg. A surge of misery shot through him as he realised with anguished disbelief that he had only imagined the kiss and her pleasured response. His face fell into a stern frown as he gathered his broken thoughts enough to answer her gruffly.

"I do not think the stinger remains."

Elizabeth heard the cold tone of his voice, and though it stirred familiar feelings of displeasure with the gentleman before her, she tried to reason that he might be in some pain and had just released her from danger. She reached in her pocket, withdrew a handkerchief, and dipped it into the cold water of the fountain before pressing it against the swelling on Mr Darcy's hand.

Both were silent for some minutes. Elizabeth tried to think of some topic of conversation, but everything her mind came upon seemed to have a hindrance of sorts in their history together. Darcy's thoughts were less congenial in nature as he contemplated how quickly he might excuse himself. The sweet pressure of her hands as she pressed the cold cloth to his injured one was nearly unbearable.

"We were all under the impression that you had left Rosings, sir," Elizabeth hedged, her curiosity on this topic fighting to be released from her lips.

Darcy cleared his throat, the deep resonance unfathomably making Elizabeth blush. "My carriage encountered difficulty."

"You were not injured?" Elizabeth eyes swept over him as if to confirm the truth.

"No, we were not injured. We were not far from my aunt's when the axle broke, and so we returned to await its repair."

"I am sure your aunt would loan you her carriage…" Elizabeth began but then stopped abruptly, seeing his frown deepen and realising that her words might make her sound eager for his departure.

"It is with uncommonly poor timing that we found Lady Catherine's carriages being reupholstered, thus unavailable."

"What—all?" Elizabeth exclaimed.

"Yes, all," Darcy said through clenched teeth. He, too, had begun to have suspicions on that matter.

As Darcy's jaw tightened and a dark shadow fell across his face, Elizabeth looked down at the fountain beside her. She realised how natural it would be for him to find her company irksome and difficult. They exchanged heated words not many days in the past. He had declared his ardent love and admiration for her, the remembrance of which brought a bloom to her cheeks. Though she did not seek his good opinion, she had had it then—even briefly—and was not unaware of the compliment thereof.

She recalled with sudden acuity her shame for her part in the argument, particularly her misguided and misinformed defence of Mr Wickham. Knowing the true history between the two gentlemen as she did now, she could not help but feel the deepest sorrow for her misjudgement of Mr Darcy.

When he gave her the letter, she had wondered briefly what more he could have to say to her. She expected little left to be said, considering their paths ought never to cross again. And if there was more to be said, why did he not speak his piece that night and be done with it? She soon had her answer for in his letter he had said, *"You may possibly wonder why all of this was not told to you last night. But I was not then master enough of myself."* Elizabeth froze, venturing to look at him through her lashes. He was looking away from her, his expression pained.

"Thank you for freeing my bonnet, sir."

He looked at the forgotten article and then at her. "I am afraid it is badly damaged."

"'Tis no matter. I should have remade it sooner or later. This will just give me an excuse for doing the task all the sooner." Elizabeth tried to smile cheekily at him, but the edges faltered when she saw him swallow, nod, and return to look at the hedge surrounding them.

Elizabeth realised with chagrin that, despite the need for the cool cloth on his hand to prevent the swelling, the need for *her* to hold it there was not present. With embarrassment, she removed one hand from where it held the cloth to reach towards her bonnet. He handed it to her immediately. With a gentle nudge from her, she returned his hand, and he took up the job of pressing the handkerchief to the injury.

Awkwardly, the lady inspected the damage to her bonnet in an attempt to hide the flush of embarrassment she felt at having held his hand for so long and without a thought! How strangely she felt the loss of it as well.

For Darcy's part, he was convincing himself that he felt relief that she no longer held his hand. Notwithstanding the cold cloth, his hand felt scorched from where hers had touched it. Had he been less selfish, he might have told her many minutes before that the pain of the sting had long departed.

The only sting he felt now was the sting of mortification he experienced in knowing that he had imagined, with quite some detail, a scenario that would never—could never—happen. Never had his musings produced such a vivid dream. From start to finish, her presence left him intoxicated. The reality struck him hard in knowing that the union of hearts he imagined was nothing but that: his imagination.

"Mr Darcy."

He turned to look down at her then, noticing the pinch of her brow and the uncertainty in her voice. "Yes, Miss Bennet?"

Her slim fingers fumbled with the lace of her bonnet for another short time before she whispered, "I owe you an apology, sir."

Darcy raised his brow, unable to imagine anything for which she might have to apologize.

Powerless to meet his eye, Elizabeth continued. "I am sorry for the unjust words I said to you regarding Mr Wickham, sir."

Elizabeth did look up at him then and saw his face transform in displeasure. Neither ventured towards the topic most obvious between them—that of the proposal. Their last meeting was so unpleasant and this encounter so unexpected that both of their attempts at civility were exaggerated. Elizabeth knew for herself that she would have gladly skipped through this uncomfortable happenstance without any reference to their troubled past if it were not for the guilt she felt.

"I had not known he was so very bad."

Darcy's heart fumbled to hear her regretful tone. He had suspected her partiality for Wickham but had hoped she would be spared such pain once aware of his true character. He was not fool enough to pretend he did not wish for her to become disapproving towards her favourite, but he did not wish for her to be injured by the knowledge. He was contemplating his response when the sounds of her muffled cries reached his ears.

He turned abruptly, surprised to see her weeping, yet his heart melted at the sight. He quickly passed her *his* handkerchief. "Please, Miss Elizabeth, he is not worth your tears."

Her eyes glistening and remorseful, Elizabeth shook her head slightly and with a gentle hand on his shoulder assured him that her distress was not for Wickham. He breathed in relief at the words but still marvelled at the reason.

"Tell me, sir. Is your sister…is she still much harmed by her misfortune with Mr Wickham?"

"She suffers only in that it has made her terribly reticent—more so than she was before. She does not trust her own judgement anymore, I am sorry to say."

Elizabeth nodded and looked away from his gaze then. "I understand her perfectly then."

She had said it so quietly that Darcy was not certain he had heard her correctly and made no reply. He was reeling with a strange awareness he could not label. He dared not give himself hope that her words meant anything more than understanding the characterisation of Wickham.

He was relieved—he could tell that much—that she believed his account. Since Colonel Fitzwilliam had said he did not see her, Darcy had that niggling doubt. It gave him a small amount of real pleasure to know that, at least in some minute way, Elizabeth's opinion of his character was not totally devoid of any good as to disbelieve his words without proof.

"How is your hand, sir?"

Elizabeth's voice jolted Darcy back to the present, and he realised they had been silent for some time. He lifted the cloth to look at his hand and noted only a slight redness. "I believe I will survive."

Elizabeth laughed at his tone, pleased and surprised by his attempt at levity. "May I have a look?"

Darcy could only nod as he lifted his hand towards her. She took his hand once again in hers, and he felt a sudden jolt pass through him at the connexion. She must have felt it as well, for she looked up at him abruptly as they studied one another.

"Is that ink on your forehead, sir?" she asked with no little amusement.

Darcy immediately raised the wet handkerchief to his head and rubbed it across his brow. He knew the moment he saw the black on the fabric that it was from writing Elizabeth the secret letter he had penned that very morning. He remembered laying his head down in anguish. The remembrance made him blush with mortification. Thankfully, Elizabeth did not question how the ink got there, and he offered no explanation.

She bent again to inspect the bee sting. As the cool, feather-light touch of her fingers brushed the inside of his palm, Darcy struggled for distraction. "I will have your handkerchief laundered and returned to you."

Elizabeth shook her head, the curls bouncing, as she dismissed his statement. "It is of no consequence. I have some shopping to do to replace the lace on my bonnet. I shall just have to endure shopping for another."

Darcy smiled, almost pained by her impertinent tone. "You need not waste your money..." He tried to protest, but she stopped him with a squeeze of his hand. His tongue suddenly lodged in his throat.

"Oh no, Mr Darcy, you must never tell a lady there is no need for shopping. If you return my handkerchief, I shall have no need for a replacement and will be severely displeased."

"My mistake."

"You may simply discard it, sir."

Though Darcy nodded, he knew he would never discard it—not in the whole of his life. "Then at least keep mine until you can replace yours. I insist." He held his breath, hoping she would oblige him—and hoping that she would not see the desperate longing in his eyes that she might keep something of his. He had wanted to give her everything that was his; he was now resigned and determined that she at least keep this.

She blushed and nodded, and he expelled his held breath in relief.

To divert herself, Elizabeth pretended further examination of his hand. He was being so kind, almost charming, and that only complicated the swirl of her emotions regarding this man. She was relieved that she could apologize and have him accept her remorse regarding Mr Wickham. That was a tremendous weight off her shoulders. Still, she could not help being confused by a mix of slowly growing admiration for him and heated remembrance of his arrogant demeanour. Furthering her disquiet was the warmth she felt whenever she held his hand and the heady memory of his near embrace as he freed her from her bonnet.

"Do you feel much pain?"

Darcy looked confused at her question. The realisation that he had much about which to be pained drained her face of its previous blush.

"It does not pain me much at all, Miss Bennet. Thank you for your kind attentions." Darcy paused, held his breath, and feeling a little confidence embolden him at having her keep his handkerchief, added recklessly, "The pain I believe would leave entirely if you were to kiss it."

Immediately, he regretted his words when he saw her stiffen and then stand. His hand dropped like it burnt her. "Miss Bennet, please allow me to apologize," he said, standing too. "I was only attempting a joke. I...I..." His voice died in mortification at the discomfort he saw on her face.

She curtseyed then and with a shake of her head pretended not to be offended. "No, no, it is only that I...I must be going. I have been away much too long. Do take care of your hand, Mr Darcy, and I wish you safe travels. Goodbye."

Before he could utter even a single word, she had skipped around him, and as abruptly as she entered his line of vision when he entered the alcove, she was gone out of it through the archway. Darcy clenched his jaw in anger. This time it was directed entirely inward. He could not pretend she held him in any favour. He had forgotten that as she kindly administered aid to his hand. Their almost civil discussion and the resolution of their disagreement regarding Wickham had fooled him into thinking that she did not find him distasteful. Had she not made her opinion clear to him that evening? Her words were etched in his memory: "… *your arrogance, your conceit, and your selfish disdain of the feelings of others were such as to form that ground-work of disapprobation on which succeeding events have built so immoveable a dislike …*"

Darcy sunk down onto the fountain's edge again. *So immoveable a dislike.* He felt the urge to write to her again. At least with paper, he was able to express himself adequately enough not to make a cake of himself. His hand turned, and he examined her handkerchief held tightly in his palm. No, he would never discard it.

∽

Elizabeth walked as quickly as her legs would take her out of the maze. She exhaled in relief when she exited, glad to have found her way easily and without many wrong turns. She almost expected Mr Darcy to pursue her. She half feared, half wished for it. And that was why she had to leave so quickly. She knew that she left him assuming he had offended her. It could not be helped. If he were to know that his jest brought with it the very great temptation to do just that—to kiss his hand—he would have been shocked, nay, disgusted with her indecent thought. She did not dare believe that he could still have tender feelings for her. It would be better for both of them if his admiration for her were to dissolve quickly. After the spiteful words she threw at him during his proposal, she expected it would not take long. In the garden, she had seen his stern frown and his troubled and pained expression, and she knew that being in her company was not easy or any longer desirable to him. Even if he did still hold her in esteem, she could not return his regard in equal measure.

Upon reaching the parsonage, she quickly ascended the stairs to deposit her bonnet there. It was only then that she realised she still held his handkerchief in her hand. It was good of him to be so magnanimous regarding her gross misjudgement of Wickham. It showed that, between the two gentlemen, there was only enough goodness for one man, and she was persuaded Mr Darcy had it all. Not wishing to explain the article of clothing with its embroidered initials to anyone, Elizabeth walked quickly to the hot coals remaining from her nightly fire. She kneeled down to toss it on the embers and destroy it. After a moment of hesitation, Elizabeth stood and walked to her trunk. Lifting the heavy lid, Elizabeth dipped her hand along the silk lining to the small pocket. Her fingers touched the object she sought and gently pulled out Darcy's letter, the folds already showing wear from her many perusals.

With hardly a moment to examine her actions, Elizabeth wrapped the handkerchief around the letter and returned both to the silk pocket, securing the heavy latch of the lid once it was closed.

CHAPTER 5

Upon exiting the maze only moments after Elizabeth's hasty departure, Darcy walked with determined strides to the stables. It was too much—far too much for one to bear with equanimity. Her proximity to Rosings, their unexpected encounter, and even her damnable scent that was etched into his mind when he released her from her bonnet—all were unbearable. Darcy cursed the injustice of it all until his riot of emotion simmered into something closer to anger then despair.

As he rounded the side of Rosings on his way to the stables, he glared at the edifice with maleficent blame. To him at that moment, his aunt's home represented all the responsibilities, duties, and expectations he had carried on his shoulders for many years. How he hated them now! They had been a source of painful adversity when he struggled with a decision regarding Elizabeth. *She* had been offended by his honest account of them. Fury snaked its way towards her again and at her dismissal of all that he had endured in coming to offer. So she did not desire his good opinion. So she disliked him immensely. What of human compassion?

He had been nothing but honest with her. He came to confess his love and for evidence of its strength provided the proof that he had desired her despite expecting to gain nothing in the match by way of connexion, wealth, or status.

The scuffing of his boots stopped abruptly in the gravel lane leading to the stables just in front of him. "… *had you behaved in a more gentlemanlike manner.*" Did she really believe his account dishonourable? Darcy recalled his words, and with a churning disquiet building deep in his stomach, he realised with crippling truth that he had been most offensive. Nay, he had been grossly and utterly disreputable. Suddenly, the entire foundation of his ire collapsed, and the world seemed to spin as his perspective spun too.

Numbly, he shuffled to a nearby bench. Folding into it with little grace, Darcy stared with disbelief into the bright sky in front of him. He tried to assuage this tempest of gloom that encompassed his every thought by reminding himself that *she* had declared his manner of proposal would have made no difference. She would have declined him no matter what or how he had said it. Her dislike was fixed, 'immoveable' as she so boldly stated. Still, he could not comprehend his imprudence. That he had said such unimaginably offensive things to her…to the woman of whom he had wished to have stewardship for the rest of his days.

In his pride and arrogance, he had expected her acceptance. His scruples he thought she would have understood. Fool that he was, he had not believed she would find any offense in hearing her family disparaged, her status belittled, and her lack of wealth so indelicately presented. *Idiocy!* True, he had not meant for those things to sound so despicable. But was there any way he could have said such things to make them less offensive? Speaking of such to her, especially while professing admiration, would have always been dishonourable. *Ungentlemanly.* Darcy groaned as he closed his eyes against the stinging sensation he felt. There was no atoning for what he had said.

His encounter with her now felt tainted with this new perception of their interview at the parsonage. How despicably he acted then and how soulfully he repented his words now. She must have been mortified to see him in the maze, her surprise more than just being awakened suddenly. Darcy could not blame her for wishing to be far from him. His proposal had hurt her profoundly at the very moment he believed he was gratifying her with his declaration of love.

How little his feelings of admiration must have been believed in the face of the other slights he presented to her. In that moment, Darcy was hard pressed to know whether he deserved to lay claim to any feelings of love. Did he know what love was?

Yet, in the maze, she had tended to his hand most gently with a kindness he now realised he had not earned. Her goodness was magnified in his heart, and it swelled with painful yearning. She could have taught him what love was.

Darcy stood and, with a gait long beyond his eight and twenty years, continued on to the stables. The only kindness he could bestow upon her now, the only reparation allowed to him, would be to remove himself from her presence and with as much swiftness as was in his power.

Finding his groom, Darcy asked, "How soon might we expect our carriage, John?"

The groom removed his hat, rubbed his head with one hand, and replaced it in almost the same movement. "We expect to 'ave 'er any day now, Mr Darcy, sir."

Darcy looked about the stable, calculating in his mind how long it might have taken to send for another carriage at Pemberley and whether he could have left by now if he had. It mattered not. He was here, and in the fog of the days immediately following his proposal, he had not thought it necessary, considering he would not encounter Elizabeth again.

With a sigh, Darcy turned again to his head groom. "John, I wish to be notified immediately when our carriage is available and wish to depart within that hour—regardless of time of day or the weather, am I clear?"

"Yes sir, Mr Darcy."

Darcy nodded and turned to leave, his swift steps taking him again to the house. He had just gained the steps when he looked up to see his cousin descending towards him.

"Darcy!" Colonel Fitzwilliam bellowed jovially.

Darcy stopped where he was and waited for his cousin to reach him. "I have just come from the stables. The repairs are nearing completion, and I wish to depart as soon as they are."

Colonel Fitzwilliam nodded his agreement as he tugged on his gloves. "Then it is good I have decided to call on the parsonage now. I may not see another chance."

Darcy turned his head down the lane that lead to Hunsford, lost momentarily in his morose thoughts again until his cousin's voice brought him to attention.

"Care to join me? I have not had the pleasure of seeing Miss Bennet since our unfortunate return to Rosings, and I am determined to remedy that." Richard chuckled with a warmth to which Darcy took an instant dislike. His cousin looked back at the house over his shoulder as he continued, "And while Mr Collins graces Rosings with his presence, I shall take advantage of his absence at Hunsford to grace it with mine."

With much effort, Darcy schooled his features to betray none of the jealousy felt towards his cousin right then, laughing as he was at his own wit. Richard's carefree delight in Elizabeth's presence, his ability to speak to her without crippling mindfulness, and most significantly, his untroubled history with the lady were all thorns for Darcy.

"I think not this time." Darcy cleared his throat, disgusted with the amount of temptation the idea presented despite the fresh memory of seeing her flee from his presence in the maze. "I have matters of business to attend."

The colonel gave a derisive chuckle as he slapped his cousin on the shoulder. "And may you have all the luck in that endeavour. You are not likely to get any business completed. Our aunt has been asking after you this past half hour. I was lucky enough to find my escape when the tea tray was brought in."

"I will take my chances," Darcy said as he again ascended the steps.

Darcy heard his cousin's departing salute but did not return it. Upon reaching the entrance to the house, he was not surprised to see it opened for him by the butler. Groaning, Darcy knew any chance of escaping his aunt was impossible now, not with her loyal retainer preparing to pass on her requests for his presence.

Instead of putting it off any further that day and before the butler could open his mouth, Darcy spoke. "Where might my aunt be at this hour, Gibbons?"

As expected, the butler seemed pleased and announced that her ladyship was currently receiving Mr Collins in the south parlour. Darcy wanted nothing but to dispose of his disjointed thoughts on parchment. However much he disliked both the company of his aunt and her ingratiating parson, they would at least serve as distraction from his troubled thoughts. Perhaps if he were to conquer his weakness for writing to Elizabeth, he ought to start when he most needed the release it brought him. Distraction was a necessary vice now. So Darcy trudged towards the south parlour.

He could hear her strident tones long before he entered the room. He bowed to his aunt and acknowledged Mr Collins before taking himself to the tea tray, thankful for the occupation it gave him.

"Nephew! Where have you been? I have requested your presence the better half of this morning. You have been abominably rude."

Darcy held his breath and the retort biting at his lips. Instead, he turned, bowed again, and addressed her. "Forgive me, Aunt, I was partaking of some exercise now that the weather has cleared."

Lady Catherine made an indistinct sound of displeasure and spoke to the room at large. "I cannot imagine that the wilderness lane you so prefer would have been dry enough. You had much better have stayed in the gravel lanes of the formal gardens."

Darcy sat himself in the chair to her right, his lips twitching to think that he would have been better served to garner this advice from her before he set out to walk. He made it a point to nearly always do the opposite of what his aunt advised and found in his experience that this philosophy proved great wisdom. If he had been told to keep to the formal gardens before he walked out, he might have gone to the wilderness lane and avoided Elizabeth after all.

"As it happens, ma'am, I did visit your formal gardens."

Lady Catherine lifted her wrinkled chin, pleased with herself. "You were wise to follow my counsel in this matter," she said as if her guidance worked ex post facto.

Mr Collins chirped his agreement in abundance, much of which Darcy ignored as he sipped his tea and wondered how long he might be required to attend his aunt before he could escape. When he finished his cup, he stood to return it to the side table and noticed his cousin Anne, sitting demurely on a sofa by the window. She looked out forlornly to the view beyond.

Immediately, Darcy knew why his presence was so adamantly desired. His cousin rarely ventured out of her rooms during the day except for the occasional ride in her phaeton. And *that* only occurred when the weather was deemed warm enough by Lady Catherine. Though he did not share his aunt's feelings on a union between the two of them, he did care about his cousin.

Darcy walked towards her now and stood to the side of the window through which she gazed. She lifted her eyes to him then and offered him a slight smile. It was returned before he brought his gaze to join hers out the window. He was startled to see that, from this vantage, the gardens below—and more particularly the maze beyond—could be seen with very little effort. Even now, Darcy mapped the pathway with his eyes through the maze that brought him to the chamber where Elizabeth had been resting. His eyes slowed as they approached the entrance to the garden room and from there he could see the fountain quite clearly.

Turning away from the view, Darcy's eyes met Anne's with the swift comprehension that she might have witnessed his entire encounter with Elizabeth, depending on how long she had been gazing from this particular vantage. The sudden twinkle in her eyes told him she had indeed seen the two of them together in the maze.

Darcy swallowed. His cheeks warming, he broke away from that knowing look and turned again towards the window. *What might she have thought of what she saw?* From this distance, she could not have seen expressions on their faces, but it would have been abundantly clear that they spent much time together alone...and holding hands.

Once again, Darcy turned wide eyes to his cousin. She did not meet his gaze but instead stood and spoke not to him but to her mother. "Mother, I have decided to partake of the warm morning and take some air. My cousin has kindly agreed to accompany me."

Somewhat alarmed, Darcy saw a blush spread across his cousin's cheeks while she looked demurely down after her pronouncement. He turned in time to see Lady Catherine's smug supremacy at this act of solicitousness on his part, however little truth there was in it.

"You may go as far as the balcony. I would not have you take a chill in the damp air." Darcy witnessed the small smile his cousin held in check as she nodded to her mother and lifted her hand ready for his escort. The clever girl knew that her mother would never have disallowed her request to go outside regardless of how fine a day, not after several days of wet weather, unless couched in such terms.

Darcy then felt a hint of apprehension as he stepped forward and offered his arm to his cousin as she all but led him to the glass doors at the far end of the room that led to a balcony overlooking the same wretched gardens. What could she be about involving him in such a scheme? Did she mean to use her knowledge of his tête-à-tête with Elizabeth to her own gain?

Darcy held no qualms that she meant to entrap him herself. That had always been her mother's designs but not Anne's. When they reached the doors, Darcy opened one for her and assisted her across the threshold with a gentle hand on her elbow. Anne walked gracefully to the stone railing and folded her gloved hands atop each other there.

Apprehensive, Darcy followed to her side, some steps apart and debating whether or not he ought to say something. An explanation of sorts was to be expected, but he knew not what. His eyes scanned the landscape before him and once again came to rest on the garden chamber.

"You have my support and my every wish of joy, Cousin."

Anne's gentle voice brought his eyes at once to her almost wistful expression. He did not immediately comprehend her meaning. Suddenly, his time with Elizabeth through this perspective looked very different. Through Anne's eyes, she must have seen him nearly embracing Elizabeth, then removing her bonnet, and then finally sitting with her, his hand in hers for quite some time by the fountain. An intimate proposal. What a glorious misunderstanding and one that, given the truth, broke his heart further. His perfected mask of cool indifference fell from his features. He turned unseeing eyes to the garden below, unable to hide the misery in his expression.

"I thank you, but there is no need for either your support or your joy."

"Do you mean to say you are not at present engaged to Miss Bennet?" Anne said abruptly, more boldly than was her wont.

Darcy turned quickly towards the open parlour door, listening for his aunt's imperious voice. Relieved to hear no alteration in her speech, Darcy released his breath and sighed. His eyes returned to his cousin. He used to hold quite a fondness for her. They had shared confidences from early in their childhoods until about the time Darcy's father took ill and he began to hear his aunt speak more and more of a presumed engagement between Anne and him. At that point, Darcy withdrew from the intimacy of friendship so as not to raise expectations that he was amenable to his aunt's wishes.

It was foolish and vain, for he knew that Anne had never held him in any particular romantic regard. In fact, he had always suspected her tender heart was turned more towards his cousin Richard. But she and Darcy had shared a friendship. At one time, he could speak to her of the anguish over his mother's death or laugh at the antics of a much younger sister. It was he who had pulled away, and now he was heartily sorry for it, especially if it gave her pain. He supposed it might have, considering the isolation she experienced at Rosings.

"… *your selfish disdain of the feelings of others …*"

"I am a fool." He groaned as he turned to rest his elbows on the ledge and buried his face in his hands.

"I do not take your meaning."

Darcy turned his head towards her, his eyes earnest and pleading. "Be honest with me now. Do not spare me. Have I injured you?" Her confusion was apparent, and her eyes searched his for understanding. He was loath to declare this additional failure but still made the attempt. "These many years…we were once good friends."

As clarity reached her eyes, she turned her face away to look at her gloved hands. "I do not blame you. I knew it was my mother's ambitions."

"I should not have acted as I have. It is unpardonable. We were friends, and I pushed you away."

He felt her hand on his forearm and opened his eyes. He looked up to meet her kindly eyes when she spoke.

"William, it is true that we were once intimates. And while I do regret the loss of your confidence, I know why you withdrew your attention. I am not so devoid of understanding as to think that my mother's wishes for us were your own." When he made to apologize, she cut him off again. "Nor were they ever my own."

Darcy was silent, considering his cousin's words. She had also addressed him by the familial shortened version of his Christian name. *That* she had not done for many years, probably out of respect for the distance he was trying to create. While he was relieved to know she understood his reasoning, it still weighed on him to know he had given her grief. Suddenly, Darcy remembered her blush when she informed her mother of her intentions to take the air with him. He hoped she was not prevaricating with him when she said it was not her wish that they marry.

"Forgive me, Anne. While I do not wish to further discomfit you, I…" Darcy wavered over his words. *Was it insensitive to question her assertions?*

Anne waited patiently for him to finish, and finally the words came rushing out of him. "You blushed—inside just now when you spoke to your mother about my escort outside."

Anne gave him an impish half smile as she turned, unconcerned by the gravity in his voice. "While I may be of uncertain health, I am by no means without talents."

Her features transformed into the picture of a demure maiden, and a warm bloom overspread her cheeks. In disbelief, laughter erupted from Darcy as he shook his head.

"Unbelievable! That is a dangerous talent to possess!"

Anne shushed him and looked apprehensively towards the open door herself. "It worked, did it not?"

"Indeed, it did. However, I cannot think to what purpose you would employ that 'talent' if you did not mean to mislead me—and your mother—into thinking…" Though Darcy's voice began with good humour, the truth of his words ended in earnest.

"I wished to speak privately with you. And I could not foresee the chance without deceiving my mother in the process—though it is true I wished to be granted the liberty of enjoying a bit of this beautiful day as well."

"You must allow me to apologize again. My negligence has also led you to live a very isolated existence." True regret filled Darcy's voice.

Anne laughed quietly, bringing him some comfort. "There may be some truth to that, but I daresay it is in the past now."

"You are too generous." Darcy vowed to himself to restore the closeness he once had with Anne.

They were quiet for a few minutes. Darcy recalled many instances when she, with some manoeuvre or another, had made his visits to Rosings more comfortable. Often, when he was most in want of release from his aunt's constant attention, Anne seemed to come to his rescue. She might stand to retire, allowing him to also retire for the evening. And more recently, when the party from Hunsford had dined with them, he had been trapped by Lady Catherine into speaking about Georgiana's piano accomplishments when all he longed to do was join his cousin and Miss Elizabeth at the piano. With sudden insight, Darcy remembered the uncharacteristic way in which Anne had inserted herself into the conversation with her mother, thus allowing him an escape so he could command a full view of Elizabeth.

Anne broke into his thoughts. "I think you know I saw you in the garden with Miss Bennet."

From either the emotions now rushing to the fore again or a lack of knowing what to say, Darcy did not reply.

"And I must acknowledge I have observed your certain partiality for the lady."

Anne's gentle probing snapped the tenuous hold Darcy had on his reserve. She had once been his confidante. He had no doubt she would execute the office admirably now. His lips pinched together briefly, one last instinct to protect the secret, before nodding to her. "I admire the lady greatly. In fact, I admire her above all others."

Anne smiled. Despite wishing to assure her the topic did not trouble him overmuch, he could not return the smile.

"I do think it will be a brilliant match. She is beautiful and warm and lively. And you, dear cousin, want for nothing but a little more liveliness, and that, if you marry prudently, your wife may teach you." She laughed at her own wit then, causing Darcy to wince. "When will you propose?"

The genuine eagerness in her voice forced Darcy to look down. He ran his fingers along a groove in the chiselled railing, the image before him growing ever more blurry as his eyes grew moist. Swallowing, he succumbed. "She would not have me."

Darcy heard his cousin gasp and turned slowly to regard her with a sad smile and a shrug of his shoulders. Her eyes slanted with the utmost compassion as understanding dawned. He watched her open her mouth to speak, but no sound came. Her words failed her. He understood the feeling. They failed him too when he thought of the outcome of that most painful evening. Darcy looked up at the sky and exhaled loudly—all in an attempt to push back the evidence of his distress from his eyes.

With gentle nudging, Anne persuaded him to reveal all. Some of it was recalled with the fevered feeling of fresh wounds, others with his more recently acquired humbled perspective. Regardless of his feelings about any given point of the evening, he shared it all with his one-time friend. Her gentleness of spirit made easier his confession of this most personal account. She neither mocked nor rebuked—though he knew he deserved the severest of tongue-lashings.

The narrative brought him current, including the tormenting pleasure of her company again in the maze. When he finally finished, Darcy felt a surprising lightness fill his breast. It had done him good to confide in Anne. He felt certain of her secrecy, which made the mortification he experienced in sharing this trust somehow lessened. When, after several minutes, his cousin still had not spoken, Darcy asked, "Have you nothing to say to me regarding my foolishness?"

Anne played with the cuff of her sleeve, the delay inflaming his impatience. Just as he might have spoken again, her meek voice reached his ears.

"What would you have me say?"

She looked at him with clear, kind eyes. He expelled his breath in despair. "I know not."

With a little hesitation in her voice, Anne said, "You have made some grave errors…not in choosing to pursue Miss Bennet, mind you…but perhaps in doing so without the benefit of considering her feelings and wishes in the process. You are a good man, Fitzwilliam Darcy, and in time, she may see that. Perhaps in the *meantime* you might make yourself into a better man, the kind of man she deserves."

"*There is, I believe, in every disposition a tendency to some particular evil, a natural defect, which not even the best education can overcome.*" Darcy turned away from her, his own words at Netherfield coming to mind. He knew her to be right though faulty in one respect.

"I very much doubt our paths will cross after this. There is little chance of her coming to see any good in me."

She shrugged her shoulders then pulled the shawl tighter across them. He straightened and offered her his arm, seeing that the air had begun to chill as the sun had risen high enough to put their balcony in the shade of the house. "It may be so, or it may not. You have yet to right the wrong with your friend Bingley."

Darcy halted his steps and looked at his cousin. "Do you think it ought to be attempted? What if Bingley's sentiments have changed or—worse still—hers have without her sister knowing."

"Cousin." Anne frowned disapprovingly. "Regardless of the current sentiments of either, it is not for *you* to choose. You have wronged your friend. At the very least, you must apologize to him. However goodly meant your interference—"

"Interference!"

Anne levelled him with such an uncompromising countenance, so very like her mother's, that it stopped him in his protest.

"It can be called very little else. The material point is that you have a tendency to make choices for others without considering their feelings."

She allowed this last to penetrate and hit its mark. From his pained mien, the message had hit squarely where it ought.

"I shall consider it." As they approached the parlour doors to return to the company inside, Darcy hesitated briefly. "Thank you."

Anne nodded as she preceded him into the room. Upon reaching the others, Darcy asked whether she felt well enough to stay or wished to retire and rest for the afternoon.

"I shall just stay a moment longer, thank you."

Darcy excused himself also from his aunt, who said nothing of their lengthy time together out of doors, instead looking highly pleased. His farewell to the parson was more succinct, allowing the man little opportunity to offer his copious felicitations.

Anne waited until her cousin had left the room before attending briefly to the conversation resuming between her mother and Mr Collins, though it could hardly be called a conversation since it consisted almost entirely of Lady Catherine's voice interspaced with occasional devoted agreement from the gentleman.

At present, her mother was advising Mr Collins in the most strident terms about the planned departure of Miss Bennet and Miss Lucas. Anne learned that the ladies were to travel to London by post the day after tomorrow.

"Have you purchased their tickets for the journey, Mr Collins?"

"I have not, Lady Catherine. The weather has prevented me from going into the village until today, and I thought it best to see to your needs first, your ladyship. I came straight away to call upon you and assure myself of your continued health."

Lady Catherine waved his solicitousness away with a swipe of her grey glove. "You must see, Mr Collins, that they travel through Bromley. The inn there is always attentive to my needs. They should mention my name and so be accommodated."

"I will see to it immediately."

"Bromley, Mr Collins. Do not forget!" Lady Catherine punctuated her advice with a tap of her cane upon the damask carpet.

Anne watched with hidden amusement as Mr Collins nodded vigorously and began a low murmur, "Bromley. Bromley. Bromley." In an elevated tone, he addressed her mother again. "It shall be done."

"Of course, there are other towns along the route to London where one might stop, but I declare that none are as suitable Bromley."

While Anne observed the interaction, she contemplated the situation with her cousin. It was grave indeed though perhaps not without hope. It had to have been an awkward meeting that morning in the garden, understanding it was their first encounter after the proposal and his giving her the letter. She did not think Miss Bennet devoid of sense, and her cousin's letter surely would have repaired some of his character in the lady's eyes.

"Mr Collins, as you must know, my mother is always attentive to those within her reach." Both Lady Catherine and the parson looked at Anne with some surprise at her joining the conversation. Before either her mother or Mr Collins could agree, Anne continued. "As such, I am sure I speak for her wishes when I say we would be pleased to have your party dine with us tomorrow evening." Anne glanced at her mother who, though slightly displeased at the suggestion, did not protest. "In honour of Miss Bennet and Miss Lucas's departure."

"Miss de Bourgh," Mr Collins said in his most reverent tone, "you and your ladyship"—here he looked towards Lady Catherine with undisguised adoration—"do us a great honour with your invitation, and I can assure you, we heartily and most humbly accept."

Mr Collins bowed deeply to Lady Catherine and then to Anne.

"Yes, well..." Lady Catherine began with feigned acceptance. "We dine at six."

Checking his watch, Mr Collins straightened suddenly. "Although it pains me to deprive myself of your company and wise counsel, Lady Catherine, I must excuse myself now if I am to make it to the village to book my relations' passage for their journey."

Lady Catherine nodded regally to the cleric and reminded him once again about stopping in Bromley. With another round of bows and goodbyes, Mr Collins took his leave. Lady Catherine turned to her daughter and said, "You were long out of doors with Darcy, Anne."

It was a question posed behind the veneer of a statement, and Anne knew her mother was requesting information. Anne withheld a smile at the thought of telling her mother that her cousin had proposed. It was the truth, though not to her. Instead, she chose to heed her mother's oft-given counsel to practice more. Thus, Anne purposefully looked down at the hands in her lap and produced a brilliant blush. When her mother nodded smugly and did not question her further, Anne added a shy smile to her charade.

CHAPTER 6

Hands cupped around her jaw, Elizabeth pursed her lips and tilted her head to the side as she studied the reflection before her. Her hair, which could never be considered classically beautiful—always managing to unravel itself from the pins that would tame it—reflected the light from the window. In the late afternoon illumination, Elizabeth allowed herself to be pleased at least by the array of chestnut hues that wove through her dark, curly locks. Nevertheless, even now, after having just replaced all her pins anew, her thick hair positively strained to be released.

Humming absently to herself, she tilted her head the other way to study her face. There was a lack of symmetry to her features in more than one area. She had neither Jane's serene blue eyes nor her rosy complexion. Her skin was fair though touched with the occasional freckle, no doubt a result of her disregard for a bonnet on her walks. Her eyes, framed by long lashes were dark brown and, to her inspection, almost questioning. Her uncharacteristic interest in her reflection could only be for the sake of one man. His expressed adoration had left her entirely at a loss for reason.

While she knew that Darcy belonged to a greater social sphere than her own, as a gentleman and a gentleman's daughter, they were equal. Yet, looking at herself, Elizabeth wondered how so great a man could have admired her and, if she were honest, which of her features he admired most.

Shaking her head, Elizabeth sighed. In all likelihood, Mr Darcy by now had easily pushed into the past any admiration he possessed for her features. Her reasoning surely had left her. One moment, she despised the man for his arrogance and conceit. In the next, she pitied him for his disappointment at her hands. And still, she also knew remorse. Her behaviour towards him, though not constituting any real regret for her decision, made her feel a shrew. She had never remembered losing her temper so thoroughly in her life.

She dared not contemplate his account regarding Mr Wickham. Her folly in that quarter would undo any sense of composure she had at present. And considering she was mere moments away from setting out with her party for Rosings to dine with him, she required all the composure she could muster.

How glad she would be to put this whole episode behind her when she returned to London on the morrow. After the encounter with him in the garden yesterday morning, and now this evening before her, Elizabeth felt her sensibility positively frayed. Distance between them was all she needed to finally comprehend the events of the last se'nnight. Some time and distance would give her sense. Nodding to her reflection as she added her wrap, Elizabeth's lips lifted into a wry smile. Sense and sensibility were what she needed now.

While her fingers fumbled over the button at her neck, her mind recollected Mr Darcy's gentle hands unfastening her bonnet. Warmth swept through her cheeks at the memory. For a man whom she had sworn to hate for all eternity, she was having a difficult time finding distaste for his gentle touch or his scent that had engulfed her.

He had little to recommend himself by way of his manners to be sure; yet, now knowing more of his character, he began to appeal to her. She could not deny she had found him handsome from the start of their acquaintance. His broad shoulders, dark features, and strong jaw might have flustered Elizabeth had she allowed them that power. This fact had spurred her distaste for him as it seemed his handsome features were wasted on such a contemptible man. Besides, her beauty he had withstood, making charity for *his* all the more difficult for Elizabeth.

A knock at her chamber door jolted Elizabeth from her musings.

"Are you ready, Eliza? Mr Collins insists we depart soon or else we risk truancy at her ladyship's table."

Smiling at her friend's playful tone, Elizabeth nodded as she stood to retrieve her wrap that hung near the door. "I am quite ready. Heaven forbid we are late on my last evening at Rosings."

Charlotte laughed and walked on to collect her sister Maria. Elizabeth paused at the threshold of her room.

Squaring her shoulders, she caught her reflection in the glass again. She used the mirror to practice a civil smile.

Pleased with the result, Elizabeth opened the door. *I can do this.* She could be in his company with neither the raging symphony of anger and dislike that played staccato in her mind since the day of his proposal nor the confounding, sweeping song of allure that flowed in the undercurrent of her breast like the deep, slow notes of a cello.

With a steady breath, she descended the stairs and joined the party bound for Rosings. Much to Elizabeth's chagrin, the cello's song was the hardest to suppress.

～

Thanking his valet and dismissing him for the evening, Darcy studied himself in the mirror only long enough to confirm he was presentable. He did not want to see the haunted expression that might be detected in his eyes. Knowing as he did that in mere moments he was to see her again, he needed little provocation to lose any of the hard-won composure he held tenuously at present.

Colonel Fitzwilliam's return from his visit to Hunsford yesterday had been torture. Oblivious to his cousin's dark expression, Richard had expounded at length on the beauty of Miss Elizabeth. She had returned from a morning walk only moments before he had arrived to call on the parsonage. Knowing as Darcy did that she had just left—nay, fled—his company before arriving home made Richard's appreciation of her flushed cheeks and bright eyes all the more excruciating. His report of her continued civility and easy manners was also difficult to hear. *She has never been easy with me. Will I ever have that pleasure? Likely not.*

Darcy at least could claim that, during the whole of Richard's speech, he betrayed nothing of his inner turmoil. If he could manage to elude his cousin, then he might have some chance to keep himself in check during the evening.

Pausing briefly at his writing desk, the tips of his fingers drifting over a blank sheet of parchment, Darcy debated, then conceded, then sat. Taking up the quill, he dipped it in the ink, tapped it once, and with a steady, practiced hand, wrote out her name.

Miss Elizabeth Bennet,

Though I deserve the torture that will be mine to see you this evening one last time before you and I part ways, you do not deserve to be discomfited by my presence once again. If it were possible, I would excuse myself. You must know it is not. I apologize for this. However, I vow with all the strength I possess not to injure you further this evening. Seeing your eyes, hearing your laughter, and drinking in your smile will be the things I trea-

sure as my last memories as I will not trouble you with my conversation. For your comfort, I will govern my actions, thinking for once of your feelings beyond my own and thus, it is my hope, securing for you a small reprieve from any distress you might have from being in company with me this evening.

Most sincerely,
Fitzwilliam Darcy

With swift hands, Darcy sanded, folded, sealed, and addressed the missive. Resolutely, he placed it with the others in the secret compartment of his travelling writing desk and left his chambers feeling better for having set his purpose for the evening.

~

When Darcy entered the drawing room, the party from Hunsford was already assembled. Darcy kept his resolve through the greetings and small pleasantries that were expected.

When she asked politely after his bee sting, he managed to keep his voice steady as he thanked her for her concern and assured her that it was well healed. His hand had drifted automatically to softly touch that spot where he had been stung. It was tender, but the recollection of her holding his hand dispelled any discomfort. It did remind him, however, to keep his distance for her sake and comfort.

Though he was always aware of her, she made as much of an effort as he did to avoid eye contact, thus confirming it was not with pleasure that she dined at Rosings and in his company.

Darcy circled the room before taking up his accustomed spot near the hearth. Turning away from the room, Darcy kept his focus on the profile of his aunt. Occasionally, he was required to make some response, but other than that, he easily refrained from any other conversation. If not for Elizabeth's gentle voice, mixed occasionally with Richard's, Darcy could almost convince himself she was not present.

If *his* wishes were his only concern, he would have turned to gaze upon her in full. He would have soaked in her beauty and perhaps even walked to where she sat near Colonel Fitzwilliam and inserted himself into their conversation. A wry smile lifted the corners of his lips. Moreover, his true wishes would include removing Richard entirely from the conversation. Darcy would have wished for her exclusive attention.

A tinkling laugh reached his ears, and before he could stop himself, he turned towards the enchanting sound. As he studied her that evening, her discomfiture reminded Darcy why he would not act on his wishes. All previous humour fled as he admonished himself to remember he was not there that evening to suit himself; he was to act in accordance with her feelings. And it was quite obvious by the way her eyes pinched at the sides and her smile weakly appeared that, although she was enjoying his cousin's wit—damn his eyes!—she was still unsettled.

Compassion for her plight softened his eyes and delayed their obedience to his vow. He ought to look away, but then, as their eyes met, strands of pleasure and pain wove themselves into a rope that coiled itself around Darcy's neck like a noose. It was hard to breathe through the longing he felt for her and the knowledge that he was the source of her uneasiness. Her pink, beguiling lips hinted at a smile, civil in its appearance and perfectly unlike the effervescent joie de vivre that usually animated her face.

Darcy nodded and turned his head, tearing his eyes away from her features to study the weave of the carpet below his feet. If he needed further proof that he made her uncomfortable, that was it. Until dinner was served, Darcy kept his gaze locked entirely where it was.

Elizabeth looked at her hands in her lap and attempted to convince herself to be pleased with successfully controlling her features when her eyes locked with Mr Darcy's. It had not been without great effort as the rumbling timbre of the cello resonated into a crescendo when her brown eyes met his, the vibrating notes no longer playing slow, purring tones but rather like the plucking beats of her heart.

It was distressing she should feel this way towards him, now of all times. She had rejected his suit, and when their feelings ought to be in accordance once more—his returning to indifference towards her and hers returning to disregard towards him—she found it entirely impossible to ignore the stirring interest she had for him. It must be conceit, Elizabeth reasoned as Colonel Fitzwilliam continued to speak. If it were not for the knowledge that, at one time, she—Elizabeth Bennet—had garnered the admiration of such a man as Fitzwilliam Darcy, she might not have this vanity. It pleased her now to know she had gained his affection even as days ago it was her avowed belief that his good opinion was never her wish.

She was distressed to admit this failing in her character. It had been a se'nnight of newly discovered weaknesses. She was prideful and had a tendency towards prejudice, and now she was vain—and interested in a gentleman merely because he had admired her!

Her admiration of him was steadily growing, based on his merits, character, and goodness so recently learned via his letter and their encounter in the garden. She was flattered to know she had inspired passion in such a man. As a shiver ran up her spine, Elizabeth acknowledged a certain curiosity to see that same passion once again pass through his eyes and to see what might be had if the impenetrable self-possession for which he was known were dissolved by emotion. It was that very idea that sent the cello's song humming through her breast.

"Here you are, Miss Bennet," Colonel Fitzwilliam said as he bowed.

Startled, Elizabeth found that, while ruminating on Mr Darcy, his cousin had escorted her to her seat in the dining room. Her distress at having found herself so distracted caused her to smile rather excessively at Colonel Fitzwilliam to make up for her poor manners and inattention.

"Thank you, sir."

Darcy clenched his teeth to see that smile and realised in witnessing it that he had unconsciously allowed his eyes to rest upon her again. Mercifully, before his cousin could respond, Lady Catherine's imperious voice spoke loudly to her guests.

"Mr Collins! You cannot sit next to your wife! Move at once." She waved him away from his seat and indicated he switch with Elizabeth. "Miss Elizabeth, you will take up the seat on Mr Darcy's right."

"No!" Darcy blurted, drawing the startled eyes of many. Elizabeth's brow pinched at his rudeness and awoke him at once to correct his blunder. "I beg your pardon, Aunt, but I only wish to say that perhaps Miss Elizabeth might prefer to sit near her friend on this her last evening."

"If Mrs Collins will not be much distressed at the loss of her friend's company, I should like to have Miss Elizabeth by my side, Mother." Anne's sudden and unexpected contribution to the conversation brought all consideration to a halt as the unprecedented statement put an end to the debate. Miss Elizabeth would take the seat her ladyship wished as it solved the problem of Mr Collins sitting too near his wife and allowed Anne to sit next to Elizabeth.

Elizabeth stood, and Colonel Fitzwilliam escorted her to the chair beside Anne as others also shuffled their seating. Her confusion might have been apparent if not for the ironic humour she perceived in the entire episode. Mr Darcy was clearly trying to avoid her as evidenced by his sudden protest. Though the sharpness of it stabbed at her heart—and stirred a little of that resident anger at his rudeness—it was entirely for naught as his cousin Anne thwarted his poorly contrived explanation, placing Elizabeth at his side. While Elizabeth's wit had a barbed edge, tinted mostly from the incivility of his protest, Elizabeth could not help feeling relieved to have some of her previous dislike come once again to the fore regarding Mr Darcy. The cello's song was hardly noticeable when replaced by dislike.

Darcy glared at his cousin after the ladies sat, and he lowered himself into the seat beside Elizabeth. Over the curls of her head, he kept his eyes locked on those of Anne and, with raised brows, tried to communicate his displeasure for this little contrivance of hers. Anne understood his expression but, instead of having any remorse for her actions, indicated to him with a tip of her chin towards Elizabeth's lowered head that he should make more of an effort with Elizabeth. It was not the first time that evening Anne had made eye contact with him across the room to reprimand him for staying aloof. He understood she wished for him to woo Elizabeth and take advantage of this last evening together to gain her approbation. Anne did not realise *that* was not a possibility, and he would not, as promised in the letter he wrote before leaving his chambers, make Elizabeth uneasy with his presence. She had made her sentiments known, and Darcy would respect them. He only wished Anne had not felt compelled to play matchmaker just now.

Darcy swallowed hard and looked down at the bent head of his dinner companion. He ought to apologize for his outburst. He ought to assure her that he was not intending to be so uncivil, but before he could, her head turned towards Anne, and they began to converse quietly.

As the courses were placed before him, Darcy had no other option but to attend to his meal. He strained to hear what Anne and Elizabeth were saying, praying Anne would not further her well-meaning motives with Elizabeth on his behalf. The snippets of conversation that did reach his ears calmed him on that front for the most part. They spoke of the change the countryside had experienced over the course of Miss Bennet's stay in Kent. With Anne's occasional jaunt in her phaeton, she had a little something to contribute, and as ridiculous as it was, it pleased Darcy to see his cousin make such a sincere effort to become acquainted with Elizabeth. He could not see Elizabeth's face as it was turned from him, but the tone of her voice gave way that she was enjoying her conversation with Anne as well.

Darcy felt jealousy tiptoe up his back at the effortless way they spoke to each other—mostly because Elizabeth seemed to be easy with everyone but him. Except for a brief glimpse of that ease in the garden earlier, he had never much seen it directed his way.

When Elizabeth returned her attention to the plate before her, Darcy prepared himself to make his apology.

"Miss Elizabeth, please accept my apology for my incivility before dinner. It was never my intention to slight you. I *did* wish to allow you the pleasure of your friend's company and conversation…and wished to spare you mine." The low tones of his voice tickled her ear, and the cello surged inside her.

His eyes were kind, but she knew her company was also not his desire.

In the relative close proximity of the seating arrangements, she detected a hint of his cologne. The intoxicating mixture of lemon and sandalwood was fresh to her senses.

"Apology accepted, Mr Darcy, as I know that my company cannot be easy or desired by you."

Surprised, Darcy spoke rather without forethought. "No indeed, Miss Bennet. While your company has never been easy, it has always been desired."

"I cannot understand you, sir. In the same breath, you say my company is not easy and then that it is desired."

Darcy did not answer right away, and to buy himself some time, he took a bite. His return to his meal caused her to turn again to hers with a pinch at her brow. His heart was in a bruising squeeze for he longed to explain how he felt, yet it seemed to him that his words might distress her. It was that pinch of her beautiful brow that decided for him. She wished to understand his statement, and he had vowed to consider her feelings beyond his own. Hoping he was not making the wrong choice, Darcy leaned closer to her, the sleeve of his jacket just brushing her shoulder.

"Miss Elizabeth." She looked up at him, and he wished very much that he could have called her "Elizabeth." Swallowing the pain that came with the acknowledgment that he might never be able to claim that privilege, he opened his mouth to speak again. "I have thought about how to explain my words to you, and I hope that, in doing so, I will not say things that you would rather not hear. But alas, it cannot be helped."

Darcy drew in breath and proceeded, locking eyes with hers. "The last is simple: your company I have always desired. The first is the part that I rather suspect you will not take pleasure in hearing."

Elizabeth frowned, expecting a slight in terms as kind as possible. What he said instead stunned her. "I am not easy in your company—and never have been—because you bewitch me. I am a man of this world and have been blessed to want for nothing. Yet when I am near you, I feel all my words flee my mind and all my wits retreat, and all that is left of this gentleman is the bumbling mute you have heretofore known."

Elizabeth could not prevent the warmth at his words that began at her neck and spread to her cheeks. They were without a doubt distressing but, likely, not in the way that he expected nor in the way she felt before when he had declared admiration for her in the parsonage. At that time, his words had been tainted with pride, making their taste bitter. Here, he was painfully humble. Elizabeth heard a naked truth along with his words. It was this truth that caused her blush, for it was the first believable proof of his warm regard. The cello's song was loud and stirring, and she began to believe it was no cello at all but her heart's song, strumming wildly. This abrupt and disquieting realisation could not be examined at present, and to cover her sudden epiphany, she lowered her lashes to break eye contact.

In a riot of emotions, she teased. "It must rather be a relief when I leave then, sir."

Darcy smiled at her though sadness touched his eyes. "Ah, but there's the rub. Though my reason returns, I am then deprived of your company."

The two returned their attention to their plates as the next course was presented. Elizabeth's colour remained high and her thoughts disjointed throughout the rest of the meal. She laughed to herself to think that his affliction had become her own.

For Darcy's part, he tried to sort out what her reaction meant. He could not help feeling a little frisson of hope weasel its way into his heart. And though he was far from believing there was any atonement for his long list of sins in her eyes, he was left with a sweetness that lifted his spirits. At the very least, he hoped they could part with less bitterness between them.

He also struggled mightily with the discovery of a small birthmark on the left side of her neck just outside the hairline. It was pink and had seemed to brighten with her blush, seeming to demand his gentle kiss. Instead, he kept his attention squarely on his plate and the task of putting food into his mouth. If he studied his meal, he could not tip his head to glimpse the sweet temptation.

At length, Darcy heard Anne ask her about her travels the next day, and Darcy learned that Elizabeth was to leave in the early morning for London. From there she would stay only a day or two and continue on to Hertfordshire. Though he expected never to have the pleasure of seeing her again, it did give him some comfort to imagine he knew where she was in the world.

Though Darcy and Elizabeth did not speak much more, there was less of the awkwardness that painted their previous encounters in the garden and earlier in the meal. The newly acquired calm between them was only displaced when Darcy stood as the ladies left the men to their port.

His hand innocently brushed against the exposed flesh of her arms as he pulled the chair back for her. The softness of her skin sparked a flame in him, a blazing passion of love and longing that filled his eyes. The touch had startled her too as she quickly looked over her shoulder at him and caught the expression in his eyes before he was able to hide it. Her mouth opened in a breathy exhale, and as his eyes slid down to witness it, the expression flared once again before he stepped back from the chair to allow her to stand, drawing his gaze away.

Elizabeth could barely mumble, "Thank you," managing a wobbly curtsey before disappearing through the dining room doors behind the others.

"The duck was rather good tonight, eh, Darcy?" Richard resumed his seat and accepted the glass of port from a footman. "You even ate it. I thought you despised the stuff."

Colonel Fitzwilliam's deeply resonant voice sounded loudly in his ears, and he turned towards his cousin with a slight shake of his head to clear it. Clinching his tingling fingers into a fist, Darcy looked down at his plate and realised he did not remember eating the foul fowl.

CHAPTER 7

ELIZABETH STEPPED OUT OF THE POST CARRIAGE INTO THE BUSTLING COURTYARD of the coaching inn. Turning, she waited for her travelling companion, Maria Lucas, to descend. When Maria reached her side, they entered the inn for their refreshments. Bromley was a popular stop on the route to London, it would seem. To her side, Maria resumed her steady account of their past six weeks in Kent, detailing every tea, dinner, and encounter with the great estate of Rosings as if Elizabeth had not been present through it all. While she might have liked to forget her time in Kent, along with its accompanying whirlwind of astounding occurrences, Maria's endless babble allowed Elizabeth to have some time for reflection as the young girl rarely required any response.

"How much I shall have to tell!" Maria excitedly exclaimed with a dramatic drop of her shoulders.

Elizabeth paused on their way to the threshold of the inn and turned to look contemplatively at the road they just travelled. Mumbling to herself, she said, "And how much I shall have to conceal!"

Her reflective glance down the road brought her attention to the coach in which they had travelled just as they lowered her small trunk to the ground. A frown pinched the sides of her lips as she watched the grooms place her belongings next to Maria's trunk. As larger trunks were hefted atop the carriage, she was satisfied that the grooms were simply rearranging the load for the new passengers, thus Elizabeth and Maria turned to enter the inn for a brief respite while the horses were changed and they continued on to London.

The sudden change in light from the midmorning sun to the darkened walls of the inn caused the ladies to pause while their eyes adjusted. The inn was clean and looked to be quite busy as travellers of all types loitered at tables around the small room. A small, modest-looking girl was weaving through the tables, chairs, and constant activity of the patrons with the ease of a minnow through sea grass currents. To Elizabeth's satisfaction, it did not look like the services she offered were any more than the drinks and refreshments she carried on her small tea tray. Travelling without a manservant was never something that brought Elizabeth much ease as she had heard many horrid stories about the difficulties one might encounter.

For the first time, Elizabeth was thankful for Lady Catherine's insistence that Mr Collins book their passage through Bromley for, as they were required to travel to London without a manservant, at least their only stop would not be at some inn of questionable repute. Once they reached the coaching inn in London, Mr Gardiner would send his man to meet them with her uncle's carriage. Until then, Elizabeth would have to quiet her discomfort and be grateful their only stop would be of short duration.

"Come, Maria. I see an empty table over here. We shall have our tea and be on our way."

Elizabeth led her younger friend to the empty table and was barely settled when the efficient little minnow was already standing at her shoulder and asking what they might desire. Elizabeth ordered them a pot of tea and some bread and cheese. Then, with the ease of a long-standing acquaintance and the experience of many sisters much younger than herself, Elizabeth entertained Maria in the way that young girls are wont to enjoy with a lively discussion of the fashions around them. Busy as the inn was, there were travellers bound from many districts and most likely all headed towards the capitol as Bromley, it seemed, was an easy middle distance from just about anywhere.

She finished her cup and, placing it upon the saucer, hailed the young server to their table.

"Is there a retiring room? My companion and I would like to refresh ourselves before being trapped in the post carriage to London again," Elizabeth said, her chin tipped up to smile at the young girl.

The girl's responding frown confused Elizabeth. Glancing from Elizabeth to Maria, the girl hesitated and then said, "Ma'am, the London post left but a few minutes ago."

Concerned, Elizabeth rose from her seat with urgency, and grasping her belongings, she said, "That cannot be—we heard no announcement."

Twisting the towel hanging from her apron, the girl shook her head with worried eyes. "I am sorry, miss. That post…"

The rest was lost to Elizabeth as she tossed a few coins on the table, and with a thudding distress, she and Maria threaded through the busy inn and exited in a rush. Her half boots skidded to a stop in front of their trunks still gathered in a pile with their other belongings at the side of the courtyard where she first witnessed them being unloaded. With a strangled cry of disbelief, Elizabeth ran a few steps into the dusty road to look for the carriage though she knew it was a hopeless venture.

"How can this be? Oh—fifty miles of good road, indeed!" Elizabeth exclaimed to no one as the once-busy inn saw only a half dozen travellers near their own private carriages. Her hand went to her head and rubbed her brow in utter incredulity. Looking down at the reticule, bonnet, and gloves in her other hand, she numbly sought a repair for such a horrible mistake. She had not thought her conversation with Maria so enthralling that they would have missed hearing the announcement for the carriage. And never before while travelling had any such misfortune befallen her. She was at a complete and utter loss as to what she might do.

Maria's wail of distress brought Elizabeth out of her stupor—and a good thing too, for she heard the distant sound of hooves on the hard pack dirt coming from behind her, prompting her to remember that she was standing in the middle of the road with a carriage approaching. Turning to Maria, who by this time was nearing hysterics, Elizabeth's jaw set into a grim line as she gathered Maria's arm in hers and nearly stomped back towards the inn, determined to speak to the proprietor about this breach and see what might be done to correct it.

~

Darcy felt the carriage slow, and as he had instructed his coachman—bless the man for his efficiency in notifying Darcy his carriage was fixed and having their belongings loaded within the half hour so that they might depart from Rosings as soon as may be—that he did not wish to make any stops on the way to London, the decrease in speed caused his already stern countenance to morph into a displeased scowl.

"What delay shall befall us now?" Darcy huffed ungraciously.

Colonel Fitzwilliam laughed though he could tell he was walking a thin line with his cousin this morning. He thought Darcy would be pleased to finally be leaving Rosings, and considering their hasty departure—early enough to avoid further delays from their Aunt Catherine—Richard would have believed that his cousin's mood would have been jubilant.

He turned in his seat and opened the small door behind the legs of the coachmen to enquire for his cousin. "Ho there, John."

Before he could ask, Darcy's bellowing voice spoke loudly as well, "Where are we, John?"

The gruff voice of the coachman could barely be heard over the clopping noise of hooves and harnesses. "Bromley, sir."

"Unless the horses have come up lame, John, I said I did not wish to stop," Darcy said authoritatively.

Colonel Fitzwilliam eyed him with censure for his tone but turned towards the window. "We felt the carriage slow, John. Are the horses well?"

"Aye, sir. It's only there be a girl in the road ahead. She be moving off now, and I shall drive on soon 'nuff."

"Thank you, John," Colonel Fitzwilliam said with a raised brow at his cousin, reminding him that his poor mood ought not to be taken out on the servants.

Darcy quickly added his own thanks to the driver and felt the coach soon begin to increase in speed. He leaned back against the squabs and looked out the window at the passing buildings. Though a popular place to stop, there was hardly anything to Bromley as a town. It twisted his poor mood to accept that Colonel Fitzwilliam was right and that he had let this cloud of discontent make him more terse then normal with his loyal groom. Considering the manner in which the groom had hastened their leave from Rosings, Darcy felt rather worse for nearly taking the man's head off.

He ought to be glad to finally be leaving a place that had caused him such heartache. He ought to see the early note from his coachmen that his carriage was ready as a blessing. After reading that the man had learned the carriage was finished late in the evening the night before while he had been dining with Elizabeth...shaking his head, Darcy focused his thoughts once again. The man had ridden one of the coach horses nearly ten miles to where the coach had been brought for repairs and retrieved his equipage late in the night so that they might depart early that morning. His valet had informed him of the carriage's return as soon as Darcy rose to break his fast. Already his servants had begun to pack his belongings and those of his cousin. Within nearly impossible times, he was on his way out of Kent—away from his aunt's home, away from where Elizabeth had enchanted and broken him, and hopefully away from all those miserable feelings.

Only, almost as soon as they had passed the parsonage—and this time Darcy did allow himself to glance out and up to the window he thought she might have claimed—Darcy felt a heaviness settle on his shoulders. It was as if all those hopeless, broken feelings of loss and longing had woven into a heavy blanket that wrapped itself around him. She would not be his; he would now have the unpleasant task of training his heart to accept it.

It was in this attitude that Darcy saw the girl his man must have been speaking of standing off by the side of the road ahead. The road curved to the right, and so she was visible from his vantage long before they would come upon her. He watched as she raised her arms and threw them down with such temper that her distress was obvious. As the coach drew closer, her features cleared through the haze of dust that had already coated the outside of his carriage.

Her dark curls glistened in the sunlight, and a lump caught in Darcy's throat. It could not be! His luck could not be so bad as to…yet, as they passed in a clatter of wheels, hooves, and harness jangles, Darcy's eyes widened in disbelief at seeing Elizabeth's impassioned eyes turn from the road as they passed to walk with determined shoulders back to the inn.

Darcy drew in a breath and held it. Everything in him longed to be by her side. In his chest, a great crack opened, and every feeling and sensation was tugged from that place and pulled out the window—as if his very life no longer belonged with him but with her.

Suddenly, his carriage stopped. The horses' displeasure at the sudden demand from their driver sounded in huffs and stomps of their hoofed feet.

Darcy turned to his companion with a frown. Automatically, he twisted to look back through the window, but they were far enough past the inn that he could see nothing in the bend of the road. Angered, he snapped at Richard.

"What is it now? Why have we stopped?"

Colonel Fitzwilliam's brows rose in astonishment at either his tone or his words; nevertheless, his cousin was not intimidated as he should have been by Darcy's abrupt tone.

"You ordered it so, your highness," Richard said mockingly as he crossed his arms.

Startled, Darcy blinked. "What?"

"Just now. You nearly knocked me off my seat when you bellowed, 'Stop!' to the driver."

Darcy sat in mute surprise. It seemed he had unwittingly ordered his coachman to stop! His mind went immediately to the image of Elizabeth in the courtyard, and he frowned at his own weakness. He had imagined stopping to see and speak to her once more. And now he had voiced his desire. For a moment, the temptation was so great then to exit the carriage. Seeing as they had stopped…

His cousin interrupted his thoughts. "What is wrong with you?"

Darcy looked over at him and, not wishing to reveal the true reason for his sudden outburst, said, "In the courtyard, back there, the girl—in the road—I think may have been Miss Bennet. She...she looked distressed."

"Then we ought to see that she is all right."

Richard made for the door of the carriage as if to exit, but Darcy caught his arm. "Certainly, there can be no need. It may not have even been her. And if it is, Aunt Catherine instructed Mr Collins to ensure they stop in Bromley. You must remember her expounding about it at length last evening. I am sure there is no need for our intrusion on Miss Bennet's travels."

He abhorred the pleading in his voice and hoped Richard did not detect it. The last thing Darcy wished was to thrust his unwanted company once again on Miss Elizabeth. Could he not be free of her? Still Richard looked at him perplexed.

"Ought we not to see that she does not require any aid?" Richard said, still perched ready to exit the carriage. "As you say, she looked distressed."

That detail eroded his will to simply drive on. In good conscience, he could not leave any lady of his acquaintance in distress when he might be of assistance, and Elizabeth owned more than half of his motivation for anything. Though he doubted their aid was needed nor wanted, he hesitated but a moment.

"You are correct; forgive me. We ought to at least make certain she does not require assistance." Darcy then opened the door to his right and called to his coachman as he exited. "Turn around, John, and rest the horses at the Rose and Crown. We shall stop after all."

Richard joined him in the short walk back, and with every step, Darcy felt the beats of his heart. How many times would he think he had seen Elizabeth for the last time only to encounter her once more? The rate of his heart and his trepidation at seeing her escalated the closer they marched to the coaching inn.

When they stepped through the entrance of the inn, Darcy's eyes immediately scanned the room as they adjusted to the dim lighting until he saw her speaking energetically with the innkeeper. As they drew closer, he could hear her fevered words.

"I am certain you are mistaken, sir. My companion and I were booked on that post carriage!"

"I am sorry, ma'am, but I do not have your name on my registry. We would have certainly notified you of its impending departure." Though the tone of his voice was civil, Darcy could tell the innkeeper was firm in his approximation of the situation.

Reaching their small party, Darcy noticed Miss Lucas was sniffling quietly into her handkerchief beside Elizabeth. It seemed that the post coach had left her and Miss Lucas behind. A surge of anger swelled up into Darcy's throat, and he had a difficult time dispelling it. In Darcy's opinion, Elizabeth ought never to travel by public carriage, and the idea of Elizabeth left stranded in a strange village boiled inside him, further fuelled by his frustration in knowing it was not his place to ensure her safety now or in the future. He may have a duty as a gentleman to see she was not mistreated, but the fact that it was not his duty forever after burned around the smouldering edges of his already charred heart.

Clearing his throat, Darcy stepped forward and addressed the innkeeper. "What is the difficulty here, sir?"

Startled, Elizabeth stepped backward suddenly at the sound of his voice behind her. "Mr Darcy!"

Darcy and his cousin bowed to her, Richard speaking first. "Miss Bennet, might we be of some assistance?"

Elizabeth looked down at her gloved hands, twisted as they were around the strings of her reticule. It was clear that their sudden and unexpected arrival was unsettling to her. Whatever else she felt upon seeing him, Darcy could not guess and did not wish to contemplate.

"Oh no, sir. I would not wish to importune you. There is simply a misunderstanding here."

Darcy looked towards the innkeeper with a raised brow, causing the man to swallow audibly before beginning to explain. "It is just that these ladies have missed the coach to London, sir, and while I am terribly sorry for their inconvenience, there is nothing I can do. They were not on my list. I assure you, I would have made certain they were on the coach if they were, sir."

"I have my tickets right here, sir!" Elizabeth objected heatedly again. She began to riffle through her reticule until she found the slip of paper for which she was searching. "Aha! Here it is."

A protective thump in Darcy's heart swelled at the thought of Elizabeth being so poorly treated as this. He and the colonel stepped forward to examine the paper with the innkeeper. There would be much to pay if negligence had caused Elizabeth this distress.

The innkeeper swallowed again, and with a slight tremor to his voice, the man spoke. "I see the problem now, ladies. I am sorry to inform you that this ticket was to take you through to Bromley only."

"What?" several people said at once. Elizabeth reached for the paper to examine it.

A second was all it took for Elizabeth to sag in defeat at the confirmation of the innkeeper's assessment. Her idiot cousin had not booked them passage entirely to London! Darcy gently slipped the paper from her hand as she stood there stupefied.

Looking at the receipt, Darcy could see that indeed the journey had been booked only through to Bromley. He passed it to his cousin's eager hands before looking over to the innkeeper again.

"Then you must book her on the next carriage for London right away. It is clear that she intended to travel to London and that this was a mistake."

Elizabeth looked up at Darcy gratefully for his interceding on her part but shook her head with frustration. "It seems my cousin was so focused on making certain we followed a certain *lady*'s counsel to stop in Bromley that he failed to purchase the ticket to London with a *stop* in Bromley and instead we are now *stopped* here."

"Come, Miss Bennet, Miss Lucas. Why do you not have a seat? Darcy and I shall see that everything is sorted out."

Though Elizabeth's eyes flashed brilliantly in defiance of the situation, she allowed Colonel Fitzwilliam to escort her to an empty table some short distance away before he returned to Darcy and the innkeeper.

"Gentlemen, it is with sincere regret that I cannot accommodate the Misses Bennet or Lucas today on another carriage for London."

"What are you saying, man? There are no more post carriages to London today?" Darcy scoffed disbelievingly and added, "I highly doubt that, sir."

"No there are more carriages, however—"

"Do you know who our aunt is, Mister…?" Richard leaned in authoritatively, the regimental military man in him coming to the fore.

"Daniels, sir." The innkeeper supplied with a bob of his Adam's apple.

"Mr Daniels. You might be interested to know, sir, that the 'lady' Miss Bennet referred to is none other than Lady Catherine de Bourgh. And it was on her recommendation that these ladies stopped here in Bromley and have thus graced your establishment. I sincerely doubt you would wish us to share with our *aunt* how poorly you have seen to her *particular* friends."

Darcy sincerely doubted that his aunt would consider her parson's relations as any particular friends of hers; nevertheless, the threat seemed to make some difference as the innkeeper's face paled and he began to rummage through his papers once again looking at carriage lists.

With a pat of his forehead with his handkerchief, the man spoke again, worry crippling his voice. "I am terribly sorry, gentlemen. I have looked, and the other two post carriages travelling to London today are full. The only space I have is an outside box seat for one—"

"That will not do, the ladies must travel together, and they cannot ride atop!" The idea of Elizabeth riding atop the public carriage like a common maid rankled Darcy. *Never!*

The innkeeper stepped aside to another book and began turning pages at a fevered pace. He stopped and, turning to Darcy, said, "I can assure her on tomorrow's carriage first thing in the morning."

"I am afraid that our arrival in London today cannot be delayed." The gentlemen turned quickly to find Elizabeth standing behind them. She stepped towards the innkeeper and continued. "But as it seems there is no alternative, then please secure us tickets for tomorrow's carriage." Elizabeth looked down into her reticule and pulled out a small purse to secure the tickets as she said, "We shall also require a room for the evening, sir."

"Might I ask why you are needed in London today, Miss Elizabeth?"

Darcy was grateful to his cousin for asking since his own curiosity was lapping at his thoughts.

Elizabeth turned a rueful expression over her shoulder. Darcy found her beauty quite arresting and admired the way her spirits seemed to be returning so quickly from the anger, frustration, and distress only moments before. Any other lady of the *ton* would have been in a fit of rage and hysterics by now. Not Elizabeth. She was angered and frustrated to be sure, but her naturally lively spirits returned when it looked as if there was nothing that could be done.

His admiration was barely concealed as she began to explain. "Miss Lucas was promised by her father a special trip to the shops in London tomorrow for her birthday. If we arrive tomorrow, they will not have time to shop, and seeing as they cannot delay their departure from London another day—due to Lady Lucas's spring ball—the much anticipated treat will have to be cancelled." Both gentlemen followed Elizabeth's gaze as she turned to look at Miss Lucas, weeping quietly at the table. "It is for this reason my friend is so distraught over this unfortunate turn of events. I do not relish having to tell her that we will be staying the evening."

Darcy stepped closer to Elizabeth and kindly asked, "Is there nothing we might do, Miss Bennet?"

Elizabeth looked up and met his eyes with her own bright ones. They held a bit of the teasing glint he had learned to love nearly from the beginning of their acquaintance, and Darcy's pulse sped at the sight.

With a raised eyebrow, Elizabeth pursed her lips in suppressed humour then allowed her features to fall dramatically. With a feigned pout, she said, "You might spare me the unpleasant task and tell her yourself, Mr Darcy."

Shaking his head as a slight smile pulled at the edges of his lips, Darcy said, "Anything but that."

Elizabeth laughed, the sound echoing through his hollow chest. "Then I am afraid not, sir. Thank you for concerning yourself here."

Darcy inclined his head in a bow and looked towards his cousin. He was surprised and momentarily wary of the speculative expression on his cousin's face. His wariness increased as it looked as if his heretofore blessedly oblivious cousin was coming to conclusions about Darcy that Darcy was not ready to have his cousin make.

Disliking the idea of leaving Elizabeth behind at the inn to stay the evening unprotected, Darcy decided he would leave one of his grooms behind to assure the ladies' safety, and he was prepared to offer the arrangements when his plan was pre-empted by his cousin.

"Miss Bennet, it seems to me a terrible inconvenience for you to have to stay here unprotected for the evening due to your cousin's mistake."

Elizabeth shot panicked eyes to meet Darcy's briefly. She began to shake her head and raised her hand to forestall Colonel Fitzwilliam, but he continued anyway. "I feel it is our responsibility, Miss Bennet, to right this wrong since it as our aunt who perpetuated it. Please allow us to escort you and Miss Lucas to London safely today."

As soon as Colonel Fitzwilliam quit speaking, Elizabeth almost fumbled the words in her quick attempt to protest. "Oh no, no, really, that is not necessary. I thank you, but we could not possibly…"

"It is no inconvenience. Darcy?"

Trapped so handily by his cousin, Darcy could only confirm the invitation though he knew that Elizabeth did not desire it. "Please consider it, Miss Bennet. It is indeed no trouble."

Darcy wanted to groan as Colonel Fitzwilliam flashed a broad smile at him and continued his persuasive argument. Darcy's only consolation was that it looked as if Elizabeth was not to be swayed.

"You have no manservant here as protection, and while I am sure you will be well taken care of in this fine establishment, it does not settle well with me to leave you here without one."

Here Darcy might have offered up the use of his groom as he had planned; however, he could not commit the words.

Elizabeth was still shaking her head, smiling slightly. "I thank you again. It is most generous of you to offer, Colonel, but I could not possibly…"

"Very well then, the lady has spoken. I shall not pressure you further." Colonel Fitzwilliam smiled congenially. Collectively, Darcy and Elizabeth drew in relieved breaths until Richard turned to the innkeeper and said, "Then we shall be requiring rooms this evening too, my good man."

Stunned, Darcy stared at his cousin with Elizabeth standing frozen next to him, her mouth open in astonishment. She seemed to recover from her shock more quickly as she stepped forward and, with an uneasy laugh, placed a hand on Colonel Fitzwilliam's arm, which rested on the innkeeper's desk. "Oh no, Colonel Fitzwilliam. Please—it is not necessary that you interrupt your trip on our behalf."

Darcy did not like the sight of her hand on his cousin's arm, and in a surge of possessive instinct, he stepped forward and, before realising what he was about, gently lifted Elizabeth's hand off his cousin's sleeve and pressed his other hand atop her small one now in *his* possession.

"It is no trouble, Miss Bennet," Darcy heard himself utter. "We have no fixed engagements calling us to London so urgently and may stay a night on the way with no trouble."

Elizabeth drew in a quick breath, withdrawing her hand slowly out of the shell of his two. The slide of her glove against his brought added warmth to her already rosy cheeks. "Mr Darcy, Colonel, really your offer is most generous and kind. However, London is barely two hours from here. There is simply no need to stay anywhere along the way on our behalf."

"Then you might consider allowing us to escort you today, Miss Bennet," Colonel Fitzwilliam offered kindly and with a satisfied countenance.

Darcy could hardly know what she saw in his eyes as he was careful to keep his face expressionless. He could not like the way his cousin had cleverly tricked her into riding with them, and she had been trapped handily by the manoeuvres of a seasoned military commander—she and Darcy both. However much he wished he could have spared her this unfortunate time in his company, it was as he told her last evening: *her* company was always desired by him.

"I…" Elizabeth began to protest again, albeit weakly.

"I might also point out to you"—Darcy was surprised to hear *his* own voice suddenly adding to his cousin's argument—"I, myself, have a much younger sister who counts among her accomplishments her ability to shop. I cannot abide the idea of preventing Miss Lucas her fun if it can be avoided." Darcy pretended to shudder. "It has been my experience that the outcome is never pretty."

A tender coil of pleasure surrounded him upon witnessing Elizabeth's burst of laughter. When she turned her merry, sparkling eyes upon him, he was as handily trapped by her as he and Elizabeth had been by his cousin.

"Very well, sirs. You have convinced me. But, Colonel, you ought to have started off your argument with the one Mr Darcy used. It might have hastened your triumph. We will accept your escort and with many thanks."

CHAPTER 8

WITH AN ODD LUMP IN HIS THROAT, DARCY OVERSAW ELIZABETH'S TRUNK secured atop his carriage. It was a strange feeling watching his beloved's belongings attached to his carriage. It was symbolic of all his wishes being fulfilled, yet there was a bitterness knowing those wishes were not reality. His hands at his side twitched into a fist briefly when his cousin's smug chuckle mocked his ears from just behind his shoulder.

Turning towards Colonel Fitzwilliam, Darcy frowned.

"Such a scowl! You ought to thank me for so handily and cleverly bringing this all about."

Darcy shook his head slightly as he returned his gaze to the bustle around his carriage. "If you had an ounce of observation, you might have noticed that the idea of travelling with us distressed Miss Bennet."

"Oh, I assure you I observed plenty." Richard laughed, forcing Darcy to clench his jaw. "Oh come on, my good man! I have done you a good deed, and you act as if I have—"

"Richard! Miss Bennet does not wish for my company!"

"She was being modest, Cousin." Richard attempted to placate Darcy, waving away his words as if they were of no importance. "If you allowed even a portion of your admiration—no, do not object! It is no longer hidden from me. If you allowed *the lady* to see it, however, you might find—"

Darcy stopped Richard gruffly. "Miss Elizabeth dislikes me heartily, Richard. Of this I am certain."

Colonel Fitzwilliam's protest was immediate as was his cousin's attempt to silence it.

"Trust me in this. There is nothing I am more certain of than that lady's opinion of me." *Nothing perhaps besides my opinion of the lady.* "Furthermore, I find it contemptible that you should—" Darcy swallowed his words as he noted the approach of the ladies.

Colonel Fitzwilliam turned to follow his cousin's gaze and laughed. Raising his voice he said, "I will see that Miss Bennet's and Miss Lucas's trunks are secured safely if you will inquire of them whether they are in need of anything before we depart."

Darcy stared at his cousin with cold eyes, for he hated to be managed in this manner. Richard could not know what he was doing, however *observant* he claimed to be. He might have seen a little more of what Darcy's feelings were regarding Miss Bennet, but he was way off the mark on his conclusions regarding *hers*.

With stiff shoulders, Darcy made his way towards the ladies standing some few feet away from his carriage. Awkwardly, he greeted them and inquired as to their needs before they departed. Though Miss Lucas seemed recovered from her doleful mood, Miss Bennet answered for them haltingly.

After the initial exchange, it seemed they were destined to stand about in silence. Elizabeth fidgeted with her reticule as the silence lengthened and felt more self-conscious of the interruption and disagreeable intrusion she was making on his journey to London. When Miss Lucas, never one to be comfortable in company with the imposing and intimidating visage of Mr Darcy, excused herself quietly, walking away towards her belongings, Elizabeth felt her pulse quicken and her cheeks pale.

What a strange and horrible penance she was experiencing for her brash words in refusing his proposal, that she should have encountered him unexpectedly not once but twice since then. Additionally, her dinner at Rosings last evening seemed oddly fitting in this unlucky turn of fortune.

Remembering the previous evening when his fingers accidentally brushed against her bare arm as he pulled her chair out brought back all the warmth that previously fled Elizabeth's cheeks when Maria left her standing alone with Mr Darcy.

His unexpected arrival at the inn and subsequent assistance with the innkeeper, while it could not be considered wished for, was not altogether unpleasant. Mr Darcy, she had learned, was a most intriguing gentleman— one she might have wished to know better. The gentleman in question dragged his boot across the dust on the ground, drawing her gaze as well. This sign of his unease reminded her why she protested so vehemently against travelling with him.

Mr Darcy spoke briefly with one of his grooms and then turned towards her. "Have you the letter for your uncle, Miss Bennet? My man will ride ahead to inform your relations of your change in conveyance."

"Yes, yes of course. Thank you."

Her hands flew immediately to the strings of her reticule, fumbling with them until she could open the small bag and retrieve the note she had just written to her uncle, explaining her delay and how she came to be travelling instead with Mr Darcy. With shaky hands, she gave the small missive to the gentleman. Their eyes caught and held only a moment before he thanked her and passed it on to his groom. Together they watched silently as the man mounted a hired horse and rode off down the London road at a pace.

She suddenly felt the need to apologize. "Sir, I am heartily sorry for—"

"Please, there is no need." Darcy swallowed and wondered how they were to survive two hours together in a carriage with so much tension choking them. Determined to put her at ease, he said, "I am sincerely glad to be of assistance, Miss Elizabeth."

She saw the softness in his eyes that betrayed the formality of his stance and the vacancy of his expression. His dark eyes emboldened Elizabeth to speak next. "Mr Darcy…I am rather concerned about the space in the carriage." Her lips were pursed in serious reflection though her eyes already danced with humour.

His brows rose in mild affront as he turned to look at his carriage and then back at her. "I assure you my carriage is adequately sized for four. I should think we will travel quite comfortably."

To his surprise, she laughed. It danced around him like fairy nymphs until the musical sound tapped and toed its way right onto the surface of his heart. The pleasure of that moment outweighed the lingering sting of his disappointment. Though he did not understand the source of her amusement, he could not help himself from smiling in response.

Elizabeth caught her breath when he met her eyes, and after biting her poor lip briefly to compose herself—and unwittingly discomposing Darcy further—she turned sparkling eyes up to him. "Not if we are to take along with us this giant beast that always seems to be about when we are in company together."

Though her words began laced with humour, they soon sobered when she once again looked at him. What could she mean by purposefully alluding to his proposal? The ache in his chest returned, and Darcy could not hold her gaze, dipping his head once again to examine his boot. What Elizabeth wished for him to say on the matter, he knew not. To him it felt cruel that she should delight him so easily with her laughter in one moment and then bring him to misery in the next.

The almost unperceivable pressure of her gloved hand on his forearm drew his attention. "Mr Darcy, sir. I am conscious of the discomfort I bring you by travelling with you, and while your words have been welcoming and indeed most gracious..." Elizabeth drew in a fortifying breath. She decided to be direct, and the words tumbled from her mouth. "...I despise that I am making this situation more difficult!"

But not sorry for refusing me, Darcy thought with tormenting acceptance. Turning his body slightly, to put himself between her and any observing eyes, Darcy gently placed his gloved fingers atop her own on his arm. He traced the stitching on her glove briefly before lifting her delicate hand in his and bowing slightly over it. He released it with some reluctance before he spoke. Bent as he was towards her, the timbre of his voice blanketed her.

"Please do not make yourself uneasy on my behalf. While neither of us expected to see the other again after last evening, circumstances have arisen." He paused briefly before continuing. "I must beg your forgiveness for my words that evening at the parsonage... Might we put this behind us and endeavour to forget it?"

Elizabeth searched his pleading expression. It should have relieved her to see his desire to forget the whole sordid affair, yet it could not. But seeing as she did that it was an almost desperate wish of his that she think no more of his words of love and admiration, she consented. Nodding her head in acquiescence, she never felt more a liar. Never could she forget the look of devotion, love, and tenderness that burned through his gaze that evening. And while his more disagreeable sentiments still smarted her bruised pride, they could not overwhelm her anymore with bitterness.

She heard herself say, "Yes, of course," and the words scratched her throat with their reluctance. She was left confused by her reaction. She did not love Mr Darcy and so could not marry him. These choked emotions must come from the remorse she felt in hurting him as she did with hurled accusations and unladylike pronouncements. But she had seen glimpses of his true character—starting with his letter and accumulating further through her encounter with him in the garden, again at Rosings, and there at an inconsequential coaching inn.

Colonel Fitzwilliam called his cousin's name, and their time for private converse was over. Darcy turned to answer his cousin, and Elizabeth's eyes studied the breadth of his broad shoulders. A pang in her heart plucked the strings of that cello, strumming slowly an echo of awareness most acute and troubling. When he turned once again to her, it was with a hand outstretched. His expression was sombre, the edges forced into a studied calm. "The carriage is ready, Miss Elizabeth."

She nodded, and as he walked her to the door of the carriage, she talked herself into a greater feeling of composure. She hoped that, by acknowledging the matter again, they could remove any awkwardness between them. Despite her efforts, she felt more unsettled than ever. They paused for a moment as Colonel Fitzwilliam helped Miss Lucas to enter the carriage and, after giving his cousin an enigmatic smile, entered after her, leaving Elizabeth alone with Darcy again.

With a tight smile, Darcy murmured, "Miss Elizabeth."

He had reached for her gloved hand, and she placed it securely within his grasp. His grip was firm and comforting. Elizabeth gathered her skirts with the other hand and bent to step up and into the carriage. As soon as she was settled safely next to Miss Lucas, he released her hand and, with a tip of the carriage, seated himself across from her. And while she had teased him about the size of his carriage, she now could see that there was perhaps some truth to her jest.

While his carriage was of impressive quality and size, his legs were long, however, and his shoulders wide. Immediately, Elizabeth tried to shift her position as her knees entangled and brushed against his as he, too, tried to adjust his legs. In the ensuing dance of knees and pardons, Elizabeth could feel the heat in her cheeks bloom hot.

She glanced at the other occupants of the carriage and saw that Colonel Fitzwilliam's expression was warm with amusement. Not for the first time, Elizabeth wondered whether he knew of his cousin's proposal. Miss Lucas seemed unconcerned as she looked eagerly out her window. Elizabeth noted the positions of *their* legs and saw that, with no little discomfort, they were arranged in such a way that neither seemed disturbed by the other's limbs. Immediately, she tried to emulate their arrangement as discretely as she could.

Spying a travelling escritoire between the gentlemen and knowing that their larger sizes made the bench on that side more cramped, Elizabeth thought of a solution to the disconcerting sensations occasioned by her leg brushing against Mr Darcy's and spoke, causing the dance of limbs to cease momentarily.

"Mr Darcy, allow me to place your travelling desk beside me here. It will fit more comfortably on the ladies' side than squeezed as it is between you gentlemen."

He seemed almost frozen, looking from the desk beside him to her. She thought she detected a trace of panic in his eyes but could not understand it and therefore decided she must have imagined it.

"I am sure we need not make you uncomfortable, Miss Bennet. I should have asked my groom to place it up top. I am sure there is time to…"

The jolt of the carriage caused his words to die away as it swayed into motion.

Elizabeth laughed at the timing, growing a little more desperate as the carriage's movement once again knocked her knees against his, nestled as they were between them.

"It is no trouble, you will see, sir. There is plenty of space," Elizabeth asserted shakily. "Your documents will be quite safe next to me, so have no fear on that account." She laughed once again to cover her discomfort and teased him. "I remember a lady of our acquaintance mentioning how many letters you must have to write in the course of a year. How odious!"

That remembrance brought a smile to his lips, and Darcy realised there could be no harm in having his case next to Elizabeth. Silently perceiving the irony, he considered it would be the closest his letters would ever be to her possession. With a nod, he passed her the case and leaned forward to help position it next to her in the carriage beside the window.

He noted she adjusted her legs discreetly so that, when he sat back again, his legs mostly straddled the case and not her own small knees. It was cleverly done, and he admired her ease in handling the situation without further embarrassment to either of them. As he relaxed back into the squabs, he also enjoyed the greater comfort as he and Richard were not packed so tightly. All in all, she could not have manoeuvred the solution more masterfully. Though he certainly had more space with which to relax, Darcy was not entirely sure the loss of the occasional brush of her skirts against his legs was worth it.

"Well, are we not a cosy lot now?" Colonel Fitzwilliam asked jovially. The other occupants merely smiled half-heartedly.

~

The journey settled into a quiet affair, and Elizabeth was surprised to find that it was a comfortable one. Occasionally, Maria would mention some vantage out her window, and Elizabeth would lean across her to see and comment back. The colonel spoke of their time together in Kent, and for a time, both Darcy and Elizabeth read.

Elizabeth held a book in her hands though she had not made much progress when Colonel Fitzwilliam addressed her.

"It is a beautiful piece of craftsmanship, is it not, Miss Elizabeth?"

"Pardon me, Colonel?"

He motioned with his hand towards hers lying across the writing desk beside her. Immediately, she lifted her hand as if the wood had scorched her. Absentmindedly, she had been tracing with her fingers the intricate carving pattern that followed around the side of the desk. Embarrassed, she looked automatically at Darcy, for her thoughts had been of him and the letter he gave her in the grove, the one he might have written on that very desk.

Darcy had been watching her over the edge of his book as she traced the pattern on the wood. It was mesmerising the way her slim fingers bent as they caressed in and around the grooves, and it captured his attention entirely, his book forgotten. He hoped the feelings surging in his breast were not discernible to his companions. Shifting his eyes, he turned towards his cousin, suspicious that Richard might have noticed his distraction with Elizabeth's movements. To his surprise, Colonel Fitzwilliam seemed to be wholly without mischief. Instead, his expression showed an impassioned interest in the topic.

Elizabeth cleared her throat, claiming Darcy's attention again.

"Yes, it is a very handsome case."

"I have one of my own, though it is not so finely built as my cousin's. It was given to me by my grandfather on my mother's side. I am embarrassed to admit it, but I am rather juvenile in my fascination with writing desks. If I had a home to claim as my own, I am sure I would have a collection to rival Darcy's book collection."

Elizabeth's brows rose in surprise as she laughed at his cousin. Darcy felt a splinter of jealousy, especially when she responded with eager interest. "We have that in common, sir! My father has three. One from his youth, one he was given during his university days, and one he uses now. I love all the little compartments and subtle design differences."

Elizabeth was immensely relieved that the colonel did not seem bent on embarrassing her about her earlier distraction. And while she was truthful in her assertion that she found writing desks interesting, she was never so voluble an enthusiast before as the topic perfectly concealed her earlier pastime.

In an attempt to include Mr Darcy in the conversation, she said, "It is a very fine desk."

"Thank you."

Darcy could not check an enigmatic smile as he considered the letters to the lady that were enclosed within. He allowed his gaze to settle comfortably on Elizabeth for a time as she and Richard discussed the different desks they had seen. He had forgotten that his cousin was somewhat of an eccentric when it came to desks. This particular desk had been a gift from the colonel's father, and Darcy recalled that Richard had helped pick it out. To Darcy, one desk was much like another, but listening to Elizabeth and his cousin's short discourse made the topic rather riveting—though it might have been the way her eyes lit up that rendered the topic captivating.

His cousin's words finally filtered through the haze of admiration in

Darcy's mind when his cousin pulled the travelling case out from beside Elizabeth and onto his own lap.

"Do you mind if I show her, Darcy? You have not any private documents contained within?"

Darcy startled and possessively placed a hand on his case to prevent its being opened as it sat on Colonel Fitzwilliam's lap.

"Oh, Colonel, I do not wish to intrude on Mr Darcy's personal business just to see the inside of the case. I am sure it is just as masterfully made as the outside."

Colonel Fitzwilliam laughed and, turning towards Darcy, said, "I am sure you do not mind, Cousin, do you? I remember selecting this case, and the inlay design features are very well done."

Darcy warred within himself. It was not as if she would find his letters; he assured himself of that fact. They were held in a secret compartment, one of many. And if she did, there was a daring recklessness that wished for her to find them and expose everything she was to him.

He withdrew his hand and feigned nonchalance. "By all means. It is of no consequence."

As his cousin held his hand out for the key, Darcy withdrew it from his breast pocket with a prayer that he was not gambling too high of stakes.

Elizabeth seemed to teeter between uncommon interest in anything pertaining to Mr Darcy's personal life and not wanting to intrude. The gentleman fascinated her, and every hour in his company drew her in further. When Colonel Fitzwilliam opened the case and passed it to her, she looked about Darcy's personal belonging with no small amount of awe. The simple collection of writing instruments and vial of ink were rendered more fascinating by virtue of their owner. As far as writing desks went, it was as lovely as she had ever seen. She traced the pattern on the fine, inlaid wood and ran her fingers across the gold-imprinted drawer hinges and pulls. She noticed each pull had a "D" on it, a perfect replica of the Darcy crest that had imprinted the deep red wax seal on the letter he gave her.

Colonel Fitzwilliam was pointing out various design features and making a point about certain areas of the craftsmanship that were particularly well done, but all Elizabeth could think was how Mr Darcy spent countless hours writing there. He might write letters of business and letters to his relations. He was a most devoted brother and likely wrote to Miss Darcy with some frequency. The idea that the green felt of the writing surface had witnessed so many of his innermost thoughts was oddly intimate to Elizabeth. Her hands slid across the surface subconsciously as if she might withdraw from them some of those secrets. It stirred in her a storm of emotions.

She had not forgotten that it was not *any* writing desk but it was *his* writing desk. Yet, she had allowed her curiosity to make her imprudent. More than imprudent—unforgivably invasive. She had cruelly spurned any right to be privy to his private thoughts by her refusal of his marriage proposal. Looking upon the case, she could imagine his thoughts reaching up to her from the memories within the box. Elizabeth dared not guess what they might say about her after the abuse she rendered Darcy at the parsonage.

With shaky hands, Elizabeth closed the case again and placed it beside her once more. Looking across to Mr Darcy, she was surprised she could meet his eyes after having encroached so on him. "It is a very fine writing desk." She cleared her throat, trying to disguise the feelings choking her. "The one that I have was my father's first, so it is very old. It is in my trunk—outside—for I did not think there would be room—in the public coach—to have it with me."

She held Darcy's gaze while she babbled, her words so disconnected to the thoughts whirling in her head. The expression in his eyes did not dispel her worry, for she could tell that he detected something of her feelings. His eyes were intense and searching in a way that made Elizabeth feel exposed. It was oddly just, considering her intrusion into his private space.

"Thank you. I suppose I do not have the same appreciation or interest in it that either you or my cousin have."

He meant the words kindly, but the strange emotion in her eyes flared again, and Darcy was captivated. She almost looked as if she encountered some great loss, and he could not understand what inspired it. They had sparkled with interest when she first took up his case, and his heart had beat wildly when her fingers brushed against the drawer where she might access the secret lever to the hidden compartment of letters addressed to her.

Then her expression had fallen to mild interest, displayed, he was sure, purely for his cousin's sake as Richard droned on and on about various features. Though he did not claim to know her well—his failed proposal as obvious evidence—he felt that underneath her polite expression was a torment. What could cause such heartache? He knew that level of anguish. He had experienced it every day since she refused him. But *she* could not have anything with which to lament so gravely.

Miss Lucas observed the exchange with curious eyes, having looked on as Elizabeth had perused the writing desk but said nothing

"Oh, Miss Bennet, I have not even shown you the secret compartments!" Richard's protests intruded upon Darcy's and Elizabeth's private thoughts, and they broke eye contact. He held his breath, only releasing it when he saw that she had no intention of taking up the desk again.

"Perhaps we should not pry into Mr Darcy's privacy any further, Colonel."

Elizabeth met Darcy's eyes again, and he realised she looked penitent. It dawned on him then that she felt regret for intruding on his private life. Did she not know that she already owned every part of his soul?

"I am sure my cousin can have nothing to hide, Miss Elizabeth. I would be surprised if he knew how to access all of them."

Darcy stunned them both by saying, "I am very much aware of the hidden compartments, Richard."

Perhaps his curt tone was more telling than he intended because Richard turned in his seat, amused and all curiosity to tease his cousin. "Shall we ask my cousin his meaning? What has he hidden, Miss Bennet, do you think? Shall we ask him why a man of sense and education, who has lived in the world, has anything to hide?"

"Nay, Colonel Fitzwilliam," Elizabeth said laughingly. "I shall not be party to any such discovery. A gentleman, like a lady, must have his secrets."

Whether it was the relief that came with knowing Colonel Fitzwilliam would not push further, given Miss Bennet's disinclination to pry, or the warmth of admiration he felt for the skilful way she dispelled the notion with her gentle rebuke, a well of mirth bubbled out of him, and Darcy laughed.

Elizabeth then expertly guided the discussion back to safer grounds. "I will confess, Colonel, that the idea of secret compartments is what really intrigues me about these clever desks." Here she patted the desk beside her and again traced the carvings with her fingers. Leaning forward with an excited expression, she continued. "My desk contains one such compartment, and the travelling case my father currently uses has four—though I have managed only to discover three of them, much to my chagrin."

"And do you use your compartment, Miss Bennet?"

She met the speaker's eyes with a slight smile. "I might if it were not so easily discovered, Mr Darcy! I think it is located in rather an obvious location." Elizabeth gave an exaggerated huff of feigned annoyance that amused the gentlemen. "What is the use of a secret compartment if someone might easily infiltrate its confines?"

"Perhaps it is only obvious to you, familiar as you are as its owner."

Colonel Fitzwilliam nodded in agreement and asked with the same anticipatory interest, "How do you know your father's desk has four compartments if you have only discovered three?"

"He has told me of the fourth. He rarely travels away from Longbourn, so the desk gets very little use. Some days when the weather is wet, I have amused myself puzzling through the desk for the last compartment."

"And your father does not mind your perusal of his desk?"

"On the contrary, I think it diverts him." Elizabeth tapped her finger against her lip as in contemplation.

The action caused Darcy to swallow noticeably, and Colonel Fitzwilliam elbowed him in the side discretely with a smug little smile.

"I think," Elizabeth said. "I wonder if he might not have invented the last compartment after all. It would be just like him to tease me in this manner, for he knows I will not give up."

The colonel laughed at such an image, and Darcy smiled.

When the carriage arrived outside her aunt and uncle's Cheapside townhouse, the gentlemen exited the carriage first and then assisted the ladies.

Darcy's hand lingered on Elizabeth's as she stepped down. He held it securely in his own and looked at her gloved fingers as if unmindful of his actions. When she cleared her throat and whispered his name, he started. He had been thinking that, despite their previous history with unexpected encounters, this perhaps would surely be his last meeting with her, and so he held her hand and looked into her eyes. The grip this had on his heart made releasing her all the more difficult.

"God bless you, Elizabeth," he whispered so softly that she could not be sure she heard correctly.

She looked at her hand in his and slowly withdrew it just before the door to the townhouse opened and her sister rushed out.

"Lizzy!"

Darcy took a step back. The two sisters embraced affectionately, and upon releasing her sister, Miss Bennet turned and warmly thanked him for bringing Elizabeth to London. "It is good to see you again, Mr Darcy. I hope you are well."

"Thank you, Miss Bennet, I am." Elizabeth introduced Colonel Fitzwilliam to her sister and then to Sir William Lucas who had by then exited the home as well to greet Maria. They were all entreated to come in for some refreshments, which Colonel Fitzwilliam eagerly accepted after setting eyes upon the lovely eldest Bennet sister.

When they were seated in a tastefully decorated parlour, Darcy learned that the aunt was called away moments before to attend an issue in the nursery and that Elizabeth's uncle was expected home from his office at any moment.

With a fleeting thought, Darcy hoped that he might be spared the introduction to these additional relations even if it meant bringing the last of his acquaintance with Elizabeth to a close that much sooner. He looked at his cousin and nearly groaned when he realised a short visit would not be likely considering the marked attentions he was giving to Miss Jane Bennet.

When an elegant lady, only a few years his senior, entered the parlour and was introduced to him as Mrs Gardiner, Darcy was humbled to realise how quickly he presumed a slight against Elizabeth's relations. Though he had not many chances to work on his temperament since his failed proposal, it was discouraging to find that it was nearly second nature for him to be judgemental. He had wished to become a better man, and he was disappointed to find that, as of yet, he was not.

His lesson in humility was increased further a short while later when he was introduced to a well-educated and cultured-speaking gentleman. *This is the brother of Mrs Bennet?* Mr Gardiner was a genteel, mild-mannered man who had a great deal to show for his intelligence through pleasing conversation and wit. Darcy soon learned that Mr Gardiner was also an acute observer, and he wished he could compel himself not to gaze so readily upon Elizabeth.

In a concerted effort to draw his own attention away from the man's lovely niece, Darcy observed the other one. Miss Bennet was politely accepting of his cousin's eager conversation. However, Darcy detected after many minutes that her smiles did not reach her eyes and that, indeed, those very eyes held a guarded nature he had not observed before.

He was certain there was a difference, for he had based his entire assertion to Bingley upon his observations of Miss Bennet. Could he have been wrong? Elizabeth had said as much during her rebuttal, but until witnessing with his own eyes, he was hard-pressed to regret his actions. He had believed then that he acted prudently for his friend. And although Elizabeth had informed him otherwise, he could not regret his actions as they were done with honest intentions. Here, Miss Bennet received his cousin's attention with a happy countenance. With his friend Bingley, Darcy realised miserably, she had received them with joy...and perhaps fondness.

Darcy turned away from Jane to observe Elizabeth. Her expression was impossible to make out. Soon Darcy announced their need to depart and thanked his hosts. He felt a sudden need to escape, and though he could have wished to delay the inevitable break with Elizabeth, it must be done. He came to her last, and when he took up her hand, he was stilled. Bowing slightly, Darcy caught her eyes with his. He opened his mouth to say goodbye, but his heart would not allow the utterance. Instead, he nodded almost imperceptibly, and after a studied perusal of every feature on her face, he turned and left, leaving his heart behind.

CHAPTER 9

DURING THE FOLLOWING DAYS, WITH LITTLE EFFORT, ELIZABETH WAS ABLE TO push thoughts of Kent—and its disconcerting stew of confusing emotions—into the back of her mind. Mr Darcy, had he known, could boast of no more than a dozen visits to her thoughts during the course of a day. Taking advantage of the warm and soothing company of her two favourite people, her aunt and Jane, Elizabeth's few days in London before departing for home were spent in almost comfortable pleasantry—with the exception of those dozen or so moments of weakness, of course.

However, on occasion, as might well be expected after so significant an event, her mind did dwell on a pair of dark eyes, the indiscernible expression of their owner upon taking leave of her, and the echo of his words from the parsonage. It could not be helped, after all, that these things might make an impression on Elizabeth, but she was not made for melancholy, and though she was still quite affected by their interchange, she endeavoured whenever possible to studiously change the direction of her musings. Jane remained unaware of any difference in her—as Elizabeth had not yet determined what might be revealed safely and had opted to keep her counsel on the whole until she could make that judgement—but Elizabeth had some suspicion that her aunt might have detected something more.

Most difficult of all for her to forget was the moment of final parting between her and Darcy. She could not deny the pleasure she felt when he took up her hand at the last. His struggle to express even the simplest of adieus pawed at her thoughts. She had almost convinced herself that she was relieved he did not waste breath on any sentiments that could have no future. When his glove had slid against hers as he turned to leave, her hand was left bereft and squeezed tightly into a fist by her side. The near silent sound of the two fabrics' liaison reverberated in her ears. And then with only one solemn, parting look, he went away.

As he quitted the room, Elizabeth felt how improbable it was that they should ever see each other again. Though, with an uncontrolled moment of bemusement, she reminded herself that she had thought the same on many occasions before, and *that* had not happened. Indeed, she half expected to run into him at the lending library or the shops she frequented with her aunt while in London. It had been her luck since receiving his proposal that they should be thrown together unexpectedly. It seemed almost probable that it should continue to happen.

When it did not, Elizabeth sighed at the perverseness of her feelings—curiosity and a bit more—which might have promoted the continuance of their acquaintance now that it was, in all likelihood, impossible. She was certain, not many weeks past, that she would have rejoiced in its termination.

Determined though she was to forget her time in Kent, much of it was too indelibly ingrained in her mind to do so. And even if she were to find success in that quarter, Elizabeth rather believed herself to be changed from the experience permanently. Her confidence broadly shaken from the realisation of her multiple failures when it came to understanding one's character, Elizabeth found herself constantly questioning her impressions and foresight.

When her home finally came into view in all its yellow stone and familiarity, Elizabeth's eyes filled with tears. It was rock and mortar, firm in its foundation, and resilient against the buffers of storms.

Her opinions upon leaving were, she thought then, the same: certain and immovable. Upon her return, she felt rather a shell of her former self. What did Elizabeth Bennet of Hertfordshire know of the world—of anything? Mr Darcy's proposal had given her an odd mix of flattered and bruised vanity. How great a compliment from such a man, yet the actual man was hidden from her view by her own constructed walls of prejudice.

Barely had the carriage stopped before Elizabeth was opening the door and bursting forth towards the house. She had maintained her reserve while in London, but with Longbourn's doors opening wide to receive her home, she felt the prickle of tears as she rushed into its embrace.

Her reception by her family was made blessedly brief as her mother fussed over Jane. Lydia and Kitty, who had met them at the coaching inn on the way from London with her father's carriage, disappeared into the house with hardly a word between fits and giggles. Mary had simply nodded her head at the returning sisters as she, with a book in her hand, passed on into the parlour.

Only Mr Bennet's, "I am glad you are come home, Lizzy," threatened Elizabeth's composure further. Gleaning from her father a modicum of strength from his gentle welcoming hug, Elizabeth managed to produce a tolerably adequate smile before excusing herself to her chambers to deposit her things. There she remained until she could restrain all discomposing thoughts well enough to appear serene.

The rest of the evening, she sat subdued as her family took turns sharing news from their times of separation. Mrs Bennet, despite all her attempts, could not gather from Jane whether she had seen anything of Mr Bingley in London and was left dissatisfied. When Elizabeth retired for the evening, Jane excused herself as well.

Elizabeth was hardly surprised when, a few minutes after readying herself for bed, she heard Jane's quiet knock on her chamber door. Her mood since coming home, she knew, was vastly different from the facade she kept during the few days in London, and Jane surely discerned a difference in her much beloved sister.

Knowing that she could no longer keep from Jane the events that occurred in Hunsford parsonage or the following encounters, Elizabeth was determined to share what she could with Jane. At length, resolving to suppress every particular in which her sister was concerned and preparing Jane to be surprised, she related to her the chief of the scene between Mr Darcy and herself at the parsonage. Elizabeth knew she needed her sister's kind guidance if she were to find any peace regarding the whole.

Jane Bennet could not have been more surprised by Elizabeth's eager candour and then Mr Darcy's most shocking proposal to her dear sister. "He proposed?"

"Shh, Jane!" Elizabeth laughed uneasily as she covered her sister's mouth with her hand. "If you are not careful, our mother will hear you, and I shall never survive the night."

"No, you are right, Lizzy. I am sorry. Mama must never know that you rejected not one but *two* eligible suitors."

Though the sisters then laughed, Elizabeth's laughter left a bitter pang of something ricocheting within her rib cage. Miss Bennet's astonishment was soon lessened by the strong sisterly partiality that made any admiration of Elizabeth appear perfectly natural.

Elizabeth watched as all surprise was shortly lost in Jane's other feelings. Soon her humorous attitude progressed without much effort to consider the gentleman's heart, causing her smile to transform into a compassionate grimace. Jane's generous nature prevailed, and she was sorry that Mr Darcy should have delivered his sentiments in a manner so little suited to recommend them; moreover, she grieved for the unhappiness that her sister's refusal must have given him.

"Oh, poor Mr Darcy! Only think, Lizzy, how great his disappointment must be."

Elizabeth nodded her agreement, not sure why she was unable to voice any response. She knew Darcy's feelings had not stayed long in the realm of regret, but that knowledge did nothing to comfort Elizabeth the way it ought.

The events in the parsonage having been dissected, the sisters soon moved on to Darcy's letter. The account of Wickham's perfidy was a most unpleasant topic to expound upon even for Elizabeth, who by that time had a couple of weeks to get used to the shocking truth. What a stroke it was for poor Jane, though, who would willingly have gone through the world without believing that so much wickedness existed in the whole race of mankind as was here collected in one individual.

Together they determined that, concerning that rogue, nothing ought to be shared abroad. Though Jane asserted that perhaps Wickham had changed and might wish to start again, acquitting himself anew, Elizabeth had no such hopes. They would hardly do any good for, that evening, the sisters had learned that the militia was not long for Meryton and were due to depart for Brighton. In an effort to put the evidence of her own poor judgement behind her, Elizabeth was only too eager to agree to remain silent when it came to Wickham's sins.

With all the compassion of a much-endeared sister, Jane listened to Elizabeth recount the days following the proposal. Their sudden meeting in the garden produced tears, and her frequent exclamations of sympathy for poor Mr Darcy were soon quieted when she saw Elizabeth's distress on hearing them. And while Elizabeth did not reveal the pounding of her heart when dining beside Mr Darcy at Rosings nor the duplicate sensations rendered from the close confines of the carriage ride, Jane received with equal parts compassion and amazement the rest of her sister's report.

"And oh, dear sister, I can only imagine how unpleasant it must have been to encounter him again at Bromley and to be left to ride in his carriage too!"

"It was not as unpleasant as I thought, nor could it have been called comfortable," Elizabeth replied with a shy smile but soon changed her mind. "No, I was very uncomfortable, even unhappy at times. And there was no one to speak to of what I felt, no Jane to comfort me and say that I had not been so very weak and vain and nonsensical as I knew I had!"

Jane quickly leaned forward to enfold her sister in a fierce embrace. "But you disguised all of this so well while we were in London. How could you do it?"

"I was not then master enough of myself to know what could or ought to be revealed."

After many more minutes of commiseration between the two, Jane surprised Elizabeth when she said, "But you do not think so badly of the gentleman now, do you, Lizzy? I mean…I thought I detected…"

"I do not think so badly of him, Jane. But as none of that matters now, I see little point in professing it."

∼

The days following Darcy's separation from Elizabeth started far less easily for the gentleman than they did for the lady. While she could hide the effect of their interactions in Kent from her relations, he was less fortunate.

It was not a long journey from Cheapside to his Grosvenor Square town home. Though the distance was relatively short, the ride seemed intolerably long to Darcy since, from the very first turn of the carriage wheels, Colonel Fitzwilliam made his presence an insufferable blister on Darcy's fragile spirit. Having to part from Elizabeth for what must be accepted as forevermore, Darcy wanted nothing more than to have the silence he required to process such an injury to his heart. But that was not to be as his travelling companion stole not only his solitude but also the longed-for silence. What should have been a time for Darcy to put a cap to the whole sordid affair, being as he had seen the last of his beloved Elizabeth, was instead a perpetual stream of searing reminders.

Colonel Fitzwilliam's soliloquy on the manifold allurements and virtues of Miss Elizabeth Bennet was not only entirely superfluous to Darcy, as he was well aware of the list in its entirety—as well as a few more—but each praise was a throbbing thorn. They had not gone many blocks before the torment, such as it was, could not be borne any further, and Darcy had determined to confess all. The confession itself, he did not delude himself to believe, would be less excruciating than listening to his cousin speak of Elizabeth, but at least it would explain Darcy's reluctance to participate and make his later requests for Colonel Fitzwilliam to cease probable.

"When are you likely to see the lovely Miss Elizabeth again, Darcy?" Colonel Fitzwilliam said.

Darcy did not answer at first, the swirling sickness brewing inside him clawing up his throat and threatening him with a sob so undignified as to strike Darcy mute with the fear of it. After several attempts, Darcy found his voice. "I am not likely to see Miss Elizabeth again after today."

Brows lowered, Colonel Fitzwilliam's first instinct was to argue with his cousin, yet something in Darcy's eyes kept him from doing so. Instead, he asked, "What makes you so certain?"

Darcy clenched his jaw and turned to peer out of the carriage window. They were still a good distance from his home. There was enough time, perhaps, yet only enough. Darcy would not be forced to provide many details, which was of some comfort.

"Miss Elizabeth is as bright, beautiful, and beguiling as you describe," Darcy said, uncertain how to voice his disappointment. *And she would not have me.* The lump in his throat returned, preventing words for a time. How had he managed to tell Anne about it in the first place? Darcy realised that the difficulty in telling was only compounded by the audience. He knew that Colonel Fitzwilliam thought well of him. In his pride, he must admit to being gratified by the older cousin's reverence and respect. It was entirely and mortifyingly humbling to Darcy to have to admit to this cousin what a failure he was. Even worse, Darcy knew that Colonel Fitzwilliam, if his situation were different—or hers for that matter—would have considered making an offer as well. What she would have answered *him* haunted Darcy's thoughts like a mocking spectre with debilitating frequency.

"Then why do you not pursue her?" asked Colonel Fitzwilliam when his cousin seemed hesitant or unable to continue. "She is, as you say, beguiling and lovely. In these aspects, you cannot possibly refute her as your match."

"No, that boot is quite on the other leg."

Colonel Fitzwilliam largely ignored Darcy's comment, prepared already for an argument. "What have you to say against the match? You are quite rich enough to take a wife with little or no fortune."

He was painfully aware of the reasons, having foolishly led with those hesitations while making his disastrous proposal. The reasons mocked him so thoroughly as to make him certain that, had her fortune, connexions, and status been rather worse than they were, he still would have given anything to have her. Before Richard could go much further, enumerating any possible reasons Darcy might fight his inclination for Elizabeth, he raised his hand to stop his cousin.

"I believe it is the custom in such cases for the lady to be in compliance for any such match to occur."

"Really, Darcy, you drive me mad with all your pompous— Wait! What did you say?"

Hands clenched into fists on his thighs, Darcy exhaled loudly. How many more ways must he abuse himself with saying it?

"She would not have me, Richard! I asked, and the lady refused. That is the end of it."

Richard sat gaping, uncomprehending his cousin. It was as spectacular a statement as it was entirely unimaginable to the colonel. What lady would refuse such an excellent temporal match besides the fact that his cousin in truth was an excellent man as well? Richard contemplated this shocking revelation for some many minutes as the man himself hung his head and took up his top hat in his hands. Darcy ran his fingers along the inner seam of the hat, presumably inspecting it. Had he not just made the most astonishing statement, Colonel Fitzwilliam might have thought Darcy was simply bored, but it was obvious that Darcy was struggling mightily with an eddy of emotions.

Richard's voice came out sombre, contrite, and compassionate—so much so that Darcy tasted the rusty tang of blood as he bit his cheek in an attempt to maintain his control. He spoke quietly in the hollow of the carriage. "I...I hardly know what to say, William. I am sorry." He saw Darcy wince at his rare use of his given name and change the direction of his gaze from his hat to the roof of the carriage, his eyes blinking rapidly, his exhausted head resting backwards. Understanding now the precipice upon which Darcy teetered, having seen many soldiers on that brink of anguish on the battlefield as they buried their brothers in arms, Richard knew his cousin did not need his compassion but a flanking manoeuvre to allow Darcy to step back from that edge.

Purposely making his voice light with feigned humour, Richard said, "Well then, I suppose I made things rather awkward by insisting she accompany us from Bromley."

After a moment of silence, Darcy met his cousin's eyes. And while he could see the gravity behind the light expression, he was indefinitely grateful to his cousin for his blithe tone. Darcy nodded his head as he answered, his own tone falling short of his cousin's congeniality. "Indeed."

"I suppose I ought to have listened to you when you said she did not wish to accompany us."

Immediately, Richard regretted his words. Darcy, clearing his throat, looked outside the window and, seeing they were arriving momentarily at his home, turned to Richard.

"Please do not speak of this to Georgiana. Indeed, I would ask you to forget I told you."

Though he nodded his acceptance, Richard frowned. His tone was more staid as he said, "Naturally, I shall say nothing to Georgiana. Though Darcy, *we* are not finished here. I want you to tell me all, and I suspect you need to speak of it."

Darcy's half-lidded expression met Richard's eyes and did not answer. The carriage door was opened by the footman, and Darcy looked away as he bent over, preparing to exit. He paused just before his head exited and his foot stepped down. Looking back at his cousin, he said, "All right."

Richard patted his cousin's shoulder once and gave him a grim smile. Together they exited the carriage and ascended the stairs to Darcy House where the front door opened with a most welcome sight. Georgiana extended her arms, and into them, her brother went, eagerly and lovingly. If he held her more firmly than he usually did or a moment longer than was his habit, none but his cousin beside him noticed. Darcy squeezed his eyes shut tightly, his head buried beside her flaxen curls as he breathed in the giggling murmurs of welcome she bestowed. Here was his only family. Here was all in the world that loved him.

CHAPTER 10

"Thank you, Carroll. That will be all."

"Very good, sir," the butler said, executing a regal bow before closing the study door behind him.

The moment he was alone, Darcy drew a deep breath as if he had not breathed deeply in ages. Taking advantage of the privacy, he fell against the plush leather of his desk chair, and in a rather uncharacteristic slouch, he stared blankly into the room. Although it had been nearly a se'nnight since his return from Rosings, he hardly could boast any significant improvement in his moods. Mostly, he had kept himself feverishly busy with whatever estate matters he could conjure. His secretary had enjoyed a rather light few days as those unpleasant tasks such as responding to social invitations from members of the *ton* or investigating charitable societies that frequently sent requests for his benevolence were also taken up by Darcy himself. He was trying mightily to bring his mind and heart back under control, yet when one is expectant of a particular blessing and it does not come about, it is rather difficult to forget.

With a sigh, Darcy sat upright again and began to sift through the numerous papers he had laid out before him. Inactivity led to distracted musings that led to painful memories. The business of the hour was not pining after Elizabeth; it was determining the merits of a particular investment. As he shifted through the papers and concentrated on the business at hand, Darcy studiously became busy again.

He was occupied safely for some thirty minutes before he realised that a document from his solicitor regarding the scheme was not among the papers before him. On discerning the document was not present, Darcy sat back in his chair, his hand rubbing his jaw as he tried to remember whether he had taken it up to his chambers the night before among the other documents he had worked on late into the night. It had been his habit since returning to take correspondence, business matters, and other such distractions to his chambers when he retired. He was mindful that, while he could not hope for good sleep—indeed as plagued as his dreams were of Elizabeth, it was hardly a surprise—he did not wish to inconvenience his staff further by remaining downstairs in his study or the library. He knew that, even if he dismissed the footmen or Mr Carroll for the evening, they would remain until he retired to his chambers. That first night home had been a long night for his servants. Since then, he had taken work with him to his chambers. They need not suffer his long hours.

Unable to remember whether the desired document was with him the previous evening, he was about to return to his chambers to sift through the papers on his writing desk there. Thinking of the writing desk stopped him in his tracks. With a sound of triumph, Darcy turned and went to the bookshelf. In the far corner of his study, Darcy stored his travelling desk on the bottom shelf while he was not from home.

Remembering he had received that particular document while at Rosings, Darcy snatched up the travelling case and placed it on his desk. It was a matter of mere moments before he had the case open and discovered the missing document among the other letters he had received while at his aunt's house.

However, after grasping the small batch of letters, it was only a matter of seconds before Darcy was reminded of yet another group of letters contained within the desk. His previous industry soon lost entirely, Darcy set the batch of business letters aside on the desk and, with exaggerated slowness, reached for the drawer behind which the lever to the secret compartment was hidden. It was as if he expected at any moment that a viper would strike him if he moved too quickly. While his body seemed trapped in a surreal otherworld—sluggish and hesitant—his mind had already sped ahead to the letters contained within. The remembered words they concealed flashed across his mind in aching acuity. *"I love you, Elizabeth. ... I wish I did not."* Darcy winced and shut his eyes as if he could shut his mind to the tormenting words—*your heated defence of Wickham*—

Groaning, Darcy shook his head to clear it and opened his eyes as his hands expertly found their way to the lever and extracted the letters hidden within.

Collapsing back into his chair, Darcy held them before him, sifting through the lot. *So many!* Looking at the letters cradled in his hands, Darcy realised humourlessly that Elizabeth's power over him was certainly more potent in direct doses. He stood, and walking slowly to the bookshelf, he gazed across the shelves. With the practiced eye of one who knew exactly what he was looking for, Darcy reached for the blue and gold binding of a rather large volume on the fourth shelf on the furthermost right side, sixth from the end.

The leather binding hissed quietly as it slid from the shelf into Darcy's hands. In one hand, he held the letters to Elizabeth, in the other, the book. Darcy took in the elegant embossed pattern pressed into the blue leather. The book was of such a size as to make another suspect it was quite heavy, yet Darcy held it easily with the one hand, its weight inconsequential.

Easily, Darcy shifted his hold on the book, and the front cover fell back to reveal the hollowed out centre. Darcy watched as, in the upset, so too did a few of the letters concealed inside shift, coming to rest against the side of the compartment. Various parts of her name became visible as the letters settled to rest again in their stack inside the book. Here was the evidence of Elizabeth's hold over him and perhaps his weakness regarding her. The letters he had written since nearly the beginning of his introduction to Elizabeth laid as sentinels to him.

With mixed emotions, Darcy placed the new additions to his furtive collection into the tome and, after only a brief hesitation, closed the book, returning it to its place on the shelf. He had promised himself multiple times that he would destroy them, but he could not.

He walked to the empty hearth in his study and glared into the silent space. His thoughts drifted to his conversation with his cousin not long after Georgiana retired for the evening on the day of his return to London. With a slow shake of his head, Darcy accepted that he could not have hoped for his cousin to wait long for the continuation of their interview from the carriage, yet Darcy had indeed hoped that Richard would have waited at least a day.

When they were both seated, nursing a glass of brandy before that same hearth—then bright with the heat of a fire in the evening to ward off the spring chill—Colonel Fitzwilliam wasted no time in broaching the topic of his proposal.

With acceptance of his fate, Darcy had begun from the beginning. With detached narrative, he laid out to his captive audience his long-held admiration for Miss Elizabeth Bennet and the anguishing objections to the match. For what seemed like hours, but could only have been minutes, Darcy related his ill-fated history with Elizabeth.

Reaching the pinnacle of the story, Darcy was able to relate the whole of that evening at the parsonage verbatim. He had reviewed it enough times himself to know exactly every word he had flung at her and every painful dart to his heart she had returned. Though he had already felt the severest of self-contempt after realising his foolishness, it still stung deeply when his cousin rung a peel over him regarding his manner of proposing.

"You said what? Darcy, you are a damned fool if I ever knew one. Did you not even think, for one tiny moment, of the lady's sensibilities? Or were you too caught up in your own arrogance, the enormous honour you were bestowing upon Miss Bennet by simply admiring her. Blast and damn, Darcy!"

Darcy winced, still smarting from the cutting truth of his cousin's rebuke. He had been entirely right and the harsh censure completely deserved.

Speaking aloud to the empty room, Darcy said, "His reproof, so well applied, I shall never forget: *'You were raised better than that, Darcy.'*"

No other words could have struck Darcy with more force at the moment, with exception to the memory of Elizabeth's own reproof at the time: *"… had you behaved in a more gentlemanlike manner."* No, the two together summed up all the shortcomings Darcy painfully and acutely felt. He knew he was a good man in essentials. But when he considered his parents—the duty he felt towards their legacy—it was important, was it not? So important that he feared he was dismissing it in offering for Elizabeth. Fool that he was.

Then Darcy considered what his parents would think of his behaviour to a lady. Duty or not, they would not have had him speak so despairingly to another.

The revelations made and confessions given that evening to Colonel Fitzwilliam were oddly cathartic to Darcy. His thoughts returned then to his discussion with Richard. After acknowledging the truth of his rebuke, Darcy had felt rather defeated. And indeed, they sat silently for so long, one might have thought both gentlemen had said all that there might be to say.

Richard had finished his drink and, with gentle probing, had asked whether, perhaps after having received his letter, there might be some hope of changing her opinion. For a minute, Darcy had contemplated such a miracle and allowed himself to imagine the utter joy that thought brought. Their acquaintance had been marked with such opposition and misunderstanding as to make Darcy positively ache with the desire to gain some measure of true familiarity. What he would not do…

Instead of giving voice to such fanciful thoughts, Darcy had replied, "The recollection of what I then said, of my conduct, my manners, and expressions during the whole of it, is now, and has been many days, inexpressibly painful to me. I cannot help but believe Elizabeth feels the same of that fateful evening."

Gently Richard protested. "You forget. I bore witness to her behaviour towards you twice after that evening. She did not treat you with that same abhorrence that marked her words at the parsonage."

"Tempting though it is to grasp onto the happiness that theory might give me, it can prove but one thing. It only lends evidence to the goodness of Elizabeth. Despite my offensive words, when forced into my company, she comported herself evermore as a true lady."

"Is there nothing I might do? Perhaps if I speak to Miss Elizabeth..."

"No, it is of no use. The only thing that I would wish—now that you know all—" Darcy swallowed the lump in his throat and then, with pleading in his eyes, said, "Please do not speak on this subject again."

With his brows creased, Richard spent a moment contemplating that request and then finally, with uncharacteristic submission, agreed to Darcy's request.

After having purged himself to his cousin that evening, he still felt the weight of his actions. Now, as he stood staring into the dark shadows of the hearth, Darcy sensed within him a growing determination.

He was not an idle and indolent fellow. As Colonel Fitzwilliam had said, he was raised by good parents to be better than he had showed Elizabeth. That ember within him began to burn a slow path inside until it filled him with impenetrable resolve. She had dismissed his suit and with good reason—though it had taken nearly a fortnight for him to be reasonable enough to allow her words some justice.

Now it was up to him to endeavour, however hard it might be, to become the man that was worthy of her and to learn what it took to please a woman worthy of being pleased. He had been selfish and overbearing, had cared for none beyond his own family circle, thought meanly of all the rest of the world, or *wished* at least to think meanly of their sense and worth compared with his own. Such he was until Elizabeth.

Though his heart squeezed agonizingly at the thought of never seeing her again, he accepted then that it did not matter whether he did or not. For his resolution to better himself ought to be done despite having no hope to redeem himself in her eyes.

Darcy stood, the heaviness in his heart still there but his shoulders pushed back as he felt the rightness of his decision. It had been his plan to try to forget Elizabeth. He knew it would not be easy, and indeed, he had found so little success in that endeavour of late as to perhaps prove its impossibility. Deciding not to forget her had never crossed his mind before.

Oh, how his heart beat with relief at the thought! Forcing it to push her out of residence there seemed as if he were forcing the very organ to quit. As he contemplated the astonishing notion that he could begin to move beyond that dark place without relinquishing her memory, his pulse gloriously surged. If he were to become a better version of himself because of her, then he ought to be able to keep her, if only in his heart.

It would not be easy, Darcy admitted as he began to pace across his study in thought. Indeed, the very idea of never seeing Elizabeth again still plagued him. And there would be times that he knew he would be weak—when the empowering energy of spirit he was feeling would not hold him up and his soul would grow dark with pain again.

His pacing took him to his desk and the open travelling case there. He could still write her during such times. He could tell her of his heart's agony. The writing had relieved his burden of emotion. He was half-tempted to do so now—to share with her this change in his heart. And he might have taken up the quill right then if the thought had not struck him that he must prove himself first.

This was a right fine plan of his, to better himself and, by doing so, pull himself out of the hell he was in. But a *plan* was all it was at that point. There had been no action, and Darcy knew it would not be easy to correct eight and twenty years of habit. And without any action towards that resolve, with that very undertaking being only in the cusp of its creation, Darcy felt oddly unworthy of even writing to Elizabeth, regardless of the fact that she would never see his words. Instead of putting pen to his new resolution, Darcy decided he must test the fruits of his labours before he could report any progress to her.

Thus, Darcy closed his travelling case and returned it to its spot on the shelves. Then drawing forth a new piece of parchment, he did write a letter—though not to Elizabeth. He had known for many days that he had wronged someone else. He had wronged her sister.

However, it was not her sister whom Darcy addressed when he placed his pen to the parchment; yet, it was with her ultimate happiness in mind that he wrote. When he finished the short missive, Darcy rang for the butler. A smile tugged at his lips as he considered how pleased Anne would be with his actions.

Earlier Mr Carroll had come to convey an invitation from his sister to take tea with her. He had told his butler that he could not, that he had too much business to attend. Georgiana, he knew would have been disappointed but also would have understood. It was not unusual for him to be unable to step away from his work to join her. Deciding he would join Georgiana after all, Darcy opened the study door himself when Mr Carroll knocked in response to his summons.

"Carroll, please see that this gets delivered to Mr Bingley, and have a footman await his reply."

If the long-time retainer was surprised by the sudden appearance of his master at the threshold of his study, he was too well trained to show it and simply took a step back as he held out one gloved hand for the missive.

"Right away, sir."

"And I believe I will take tea with my sister after all. Please have a fresh tray sent to…"

"…the blue parlour, sir. Georgiana and Mrs Annesley are currently working on their embroidery there."

"The blue parlour then. Send a tray, Carroll."

"Certainly, sir. Anything else?"

Darcy paused some few steps away, as he had already begun walking towards that part of the house where Georgiana was. Turning, he said, "I have invited Mr Bingley to dine tonight. If he accepts, you will inform Cook."

"Turner will be in raptures, sir."

That comment, made with nary a change to the butler's sombre mien, made Darcy's lips twitch with wry humour. His cook was half in love with his friend. Mr Bingley never failed to praise her meals to such an extent that Darcy at times had a real fear of losing her loyalty. Mr Bingley's naturally affable personality made him quite voluble, especially when he knew that Darcy's cook was so well pleased by his praise. Wherever Bingley could do good or bring joy, he was sure to do so. Guilt pricked at Darcy. Bingley was so apt to please others that he often forewent pleasing himself.

Indeed, Darcy remembered how easy it had been to convince Bingley to stay in London after leaving Netherfield once he had suggested that, if Miss Bennet was not truly endeared to him, his continued presence in Hertfordshire might grow to make her uneasy and perhaps a little unhappy, especially with the speculation beginning to circulate. Bingley had been easily convinced he could bring Jane Bennet greater happiness by staying away.

Regret began to oppress Darcy until he reminded himself that this evening he hoped to make things right in that quarter. At least one of them ought to have a chance at happiness. And Darcy was convinced that Bingley and Miss Bennet deserved it all. And if a little of that radiated out to her sister, if even a portion of Darcy's efforts to right that wrong made Elizabeth happy, then Darcy could be content. Never had he wished that making her joyful was more in his power than at that moment. The very thought that he might please her constricted his heart most assuredly.

"Then I hope, for Turner's sake, that my friend has no other engagements," Darcy said to Mr Carroll, finally coming back to the present.

Darcy resumed his walk through the house to Georgiana. He quickly rounded the baluster to the staircase as he took the stairs at an unreserved two at a time. As he approached the blue parlour, he came upon two housemaids in close conference. It was clear that he had surprised them with his quickened pace around the corner, and indeed, he had also been caught off guard.

Mechanically, Darcy stepped aside to avoid a collision and murmured his pardons. The girls, too, stepped aside, echoed their own in reverent tones and, pressing themselves to the wall, looked down at their shoes as was the custom when a member of the household or a guest was near. Servants were trained not to be seen.

While Darcy had never treated any of his servants with the ruthless disregard that many of his class did, he was still largely in the habit of hardly thinking of them. With the exception of those servants like his housekeeper and butler—whom he had known since he was in short pants—and his valet—who had served him since his university days—the many servants that depended on Darcy for their livelihood enjoyed good employment at the hands of a fair but distant master.

Darcy resumed his walk, thinking idly how one of the maids had looked distressed, but quickly discharged the thought as he had reached his destination.

When Bingley's reply to his invitation came some half hour later while he visited with his sister and her companion, Darcy felt a moment's trepidation at seeing his friend's acceptance. Though not a coward, Darcy knew that if Elizabeth were to ask for one of his faults then—as if she did not know as many already as she had at Netherfield—he would have to confess that admitting when he is in the wrong was difficult. Yet, laughing humourlessly to himself as he tucked the missive in his breast pocket, he was no stranger to duty, and unpleasant or not, he would do what was necessary.

CHAPTER 11

~~~

Once the meal was completed, Darcy asked Bingley to join him in his study. Excusing themselves from Georgiana for the evening, the gentlemen bowed and exited, leaving her to puzzle over her brother's continued strange behaviour.

"While I am pleased to have your company—your sole company—this evening, Darcy, I would have been just as pleased to share it with your sister. I feel uneasy leaving her in solitude."

Darcy closed the door firmly behind his friend and, taking a deep breath of fortification, exhaled in a rush of words that he was thankful were steadier than he felt.

"I thank you for your kind consideration for Georgiana. However pleasant that aspect is to me, I had invited you with the goal of speaking to you on a matter of some importance—and privacy."

Bingley nodded his head in acquiescence to his friend. "By all means, Darcy, I am at your service as in all things."

Inviting his friend to seat himself, Darcy went to the sidebar and poured two drinks.

"Thank you." Bingley sipped from his glass with appreciation and lifted it in gratitude to his friend before settling back into his chair. "I have not yet heard you speak of your trip to Kent. Tell me, was it pleasant?"

Darcy paused with his glass midway to his mouth only briefly before raising it again and swallowing a portion. While settling into his seat, Darcy managed a tolerably unaffected reply. "Memorable to be sure."

"I am pleased to hear it. And your relations, they were all in good health?"

"Perfectly so, I thank you."

For some minutes, the two gentlemen sipped their drinks in companionable silence. Darcy found himself thinking on how he might bring about the subject while his friend was completely unaware of the turmoil hidden in the man beside him.

"And you, Bingley? How was your Easter holiday? I had thought your plans were to remain in London."

Bingley smiled at his friend, reminding Darcy of what a very congenial and pleasant fellow Bingley was.

"You were not misinformed. I stayed in town and had a rather quiet respite."

"And did you attend anything of interest?"

Bingley looked up from his drink with a droll smile, and his brow rose. "Are *you* asking about my social engagements? You, Fitzwilliam Darcy, interested in what balls or soirees I may have attended?"

Darcy laughed along with his friend, less so out of real humour than his trepidation. Clearing his throat, Darcy ventured further. "I do not wish to hear every minute detail—*that* I assure you. I just wondered whether... perhaps you had made any..."

Bingley listened attentively with the same amused expression on his face as Darcy struggled to articulate.

"Have you any new acquaintances?" Sipping his drink, Darcy added, "Of the female variety."

The humour displayed so naturally and readily on his friend's face fell quickly away and inspired Darcy to finish his drink. The whiskey burned down his throat and settled most uneasily in his gut.

With a nonchalance that did not fit well, Bingley replied with practiced ennui.

"I do not believe any ladies stood out to me, Darcy. Wait—" Bingley held up his hand to stop Darcy speaking, as they both knew at that moment that their discussion might at least in part reference a certain lady in Hertfordshire. "I am well aware of your concerns, Darcy. And let me at once put you at ease on that account. I am perfectly and entirely past any infatuation I may have had for the ever lovely Miss Bennet."

Darcy found himself to flinch on hearing the name "Bennet" spoken aloud.

For a minute, Darcy studied his friend. Anne's counsel to allow Bingley to make his own choices rang loudly. He ought to accept and leave Bingley be, especially considering his most emphatic reply. Yet, Darcy was most fervently compelled to once again persuade his friend to return to Hertfordshire. With lancing blows to his crippled heart, Darcy knew that, despite the chance to grant some happiness to Elizabeth, if Bingley did not love her sister anymore, he ought not to encourage his return. Besides, if Miss Bennet's admiration were no longer returned, it would not ultimately bring either happiness in the end.

So it is over. His final link to her, flimsy though it was, was at an end. While he had hoped he might reunite Bingley and Miss Bennet—and his mind whispered, *maintain a connexion to Elizabeth*—all such hopes had dissolved away as a sand castle near the shore. All that remained were ruins.

Hard though it was for Darcy, he nodded and accepted his friend's words. And detecting in his friend a wish to change topics, Darcy complied by saying, "You ought to see the horse my uncle has purchased recently."

"A prime piece of horseflesh, is it?" Bingley jumped on the new subject.

His friend leaned forward as if interested, so Darcy pushed aside his disappointment and accommodated Bingley. He went into detail then about the size and pedigree of the horse while Bingley listened attentively though not venturing any questions of his own.

"I am half tempted to try to buy her out from under him, if it were not for my own Salazar—"

"—I mean it was only natural that I should have admired her."

Bingley's outburst stopped Darcy. He felt the slightest tug of a smile and said, "Might I assume we are no longer speaking of my uncle's horse?"

"I apologize, no. My mind was elsewhere." He shook his head and waved him off. "Continue."

"I have no objection to speaking of Miss Bennet."

Darcy held his breath as Bingley eyed him carefully in consideration. It was clear that his friend was struggling with indecision. A thread of hope started to twist in Darcy's mind at the chance to bind himself secretly to Elizabeth—to have at least one connexion to her. Still, he would not force his friend. It must be Bingley's choice.

"Considering her exquisite beauty and gentle manners, it was only natural that I would admire her. It could not have been helped, could it? It was not as if I could have avoided falling in lo—" Bingley's rush of words cut off abruptly as he took a drink from his glass and then stood. "She had a talent for putting me at ease." Darcy watched him meander towards the bookshelf and remove a book. "You are very generous to allow me this moment of reflection." As he spoke, he idly examined, paged through, and replaced books. "Her eyes, Darcy, they were the bluest of blues…could get lost in them. And when she smiled…I remember you saying she smiled too much. I assure you it was not enough for me. I grew to crave those smiles. When she smiled, I was convinced that heaven could not have created her for any other purpose than to lead a man's heart into captivity."

Darcy was amused by his friend's fevered speech, the words coming so quickly they were almost hard to comprehend. The words poured forth with such raw emotion that at once, Darcy knew they sprang from that internal strain. His amusement fading away, Darcy felt keenly in tune with his friend. They shared a brotherhood of loss—both at his hands.

Bingley continued despite his one-sided conversation, reasoning and justifying that Miss Bennet's charms could not have been ignored and perhaps convincing himself that he was not foolish for having fallen for them. With sudden alarm, Darcy observed that his friend's distracted inspection of the bookshelf brought him dangerously close to a book of blue and gold binding shelved on the fourth shelf on the furthermost right side, sixth from the end!

"Bingley!" His heart pounded with fear that, in the next moment, Bingley would discover that the pages in the particular tome his hand rested upon were glued together—and instead held Darcy's own well of emotion.

"I beg your pardon," Bingley said gloomily, his hand sliding mercifully down the book, across the shelf and to his side in defeat.

Drawing in a breath of relief, his heartbeat still pounding loudly in his ears, Darcy stood and came to his friend. Placing his hand on Bingley's shoulder, he ushered his friend safely out of reach of that book and back to his chair.

"Bingley, your admiration for Miss Bennet was natural. Furthermore, it showed great intelligence and particular taste."

Bingley's mouth opened to speak but the torrent of words had left him as he stared mutely at Darcy, whose tone was calm, gentle, and sincere.

"I dare say you could not have chosen a more worthy lady, Bingley."

His companion looked down at his boots and remained silent for a time. When he did speak, it was devoid of all the animation of his earlier utterance. "I...thank you, Darcy. If only I could have made her love me."

Darcy's hand went straight to his heart, rubbing there as he looked away. He knew that exact wish. If only he could have made Elizabeth love him.

But Bingley's situation was different, and while that added to the ache within, it meant that Darcy knew precisely the significance of the knowledge and *hope* he could impart to Bingley now.

"Do you still admire her?"

Terrified eyes met Darcy's then. "I do. God help me, I do."

"Bingley..." Darcy began, stopped, stood, and walked a few paces before turning once again to his friend. "Bingley, I think you should return to Hertfordshire."

"No." His response was so quick in coming that it surprised Darcy.

"Why ever not, man?"

"She did not love me. I cannot make her unhappy." Bingley twisted his signet ring and lifted his gaze to meet his friend's. "Even if seeing her again would bring me immeasurable pleasure."

Pressing his lips together, Darcy said, "There is something I must say to you, Charles. While I visited with my relations in Kent...I happened to renew a mutual acquaintance of ours. She, too, was visiting her relations there. Miss Bennet's sister Elizabeth was visiting her cousin Mr Collins, my aunt's rector. Or rather she was visiting his wife, the former Miss Charlotte Lucas."

What came forth then was a delicate and careful dance on Darcy's part to relay to Bingley the whole of the time spent in Kent without divulging confidences. Finally, Darcy professed that Miss Bennet admired him while in Hertfordshire and, still more significantly, admired him still.

When Darcy finished speaking, he expected his jovial friend to emerge with renewed purpose the way his own heart might have if told Elizabeth returned his love.

Instead, and to Darcy's growing concern, Bingley remained puzzlingly silent. Uncertain how he might condole with his friend, Darcy continued with the rest of his planned revelation.

"Furthermore, I owe you my deepest apologies for persuading you not to return to Hertfordshire." Bingley waved Darcy's words away—the first animation from his friend since the earlier disclosure. "Still more, I must apologize for a more grievous sin perpetrated against you. During the whole of this winter, from the festive holidays until sometime this week, Miss Bennet was visiting relations in London. I had knowledge of it and did not tell you."

Bingley's head snapped up as he gawked at his friend. "Thank you for what you have told me this evening, Darcy, but I think it is of little use. Miss Elizabeth must be mistaken about her sister, for if, as you say, Miss Bennet was in town all this time and did not make any effort to further the acquaintance, I am persuaded to think our earlier assumptions to be correct. She did not return my admiration."

"Miss Bennet did call upon your sisters while in town, and after a fashion, they returned the call."

"Pardon?" Bingley's voice held none of its previous detachment. Darcy began to repeat himself when cut off by Bingley. "No, no I heard you before. What do you mean by 'after a fashion'?"

Bingley was by then rightfully unhappy, and Darcy hated to add to it. His sisters held the majority of the blame, but he could not acquit himself entirely. After all, it was his advice that led them to act in such a manner. "Your sisters apprised me of Miss Bennet's visit. I believed at the time that you were not yet recovered from your admiration for Miss Bennet, and since I was still mistaken as to her feelings for you, I determined it best that you not see her. I advised your sisters to gently inform Miss Bennet that a further acquaintance was not desired. I believe they chose to interpret this as waiting several weeks to return Miss Bennet's call and making their own visit quite brief."

There. It was done. Seeing Bingley's reddened countenance and hearing his following words disheartened Darcy further.

"I believe, under the circumstances, you will understand when I tell you that this revelation will prevent my sisters and me from accompanying you and Miss Darcy to Pemberley later this summer as planned."

Startled into silence for a minute, Darcy was faced with the results of his perfidy. So, he was to lose his friend over the matter as well. It was no more than he deserved, but he had believed—nay expected—that Bingley's amiable character and forgiving temperament would prevail in the end to save the friendship now dissolved between them.

Darcy stood, good manners prompting his friend to stand also. He extended his hand to Bingley and was inordinately pleased to see it accepted. "For what it is worth, my friend. I *am* truly sorry."

Bingley's grasp was firm and his gaze levelled boldly on Darcy's.

"You should not have meddled in my affairs."

"You are most correct."

All the while firmly grasping Darcy's hand, almost in challenge, Bingley continued. "Then I have your word you will not do so again."

The singular nature of Bingley's words lent towards a hint of a future, and Darcy was grateful for it, eagerly and sincerely agreeing.

"Then I forgive you," Bingley replied with a satisfied nod of his head and released Darcy's hand.

Darcy watched as he brought his empty drink to the sideboard and prepared to leave. Not knowing where that left their years of friendship, Darcy was unaccustomed to the feeling brewing inside. In all his life, he had people clamouring to be a friend or more with him. In the past fortnight, two of the people he cared most for chose to walk away from that role.

Before Bingley exited the study, Darcy said, "Will you not reconsider being part of the party at Pemberley? You have always been welcome there, and I hope you know you always will be."

"I really cannot."

"I understand."

"I am going to Netherfield, and I cannot be persuaded against it this time—not for *all* of Pemberley."

A slow smile began at the edges of Darcy's lips to match the wide grin of his companion. With a relieved laugh, Darcy patted Bingley's back, only managing to nod as speech was beyond him. He deserved no charity from Bingley, yet he knew he had received it. And he was satisfied for now.

CHAPTER 12

SPRINGTIME HAD COME TO HERTFORDSHIRE, AND THE WARMTH OF SUMMER seemed pressing on its heels as Elizabeth walked along the little wilderness near her home, admiring the brave new blooms of colour sprouting along the path. Though it was less than two weeks since her return, she felt refreshed in the warmth of her old comfortable paths and predictable social circle.

There the faces and landscaping were the same, which lent Elizabeth a security that she had been without on her travels. No, perhaps security was not quite the right sentiment. Every new sight and prospect of verdant landscape was exciting in Kent. And while Elizabeth might admit that she enjoyed the adventure of knowing more of the world, at the moment her contentment entirely sprang from being at home. She had been like a confident but naïve animal eager for some new excitement. But her confidence regarding two gentlemen proved wholly ill-conceived, and now that confidence was gone, the animal retreated to the safety of home to heal from those wounds.

When she thought of Mr Darcy and the words they exchanged throughout all of their experiences in Kent, she knew shame beyond any she had felt before. She had acted more than poorly; she had acted entirely and without question imprudently. Her judgement in that quarter could not have been more wrong unless she considered her judgments regarding the false and despicable…

"You are rather quiet this morning, Lizzy."

Her companion's voice bringing her out of her quiet musings, she captured Jane's arm in hers and pressed her beloved sister against her side in closer confidence.

"I was thinking of Mr Wickham."

Pulling away to view her sister's face, Miss Bennet frowned. "I hope you are not blaming yourself again."

A breathy exhale was the only answer given, and for a time, the two sisters walked about in silence.

"Lizzy, you must listen to me now." Jane stopped, causing her sister to stop also. Facing Elizabeth, Jane spoke with a mix of compassion and force that only she could have contrived. "Ignorant as you previously were of *everything* concerning the two gentlemen, *detection* could not be in your power and *suspicion* certainly not in your inclination."

Elizabeth smiled at her dear sister and, giving into the impulse of the moment, pulled her into a quick embrace.

"You are very good. And I thank you for so sternly reminding me of that. If you will say but a few more words on the matter, perhaps adding a word or two praising my general intelligence, my conscience and guilt will be entirely swept away."

Jane laughed, as Lizzy knew she would, and pulled her sister's arm again into her own to continue their stroll.

With less animation and more sombre tones, Elizabeth said, "I am rather uneasy about something."

"A burden shared is a burden halved. What is it?"

"We had decided that exposing Mr Wickham's general character was... that we ought not to do it."

"Oh, Lizzy, how can it be done without injuring others in the process? I am afraid that little good can be found in exposing Mr Wickham's evil deeds."

"True, however..."

"And if that gentleman is eager to re-establish his honour—what then? The regiment leaves in a few days. After that we may never see nor speak his name again."

Elizabeth was a beat behind in her response as she contemplated Jane's words. While she had no such confidence in Mr Wickham's wish for redemption, she still could not be happy sitting idly while he moved about their friends and neighbours. In the time since she had returned, she had been in company with him twice, and each time she was able, with very little effort on her part, to avoid conversing with the deceitful gentleman.

"I still do not feel quite easy about it. I cannot believe as you do that he wishes to amend his ways. That which is inherently bad remains bad. That which is inherently good stays good." Mr Darcy came to mind, the crease returning to her brow. "And even if, by chance, Mr Wickham wished to 're-establish' his character, he has wronged me!"

Jane smiled sympathetically. "I see what it is now. Be careful that this desire of yours to expose Wickham is not to assuage your own guilt in believing him."

Biting her lip, Lizzy confessed. "I will not say that my pride, which has been injured by Mr Wickham, will not rejoice in seeing him exposed. And I will further allow that part of my reservations include a desire to confront him personally for his deceit. But I also feel this inclination to protect my friends and family here in Hertfordshire from him."

"Lizzy…"

"Jane, if from the start we knew of Mr Wickham's character, would you not wish the same? Would you not have done all in your power to protect our sisters, friends, and acquaintances?"

Sighing heavily, Jane answered. "Just take care, Lizzy. Mr Wickham may yet have tendencies in his character more evil than even you and I know. Take care that you do not do anything foolish."

"I am more apt to believe Mr Wickham a coward than sinister, but I will heed your advice, dear sister. And if and when I choose to speak to the gentleman, I will 'take care.'"

"That is all I can ask," Jane said with a twinkle in her eye. "Foolish, headstrong girl!"

The two laughed at such a display from Jane and continued their walk about the gardens. On Elizabeth's part, she felt more ease now that the indecision was gone. She would do as she promised Jane and not act without thought, but should the moment arise, she *would* act!

~

"Thank you, John," Mr Darcy murmured to the footman as he handed Darcy his hat and walking stick. Placing the top hat firmly in place on his head, Darcy looked up the stairs just as his sister was descending.

"What is this, Georgiana? *You*, foregoing your usual tardiness and presenting yourself ready at the appointed time?" Darcy teased, his eyes crinkled in amusement as he took in her slightly pinked cheeks.

"You are so very witty, brother of mine. Your clever repartee never ceases to amuse." Her dry tone and quick rejoinder pulled from Darcy a deep, rumbling laugh.

It almost reminded him of… Clearing his throat, he replied with a formal bow. "I aim to please, my dear."

Mildly bemused, Georgiana laughed and shook her head, looking at him with the slightest puzzlement in her eyes. While he was the kindest, most attentive brother ever, he was not always the most playful.

"If it will bring you some comfort, I will say that I am not entirely ready for our walk. I am, as you see, not prepared to go out." She turned to allow a maid to slip her pelisse over her arms and button it.

His sister retrieved her bonnet and gloves, seemingly taking an exaggerated amount of time adjusting each article of clothing. When she turned, fully prepared for their walk, he feigned a sigh, pulling out his pocket watch. Before he could make some wry comment, Georgiana swatted his hand and said with a giggle, "Let us be off!"

Their destination was not far, it being a lovely, small piece of parkland in the square in front of Mr Darcy's London home. It was always an easy distance and pleasurable exercise for the siblings to partake. Whilst in London, and if his obligations allowed, Darcy tried to walk with his sister at least once a week.

As they ambled along a cobbled walkway to the entrance, Darcy listened intently as she spoke, first of her studies with her music master and then of the shopping trip she had recently taken with Mrs Annesley. Georgiana was youthful pleasures personified, and it pleased Darcy to hear her speak so joyfully. She had improved much since her misfortune at Ramsgate. Her tendency to withdraw into herself had lessoned, and Darcy was warmed to see her display so much contentment.

She remained reserved among others outside her intimates, and that, too, gave Darcy some pleasure. He noticed that, when they neared others, she would stem her speech until they were passed. While he would not have her uneasy in society, her reticence might protect her from those that would do her harm. Grinding his teeth, Darcy contemplated that such wariness, a result of her experience with Wickham, was at least one good thing to come from the whole sordid affair. It showed Georgiana had learned to be vigilant, and Darcy could not but find that good.

Georgiana made some comment on his mood, and Darcy brought his thoughts back around to attend her.

"I am in good spirits this morning, Georgie." He plucked a finger on her nose and continued. "Can I not be happy to escort my favourite sister on a walk about the park?"

"Your flattery is a little rusty, brother dear. I am your *only* sister!"

Darcy chuckled and patted her gloved hand on his sleeve.

"You just seemed…" She paused, and Darcy looked at her expectantly. When she spoke again, it was with the same halting hesitation that caused him to think at first they were near others. Soon he realised it sprang rather from her hesitancy to disturb him. "Upon your return from Kent, you seemed unhappy."

Darcy turned his gaze to the path ahead. His firm jaw worked back and forth as he prepared himself to speak. He had spent so little time with Georgiana that he did not expect her to notice, though now he suspected his neglect likely first attuned her to the difference in his demeanour. He could not account for his more positive outlook except to admit that the lovely dream of Elizabeth helped. And though it was a near impossible task to live with his memories of her while knowing he could not have her, he had determined to be a better man and promised himself that, as a reward, he would not force her memory gone.

"Do you think I am disdainful of the feelings of others?"

His abrupt change of topic further marred Georgiana's lovely countenance as she tried to make sense of her brother's contemplative visage.

"I do not understand what you are asking."

Darcy looked briefly at her before returning his gaze ahead. "Perhaps it is not fair to ask you to judge your brother in this manner. Forgive me."

Eager to be of service to her brother, Georgiana protested. "Oh no, please. I should like to help."

With a sigh, Darcy nodded. "I was made aware recently of some... defects in my character, and I am endeavouring to mend them."

"Defects? Upon my word!" Georgiana's quick defence brought a wistful smile to his lips, and he raised her gloved hand to his lips to kiss her fingers.

"It warms my heart to hear you defend me so valiantly, Georgie. I have not always been the best of brothers to you—"

"If you do not wish to hear my protests, Brother, speak no more absurdities!"

Nodding, Darcy tucked away the warmth he felt from her defence into his heart, and he sobered as he continued. "I have been made aware that I can be selfish, conceited, and disdainful of others."

"While I cannot agree with the foolish person who labelled you as such, I will attempt to address the claims as objectively as I can."

Her name is Elizabeth, and she is no fool. Darcy smiled at his sister, bemused by the fire in her eyes. *And I think you would have adored her.*

Squaring her slim shoulders, Georgiana addressed the first of the unfounded accusations. "Selfish. You are the most unselfish person I know. You are always free with your time whenever you can allow it to spend it with me. You give your money freely to many charities..."

"Georgie, I have realised my tendency to put my own wants above those of others. Is that not the definition of selfishness?"

His sister was quiet for a moment. "But you are a Darcy. Our parents would expect you to put your own family circle above others. While I am certain that the rest of the world has merit, they are not Darcys."

Astonished by her blunt response, Darcy laughed. And he could not admonish her pride. Georgiana was good and wholesome, yet she, in so few words, had described his own actions in public as to make them reasonable. Like his parents, Darcy had given Georgiana good principles but allowed them to be followed in pride and conceit. Had she said that to anyone else, she would have rightly been labelled the same as he was by Elizabeth.

It was testament to Darcy how far he had to come that he could see the reasonableness in her statement while still detecting the conceit. Her innocent and shameless riposte proved that she believed it as fact.

"I cannot say that you are not a little conceited," Georgiana began again, drawing her brother's direct attention. "But a little conceit is not a very bad thing, I begin to believe. Only think, you come from a family of long standing. Our name traces back to the Norman invasion. Pemberley is often heralded as one of the most glorious estates in all of England. Is that not something to have pride in?"

"Pride, where there is a real superiority of mind, pride will be always under good regulation." Darcy stumbled. He had said that to Elizabeth while she resided at Netherfield to nurse her ailing sister. She had accused him of pride and vanity, and he had defended pride in such a…such a ridiculous and *conceited* manner. And here again his sister, the pure and warmest heart he knew, defended his pride. He groaned under the realisation of still another instance where her words were reasonable yet confirmed Elizabeth's accusations as well.

"Pardon me, Georgie, but I must stop you there." He led her to a small bench at the side of the path. "I have failed you, my dear. I am afraid that I have…" Darcy paused, rubbed his hand across his jaw as his mind sorted out the thoughts racing through him and weighing on his heart. "I was spoilt by our parents, who, though good themselves—Father, particularly, was all that was benevolent and amiable—allowed, encouraged, almost taught me to be selfish and overbearing. To care for none beyond my own family circle, to think meanly of all the rest of the world, to *wish* at least to think meanly of their sense and worth compared with my own. I have, in turn, spoilt you in this same manner."

She could not keep quiet any further. "Oh, Brother, that is not true. You are good in your heart and as a man. Indeed. You are good! Our parents, who were also good, did their best."

Darcy continued without correcting her. "We are Darcys, and while I will not say that we ought not to have familial pride in our name, it does not mean we are better than others—or rather, that our decisions, beliefs, and worth are valued greater than others."

Georgiana sunk under the heaviness of his words. She recalled the words she had most recently spoken and began to see the ugliness in them. "Oh, how horrid I must be!"

"Georgie! No!" Darcy took up his sister's hand. "It is not you. I am to blame here. I am endeavouring to be more aware of this habit of mine."

Georgiana was quiet for some time, and Darcy feared that his candid discussion with his sister and gentle correction had dimmed her confidence again. When she spoke, Darcy could barely hear her whispered words.

"Who said this to you? Who called you these things?"

Elizabeth. "It does not matter. What matters is that this person was accurate, at least in my assessment."

"It is always difficult to look upon oneself and see with painful acuity our faults and mistakes." Darcy winced and knew that, in part, Georgiana knew this from personal experience. "But I am convinced that it is a necessary part of healing."

Healing. It was not what he expected to hear her say. Yet was Darcy not in need of healing? "You are wise beyond your years, darling,"

She looked up at him with glistening eyes. "I will say that, while I can see now the lapse in our education, I will not now or ever see you as anything other than truly good, Brother. Perhaps we both have need for improvement."

"Thank you. You must permit me to say that you are perfect to me. I cannot think ill of you. You are my dearest, most—"

"What was her name, William?"

Sputtering, Darcy cleared his throat and looked at his sister. "I beg your pardon?"

"What is the name of the woman who told you such things?'

Looking away, Darcy tried to hide the fact that his muscles had all frozen in response to her question. "What makes you think a lady is the source of this?"

"Come now, Brother." With a sigh, Georgiana explained. "It cannot have been Mr Bingley or our cousin Richard. Though being the only gentlemen I believe who could have spoken so boldly to you without consequence, I cannot think of any reason they would have to address you on these matters. It cannot have been any ordinary gentleman acquaintance of yours, for you would have been angered enough to defend your honour. It must have been a lady. For only a lady—particularly one you may have *admired*—could have caused such anguished introspection."

Darcy caught his sister's gaze and detected some insecurity defying her confident assessment of the situation. Her boldness made him relent.

"Very reasonable deduction, Georgiana. It so happens that you are correct—"

"And you admired her?"

Darcy chuckled despite himself. Suddenly, her eagerness to focus on that minute detail was endearing. With a firm look at his sister, he confirmed her initial suspicions. "It *was* a lady."

Georgiana bit her lip with indecision. She could tell that her brother did not want to admit admiration even though anything less could not have been possible given the seriousness of his introspection. If he esteemed her less, he might have said more. If her brother loved another who thought ill of him, it would be a serious blow and a motivator for change if ever she knew one. Still, he might admit to a name.

"And…her name?"

"Elizabeth." The word poured from Darcy's lips before he could stop it. She was always on the edge of his thoughts and the cusp of every breath.

Georgiana hid a secret smile as she pulled up the edges of her gloves. She noted that he did not say Miss ——. No, to him, she was "Elizabeth." Such a lapse in propriety spoke all that Georgiana needed to hear on the state of her brother's heart.

Standing, Georgiana proposed they resume their walk. She did not question him further, for which he was grateful. While her own pride smarted at the realisation that she, too, needed work on her own selfishness and conceit, and knowing as she did that this *Elizabeth* was the source of his unhappy revelation, Georgiana still could not but desire to make the lady's acquaintance.

On their return, the two Darcys spoke of ways they hoped to improve themselves and promised to help each other. Prompted by the memory of the unhappy maid he had encountered in the corridor of his home a week or so past, Darcy decided to begin there immediately.

Upon releasing Georgiana with a warm embrace when they reached their home, Darcy summoned the housekeeper to his study. The long-time retainer was confident in her manner with the master, having known him since he was in short pants and sliding around the newly waxed floors in his stockings. When Darcy asked her to have a seat, she began to feel apprehensive as her usual interviews with him were brief and to the point.

"Mrs Carroll, I want to first say that I am pleased with all of the work you have done here at Darcy House. I know that my home would not run nearly as smoothly without you."

The housekeeper gave a pinched smile by way of response, growing more confused by the minute. Her thoughts ran quickly through various recent decisions to evaluate whether any of them might not have met with the master's approval: books were all in perfect order, every shilling accounted for, the cook and maids were well trained…

"Now, this is not easy for me to admit." Darcy's words brought the housekeeper out of her reflection. "I have been neglectful in one area of my administration with the staff."

"Mr Darcy, sir, I cannot accept that. You are a very good master."

Darcy smiled kindly at the woman's loyalty. He adjusted the items on his desk and, seeing his daily planner, pulled it in front of him. "I should like to know more of the daily lives of my servants. Mind, I do not mean to say that I wish to hear the gossip below stairs, rather that I would like to be made aware whether there are any…life changes or circumstances whereby I might be of some assistance."

"I assure you, sir, that you pay each of your servants a fair wage, sir. I am sure there is no need for further—"

Darcy gently stopped her by raising his hand. "It is not my plan to interfere in their personal lives. But I should like to be made more aware —" With a frown contorting his handsome features, Darcy began again. "Some days ago—no, it was more than a se'nnight—but that does not matter." He paused thoughtfully before continuing. "I came across one of the maids in the hallway upstairs, and she was speaking to another maid. It was clear to me that the maid was upset."

Mrs Carroll sat up straighter, affronted though she tried not to be. "While I cannot claim that quarrels among my staff never happen, sir, they are quite rare."

"Oh no, you mistake me. I did not mean to imply that the girls were fighting. Nor that you would allow any quarrelling under your excellent command." Darcy smiled to appease his faithful and revered housekeeper; endeared as he was to her as almost family, he could not help being amused by her affront.

"The maid was distressed. It made me realise that I do not know the circumstances of my servants. In the past I have been…I have allowed you to handle these matters as you see fit. I trust your judgement, and I see no reason to change the way you manage those under your employ. However, I should like to be made aware just the same should I be able to be of assistance."

Mrs Carroll nodded her head in understanding. Though she felt that Mr Darcy was as generous a master as he need be, it made her proud to see such further evidence of his goodness. She raised her chin and smiled brightly.

"Very good, sir. If I understand you correctly, you wish to know more of the servants."

"Yes! I wish to be more cognizant of the needs of those in my household."

"Very admirable, sir, though I must say that you are already the best of masters. As this is your wish, let us start with that maid. Do you remember what she looked like?"

Darcy looked down slightly ashamed. "I am sorry to say that I did not note what she looked like. Perhaps her hair was red?"

Mrs Carroll chuckled. "It is of no trouble, sir. It is more than likely that this circumstance was of a trifling matter. These girls are young and are easily offset by some inconsequential thing. Though I will say, none of our maids have red hair."

Darcy winced but smiled good-naturedly. "You see I have much to learn. I would like to include this in our weekly meetings."

"Shall we begin now, sir?"

"Oh no. I am sure that I have kept you from you duties long enough. We shall start next week."

Standing, Mrs Carroll curtseyed. After ascertaining the master's desires for his noonday repast, she left to return to her office. Though it was puzzling that Mr Darcy would make such a request, it did not surprise her that he should wish to improve himself or do more where he might. With a quick swipe at her wizened cheek, she concealed an unforeseen tear. She was pleased with the man he had become.

~

Elizabeth turned at the sound of her name being hailed. She had walked to Meryton with her younger sisters. Lydia had been invited to go to Brighton with her friend Mrs Forster. It was a scheme Elizabeth severely opposed and had yet to be sanctioned by her father. Lydia, of course, was certain of his acceptance and thus wanted to get a few ribbons to trim a bonnet of hers. Elizabeth, already wary of the possible horrors of Lydia nearly unsupervised in a town full of officers in Brighton, was compelled to walk with Kitty and Lydia to Meryton when it was proposed. She may not be able to rein in Lydia if she travelled to Brighton, but she could do her part during their time in Meryton.

Elizabeth's heart sank and her lips pinched in a tight smile when she saw that her caller was none other than Mr Wickham. He bowed to the ladies, and Elizabeth shot her sisters a look when they giggled.

"Ah, the Miss Bennets, out for a stroll this lovely morning."

"We are going to the milliner's shop, for I am to accompany Mrs Forster to Brighton as her *particular* friend."

Elizabeth tried to silence Lydia with a firm, "That has not been decided yet, Lydia. Papa has not yet granted you his permission."

Lydia scoffed and waved her away. Elizabeth was disgusted to see a gleam in Wickham's expression before he turned his attentions to her.

"Miss Elizabeth, it would give me great pleasure if you were to be among the party bound for Brighton."

Elizabeth was quick to cut her sister's protests off with her own. "That is very kind of you, sir. Yet, I am travelling with my aunt and uncle to the Lake District this summer."

"Brighton's loss." Wickham gallantly gestured to the door of the shop and made to open it for them. As much as Elizabeth would have gladly left his company, it looked as if he was wishing to accompany them as he had on many occasions in the past.

Elizabeth clenched her jaw as she entered the shop. She was ashamed anew at all the time she wasted in his company before she learned of his duplicity. After her eyes adjusted to the light of the shop, she surveyed the other patrons. When her eyes rested upon her neighbour Mrs Long, studying some lengths of fabric, an idea formed in Elizabeth's mind.

Turning a bright smile to Mr Wickham, Elizabeth endeavoured to act as she had always acted with him. "Mr Wickham, I hardly think you need join us. Unless you are an expert on lace?"

Wickham chuckled, obviously pleased with her teasing. "I am an expert on many things, Miss Bennet, and have yet to reveal them all." He paused to look at her flirtatiously as he had always done before. Only now, it made Elizabeth rather sick. "But lace, I am afraid, is not one of them."

Deceit, dishonour, and disgrace among the lot, I am sure! Elizabeth led him towards a display of lace, engaging him in small talk as she went. He was as attentive as ever. Elizabeth kept an eye on her sisters who, as soon as they entered the shop, were quickly diverted by seeing Maria Lucas and sharing their news of Lydia's invitation to Brighton.

"I never told you of my recent travels to Kent."

Wickham leaned cavalierly against the nearby shelves. "I should like to hear about them."

"I am sure you heard from my cousin while he was here that his patron is Lady Catherine de Bourgh."

Wickham laughed and gamely added, "She is a fierce old bird if I recall correctly."

Elizabeth hated to agree with such a man, but she could not help it. "That she is." She laughed, thinking of the many times Lady Catherine had bristled when Elizabeth answered in a manner brooking her disappointment. "Her house is but a mile from the parsonage."

Wickham nodded, encouraging her to go on. He appeared to be a perfectly attentive gentleman, but Elizabeth noted the way his eyes occasionally flickered when the rustle of skirts nearby could be heard. She wondered that she had never noticed such behaviour before.

"Her ladyship had some guests during a portion of our stay in the county," Elizabeth began, turning towards the shelves and picking up a piece of lace to examine it. While she bent to look at it, she checked to see that Mrs Long was still carefully examining the lengths of fabric on the other side of the shelves. Pleased to see that she was occupied, Elizabeth raised her voice just a touch.

"Her nephew Mr Darcy came on his annual visit to Rosings Park."

Wickham's smile turned compassionate. "You have been most unfortunate indeed, Miss Bennet."

"It certainly felt like it at the time."

"And did my old friend make his proposal?"

"Pardon?" Elizabeth looked up startled.

"To Miss de Bourgh. I believe I told you that they are expected to marry."

Laughing, Elizabeth changed her focus to another piece of lace to hide her blush. "Oh, of course. Yes. Now I recall you mentioning something of the sort. If he proposed to Miss de Bourgh, I was not made aware of it."

"Then I doubt very much that he did. Darcy could not have made a proposal at Rosings without his aunt crowing about it to all. It has been her particular wish since his infancy."

"Then I fear she is bound for disappointment."

"I hate to correct a lady, but you do not know Darcy as I do, Miss Bennet. He will always do his duty." Wickham's words were harder in the end, and Elizabeth was grateful for the opening.

"Except where it concerned you, Mr Wickham."

Wickham straightened and pulled at his cuffs. When he looked at her next, his countenance betrayed nothing but sadness and loss.

"True, though had I means to support myself, I could not have met you."

Elizabeth's smile was forced. "You are too kind." Changing the topic, Elizabeth said, "You know my cousin is ordained and, before he was so fortunate as to be distinguished by Lady Catherine, had little to no connexions."

Elizabeth watched as Wickham resumed his polite expression of earnest attention.

"I wonder, sir, if you could not seek your revenge on Mr Darcy in another way."

Mrs Long stilled, telling Elizabeth she had caught bits of their conversation as Elizabeth had hoped. Being the consummate gossip, she would play right into Elizabeth's plans. Wickham, she noted had given her his full attention. A slight twitch to his smile exposed how very much he liked the sound of her words.

"I am not a vengeful man."

"Certainly not, forgive me. I misspoke. Especially bound and educated for the church as you were. I only thought that if Mr Darcy wished to deny you the living due to his jealousy, you might have become ordained—having already received the education at his father's hand—and sought another living. Mr Darcy could not have prevented another from bestowing upon you their patronage, much like Lady Catherine did with my cousin."

Elizabeth looked up at Mr Wickham with pretended excitement. He could not interpret her words or her expression any other way than that she had struck on a solution to his troubles and was pleased for it.

Wickham cleared his throat and looked distinctly discomfited before he transformed his features into some semblance of peace.

"A happy notion, Miss Bennet. Alas, one that I cannot pursue."

"No?"

"It was Mr Darcy senior that wished me for the church. And while I would have gladly honoured that and enjoyed the profession, when his son took that from me, I confess I could not seek another living without feeling emotions unbefitting of a clergy towards one of God's children, particularly Mr Darcy the son."

"But surely, to secure yourself a means of support?"

"I am a lowly militiaman, Miss Bennet," Wickham said with a clenched jaw. After placing another smile on his face, he continued in a gentler tone. "I have resigned myself to serve and administer to my fellow militiamen now. This is my Christian calling now."

Elizabeth had planned to expose his dealings by pushing more holes in his story, but her temper had the better of her. His falsehoods and his expressions of piety were grating on her already pressured patience with the man. Though Jane would object, she no longer could hold out on confronting Wickham.

"That is admirable, sir. Truly it is. Especially as you cannot have need for the earnings of a militiaman, considering the legacy from old Mr Darcy's will, that of one thousand pounds. Then again there was the generous allotment of *three* thousand pounds his son gave you in lieu of the living."

A stifled gasp came from the other side of the shelf and Wickham's eyes flickered about and then settled with some trepidation back on Elizabeth.

"You look surprised, sir. I did tell you that Mr Darcy was among the company at Rosings Park while I visited with my relations in Kent, did I not?"

Wickham stuttered, appearing to struggle for composure. Adding further to his discomfort, Elizabeth said, "I made another acquaintance while I was there. Perhaps you will remember him from your days at Pemberley. Colonel Fitzwilliam was among the party at Rosings. Charming young man, though I imagine a fierce soldier."

Wickham noticeably swallowed. "Miss Bennet, I...I apologize but I must leave you now. I am expected elsewhere."

"Shall I give him your regards, sir? Being in the profession himself, I am sure he would be vastly pleased to hear that his childhood friend had also joined His Majesty's ranks."

Wickham did not respond, only gave a tight-lipped bow and strode off.

Elizabeth turned back towards the shelf of lace with a rather pleased smile. She had confronted Wickham and saw that, just as she had predicted, he was more coward than anything else. Along with that, if Mrs Long was feeling quite herself, most of Meryton would shortly know of his duplicity.

~

Over the next weeks, Darcy met with his housekeeper regarding their usual business and also began to learn more of his staff. Though it was not his intention to pry into their personal lives, he became more sensible of their needs.

Many times, there was nothing further for Darcy to do as his excellent senior staff performed their parts admirably. For instance, Ben, a footman, had broken a finger restocking the cellar. While the required medical attention was given to the man, it was a matter that, previously, Darcy never would have known. Still there were times, much to Darcy's satisfaction, that he was able to lend some kind assistance. One such meeting with Mrs Carroll revealed to Darcy that the lady's maid to Georgiana had received some unwanted attention from a footman employed at the house of Lord — next door.

"I have advised the girl to avoid the gentleman whenever possible. And of course, it is our policy that all staff run their errands in pairs."

"I have a mind to speak to his lordship about his footman."

Mrs Carroll's eyebrows rose sharply. It was above and beyond anything expected of him or considered his duty. Usually such cases were resolved butler to butler.

"That would be very kind of you, sir, but you need not trouble yourself."

"Consider it done, ma'am. I do not like to think that any of my staff feel unsafe living here. And I know his lordship would not tolerate untoward behaviour from someone in his employ."

"Very well, sir." Recovering from her surprise and pleasure, Mrs

Carroll looked down upon her list to see if there was anything else she had noted to share with Mr Darcy. Glad to see the last item was a happy one, she smiled and looked up at her curious master. "There is just one more thing on my list, sir. Mary has had a new sister born. Mother and baby are doing well, I hear."

"Mary is an upstairs maid with brown hair?"

Mrs Carroll chuckled and nodded her head. "Very good, sir. You are becoming quite proficient with the names."

Darcy smiled, pleased with himself. His eyes strayed briefly to his bookcase and a certain volume there. *Elizabeth would have cared enough about them to know their names—had she been mistress of my home.*

He was startled slightly out of his wistful musings when Mrs Carroll closed her book and said, "Well that is all I have, sir. If there is nothing else, shall I leave you now?"

Darcy nodded and thanked his housekeeper. These past couple of weeks had helped him to think less of himself and to be more aware of the feelings of others. His home was a small place to start, but he knew it had made him more mindful when he engaged with others.

After Mrs Carroll exited the room, Darcy turned and gently pulled out the tome containing his letters to Elizabeth. He had not written her since he had first determined to become a better man—to become a man worthy of her. Colonel Fitzwilliam had honoured his desire not to speak of her, and although he had not asked the same of Georgiana, his sister had not breathed Elizabeth's name since he first revealed it to her. But though her name had not been whispered by those who knew of her, it did not mean she was far from his thoughts. Every action, every decision he made was with thoughts of her.

Opening the book, he peered at the nearly dozen letters he had written to her. He lifted them up and felt their weight. They were light, only a few sheets of parchment, but each contained a part of his burden over nearly a year of falling in love with her and learning to accept his failings. He so dearly craved to write to her again, to tell her of the improvements he had been making, to beg her to reconsider. It was that last wish that stopped him. He could not yet be the better man he hoped to become until he was doing it not only for her but also for himself.

Replacing the letters in the book, he closed it and returned it to the shelf. He would write to her; he had no doubt. He had not the strength to completely break the habit, but he was resolved not to write until he felt he was more worthy of her.

CHAPTER 13

Elizabeth stooped to retrieve the basket of clippings from the garden and, intending to take them to the distilling room off the back of the house to dry, walked leisurely along the path towards her destination. Idly her fingers pressed a sprig of lavender between them, releasing its perfumed aroma into the air. Her path took her along the side of the house where her steps soon paused outside the open window of her father's study. She could hear his voice elevated in mischief as he spoke with her mother.

Stepping around the bend, she leaned against the window frame and caught her father's eye. He winked at her as he turned again to his wife, whose report was of particular importance, at least to Mrs Bennet. Her cheeks were infused with heightened colour, her breath laboured in excitement, and her hands, which never could stay still during the best of moments, were in high agitation.

"Well, well, and so Mr Bingley is coming down, Mr Bennet," she trilled again in Mr Bennet's ear. Though it was not news to him, he did not interrupt his wife, his twenty-plus years in matrimonial association having at least taught him the wisdom of that. Instead, he snuck amused expressions without at Elizabeth when Mrs Bennet paced about the room. "Well, so much the better. Not that I care about it, though. He is nothing to us, you know, and I am sure *I* never want to see him again. But, however, he is very welcome to come to Netherfield if he likes it."

Elizabeth caught the gleam in her father's eye and, suppressing a laugh, admonished him silently through the gestures of her hands.

"And who *knows* what may happen?" Mr Bennet then added with implication.

Mrs Bennet responded immediately, stopping her fevered pacing and looking at her husband. "Aye, husband, imagine!"

"But this can be nothing to us." Mr Bennet suppressed a smile as he looked up at his wife's chagrined countenance. "You know, Mrs Bennet, we agreed long ago never to mention a word about the gentleman. In fact, I believe that was your wise idea when last he up and left the neighbourhood so abruptly."

Mrs Bennet, struck mute in the face of her own declaration months previous, was at once displeased to hear it repeated to her when she most wished to speak of the gentleman. For she had just had it that morning from her sister Phillips, who had learned from Ms. Allman, who had overheard the housekeeper of Netherfield make her order at the butcher's.

Outside, Elizabeth shook her head at her father, knowing full well that he was sporting with his wife. Presenting him with a disapproving expression that could not hold up long against his smile and twinkling eyes, Elizabeth walked on just as his words came again through the window.

"And so is it *quite* certain he is coming?" Mr Bennet's tone could easily be mistaken for any gossiping old hen as he relieved his wife's suspended state by encouraging her to continue where he knew she wished most to go.

"You may depend upon it!" Mrs Bennet burst forth in relief. "For Mrs Phillips heard it from…"

Elizabeth laughed to herself as the voices drifted out of hearing. Though she could not approve of her father's teasing ways with her mother, such a topic could hold no other emotion but eager anticipation. The news of Mr Bingley's return was received by the eldest Bennet daughters a full se'nnight before their mother caught wind of it, and it came from a surprising quarter.

A letter addressed to Jane arrived from none other than Miss Bingley. Surprising as it was for both Elizabeth and Jane, they secreted the letter in Jane's room before it could be seen by any of the rest of the family. If Elizabeth, when Jane showed her the letter, did not expect it to contain a continuation of the writer's previous ill manners, she had formed no expectation at all of its contents. She was at once apprehensive and afraid for Jane. It had been many months since her sister had given up any expectation of acquaintance in that quarter. To receive such a letter without warning and with every potential for upset disturbed Elizabeth's most beloved sister most heartily.

"What can she mean, Lizzy, in writing to me after all these months?"

"I am sure I do not know." Every protective instinct rose in vigour within her.

Jane tossed the missive to her sister, unopened, as if it might burst into flames at any moment. Eyeing it with trepidation, she said, "I cannot read it, Lizzy. I cannot."

Taking up the letter, Elizabeth turned it over. Curiosity burned her fingers where they touched the fine parchment. Though she was not unmindful of her sister's turmoil, Elizabeth laughed at the absurdity that a single piece of post could wreak such havoc upon them. Her thoughts took flight immediately to the writer's brother and then, naturally, to his friend. In an attempt not to lose herself in meaningless contemplation of Mr Darcy, Elizabeth spoke. "What reason do you suspect Miss Bingley has to write you, Jane? She made it quite clear that any acquaintance with our family was at an end with the abominably rude way she treated you in London."

Jane sunk deeper into her pillows, her face awash with pain as she whispered, "She can have only one thing to wish to tell me—one thing that would bring me pain and seal her triumph. She must write of her brother's marriage. She as much as hinted at it when they all quitted the neighbourhood last autumn. It is past May, and such a thing must surely come to pass by now."

"Oh, my dear Jane, you do not persist in believing her allusions to Miss Darcy?"

Elizabeth took up her sister's hand, and she saw Jane turn her head away as a tear rolled down her cheek. Elizabeth could not believe that Mr Darcy would allow Miss Darcy to marry Mr Bingley, not at her age with her past, and certainly not knowing as he did of Jane's heart. She may have misjudged him before; however, his proposal and the subsequent events in Kent brought to light a better understanding of him, and this—this!—she could not believe of him. She knew him to be a better man. Still, it had been many weeks since he had last bid her adieu at her uncle's house in Cheapside.

"I cannot believe Mr Bingley is to be wed and most assuredly not to Miss Darcy." When her sister persisted in silence, Elizabeth continued gently. "Shall I open it and end this uncertainty for both of us?"

By way of agreement, Jane squeezed Elizabeth's hand. Carefully, and with no little anxiety, Elizabeth opened the letter with the other hand and pressed it flat against her thigh. As she began to read silently, her smile grew. It was not at all what either of them could have anticipated and certainly not what plagued her sister with such grief at that moment. Assuming she was being observed by Jane, Elizabeth looked up with the greatest of smiles, only to find Jane's eyes squeezed shut in guarded anticipation of dreadful news.

Shaking her sister's hand in hers, Elizabeth tried to coax Jane to look at her. "Sister, it is not what you think."

Jane stilled.

Elizabeth rushed to ensure her sister's continued recovery. "Jane, it is quite the opposite. Mr Bingley is even now making preparations to return to Netherfield."

"What?" Jane's head shot up, and she snatched the letter out of Elizabeth's hands with both of hers, causing her sister to laugh.

Jane read silently, her eyes scanning quickly across the script. "It says here that he is coming within a fortnight. And he is coming alone! Miss Bingley says she cannot accompany her brother due to a pressing summons from her aunt in the North." Jane looked up, her eyes shining with hope. "What do you think of that Lizzy? She writes that her brother is to return without her."

"Read on," Elizabeth said with an indulgent smile.

Jane bent her head again to the letter. She gasped when she read Miss Bingley's entirely unexpected request that she agree to introduce him about the neighbourhood again upon his return. Elizabeth watched with a pleased expression, knowing there was still more to the letter that would shock her sister.

An audible whimper told Elizabeth that Jane had reached the most surprising part of the letter. Jane lifted bright eyes to her sister and repeated the words of the letter verbatim. "'It is at the particular request of my brother that I ask this of you, my dear Miss Bennet.'"

Suppressing an eye roll at Miss Bingley's oft-used endearment and not at all believing the writer's sincerity, Elizabeth smiled at her sister. It was Elizabeth's suspicion after reading the letter herself that Miss Bingley had written the whole under extreme persuasion, perhaps under duress. Never would she, after treating Jane so horribly, write such an excessively affectionate letter. Expressing endearments, asking favours of such magnitude —her request was tantamount to allowing her brother to announce his intentions to the neighbourhood!

No, Elizabeth suspected Mr Bingley had somehow become informed of his sister's duplicity and orchestrated his sister's penance while also gamely warning Jane of his return and pronouncing his intentions. The fact that Miss Bingley would not accompany her brother spoke further to Elizabeth of his disfavour with his sister. A summons from an aunt up north, indeed! The source of his intelligence troubled Elizabeth even more than the startling letter. For she could not imagine Miss Bingley confessing such sins. No, she could only think that Mr Darcy had spoken to his friend. The warmth that thought tendered was quite enough to make Elizabeth's eyes water as well. She was beginning to believe that, where Mr Darcy was concerned, she knew not herself. Firmly promising herself to think on *that* at a later time, Elizabeth endeavoured to force it from her mind.

"And what is your reply to be?" Elizabeth's tone was quiet and serious.

Jane looked down again at the letter, the last of which asked if she would be willing to perform such a role for Mr Bingley. It was clear to both sisters what the letter really was asking. Would she welcome Mr Bingley back to the neighbourhood, and if so, would she welcome his suit? The last portion of the letter could have only been dictated directly by Mr Bingley himself, for the tone itself held none of the platitudes of the previous lines. It tasted of suspended hope and unmitigated fear.

When Jane looked up, her shoulders began to shake as happy tears rolled down her glowing cheeks.

"I must, Lizzy. I must. I cannot give him up!"

Elizabeth chuckled compassionately as she engulfed Jane in her arms. Rubbing her back, she agreed. "It is absolutely necessary that you take this chance at happiness now that he has given it to you."

Jane pulled back, questioning in her eyes. "You believe he is behind this letter, more so than his request that I bring him around the neighbourhood again."

"Of course, he is! I think there is a very good chance he had never learnt of your presence in London as they led you to believe, but he has since learned of his sisters' disgrace. I never doubted he loved you, Jane." Having never revealed to Jane her certain knowledge that Mr Bingley did not know of Jane's visit to London, it was all Elizabeth could do to keep from eradicating all traces of distrust from her dear sister's eyes by retrieving the oft-read missive as proof. Still, some things were too personal, too sacred, to share even with Jane.

It was a pleasure beyond anything Elizabeth could have suspected to see her sister once again happy and settled in heart. Marvelling again at the power one letter could have on one's fate, Elizabeth discussed with her sister what ought to be done next. They agreed they had better speak to their father on the subject, especially considering the social implications of such a request. It was Jane's sincere hope that Mr Bennet would not be opposed to her accepting Miss Bingley's—rather Mr Bingley's—request, and as Elizabeth suspected, the man only waited long enough to assure himself it was Jane's true wish that she accept Miss Bingley's proposal before granting his permission to reply in the affirmative.

However, as often is the case in insubstantial country towns, as soon as one topic of sizeable speculation can be shared abroad, another soon takes precedence and is at the lips of all of its principal residents. Such was the case with poor Mr Bingley's return, for no sooner was it generally learned abroad, than it was eclipsed by news with a greater potential for shock! Fresh intelligence had the inhabitants reeling and their matron's tongues whipping about with astonishment. Mrs Bennet, being not immune to the contagion of gossip, soon brought the news to Longbourn.

"You will not believe what I have learned, dear girls. Gather around for you must hear what is even now being spoken of on the streets of Meryton."

Only the youngest two Bennet daughters hovered closer to their mother, the others having learned long ago that most news brought to them through their mother was never of import or interest. However, both Jane's and Elizabeth's heads popped up from their embroidery when Mrs Bennet spoke her next words.

"Mr Wickham has left! Vanished from the neighbourhood days before the regiment." The reminder of the soldiers' departure a fortnight before brought forth renewed moans of grief from Kitty and a smug chuckle from Lydia. *She* could not bemoan their departure, for Mr Bennet's permission to travel to Brighton had been granted. It was only a matter of waiting while Colonel Forster moved his troops to Brighton and returned for his wife before Lydia would have her fondest dream realised, and she would leave with her particular friend to follow the soldiers to the coastal town.

Elizabeth looked at her sister on the news of Wickham's departure. She had not seen him since their encounter in the milliner's shop some weeks past, and she assumed he wished to keep his distance from her since he knew she was not fooled by his tale of woe. If the timing of Mrs Bennet's report was true, he must have left immediately thereafter. Elizabeth had told Jane of her confrontation and hoped Mrs Long would prove more valuable in spreading the truth of his history, but she had heard nothing.

"It seemed he sold his commission, though how nobody can quite figure—"

"Sold his commission! He would not!" Lydia burst forth, distressed then at the idea that such a man would choose *not* to be a soldier.

"Oh but he did, child, foolish man that he is! Not only that, but I have heard he has left debts behind him among all the principal tradesmen, a few of his fellow militia men, and…" Mrs Bennet paused for dramatic effect, Lydia and Kitty leaning forward in eager anticipation. Elizabeth herself found herself slightly bent towards her mother and, after realising her attitude, sat up straight in disgust.

"…there is now evidence that he was never victimized so brutally by Mr Bingley's friend." Here Mrs Bennet shot an affectionate glace at her eldest before continuing. "That Mr Darby, Dercy—"

"Darcy," Elizabeth automatically supplied.

Thankfully, Mrs Bennet continued on without pause. "Darcy. That was it, thank you, Lizzy. Mr Darcy paid Wickham for the living promised and Wickham squandered away the funds!"

After that, there was much discussion on the shocking departure of Mr Wickham though, much to Elizabeth and Jane's chagrin, the majority of the disapproval voiced concerning his many sins revolved entirely around his unfathomable decision to leave the militia. For Elizabeth's part, she was amused to consider her mother's claim of "evidence" concerning the true history between Wickham and Darcy—evidence that could be none other than sourced through her own lips and spread as hearsay from Mrs Long.

That evening, as Elizabeth sat at her window long after dark descended on their thoroughly scandalized part of England, she was surprised to find that she did not feel pleasure at seeing Wickham lose his favour among her friends. She had protected them from a misapprehension regarding his character and ought then to feel pleased with her success.

Instead, her thoughts tended towards unacknowledged disappointment. Even as she sat at the window, she wished the moment could have been shared with Mr Darcy—that he could see the effect of sharing such intelligence with her and that he might learn once again to think kindly of her after seeing his good name so masterfully exonerated among her acquaintances.

Shaking away her confusing and no doubt fanciful notions of pleasing Mr Darcy, Elizabeth moved to her bedside and watched the flickering dance of the single candle. She did not know why she wished for his good opinion—or rather, she knew it could do her no good to wish such a thing. Unconvincingly, Elizabeth assured herself that she did not long for a renewal of his offer. Laughing at herself for such a ridiculous idea, Elizabeth bent and, with unnecessary vigour, blew out the candle, plunging the room into blackness.

She sat there until her eyes slowly adjusted to the dim moonlight filtering through the window as the greater light had been chased aside. Though planning to climb into her bed to retire for the evening, Elizabeth soon was distracted as parts of her room slowly began to come into focus in the dark. Then, without pausing to question her motives, she stood and padded towards her writing desk. Knowing fingers soon found an indention in the panelling near the back of the row of drawers. Soon her fingers had triggered the release to the one hidden compartment. She did not need the light for that and felt glad to be without it.

Into her awaiting hands fell a small folded square of fine linen. Though she could not see the embroidered initials on it, her mind's eye could picture them easily.

Returning to bed with her illicit object, Elizabeth lay atop the counterpane, staring up into the shadows above her head. Moonlight filtered through the oak tree outside her window and cast leaf mosaics across the ceiling of her room. The mosaic shifted and swayed as the branches bent with the breeze outside her window, much like the twisting, ever-shifting emotions she was experiencing within. All the while, Elizabeth clutched the handkerchief at her breastbone, the one with the initials "F. D."

CHAPTER 14

~~~

THOUGH WICKHAM'S DEPARTURE HAD STOLEN THE NEIGHBOURHOOD'S attention from Mr Bingley's return, it could not have the same effect on the inhabitants of Longbourn. Miss Bennet and her next eldest sister were acutely aware of the days that passed before his proposed day of arrival. Given that Jane had written to accept the request to personally reintroduce Mr Bingley to the people of Meryton, her heart beat wildly when that day finally arrived. With her serene deportment, one who might not know her as Elizabeth did and might have presumed that the gentleman's return was of little consequence to Miss Bennet.

Knowing as she did Jane's true state of being, Elizabeth ventured to her father's study in the hopes of speeding up the inevitable moment that, the more it was prolonged, only increased her sister's disquiet.

"As soon as ever Mr Bingley comes, Papa," pleaded Elizabeth, "you will wait on him, of course."

Mr Bennet chuckled at his daughter's demands. Even knowing from whence the urgency of her request came, Mr Bennet still could not help but sport with her.

To that end, he replied, "No, no. Your mother forced me into visiting him last year and promised, if I went to see him, that he should marry one of my daughters. But it ended in nothing, and I will not be sent on a fool's errand again."

"Papa!"

Suppressing the mirth threatening his composure, Mr Bennet pressed on. "'Tis an etiquette I despise," said he. "If he wants our society, let him seek it. He knows where we live. I will not spend *my* hours in running after my neighbours every time they go away and come back again."

While dismayed by her father's unlooked-for obstinacy, it was not entirely without believability, for he, against Elizabeth's explicit concerns, had allowed Lydia to leave for Brighton a few days before. Elizabeth opened her mouth to unleash such speech as would shock her father at that profound example of injustice when her fiery gaze met his humoured eyes and mouth agape, and she realised he had been sporting with her.

All righteous protest left her then, and with a bemused chuckle, Elizabeth collapsed into her favourite chair with relief. "You are a cruel old man, Papa."

Laughing openly now with his daughter, Mr Bennet removed his spectacles to wipe away the moisture gathering at his eyes from his mischief.

"But you will visit him, Papa."

Mr Bennet smiled at his daughter, admiring her compassion on behalf of her sister's wellbeing and also for her good-natured temperament. Leaning towards her, he bestowed a gentle pat on her knee.

"Of course, my dear. Although Mr Bingley has declared his intentions toward Jane with his request, I know my duty must first be done to bring it about."

"Thank you, Papa. I did not like to believe you capable of neglecting Jane in this matter."

Adjusting his position in the seat, Mr Bennet became sombre. "How is she, Lizzy? How is Jane fairing with regards to Mr Bingley's return? Tell me truly."

With a sigh, Elizabeth shared that, despite the assurances that could be garnered from his request for her company, Jane was uneasy for the moment that would bring them face to face. After so long a separation, she feared he might not feel as inclined for her company as he at first declared once finally reintroduced to her. Furthermore, she was wary of both guarding her heart too closely, as she had before, and guarding it not enough.

"Well, we shall have to see, I suppose," Mr Bennet declared calmly, though he already had plans to acquaint the gentleman with his own terms in regard to Jane's squiring him about the neighbourhood—terms whose meaning no gentleman, when faced with such demands from the father of a young lady, could mistake.

However serene and calm her countenance, even Jane could not control the panic that commanded the tempo of her heart when Mr Bingley was seen riding up the gravel lane that led to Longbourn. Her face paled, and she unconsciously squeezed Elizabeth's hand, suddenly unsurprised to have found it within her own.

When at last Mr Bingley was presented at the parlour, her pallor fled, replaced by a rosy flush when his eyes settled on her. In that moment, even Elizabeth could see the love mired by trepidation in the open expression of his eyes.

Almost as soon as he had greeted Mrs Bennet, as was custom, Mr Bingley turned to bow before the object of his interest. Such a slight could not produce any offense on the part of Mrs Bennet who sat taller still with a pleased expression that could not have been removed if all the militiamen in the kingdom had chosen to resign their commissions.

Though overjoyed for Jane, a pang resonated within Elizabeth's heart the moment the gentleman bowed and extended his greetings to her sister, making her realise that she had wished for his friend to accompany him.

That Mr Darcy had not joined his friend was no surprise since she knew the manifold reasons the gentleman would forever distance himself from Hertfordshire. Nay, Mr Darcy would not willingly put himself in her company again. And with that, Elizabeth felt the moment of happiness for her sister become tainted with envy.

Despite that unexpected privation, Elizabeth was truly happy for Jane. Eying her sister as she made her own greetings with Mr Bingley, Elizabeth could see that Jane was glowing with joy—joy that seemed mirrored in the gentleman in front of them.

"Miss Bennet, Miss Elizabeth, it is truly wonderful to be back in Hertfordshire. Why, I do believe it has been above six months. We have not met since the twenty-sixth of November, when we were all dancing together at Netherfield."

Elizabeth was pleased to find his memory so exact, and a glance at her sister saw that Jane, too, shared the sentiment.

"I believe you are correct, Mr Bingley," Jane murmured with a bloom in her cheeks.

It was not long thereafter that a walk was proposed, and the young ladies of the house exited with their bonnets to ramble the gardens of Longbourn.

While preparing to go out, Jane requested Elizabeth stay firmly by her side, and her sister had no qualms with such a request.

Mr Bingley was likewise somewhat unsettled at that first encounter with the ladies of Longbourn, but true to his affable nature, he soon relaxed into the ever-pleased and willing-to-please gentleman they all had known previously. And while Elizabeth, as promised, did not leave her sister's side, she soon found herself an unnecessary third to a two-person conversation between the principal would-be lovers.

Quietly she strolled beside Jane, and the only indication that her presence was still desired and acknowledged was the occasional squeeze of her arm, linked as it was through Jane's. Mr Bingley and her sister were growing quite inattentive to their surroundings and others in the walking party, wholly engrossed in each other so swiftly upon that visit that every hope Elizabeth tendered for her sister felt certain to come true. Elizabeth could not feel slighted, for she knew that general incivility was the very essence of love, and by the looks of things, her sister and Mr Bingley were as much in love as they ever were before.

So little was required of Elizabeth in the discourse between the other two that she was left wholly to her own thoughts—those thoughts tending frequently towards what it might feel like to experience such a mutual affection for herself.

~

Darcy's chuckle settled into a discreet smile as he watched his sister refill his cup of tea. She had been regaling him with her misadventure from her walk in the park the day before with a particularly intrepid woodland creature. The squirrel, thinking she might offer some morsel of foodstuff, had been insistent on scurrying about her feet, prompting startled shrieks from his sister until Mrs Annesley could persuade the animal to try his luck elsewhere by means of a few close swipes of her parasol.

"You laugh, Brother, but I tell you that creature was positively mad."

Georgiana feigned disgust at his finding humour in the story. Her frown only caused him to burst with laughter. "Shall I send along a footman for your protection next you go out, or shall you succumb to the pirate squirrel's demands and bring a basket along with you?"

Georgiana provoked another laugh when she scowled good-naturedly then stuck her tongue out at her brother. Although inordinately pleased to see him light-hearted after so many weeks of a distracted state of mind, Georgiana would have rather not seen it at her own expense.

A knock at the door produced Mr Carroll to interrupt their tea with the post. She was pleased, although a little surprised, to receive a letter from her cousin Anne. After placing the letter aside her saucer, Georgiana noted that her brother seemed engrossed by one letter in particular.

With a sigh, Georgiana replaced her cup and took up her own letter. It was not in her nature to question her brother, but for many weeks, she had been struggling under a new reversal of roles whereby she worried for him. Though he had not been himself since returning to Kent, she could see he made a valiant effort each day to appear as if nothing were weighing on him.

It seemed the ghost that dwelled behind his expression every moment had returned even after their jovial recital moments before. While she broke the seal to Anne's letter, Georgiana searched her mind for similar stories that he might find humorous and prompt the return of his easy smile.

Dearest Georgiana,

Allow me to apologize for neglecting my dear cousin so long in not writing you. You are hardly the little girl who used to prance about the gardens below my window, and as outnumbered as our sex is in this family, we must not allow those creatures to gain the advantage of us.

Georgiana giggled, pleased and flattered by her cousin's words, and took up a biscuit to nibble as she read on, unknowingly drawing from her brother the aforementioned desired smile at seeing her pleasure.

Now that you and I have firmed our alliance, we must rely on each other to manage these hapless men and keep them from their own self-destruction. Fear not, dearest Georgiana, for I do not intend to alarm you with my words. You will, I hope, have noticed a certain difference in your brother. I am convinced of this as he has written me but once since leaving Rosings, and I have seen it shadowed in his words even then.

Georgiana gasped quietly, but her brother, by that time engrossed in his own letter, did not notice. How blessedly relieved Georgiana was to know that her observations of him were not a fancy of her own mind.

All I ask of you at this juncture is that you persist in speaking with William. He will naturally wish to keep his counsel, but I firmly believe he will not get the better of what plagues him if he keeps all the burden to himself. Can I ask this of you, sweet Georgiana?

Write me soon, for despite your brother's folly, I should like to know more of the lady you are becoming.

Sincerely,
Anne de B.

Georgiana, after reading and rereading Anne's letter, peeked at her brother. He sat with his own letter spread out before him as he contrived a relaxed pose. The longer she studied him, the more Georgiana realised that his expression was tight, his jaw firm, and the letter—which she could see was short due to the light streaming through the window and then through the thin parchment—was taking her brother an inordinate amount of time to read.

"And who has written you, William?"

Darcy looked up suddenly and blinked. Clearing his throat, he smiled. "It is a letter from Bingley."

"Oh, how strange that he should write you."

"Not very strange, poppet. He left London not long ago for Hertfordshire."

"Oh"—Georgiana giggled—"that makes more sense. I should have thought his writing you in London an odd thing considering he might just as well visit."

Darcy smiled though it did not reach his eyes. When he ventured no more, Georgiana, fortified by Anne's words, pressed forward. "What has Mr Bingley to say? I hope he is enjoying his trip." Grimacing, Georgiana felt her own nervousness was obvious.

Her brother thankfully was oblivious to it and answered gloomily for such an innocuous topic. "He is...I think he is enjoying Hertfordshire quite a lot."

"You ought to visit him as you did last autumn. He stays at his estate there, does he not?" Georgiana said rapidly, not knowing where the thought came from, her discomfort with his tone adding to her own disquiet.

Startling her, Darcy's head snapped up in alarm at her words. Georgiana struggled to know what she might have said to cause such a look, and breaking his gaze, she searched frantically for a safe topic.

Before she could utter a single word, he did so himself, once again looking down at the missive. "I very much doubt she would welcome me."

"Oh, have you quarrelled?" Compassion filled Georgiana. Arguing with his good friend might explain his unhappy mien these past weeks, but... "Did you mean to say 'he,' not 'she'? You speak of Mr Bingley, yes?"

His unfathomable expression caused Georgiana to grow ever more uneasy. *Anne is entirely mistaken; I cannot do this.* Her brother was as much a father to her as he was a brother, and she was not possessed of that strength of character to meddle in his affairs.

Darcy's surprising laugh brought Georgiana out of her thoughts.

"I suppose I ought to prevaricate and tell you I meant to say 'he.' But that would not be the truth. Whether I meant to say 'she,' I did, and the truth is this: there is a *she* in Hertfordshire and *she* would not welcome my visit."

It took every ounce of courage in Georgiana to utter her next words. "Will you tell me about 'she'"—nervously snickering, Georgiana corrected herself—"I mean 'her.' Will you tell me of *her*, Brother?"

Darcy returned her laugh though it was quiet and hollow. But he nodded his head, much to Georgiana's relief, and patted the seat beside him on the sofa. Darcy lifted his arm above her to settle her near his side as he had often done when she was young while he read to her. The gesture nearly brought Georgiana to tears as she snuggled in beside her brother. Unbeknownst to her, Darcy knew that he had offered her that spot for his own comfort and so that he might not have to look into her eyes when he shared his story with her.

Bingley's letter had provoked such powerful feelings that he had felt rather lost. The missive had only stated that his friend had returned to his estate and was greatly relieved at his reception from Miss Bennet. Little could his friend know that his words would draw open in Darcy the deepest of caverns in his chest, reminding him acutely of another Miss Bennet.

Though the letter was short, Darcy could fill in every word it did not possess. He easily conjured up Elizabeth's expression upon seeing her sister reunited with his friend. He could see her pleasure at their renewed friendship. And choking off his ability to speak just then to his sister was how easily, if he indulged himself fully, he could even picture Elizabeth dressed for summer time, her sun-kissed cheeks and strands of hair brightening in its rays.

Georgiana shifted beside him, and he looked down at her own blond locks nestled next to his shoulder. His arm came down around her then, and he cleared his throat in anticipation, thankful for the strength Georgiana gave him. She stilled, silently and patiently waiting for him to begin.

"Shall I tell you a story? Just as I used to?" Darcy's lips pressed into a thin line of suppressed emotion and, not waiting for a response, began. "*She*…is one Miss Elizabeth Bennet. And my story with her begins in Hertfordshire."

"Elizabeth!" Georgiana suddenly shot upright, startling Darcy and piercing him with a pang he knew he would forever feel when her name was spoken aloud. "'Elizabeth' was the name of the lady whom you mentioned on our walk weeks ago, the one who disparaged you—"

"Not 'disparaged,' Georgie, 'corrected,' and aptly so." He could not let Georgiana think poorly of Elizabeth, as fruitless as such a desire might be. When Georgiana settled again next to him, he continued his narrative.

Though her brother's story could not have surprised her more, having never known him to be under the power of any woman before, Georgiana was riveted to the sad tale. At times, she felt elation for Darcy, witnessing in her mind's eye as his words painted an image of the frightening exhilaration brought by the first stirrings of admiration then the altogether consuming fire that steals admiration and replaces it with the hot coals of love. How remarkable Miss Elizabeth must be, for Georgiana imagined only the most alluring of women could provoke such passion in a man. How amazed Georgiana was then to hear her brother speak not only of the lady's beauty, though it was clear he thought her a beautiful creature, but of her character and goodness. His was not a passion born of short duration, but one of steady growth, creeping like a vine around its host until it completely obscured anything else.

She could not bring herself to be angry with her brother for leaving Hertfordshire, for escaping such a passion. Just hearing it through his narrative frightened Georgiana with its strength. She wished he had stayed though—had stayed and wooed Elizabeth—at least for his own happiness if not to prevent whatever inevitable sad precipice she sensed was coming.

Georgiana could not claim to have known or even understood a fragment of what love meant when her brother's story caused her to reflect briefly on her misjudgement of Mr Wickham. And for certain the man did not love her, not like her brother loved Miss Elizabeth. She was convinced of that when she listened, silent and grave, as he confessed his trepidation upon seeing Miss Elizabeth again at Rosings, of their subsequent misaligned courtship—one seen only as such through his eyes—and lastly of his doomed proposal. How she ached for her brother then, for his disappointment and humiliation, and for his enduring loss.

Any subsequent softening of the lady's regard that might have been gleaned from their successive unexpected encounters could only be overshadowed in Georgiana's mind by the profound discomfort her brother must have felt in Miss Elizabeth's company after such a rejection.

"And so you see, my story concludes. Miss Elizabeth resides at her home in Hertfordshire, a mere three miles' walk from Bingley's estate. Furthermore, my friend's express intent is to court Miss Elizabeth's elder sister." When Georgiana still did not say anything after his speech, Darcy looked down at the nestled being beside him. "Ah, I see I have put you to sleep with my dreary tale."

Smiling, Darcy was startled when a chirp of distress was his answer as his sister, instead of speaking, launched herself into arms, her slight limbs wrapping firmly about his neck. The longer she held him tightly, the more his smile slipped from his features as his eyes closed in feeling.

Georgiana mumbled into the collar of his coat.

"What was that?"

Pulling back to look into his eyes, hers wet with tears, Georgiana repeated herself. "I am so very sorry!"

Though her compassion soothed, he did not relish distressing his young sister. He withdrew from her arms, placing her again beside him and handing her his handkerchief. "Now, now, Georgie. You must not distress yourself over much. I am not broken. I am, if not entirely mended, on my way towards it."

Upon uttering the words, Darcy realised they were true. His endeavour to be a better man for Elizabeth had brought its own measure of peace. Though he knew he would never entirely be saved from the pain of her loss, he knew he was on his way towards a feeling of calm he had never hoped to feel.

"Is there not anything I might do to aid you in this, William?"

Smiling, Darcy shook his head. "You are everything I need, darling. Time is what will aid me most. I have endeavoured to be a better man from her instruction. I do not doubt it was an accurate observation on her part, and I did not like that image of myself."

"I have seen your attempts, and I believe Miss Elizabeth would think kindly of your efforts."

At the thought that Elizabeth might think kindly of *anything* regarding him, let alone see and approve of his attempts to be worthy of her, Darcy's heart surged with pleasure.

Georgiana slouched against her brother. Thinking only of the admiration she had for Elizabeth and for the type of lady who could inspire even the best of men to wish to be better still, Georgiana spoke rather without thought for how her words might affect her brother and, with no little regret, said, "I should have liked to meet Miss Elizabeth."

"I often imagined such an introduction," he said a little sadly.

"Oh, Brother!"

He hushed her with a finger to her lips and a shake of his head. "Worry not. But allow me to say that I do believe Miss Elizabeth would have adored you."

Georgiana blushed, amazed that her brother, despite his own personal pain, could detect her own insecurities regarding such an introduction and, with one sentence, fill her with comfort regarding even the unlikeliest of events.

After a time, Darcy stood, leaving Georgiana seated and looking up at him with such awe. He was surprised that, after hearing about all his folly and misjudgments regarding Elizabeth, his sister could still look at him in that manner. He supposed he ought to be glad for such an ally. God knew how essential she was to him then.

"I ought to return to my study and address some matters of business. I did not mean for our tea to become such a concourse on the vagaries of life."

"I am glad that you told me."

"I am too, Georgie. I am too."

He assisted his sister to stand and lifted her hand to his lips. With a sincere smile, he said, "I shall see you at dinner."

Georgiana returned his smile and watched him exit the room. With unladylike grace, she collapsed into the cushions, at once exhausted and exhilarated to have learned so much of her brother's heart. His description of love was both alluring and alarming. For her part, she hoped it was many years before she experienced true love for herself. At the conclusion of that thought, Georgiana wondered whether God's creatures were granted but one such empowering, eclipsing love in their lifetimes. If so, she mourned anew her brother's loss. For his sake, she wished that was not the case, but should it be so, she wished most fervently that there might be some way for him to rewrite his story with a better ending.

~

Writing was exactly what Mr Darcy was doing. Though not rewriting his own story, however much such a notion might be coveted, he was writing a letter. He had vowed not to write her again until he had moulded himself into a better man. *Perhaps now, this might be my last.*

After a moment of reflection, he wrote his parting adieu: *Yours forevermore, Darcy.*

Sighing, Darcy rubbed his face while he waited for the ink to dry. He folded the missive, then addressed and sealed it. It was to her, always her: *Miss Elizabeth Bennet.* Unfortunately, she would never read that letter or any of the many others he had written her. Knowing she would not receive it did not deter him from doing it.

Looking at the letter sitting at his desk, he laughed humourlessly to himself for being so ridiculous. Darcy went to his bookshelf, removed the large volume, and brought it to his desk.

Tenderly, Darcy placed the latest letter atop the others then closed the book and replaced it on the corner of his desk instead of returning it to the shelf. He ought to have returned it to the shelf, but he was not yet ready to put that much distance, even the extra few feet, between him and this last connexion he held with Elizabeth. Drawing a deep breath, Darcy pulled his estate book in front of him to look at the agenda for today. He knew he had a meeting scheduled soon with his solicitor. Glancing down at the date, he stilled. *Has it really been two months since*

Hunsford? Nearly undone, Darcy allowed his head to drop to the desk. He was still tortured by that day, his terrible words, and the fire in her eyes haunting him. Worst was the indelible fact that she was lost to him forevermore.

Despite his recent assurances to Georgiana and his own realisations, the loss was still profound and likely to remain so the rest of his days. Suddenly, the parting appellation in his most recent letter came back to his mind with full poignancy. His heart might forevermore be hers, but she would never be his.

Resting his hand atop the tome, Darcy reflected on the way his tea with Georgiana had left him so jumbled. A knock at his study door was a welcomed distraction as his notes for his solicitor had still failed to draw his attention even after thirty minutes.

"Enter!" Upon seeing Mrs Carroll, Darcy attempted a sincere smile.

"I wonder if I might have a moment of your time, sir."

Darcy gestured for her to have a seat. "Yes, yes of course, Mrs Carroll. What is it you wished to speak to me about?"

After his housekeeper took her seat, Darcy resumed his, attention focused entirely on the long-time retainer.

"Normally, I might make adjustments for such a thing within my own books; however, I cannot see how I might make the necessary changes now that I have already brought up Sally from the kitchens to her new position..."

"Are the household funds insufficient to provide you with the people you need?"

"No, no, I assure you, it is normally quite sufficient only..."

Darcy was already paging through his estate book, having had it before him. He noted the household allotment and determined to raise it before Mrs Carroll had even finished her speech.

"Think no more of it, madam." Writing down the new number, Darcy passed the sheet to Mrs Carroll, whose face was turning quite red at his actions. "Consider this the new household budget. I apologize that I have not increased it since my father's time."

Startled, Darcy had need to sit back as his housekeeper nearly stood out of her chair, reminding him with the affront displayed so clearly on her face that this woman had rebuked him as a child on more than one occasion when he misbehaved.

"Mr Darcy! I had no notion when I came to you today of asking for an increase of funds. I assure you that I run a very tight household, and what funds I have are quite sufficient."

Darcy struggled mightily to keep his twitching lips from turning upwards into a smile, considering how his housekeeper had just taken her master to task over his benevolence. He was no disobedient child anymore.

"Mrs Carroll, I am heartily sorry if I caused offense." She was suddenly contrite, and Darcy quickly went on to reassure her. "You need not fear that your reaction caused any offense on *my* part either. Now, how might I assist you? I promise not to interrupt."

The housekeeper hesitated, obviously stunned by her own fierce reaction to his increased funds as well as his kind and wholly undeserved charity towards her outburst. "It was your request that I inform you of any circumstances among the staff whereby you might be of further assistance."

Darcy nodded but otherwise remained silent, drawing a tenuous smile from his housekeeper.

"There is a maid, and I believe it may be the one you first encountered many weeks ago that was upset: Kenna. Currently, you employ her as a laundry maid, but I have learned recently that her mother is ill. It is uncertain whether the poor lady should ever leave her bed again. Kenna has a young brother, still too young to work, and so for the last few weeks, she has been the sole provider for her family. Her father either died or ran off some years ago."

Mrs Carroll felt confidence anew in her decision to approach her employer after seeing compassion in his mien.

"As I mentioned earlier, we have only recently moved Sally up from the kitchens, so there is no position available whereby we might improve Kenna's situation."

"What is it you propose?"

"I had thought that, although we are fully staffed for upstairs maids, we might promote Kenna to that position anyway. We would only be overstaffed for the summer, for Mary has asked whether she might move to work at Pemberley to be closer to her family, and I have arranged with Mrs Reynolds to receive her starting in August. Even a few months of the advanced pay will be of some help to Kenna's family, but if you think it not a good scheme, I shall wait to bring her up until the end of the summer when Mary leaves."

"You must bring her up now. And despite my earlier assumption and the unintended offense it presented to you, the household budgets do need updating, and that sum you now hold in your hand is to be your new working amount. It will more than cover the duplicate employment among the maids and, furthermore, will allow you more flexibility for such circumstances as these."

Mrs Carroll gave her master an indulgent smile. She was at once reminded of her affection for him and pleased to see the good master and man he had become.

"I thank you, sir. That is very generous and I am sure that Kenna will appreciate the new position. She is a hard worker and might have been promoted earlier had a position been available. You will not regret her service."

"I am sure that I will not. Is there anything else?"

The woman stood, bringing Darcy to his feet out of respect for her. With a curtsey, she said, "No, no, that will be all. Thank you."

When she began walking towards the door, Darcy stopped her with a question. "Does this maid, Kenna…has her mother been seen by a doctor yet?"

Mrs Carroll gave Mr Darcy a sad smile and a nod of her head. "Yes she has, and unfortunately, her mother's illness is no longer in the hands of a physician but more aptly in the hands of God now."

Darcy responded with a solemn nod, and the interview was over. When Mrs Carroll exited his study, Darcy sat once again to address the list of notes for his solicitor. His eyes strayed to his volume of secreted letters and thought how quickly loved ones could be snatched from one's life. If only he might contrive a way to snatch one back, Mr Darcy might truly be a fortunate man.

CHAPTER 15

A MORDANT SMILE BROKE ACROSS DARCY'S LIPS AS HE PLACED THE LAST OF HIS business letters for the day on the silver salver that sat on his desk. Miss Bingley's words from so many months ago echoed in his mind with amusement. *"How many letters you must have occasion to write in the course of the year! Letters of business too! How odious I should think them!"* For once, Darcy may have to agree with Miss Bingley. After receiving a notice from his steward at Pemberley regarding a number of issues at the estate, Darcy did indeed have a great number of letters to write—odious business letters to be sure.

He ought to have left for Pemberley by now. The letters from his steward were indications that the estate had too long been without its master. Still, for some reason, Darcy was loath to leave London. It was not as if *she* was there. He knew for certain from Bingley's letter that she was with her family in Hertfordshire. Still, Pemberley was even farther from Hertfordshire than London. However, he would need to go—and soon. Perhaps later in the summer.

At least London in the summer was rather thin of its principal citizens to be of much bother to Darcy. Most of the *ton* had fled the city for their country estates, fresh air, and sport, thus blissfully saving Darcy from any social obligations.

Before his confession to Bingley, he had plans to go to Pemberley with a small party. As Bingley would remain in Hertfordshire—and there was no way Darcy would be inviting Bingley's sisters to Pemberley without their brother—it would only be Georgiana and

Colonel Fitzwilliam on a short leave from his duties, which suited him perfectly.

The tome sat beside the silver salver of letters. Darcy reached for it, intending to shift through its contents, trying to remember just when each missive had been forged and with what secret emotion. A feeling he had not felt nor expected to be able to feel for some time stole through Darcy's chest—a wistful nostalgia that was not entirely painful. As he allowed his mind to drift from matters of business to matters of pleasure, Darcy savoured the feeling. Despite the tumultuous tide pulling against him and causing him to fall in love with Miss Elizabeth Bennet, he counted it a blessing to love her. The pain from Hunsford was still there, yet Darcy believed he could now say he had been moulded into that which his parents might have wished for him, and all through her influence.

Darcy started to lift the cover of the volume when the clock in the hall struck the hour, reminding him he was due at a meeting with his solicitor. The unexpected business of the morning had stolen much of his time. Sighing, Darcy slid the book back to the corner of his desk where it had sat for the last few days.

When the clock struck again, Darcy pushed back from his desk. He gathered the papers needed for the solicitor's office into a small leather binder, looked around his study to see whether he was missing anything, nodded, and exited the room.

"Ah, Carroll. I am pleased to have caught you before I departed," Darcy said as he allowed a footman to assist in placing his greatcoat about his shoulders.

Dipping his head to take a look out of the window to the street below, Darcy was pleased to see that his efficient staff had his carriage ready but less pleased to see that rain had settled over London. A wet day travelling the streets of the capital city was never pleasant, but at least it would not be unbearably hot.

"How may I be of service, sir?"

As Darcy pulled on a pair of leather gloves, his attention focused on the task, he answered with a smile, "I left letters on the salver in my study ready for the post."

"Of course, sir," Mr Carroll said as he handed Darcy his top hat.

"Also, inform my sister that I shall be out most of the day with my solicitor and shall not be able to take tea with her."

"Very good, sir." The butler stepped aside grandly and held the door for his master.

Darcy looked at the steady rain falling then, much more than the misting of a few minutes before.

"Shall you like your umbrella, sir?"

Giving it but a moment of thought, Darcy smiled at the butler and shook his head. "I have braved worse storms then this, and in any case, it is not far to the carriage. So I thank you, no."

"No doubt, you will brave many more, sir. Have a good day."

With a nod, Darcy pulled up the collar of his coat and ducked into the steady rainfall, dashing quickly to the open carriage door and within. His butler closed the door only after assuring the carriage was away. Turning to look about the entryway after Mr Darcy left, Mr Carroll tugged at his vest and went about his business for the morning.

～

Kenna was nervous—terrified really. She had been promoted from a laundry maid to an upstairs maid, and it was her first day. The relief she felt when Mrs Carroll first told her of her move upwards in fortune was something she would remember for the rest of her days. She was certain the housekeeper did not know of her circumstances at home. She had told no one but another of the maids a few weeks prior when the worry for her mother had been too much and she unguardedly poured forth her troubles. She had been interrupted by the master that day as he rounded the corner, and the startled feeling she had, worrying that he might think she was not performing her duties, forced her to close her lips quite tightly during her working hours. She could not risk her employment, less now than ever.

She loved working for the Darcys in their London home. They were good employers, and the promotion, with its higher remuneration, was sorely necessary as she supported her sick mother and young brother.

She closed her eyes against the ever-present fear when she thought of her mother at home, too ill to get out of bed while the landlord ever hounded for the week's rent. She was fortunate in the Darcy's servants' quarters, for she did not like staying in the dark, damp flat that her mother and brother boarded. If only she could have secreted them away into her own comfortable quarters at Darcy House. Pushing away the picture of her five-year-old brother tending to her mother alone during the day, Kenna squared her shoulders, and once again, her lips formed a tight line.

Anxiously tugging at her new pinafore and smoothing her new grey dress, she assured herself she was ready for the day. Taking a deep breath, she knocked on the housekeeper's door to receive her assignments for the day.

Mrs Carroll was a fair woman. She had always treated the staff with respect, but she only tolerated a job well done. Hands shaking slightly but hidden behind her, Kenna tried to place a pleasant smile on her face as she entered the housekeeper's office when she heard her summons.

"Ah, Kenna. I see that your new uniform fits you well."

"Yes, ma'am," replied she with only a small tremor to her voice.

"Well, I am glad to hear it. I can see you are ready for your first day. Mind that you do a good job. I will not accept poor work."

"Yes, ma'am."

"I have put you in charge of polishing any of the wood in the main rooms of the first floor. There is a lot to do. Do you think you can handle that?"

"Yes, ma'am."

"This includes any furniture, mantels, and mouldings. I would normally have one of the other experienced maids accompany you on the task, but I have assigned them elsewhere. I trust that you do not mind a little hard work, for you will have much."

Mrs Carroll smiled inwardly. She could tell the young girl was nervous, for that time she gave only the merest nod. It had been her experience, though, that nervousness translated into a wish to prove one's self.

"Very good, then. Get started. The master is out much of the day, which will allow you access to the principal rooms uninterrupted. I should like to see you finished before he returns."

Kenna nodded, curtseyed, and exited the room as quickly as she could, breathing a sigh of relief to be finished with the interview. Moving quickly to the supply closet beneath the grand staircase, she gathered the rags and oils needed and began in the parlour.

As the hours went by, she was careful not to miss a spot. Though her arms ached from movements different than she was accustomed to in the laundry, she pressed on. Every time the hall clock chimed, the new hour increased her urgency. Without knowing when the master would return, she could do nothing but think each chime stole from her time to do her work. And as Mrs Carroll said, there was much of it.

Tenderly she took everything off the shelves and tables so she could wax the wood surfaces beneath them. When she had finished, she would replace everything exactly as she had found them, pausing only momentarily to inspect her work. She understood the Darcys were not the sort of gentry to inflict punishment if a vase or trinket was not returned to its exact location; however, Kenna could do nothing but an exacting job.

The last room was the master's study. With a sigh of relief and pleased that, despite the long hours, she had accomplished so much, Kenna gathered up her supplies in the basket and made to exit the room she just finished. She paused at the threshold to glance about the room, inspecting every detail and assuring herself she had not forgotten anything. Then as had been long trained in her, she opened the door just a crack to ascertain there were none of the family or guests about before carrying her basket to the master's study.

Unbeknownst to Kenna, only the housekeeper was allowed to clean Mr Darcy's study. She entered the study cautiously, determined to do an especially thorough job. That was the room she assumed would garner the most scrutiny, and a sloppy job would most assuredly be noted by the master. As she quietly worked her way around the room, she came to the desk last. She carefully removed the few books then a large tome. She was surprised by how easily she lifted it, clearly pleased by this evidence of the strength her arms had already gained after the long morning. Last, she lifted the letter tray and the inkstand to join the other items on the floor beside the desk so she could polish the surface.

After finishing the surface, she allowed the oils to permeate the wood as she moved around the desk, paying attention to the intricately carved embellishments that decorated the sides and the massive legs. Each drawer face was carefully polished, any residue expertly removed from its golden-hued handles and locks. When she had deemed the sides perfectly gleaming, she wiped at the desktop again to ensure the polish could not damage any of Mr Darcy's belongings.

As with all the other rooms, when she completed polishing the piece of furniture, she was careful to place each item exactly as she remembered it. Nearly everything was returned, and placing her hands on her hips, she felt a moment of supreme satisfaction that Mr Darcy would not be disappointed in her work. She bent to retrieve the last item, the large tome, and was just about to place it where she had found it next to the letter tray, when Mr Carroll entered the room, startling her.

Seconds seemed like a lifetime as Kenna watched in horror as the tome slipped from her hands, falling down to the perfect surface of the desk and catching the silver salver of letters, causing both to tumble to the floor with a great and ominous clatter of metal, leather, and parchment. She stood frozen, staring down at the mess about her feet for what seemed too long, her heart still unable to gain a steady tempo and her future hopes shattered amongst the chaos. Disbelief tinted her recall of all that had just happened.

At once, time sped back up, and the poor maid was struck with what she had done. Immediately, Kenna fell to her knees. Clumsily, she began to gather up the many letters, her numb fingers fumbling to hold them all through their shaking. She squeaked a succession of apologies as she worked.

"What are you doing in here?" Mr Carroll asked angrily, his voice in her ears causing her to wince.

"I am sorry, sir. I was polishing the wood, but I am done now." Her fingers ineptly bent around the many letters all around her, and spying the silver salver, she quickly retrieved it and placed all that she had gathered on the tray. Furiously, she reached for more letters scattered at her feet. So many letters, and as her eyes began to swim with tears, they sought any she might have missed.

Mr Carroll walked over to her side, the thump of his shoes adding weight to the already unbearable worry on her shoulders. Kenna expected that she would be dismissed at any moment and feared for that instant he would say the words, but until he did, she continued her rapid work to tidy the mess she had made. Mr Carroll bent to pick up the large tome that had fallen. Kenna's eyes squeezed shut, imagining what damage the fall could have accomplished for such an old book and mentally calculating how she would ever pay such a sum to replace it. *The master will most certainly not be pleased with my work here today.*

With her head bent, she did not see that the butler *was* inspecting the book, though not in the way she imagined. Mr Carroll recognised it as the one with the secret compartment, and thankfully, the master never used it as far as he knew, for it would not be good for anyone to know about it. He had been around when the previous Mr Darcy, the current's father, commissioned the book. During *his* stead as master, the book saw much use. Mr Carroll shifted the book in his hands to lift up the front flap to peek inside, grateful to see it was empty. When the maid stood with the letter tray, he placed the book on the desk and took the tray from her.

"Mrs Carroll is the only one allowed to attend the master's study, girl," he said sternly. Surmising the crash was caused by his unexpected entrance, Mr Carroll still was suspicious as to what the girl was doing in the study at all.

Kenna lowered her head, the tears that had started to form in her eyes nearly falling over each other as they spilled down her cheeks. Fear gripped her heart at the thought of losing her position. Looking up at the butler, she could see no other alternative but to beg. "Please, sir! I did not know. Honest, I did not. It is my first day. Please, please do not sack me. I swear it will never happen again!"

Mr Carroll stood for a minute examining the girl. He knew her situation at home as he deemed it the butler's job to know everything. He considered her words, knowing full well that she most likely spoke the truth, but wanting to ensure the mistake did not happen again, he allowed a troubling moment to pass before he spoke. Finally, he replied, "All right then, you are lucky I do not send you straight to Mrs Carroll's office for your last pay. Be off with you now, and make sure you do not make the same mistake."

Relief washed through Kenna, nearly causing her to fall to her knees again. The oppressive weight on her chest lifted, and she bobbed a grateful curtsey. "Oh, thank you! I promise never to come in this room again!"

Nodding, he watched the girl gather her cleaning items, placing them quickly in her basket, and leave the room as swiftly as her small legs could take her. After a moment, Mr Carroll gathered the letters from the tray and placed the empty tray on the desk. He had only come in to fetch the letters Mr Darcy had specified.

Looking down at the bulk in his hands, he thought briefly on how many more there were than usual. That observation made him frown. Ever since his master returned from his annual trip to Rosings, he had kept himself excessively busy with estate business that he usually left to his solicitor or steward. For a man who knew everything, Mr Carroll disliked not knowing what was troubling Mr Darcy.

Shrugging, he walked out of the room and gave the letters to the awaiting footman to post.

***

Elizabeth breathed in the cool morning air as she rounded the bend in the drive that led to her home. Having been out walking most of the morning, she felt refreshed and awakened, ready to break her fast with the family. Never a late riser, Elizabeth took her walks early in the morning, often absent for many hours before returning late morning when the rest of her family was just waking and preparing to breakfast together.

It had been a beautiful summer, flowers in all colours blooming in rapid succession. They had not had much rain, though it was not uncommon for their part of the kingdom and for that time of the year. Elizabeth tipped her head to look up at the sky, eying greying clouds to the south and seemingly moving their way. She smiled, thinking perhaps, if it were to rain that day, it was fortunate she took her walk as usual that morning.

As she neared the front step of her family's home, she saw the post rider slip down from his horse and begin to unload the bags at the mare's sides. As that was no significant spectacle, Elizabeth planned to walk on as she usually did just as Mrs Hill stepped across the threshold to address the rider. Elizabeth glanced absently at the rider as she passed. She noted he removed several small boxes and began to hand them to the housekeeper. Mrs Hill struggled with the many packages, juggling them to find an easy way to carry the burden, when the man extended his hands to add a handful of letters as well.

"Goodness me, you will have earned your pay today, Sam."

With a chuckle, the rider nodded his head and patiently waited for Mrs Hill to adjust the packages to free a hand for the letters. Elizabeth smiled and walked up to Mrs Hill.

"Allow me to help you with those, Hill. Shall I take the packages?"

Thankful for the help, though mindful of the dust of the road clinging to the small boxes, she said, "If you will take the letters, Miss Lizzy, I know these packages are for Cook. She ordered some spices from London to replenish her stock. With Mr Bingley's frequent visits these past weeks and all the fancy cooking your mama has requested, the kitchens began to be a mite low on some items."

Elizabeth chuckled at the image of her mother and what Cook must think to have her usual fare replaced with such intricate entrées nearly every night. "Are you sure? I can manage the packages for you. They do seem quite cumbersome."

Mrs Hill smiled indulgently. "Thank you, Miss Lizzy, but I cannot think of you getting road dust from these packages on your lovely dress. Take the letters, if you please."

Knowing she had more road dust on the hem of her dress than the boxes did on the whole, she, too, smiled but did as Mrs Hill said and accepted the stack of letters from the postman. Seeing the housekeeper shift the packages ominously to one side so she could reach into her apron pocket, Elizabeth lent her other hand to balance the stack of parcels in Mrs Hill's arm. When Hill placed a stack of coins in the man's hand, he tugged at his forelock and swiftly gained his mount again, already turning to continue on his way.

"Very well, then. Allow me to get the door at least," Elizabeth said as they reached the front door.

Chuckling, the two entered the house, Mrs Hill walking directly towards the kitchen. Elizabeth went to the side table, removed her gloves, bonnet, and pelisse, and then picked up the letters again. She began sorting for her family when her eyes caught her own name on one. Her fingers stilled, looking at the letter. Her heart now beating wildly, she stared at the letter before her. She knew that handwriting like it was her own. She had read his letter so many times that she had its contents memorized. *Why is Mr Darcy writing to me? What could he mean by this?* Seemingly, as if coming out of a dream, Elizabeth was at once awakened to the scandal such a letter delivered to her home might cause, and that realisation was sufficient to thaw her fingers and prompt her into action.

Quickly Elizabeth looked around; upon seeing nobody, she slipped the letter into her pocket. It would not do to have anyone know Mr Darcy had written her a letter. The writer had a very masculine hand, and it would be obvious even to Mrs Hill that such an impropriety should not be allowed.

Curiosity had driven Elizabeth to hide the letter. For she ought to have immediately taken it, unopened, to her father. That was the proper thing to do. But curiosity was a dangerous thing, and not knowing or understanding why Mr Darcy would take such a treacherous and bold step, she instead chose to secret it away. The very thought, the knowledge of the parchment even now seemingly weighing down the pocket of her dress caused a terrified thrill to steal through her.

After insuring the letter was safely tucked inside the pocket, Elizabeth looked down to resume her sorting—her mind barely able to focus on her task—only to find another letter addressed to her from Mr Darcy! Eyes widening, she quickly secreted that one away too. Shock and disbelief filled her mind as the next in the stack revealed yet *another* letter also addressed to her from him. Her fingers began to shift through the letters at a faster speed, flipping each new one only to find another! There were at least a dozen, though she could hardly have had the presence of mind to actually count them at the moment. Swiftly gathering up the pile of letters, she concealed each into her pockets before she at last came to the end of the pile. She was trembling, confused, and her pockets were bulging.

A noise at the stairs drew Elizabeth out of her shocked state, her heart suddenly in her throat at being discovered, and she looked to see Kitty descending. Elizabeth's face must have been expressing some degree of her turmoil for Kitty huffed at her and scowled back, believing Elizabeth was frowning at her.

Kitty entered one of the rooms, and Elizabeth was alone again. Her family! Even at that moment, they all would be coming to break their fast, and Elizabeth was in no state to encounter them, not with the knowledge of her contraband choking her thoughts. She was suddenly aware that, if Jane or her father had encountered her, she would not have been dismissed as easily as Kitty had. *Good gracious—Papa!* If he were to find her, she would have to tell him about the letters, for he would see right through her charade, and he would demand them right away. Although Elizabeth knew that Mr Darcy should not have written her even one letter, let alone a dozen, she was loath for her father to have them just yet. She had to read them and know what they contained.

Quickly, she forced her mind to gain control of her limbs, and she began walking towards the stairs, intending to gain her room as soon as possible. She had just passed the cracked door of her father's book room when he called her name. Boots scuffing to a stop, along with her heart, Elizabeth took a few long breaths in an attempt to slow her breathing before she coolly stepped backwards to peer around the door of the book room. She knew not whether her voice would betray her should he ask anything of her and hoped that he wished only to say good morning.

"Did you enjoy your walk, Lizzy?" Mr Bennet said as he stood, pulling on his waistcoat, no doubt also preparing to join the others in the breakfast room.

Elizabeth swallowed and, with great effort, attempted to smile at him. Knowing she could not at that moment utter a single word, she was grateful an eager nod would be sufficient for his inquiry.

"I thought it looked as if it were likely to rain," Mr Bennet said as he walked along the outside of his desk to peek quickly out the window before his steps brought him nearer to her at the door.

Elizabeth shrugged and attempted another smile.

Her father reached her side then, and unable to hide behind the side of the door anymore, Elizabeth stepped to the left to allow her father to cross into the hall. Her ruse was up, for he looked at her oddly. Every letter in her dress felt a thousand stones and, she was certain, caused an uncomely swell on the side of her hips.

"Are you quite all right, Lizzy? You look a little pale."

Elizabeth knew then that she must speak, for she could not simply nod and smile anymore.

"I am well, Papa, though I ought to go quickly and change my shoes. Mama would not like me wearing my walking boots at the breakfast table." Elizabeth sighed, amazed at the steadiness in her voice.

Mr Bennet smiled and nodded, dismissing her. Elizabeth could not have been more relieved as she made her way towards the stairs, careful not to appear in any rush.

She had just gained the first step when her father's voice once again called her name, this time with a little something different in his tone that immediately intensified her heart rate once again.

Turning slowly to look over her shoulder, Elizabeth waited for him to speak.

"I think you may have walked a bit far today, Lizzy. Truly you look rather odd."

Elizabeth managed a squeaky laugh then, hoping to end her father's inspection as soon as possible. "Thank you, Papa. That is just the thing every lady wishes most to hear."

Chuckling, Mr Bennet shook his head at his daughter and waved her off as he continued to walk towards the breakfast room. "Oh, be off with you!"

Hastily, now that freedom was before her, Elizabeth rushed up the stairs to her room, thankful not to encounter anyone else along the way. Securing the lock on her door for good measure, Elizabeth stepped to the foot of her bed. Fumbling with the latch to the travelling trunk that sat at the end of her bed, she opened it and slid her hand down into the fabric pocket on the back panel of the trunk. Her fingers located what she was searching for and pulled it out.

It was her letter from Mr Darcy from the day after his calamitous proposal at Hunsford. The edges were worn from the many times she had opened, read, and closed the letter since then. Elizabeth pulled the letters from her pocket and compared the handwriting just in case by some miracle she was mistaken in the sender's identity. She was not, for they matched. That thought shot a thrill through her even as a bundle of other untold emotions surged forward, all volleying for prominence. Hearing a noise in the hallway outside her room, Elizabeth quickly tucked her new letters with the old one in the depths of the pocket. She closed the trunk, sitting atop it as if to prevent their escape. After only a second, the footsteps outside her door continued on towards the stairs, and Elizabeth again breathed.

A small chuckle began, rumbling up slowly from the depths of her middle and gaining strength. Nothing was funny about the situation in which she found herself. Everything was terrifying and wonderful, yet she could not control the laughter that doubled her in half. Her hands went to her temples, fingers lacing into the curls on the side of her head. The whole of the last ten minutes was entirely unbelievable and surreal. Her thoughts quickly sped to the providence that allowed her to be the one to come upon Mrs Hill with the letters. Imagining even the circumstances that would have resulted had Elizabeth taken the packages instead of the letters caused the unexplainable laughter wracking her sides to double her over again. It was the inexplicable laughter of those who faced death and came out alive on the other side—she was sure of it.

Elizabeth stood to approach her dressing table and looked at herself in the mirror. Her cheeks were rosy and her eyes wild with energy. No wonder her father had questioned her. She looked down at her morning dress to where her pockets now hung empty. Reaching in, she felt their burden removed and could see in the mirror that her hands, bulkier than even the letters could have been, hardly displaced the folds of her dress. The laughter, having died away, came back again as she realised it was the pounding of her heart that made her pockets feel cumbersome.

She could not read them immediately, she concluded with a few fingers through the locks of her hair. She was even at that moment expected to join her family at the breakfast table. Hearing hoof beats, Elizabeth glanced outside the window and saw that Mr Bingley was again arriving before breakfast, likely to stay past supper. His request that Jane squire him around lasted only a se'nnight before he began to vigorously court her and so spent little time away from Longbourn in the course of the day. Her oft-required role as chaperone would keep her in company for the duration.

Elizabeth knew the soonest she might read the letters would be when she retired that evening. She nearly shook with a mixture of frustration, eagerness, and fear at the thought of waiting—frustration for having to wait, eagerness to see what he might write and why, and mostly fear because, in her heart, she felt that he might hate her after her terrible accusations. *Perhaps he wants to make certain I know that his regard for me has gone.* That thought made her shudder and, not wishing to add pain to the expression in her eyes, quickly distracted herself with the tasks required to ready herself for the day.

Hardly ten minutes saw her shoes changed, her hair rearranged, and her breathing slowed to a more moderate pace. Gracefully, Elizabeth descended the stairs and joined her family in the breakfast room. If her appetite was not as robust as it usually was, she thought it unlikely anyone noticed. The clock in the hall struck the hour, and so began the interminable number of such chimes until Elizabeth could retire that evening.

CHAPTER 16

Occupied as her mind was, Elizabeth proved to be a very poor chaperone for her sister and Mr Bingley. Her attention to her surroundings, be it indoors or out, was pitiable at best and wholly absent the rest of the time. While her temporal state sat fixedly among company, her mind was constantly wandering up the stairs to her room, into the trunk, and beneath a dozen stamped crests.

As a result of her inattentiveness, to which neither benefited party took considerable objection, the courting couple could be observed in closer conference than propriety perhaps might allow. In fact, while walking amongst the hedges near Longbourn, the individuals in question were entirely out of sight for many minutes before Elizabeth was of a mind to notice.

What she was of a mind to concentrate on was the most singular and unfathomable happenstance that might cause so private a man as Mr Darcy to risk writing her. And why write so many letters? Since coming back from Kent, Elizabeth had come to feel quite differently about the writer. Although she did not think she loved him, she had come to admire and esteem him greatly. Certainly, she began to think more kindly on him than she was wont to do before. His actions to separate her sister and Bingley and his judgments of her family still smarted, but after returning to the bosom of her family, she was forced to see them in a new light and acknowledge their many improprieties. She was also forced to admit that Charlotte was correct: Jane's serene but reserved manner had perhaps aided in making it possible for Bingley to doubt her affections. With his return, she had admonished Jane to be more open with her heart if it pleased her to do so. Still, acknowledging the accuracy of Mr Darcy's original observations was a bitter pill for Elizabeth to swallow.

Of course, it took much less time for Elizabeth to accept the details he provided regarding his past with Wickham. She could not but believe him from the start with what he related about his sister and that blackguard. Her heart went out to the girl, and her conscience grated on her for the horrible accusations she had flung at Mr Darcy. She knew how much they must have hurt him, and her sorrow was heavy because of it.

How differently did she now see those few encounters after his proposal! At the time, she thought mostly, if not entirely, of her own discomfort at the trick of fate that threw them together. Having many months contemplation to soften her regard and increase her compassion, Elizabeth now was awash with abject grief at what Mr Darcy may have felt after encountering *her*! If he did indeed love her still, then his desolation and disappointment would have been great indeed. If not for his words at the Bromley coaching inn, indicating she ought to forget their ill-advised interview in the parlour of his aunt's clergyman, Elizabeth might worry for any pains he still suffered. No, from that day forward she was assured that he had somehow begun the process of forgetting her.

Why might he have posted them? And what could be the purpose of throwing two people into the greatest turmoil by ensuring their delivery, especially at such great risk? Again, Elizabeth found herself conflicted and, striking upon the idea that she might discover Mr Darcy's present location, called out to her sister's suitor.

"Mr Bingley!" Coming around the hedge in the walking path, she saw the couple engaged in earnest conversation. Had Elizabeth been less preoccupied with her own thoughts, the faces of both as they hastily turned around and away from each other, would have told it all.

"I apologize, Miss Eliz—"

Having little patience for whatever Mr Bingley had to say, Elizabeth waved him silent. "Mr Bingley, might you know whether your friend Mr Darcy currently resides at his country estate?"

Confused, still Mr Bingley answered promptly, sending a questioning glance at his beloved. "Mr Darcy usually spends most of the summer at Pemberley."

Elizabeth frowned, her brows pulling together as she contemplated that piece of the puzzle. *But the letters were sent from London!*

Not understanding from whence the question came, and stemming from his own embarrassment at nearly being caught bestowing a kiss on Miss Bennet, Mr Bingley eagerly furthered Miss Elizabeth's conversation.

"Although, I am certain he has not left London as of yet."

Elizabeth's head snapped up. "Pardon?"

When Mr Bingley repeated himself, again sending a confused look to Jane, Elizabeth returned his answer with only a contemplative look of her own. Confused, he and Jane watched as she turned herself about and, mumbling incoherently, walked again around the corner of the hedge, leaving them alone.

"Whatever could be the matter with your sister?"

Jane stepped towards him then, perplexed yet unworried. Confident that Elizabeth was entirely aware of her actions, Jane concluded their chaperone was only reminding them they were not totally left alone.

"Perhaps 'twas only a warning," Jane said, a blush coming to her cheeks.

Mr Bingley smiled down at her and took up her hand, bestowing a kiss. "Jane…" The smile deepened as he saw her blush darken at hearing him say her name. "When may I speak to your father?"

Miss Bennet raised her eyes to his and, with a smile, reminded him of their agreement. "Charles, you know by now how my mother is. Once it is known that we have come to an understanding, all of our time will be spent speaking of lace and trousseaus."

"I know, my dear. You are, of course, most correct. I only…" Mr Bingley placed another kiss on the hand still held in his.

"Shh, I think Elizabeth is coming around again," Jane whispered, a little panicked as the two once again stepped apart to a respectable distance.

At the break in the hedge leading around the curve of the walking path, Elizabeth could be seen though she did not turn in their direction but rather walked on by, soon hidden by another hedge.

When they were once again safe, Bingley turned to his unofficial betrothed. "Did you perhaps tell your sister of our understanding? Is this the reason for her generous nature today?"

Jane shook her head, a little puzzled then, realising that Lizzy had been particularly distracted that day. "No, I did not."

"You would not offend me if you wished to, my dear. I know how special she is to you."

Again shaking her head, Jane said, "I do not think under the circumstances that Lizzy would begrudge me this secret. Besides, I begin to think she possesses a few of her own."

∼

Later that evening, Elizabeth entered her bedchamber with a sigh of relief and closed the door. She stood there with her back against the door, looking at the chest at the end of her bed. Several deep breaths later, she walked slowly to its side and sank to her knees. She retrieved all of the letters and sat on her bed. Her fingers ran lightly across her name written by his hand. How stirring such a sight was—her name written in his script —intimate in a way she could not describe.

Now that the moment had arrived, Elizabeth was hesitant to open the letters. The day had been so long already, her head ached from anxiety, her mind was tired, and her heart was weak with speculation. Despite her claim that her courage always rose in the face of intimidation, these letters more than intimidated her, and her courage was deficient. As long as they remained closed, her heart could remain protected from whatever charges he might lay at her feet.

Her fingers sifted through the pile over and over again, and with a heaviness in her heart, she set the letters on her night stand.

As she readied for bed, she reasoned that even Mr Darcy would not need ten letters—no, there were indeed a dozen, now that she could count them—to write any disapprobation he might have for her. Therefore, there must be something more contained within. Elizabeth chuckled to herself. *Who writes a person twelve letters?* The gaping neck of her nightgown slipped off one shoulder as she sunk on the edge of her bed. Her plait of dark, chestnut hair fell around the side of her shoulder to rest as she reached for the letters. While she knew the day had been no figment of her imagination, her heart took flight as soon as her fingers curled around the missives.

Climbing under the counterpane again, she rested the pile upon her bent knees. After examining the letters, she saw that they were all posted on the same day, and therefore, she could not tell which one ought to be read first. Holding her breath, she broke the seal on the top one. Before she could unfold it, her attention was once again caught by a knock at her door. Quickly, she deposited the letters beneath her leg under the blankets.

Jane entered with a cup of tea. "Elizabeth. I thought you might like a cup of Hill's sleeping tea. You have seemed out of sorts all day." Elizabeth acquiesced, revealing to Jane that she suffered a slight headache, which was true. She did not need to explain a desire for quiet solitude.

"Promise me you will rest, Lizzy. Though you say your headache is minor, without proper rest, you know these trifles often lead to a full megrim."

"I promise, thank you, Jane," Elizabeth said kindly.

She could not hasten her sister's departure without drawing questions Elizabeth would rather not answer, yet she was mad for privacy! She had been tormented the entire day by the stack of parchment concealed under her leg, and while her sister's solicitude was appreciated, Elizabeth could only wish her far away at the moment. Luckily for her own composure, Jane soon departed.

Once again, Elizabeth unfolded the letter of which she had only broken the seal moments before. The date at the top of the page shouted out to her: *January 6, 1811.* Elizabeth's brow furrowed. *January? But that was before Rosings.* Confusion led her to open the next letter. It was dated September of the year before. *But that was when he only just arrived in the neighbourhood.* She made quick work of the rest of the letters, each dating from various times throughout her acquaintance with him. At least three were written after his proposal, and Elizabeth was thankful to put them at the bottom of the pile—afraid of what they might say.

Elizabeth sat back and gazed at the open letters, now arranged by date on the bed before her. She rubbed her face and looked away, only to have her eyes return to the stack. *Why has he written me all of these letters?* She could not understand. But whatever the reason, the question that was foremost on her mind was: *Why in all that is holy did he decide to post them to me now?* Bingley confirmed that Mr Darcy was in London, which meant only one thing: he must have a reason!

Hesitantly, Elizabeth took up the first letter, dated September 15. Her mind went back to that time and tried to think of anything she could remember about the date. Finally, she was struck with the answer. It was the day after the assembly. She had only met him the day before. Again, her mind was shouting: *Why? Why? Why?*

Miss Bennet,

As you know, we were introduced last evening at the assembly held in Meryton.

Elizabeth had to laugh. His formal beginning only added to the absurdity of the letter's existence.

I take the liberty of writing to you to apologize for my discourtesy last evening. I have come to worry over the last few hours that you may have heard my ill-chosen words to my friend Mr Bingley. He wished for me to dance, and I was not in the mood to do so. You see, I had only arrived in town earlier that day, and I had encountered carriage troubles along the way, leaving my patience low and my head aching. I felt as if my head might explode if I danced much, surrounded even more acutely with all the din and scents of the dance floor. As it was, I could not dishonour my host's sisters by not asking them to stand up with me, but that is all I was apt to handle.

Since the time during which those words spilled from my mouth, I have been most ashamed of them. For I abhor deceit, and to call you merely tolerable, but not handsome enough to tempt me, was a falsehood of the worst kind. It did not take me long to see what uncommonly attractive eyes you have, among other light and pleasing features. I feel some great relief saying these things. Now that I have written them, they cannot haunt me.

Regards,
Fitzwilliam Darcy

Elizabeth was astonished at the contents of the letter. It occurred to her that possibly Mr Darcy could never have intended to send it to her! Her lips curled into a smile as she read the letter again. No gentleman would have talked about being unwell in a letter to a lady. Surely, that proved he did not mean to send it to her. *But why send them at all?* His words about her eyes caused a flutter in her breast that she tried to ignore as she took up the next letter. It was dated some three weeks later. She concluded it must have been near the time she came to Netherfield when Jane was sick. His handwriting differed slightly, and Elizabeth thought it looked as if it might have been written in some agitation.

Miss Bennet,

That is enough, madam!

Elizabeth frowned but, sitting back, read on.

Is it not enough that you haunt my dreams? Must you now stay under the same roof? I have just received news from Bingley that you are to stay to nurse your sister. Please be assured that I hope for her full recovery despite my ill temper. When you arrived this morning, your eyes bright and your face flushed from the exercise, I was nearly undone! It would not do to take you into my arms at that moment and kiss that rosy cheek.

Elizabeth blushed to read such words, heart pounding at the thought. How differently she viewed that moment so many months ago. Never would she have guessed the stern expression Mr Darcy had bestowed upon her was anything other than disapproval. But she saw that she was wrong—entirely wrong—for it was passion.

I do not know what spell you have cast over me, Miss Elizabeth, but I beg you to release me. When you are not near me, I think of you. When you are near me, I cannot think at all. Never have I struggled thus with any other woman. I wish I could condemn you for coming to your sister and pretend that you came only to secure me, but I know it not to be so. You came because your compassionate, sweet nature called you to your sister. You came because your heart was engaged in her comfort. This knowledge is like sweet torture to me. For you are one of the loveliest beings I have ever met. How can you be so, yet I cannot have you? There—I have said it. Perhaps now I can manage to forget it.

Sincerely,
Fitzwilliam Darcy

Elizabeth's astonishment was beyond expression. She was positively reeling after the letter. Here was the beginning of his falling in love with her! She marvelled and laughed at how he blamed her for such a thing when she was yet unaware and certainly not asking for such regard. His letter began with fevered energy and ended with such sweet tenderness. *It had obviously been written to gain some relief,* she thought. This further proof that Mr Darcy had not wished to send these letters to her made her question whether she ought to read any more. There must have been some mistake that sent them to her at all!

Curiosity drove her on though and so she numbly took up the next, dated only a day later. She noticed that not only were his musings becoming more personal but also his addresses and closings. The thought sent a chill up her spine.

Dearest Miss Bennet,

I realise you are here to care for your sister, but I find that am so ungenerous as to wish you by my side instead. This afternoon I walked the house hoping to encounter you. I have a weakness for you that I cannot explain. I crave seeing that arch smile you give me when you tease me—that lovely eyebrow of yours raised in challenge. Oh! What have you done to me? It is wholly unfair, Elizabeth.

Blinking, Elizabeth tried to calm her racing heart. He referred to her by her Christian name. Of course, it was in a private letter she was never intended to read, yet it affected her quite as forcefully as if it had been spoken aloud in his baritone voice.

Your wit astounds me, your grace beguiles me, and heaven help me, I am undone by your beauty. This evening, while you read your book in the parlour, I watched you worry a curl by your ear. I assure you the distraction caused me to lose the game of cards. All I could think was that I wished I could worry them all! You see what power you have over me! Part of me wishes I could command you, "Be gone!" but then I am left with the misery of waiting until I can see you again. How am I to survive the next few days whilst you are here? I have never prayed for anyone's recovery as fervently as I have prayed for your sister's, of that, I can assure you.

Most kindly,
Fitzwilliam Darcy

Elizabeth reached up to touch the curl at her ear, the one she knew she always played with. Her fingers felt her face and realised her cheeks were wet with tears. She had to admit what she did not wish to confess—that she was in love with Mr Darcy! Until she began reading the letters, she did not want to acknowledge the truth, for it only caused her heart to ache at the loss of him. Now, in the face of such feeling as expressed in his letters, she could not help but accept the state of her heart. But why had he sent them to her? *Was it some kind of cruel joke? A wish to purge himself of any reminder of me? An attempt to pain me with the proof of what I had lost?* No, she could not believe that. She knew he would not have wished to pain her no matter how little he regarded her now—which left her again wondering how or why the letters came to be posted in the first place.

Though her head had begun to pound fiercely, Elizabeth did not want to stop reading the letters. The next one was dated November 27, the day after the Netherfield ball. Elizabeth remembered their dance and their heated exchange. Shame washed through her at how vehemently she had countered him regarding Wickham. She wished again that she had not been so quick to believe one man against the other. But wishing did not change things, and with a sigh, Elizabeth began reading.

Miss Elizabeth,

It is with the heaviest of hearts that I write this letter to you. For if I can help it, I shall not see you again. To dance with you last evening was bliss beyond my dreams, yet I cannot have you. Not even your reference to Wickham could have ruined that short half hour with you. The exquisite look of you, the warmth of your hand, and the fire in your eyes will forever haunt me. Why do they haunt me, you might ask? It is because I must accept the truth of our situations. I have a young sister to think of. She is all that I have left in this world. I am expected to marry both fortune and connexions. Doing so would ensure her place in society. It pains me to say so, but you, darling Elizabeth, have neither.

Your sisters and mother behaved so improperly last evening. I cannot think of the joy I felt in dancing with you without also remembering the mortification I felt when witnessing their behaviour. I know it is callous of me to write such words to you, but I do so now that they might aid me in accepting the truth. I hope by writing these words that I will become capable of teaching my heart to move on. I must forget you, Elizabeth.

Today, we will leave and follow Bingley to town. I have to get away, but also I must see what I can do for Bingley. I observed that your sister does not care for him the way he does for her. She is polite and receptive to his attention, but nothing in her manner suggests that she returns his affections. I cannot have him marry where there is unequal regard. If I thought that your sister might be injured by my interference, I would not do so. But I am convinced that her heart is untouched. I shall forget you, Elizabeth. I shall.

Still, I wish you the very best,
Fitzwilliam Darcy

Elizabeth fell back against her pillows and wept. His vow to forget her stung the most, for she was certain that, after her refusal at Hunsford, he had done just that. After several minutes, she sat up. Knowing only pain could result from continuing but like a moth to the fire, she reached for the next letter. Perhaps she deserved it after what she had done.

She continued through the next several letters. He had written many while he was in London before going to Rosings. Each one having parts that made her laugh and cry. Despite her pain, she laughed when she read:

I am trying my best to forget you, Elizabeth. I forget you when I am reading that book that you favoured at Netherfield. I forget you when I see a little trinket in a store that I know would bring out the sparkle in your eyes. I forget you when I am at the theatre and someone walks by wearing lavender. I forget you when I automatically turn, hoping to see your lovely chestnut curls. I forget you when I look around the ballrooms and no other lady holds a candle to your beauty. Oh, heavens—Elizabeth, why can I not forget you?

She cried when she read:

I know it does me little good, but I cannot help but wonder what might have been had our situations been different. Would that I could call forth your laughter to my ears and feel your hand in mine.

When she picked up the next letter, she could see from its date that it had been written from Rosings. Knowing what she did, she was hesitant to read further. It was like knowing the ending to a Greek tragedy but not being able to stop the course of events from happening nonetheless.

Dearest,

You might wonder why I call you such, for after all my letters, you can see that I have not been able to forget you. I cannot imagine anyone else becoming so dear to me; yet, coward that I am, I cannot declare myself.

Why did you have to be in Kent? At first, I was angry to hear you were so nearby, for surely you had come to torture me. I thought that I had suffered quite enough. But the moment I laid my eyes upon you, I was as in your power as ever I was before. I could not hate you or blame you. I could only love you.

Do you hear me? I have said it. I love you, Elizabeth. Lord, I wish I did not, for I cannot see my way through to offering for you. This struggle, this torment is constantly bearing down upon my heart. It is cruel, and I wish I could simply forsake it all. I was set to leave after yesterday yet again. Fool that I am, I cannot drag myself away from you. I have postponed our departure twice now.

We have walked the grounds of Rosings together, you and I. Your companionship has been like a salve to my longing heart. You are so kind even when I do not know what to say. You do not force the conversation as other women might. I am not naturally talented in conversation, but you do not push me as we walk quietly together and your compassion warms my heart even further. I cannot help think that I am leaving you in suspense, waiting for me to speak of my feelings. I am not certain how much longer I can bear this. I will have to either leave or declare myself to you. Heaven help me either way.

Yours,
Fitzwilliam Darcy

Elizabeth had to take a few moments then to calm her heart. She knew what happened next, and the pain was fresh in her mind. Not three days later, Mr Darcy had made a decision. He had offered for her, and she had thrown his offer in his face. The tears now streamed down her cheeks despite her resolve to compose herself. Though his proposal was then unwelcome, she could not help but wish that somehow their future could have another chance.

His letter, given to her in the grove the next day, had begun the change in her heart. It had opened her eyes to his side of the events. These subsequent letters seared her heart as a testimony of his struggle with his love for her throughout.

Looking down at her bed, she had only three letters left. She remembered that all three were dated after his proposal, one after he left Rosings. She was afraid to read them. Afraid of what they might confirm. Afraid that they would prove he had found no way to forgive her, his love dying with her red-hot words that fateful day. His reversion to formal address was the first sting.

Miss Bennet,

I cannot even begin to describe the wounds you have inflicted on me. Your rebuke, your hateful rhetoric is burned into my mind. Thank you very much for giving me such a powerful tool to use in forgetting you this time. Blast! If I knew you held me in such little regard, I never would have been fool enough to offer for you. You said you hoped my struggles in fighting my love for you would aid in allowing it to dissolve. I sincerely hope you are correct, for I cannot think that I would wish to love you after what has happened. I hope that my letter made you regret your heated defence of Wickham. I hope that it made you regret what you so quickly threw away.

Elizabeth could not keep reading. Every word was the same as the self-loathing thoughts she had often had. That he could feel this way only confirmed her greatest fear. She had turned his love to hatred. Despite herself, she forced herself to read on—to know the full extent of his judgement. Here, Elizabeth noted the following words were blotted and smeared.

What is wrong with me? For I could never wish you pain no matter how much my pride is bruised and my heart is broken at your refusal. How could I have been such a fool, Elizabeth? You have reduced me to nothing. I wish there was a way to forget it all, even you. I want to hate you, yet all I can do is to find that I still love you. 'Tis too cruel.

Still, God bless you,
Fitzwilliam Darcy

Never had she loved him more than she had when reading the last of that letter. The date of this letter was the very day they met unexpectedly in the maze. Suddenly, her memory flew to the ink she had spied that day on his head. Her eyes fell to the portion of the letter with illegible words. The image this discovery brought to mind—perhaps troubled so deeply he bent his head to the desk—pained her anew. How she must have broken him! Yet his words were tender and his actions in the garden maze kind. While his hurt and anger had been so apparent in the beginning, fresh from the wounds at Hunsford, they melted away to love again, and he was a far better man than she had ever known him to be.

Wearily, she reached for the next letter. No sooner had she begun to read than she saw that it had been written the last evening she dined at Rosings. His thoughts and actions spoke only of her comfort, yet that evening she had seen the aloofness as disregard, his protest over the seating at dinner as a wish to pain her. That memory of the evening was bittersweet, for even now she felt the slow stirrings of that cello's song when she thought back to their conversation at dinner and of the heat in his eyes when his fingers brushed her arm while pulling out her chair.

Now the pain in her head throbbed in time with her heart. Elizabeth was certain now that what started off as only a minor discomfort was indeed brewing into a severe megrim. Her heart was full, yet she needed to continue. Only one letter remained. It was dated not a fortnight ago.

My dearest Elizabeth,

Elizabeth wept again with a stupid feeling of relief that he had so recently addressed her thus. Encouraged by this endearment, she read on.

Yes, Elizabeth, you are my dearest and shall be forevermore. I am tired of trying to forget you. Instead, I have resolved to forever remember you as the best there is. I am determined now that you shall be mine, if only in my heart. I cannot forget you, and so I am resolved to become the man you deserved. I do not expect to ever woo you or gain your favour, but I hope to cool the longing in my heart by becoming the kind of man that would be worthy of your hand.

I was not worthy at Rosings. You are a woman worthy of being pleased, and I knew not how to please you properly. I have looked upon our entire acquaintance with new eyes. You have taught me a lesson, hard at first, but most beneficial. If God should ever grant me the blessing of proving to you how well your rebukes were taken to heart, I will do my very best to show you the changed man you have occasioned.

Accepting that I will forever love you has set me free, though not without pain. I will always long for you—of that, I am sure. But there is no conflict in my heart, no burden. There is simply not room enough for anything but you. I wish you every happiness in this world, Elizabeth. Would that I could grant you them myself! If it were in my power or were my right, I would steal the very moon from its spot in the heavens and gift it to you. I am resolute to try to forget my heartbreak and instead allow only my love for you and my attention to improvement to rule my heart and mind. Elizabeth, what have you not done for me? I have not deserved you, but I will ever strive to.

Yours forevermore,
Fitzwilliam Darcy

Elizabeth did not know what to think or how to act. She simply held the letter to her heart and thanked the Lord that he still loved her. How it could be, she knew not. Though she had very little strength in her—and despite her relief at his continued regard—her head could now not be ignored. She returned the letters to the safekeeping of her trunk, barely avoiding injuring herself further when, upon standing, she felt the room sway. Reaching feebly for the now-cooled cup of tea, she forced the liquid down her throat though her stomach churned. It would soon take over her senses and put her into a deep sleep, one she was sure her head—let alone her broken heart—could well use.

Before the clutches of Morpheus could fully claim her, she determined that, should she be granted such a blessing as to see Mr Darcy again, she would do her best to act in accordance with what would constitute her happiness.

CHAPTER 17

A SOFT TAP ON THE DOOR BROUGHT DARCY'S HEAD UP FROM THE BOOK HE WAS reading in one of the armchairs in his study. He recognised Georgiana's gentle knock and called out to summon her.

Smiling, Darcy watched as she peeked around the door. "I hope I am not interrupting."

Darcy closed his book, using a finger as a marker as he stood to escort his sister to the companion chair near the armchair he just vacated. "You are always welcome, Georgie, regardless of what task I was engaged in. And it so happens, I was doing nothing more productive than reading."

"Oh, then do not stop on my account. I shall just sit here if you do not mind."

Darcy released her hand as she sat and, with a smile and nod, resumed his own seat. It was soon clear by the way Georgiana sighed and looked about the study that she had not sought his company for any specific matter. More likely she was bored.

Opening his book, he wondered how long it might take Georgiana to—
"What is it you are reading?"

Darcy suppressed a smile and looked up, answering her.

"Oh, history. Pah!" she said with a comical wave of her hand.

"It is certainly not for everyone, I suppose," Darcy replied, returning his gaze to the page. Only a short moment later, she spoke again.

"I concede it must have its uses at times. For there is the saying that if we do not learn history, we are likely to do something again—or some such."

"Edmund Burke," Darcy supplied, putting his finger again to hold his page, amusement colouring his features.

Georgiana looked thoroughly confused, drawing Darcy's smile broader. "Is that one of your friends?"

Chuckling, he shook his head. "That is the gentleman whose quote you butchered a moment ago. *'Those who don't know history are destined to repeat it.'*"

Georgiana laughed too and, shrugging, stood up to walk to the window to gaze out. "Well, I believe I am safe regardless of how much history I know, for between the two of us, *you* know plenty."

Darcy waited for more from Georgiana, certain that, the moment he opened his book again, she would speak. After many quiet minutes—and seeing Georgiana's attention occupied watching the people and carriages below—Darcy once again resumed reading.

He had read no more than half a page when she spoke again. This time he reached for the marker on the table beside him and put away the book entirely.

"Oh, it looks as if Mr Wilson across the square has bought himself a new curricle." Georgiana threw her brother a glance before returning her attention to the action outside. "Though it looks as if his skills with the whip are in need of improvement." Georgiana winced as she witnessed her neighbour execute a rather close turn.

Darcy laughed and joined his sister at the window. It was no news to him that Wilson was a poor driver; it was rather a running joke at their clubs. No sooner had he joined Georgiana at the window than she seemingly lost interest in those outside and began walking about his study, her hand trailing across the bookshelf, perusing his collection. Darcy crossed his arms, leaning against the window as he studied her in bemusement.

"Georgiana…"

His sister looked up from the book she had absently pulled from the shelf with an answering hum.

Darcy laughed, walking towards his sister. Taking up the book she held, he replaced it on the shelf again. "I think this particular book will do nothing to cure your boredom."

With a squeak of mock outrage, Georgiana protested. "What makes you think I am bored?"

His brow rose, scepticism clearly written all over his features.

With a sigh, Darcy watched his sister collapse in a heap of silk and limbs into his oversized desk chair. "Oh, I suppose you are correct. There is simply nothing to do!"

Darcy laughed at her theatrics. "That was rather dramatic even for you, my dear. Whatever do you mean there is nothing to do? You could practice the piano, go shopping with Mrs Annesley, or any number of things. You know you need only ask and I will join you on a walk or even open our box at the theatre."

Georgiana grimaced at his suggestions, picking up one of his quills and playing with the feather across her slim fingers. "I have had quite enough of the city if you must know." Becoming animated, Georgiana sat up straight and looked at him hopefully. "When might we go to Pemberley? Please, Brother, say we are to go soon!"

Darcy laughed aloud again and took a few steps towards her. "In a few days, if you desire. However"—Darcy paused, enjoying the excitement in his sister's expression—"if you can endure only three more weeks of this tedium, Cousin Richard will be on leave again. Then we might all journey to Pemberley."

Indecision was clearly written all over her face. Darcy could see that the allure of leaving town for their beloved home held much attraction for her, but he knew also that she greatly enjoyed her cousin's company above all others, save himself.

The moment her shoulders sagged slightly, Darcy knew what her answer would be. "Then you have made your decision, have you?"

Georgiana eyed him with a mock scowl. "'Tis not fair—you know me too well." With an exaggerated sigh, she pouted. "But, Brother, what shall I find to do for three whole weeks?"

"Oh, you poor child," Darcy said with a great laugh. "Perhaps you might consider the occupation I was recently endeavouring to do and *read*!"

Georgiana, frowning and leaning forward, reached for the large tome she saw before her on his desk. "I am afraid I have quite gone through all of my books, and you will next tell me I ought to read some of your own dusty, ancient ones."

Darcy's laughter died in his throat as his attention was caught by the book she was even now sliding towards herself. Stepping quickly towards his desk, he rescued the tome from her hands and tried to act casually as he walked it back to its rightful location on the shelves behind him. His heart had nearly come out of his chest at the sight of her hands on that volume. For surely, she was moments away from discovering a secret that he would not have another soul know for anything. He may have told his sister all about Elizabeth, but that did not mean he did not intend to keep a few matters closer to his heart.

"That book will surely put you to sleep, my dear," Darcy said with hardly a change to his normal pitch. He safely deposited the book where it belonged, cursing himself for not restoring it to the shelves days ago. Darcy imagined for a moment what turn of events could have come about had the letters found themselves in the wrong hands. With a shudder, he turned again to his sister. "And so, I propose a trip to Hatchards!"

Georgiana squealed, entirely distracted from her brother's odd behaviour, and clapping her hands together, stood to embrace him. Her subsequent rambling tugged at Darcy's lips, forcing from him a smile.

"There is this new set of books—novels really—I should very much like to inquire about."

Darcy walked his sister to the study door, glancing briefly over his shoulder at the book of blue and gold binding now safely shelved on the fourth shelf on the furthermost right side, sixth from the end.

"Another novel! I should think you have read every last one in the kingdom."

Georgiana laughed, and Darcy closed his study door behind them as they walked towards the front of his town home. "That is what I am telling you. This is a new author, her first work, and it is published in three volumes."

Darcy ordered their carriage brought around and, while they waited, leaned against the baluster of the staircase, amused by his sister's enthusiasm for romantic tales.

"Very well then, this shall be our quest. To find you a novel you have not read. By any chance, Georgie, has this author a name whereby we might begin our search?"

"It is simply written 'by a Lady.'"

Darcy groaned good-naturedly. "Splendid."

∾

The megrim begun and intensified by the emotional tempest of Darcy's letters did not abate for Elizabeth all of the next day as well. When finally she awoke on the third day without the galloping horses and their pounding hooves given free rein within her skull, she nearly sang with joy. Upon first ascertaining that she felt well enough to sit and partake of a little sustenance without the rolling of her stomach, Elizabeth slipped from her bed and to the trunk at its foot.

Given the last few days, perhaps it was foolish of her to seek immediately those simple cuts of parchment just as soon as she was well, but no other option was possible for Elizabeth.

When the letters were delivered, she had read them rapidly, but in the following days, not being in a state to peruse them again due to her ailment, she had begun to wonder whether they had all been part of the megrim's creation. With swift hands, Elizabeth lifted the lid and reached into the silk pocket. Her breathy sigh indicated her relief that the letters had not been some terrible, wonderful, and glorious dream.

Looking at the missives in her hand, Elizabeth pondered that, despite the pain associated with some of the words written in his hand, the majority introduced Elizabeth to her own heart. They had taught her what that organ had held inside for many weeks but denied time and again. They also were her only tangible proof that the gentleman might still hold tender regard for her.

The very warmth and hope of this assurance was sacred to her. She pressed the letters to her heart, imprinting their meaning there.

Over the course of the next hour, Elizabeth reread each of the letters, laughter and tears accompanying the journey again. His writing was masculine, giving more strength to the words of love yet convincing her of the promise of tenderness by those same hands if only the chance might be presented to them both.

This was the only point of disquiet for Elizabeth, for a nagging voice in her heart whispered that, despite all the assurances built or the hope contained in these letters, it could all be for naught.

"It cannot be for nothing," Elizabeth quietly declared to the empty room and to that doubting whisper.

She could not imagine any scenario that might bring them together, for Elizabeth could not count on reuniting with him at the eventual matrimonial union between Jane and Mr Bingley. His friend might choose not to attend, given his belief in her indifference or, worse still, her dislike. It might be too painful a venture for the man whose words in the letters upon her lap indicated months of continued heartache. Beyond this connexion, there was none. But despite her doubts, Elizabeth could not help thinking some happenstance—as it had so many times before—might bring them together. And if such fortune should befall her, she would do as she had already promised herself: she would act with her heart and hope that, in the interim, nothing would happen to change his.

~

Sitting upon a bench in the garden in full view of the house—given Elizabeth's indisposition and her younger sister's unwillingness to chaperone—Jane and Mr Bingley spoke together of their future. When her ardent suitor came to the end of his speech, his beloved asked him of his plans for their wedding.

"Do you suppose you will ask one of your brothers to stand up with you at our wedding, Charles?"

She had but one name in mind, and her purpose in asking revolved around him. Over the course of the last few days, Jane had begun to reflect much on her sister's odd behaviour in the garden the day she took ill. While at first Jane had thought very little of it, a slowly growing suspicion began to take root in her mind regarding the man about whom Elizabeth had inquired. It was her dear Charles's closest friend, Mr Darcy. While she had no real proof, Jane began to suspect her sister to have moved from indifference to admiration and from admiration of that gentleman…to love. Why else might she be interested in his whereabouts? And then so agitated by it?

"I had thought to ask Darcy to stand up with me. Does that not meet with your approval, Jane?"

Glowing, she assured him it did. "I am very glad to hear that, my dear."

Now it was the gentleman's turn to ask his darling a question, and he did so with humour clearly writ in his voice. "Now tell me truly, Jane, are you marrying me only to gain access to my austere friend?"

Jane laughed as he had hoped very much that she would. Her eyes were bright and full of love, and Mr Bingley had only to wish they were not so close to the house. Nor in such full view! A moment before, he was certain he saw the image of Mr Bennet taking in the view of the gardens from his study window—of all the rotten luck.

"I only ask because, well, because I think it could be possible that—"

Still feeling playful, Bingley interrupted. "He would not do it, you know. Even if you had thought of jilting me at the chapel and eloping with —*oomph!*"

"You horrible man!" Jane said as she playfully poked him in the side with her fan. "If there ever was a man I might be persuaded to elope with, it would be you!"

Mr Bingley groaned quietly, his eyes going serious and dark. "You ought not to say such things unless you are quite ready for me to march right to the window out of which your father so fixedly gazes and shock the poor man when I climb through it and ask for your hand."

Jane sobered, at first unaware of the implication of her words. Her cheeks stained pink and her eyes lowered to her lap, a secretly satisfied smile pulling at her lips. "I will take note of your opinion, sir. However, you might just as well enter through the house."

"Jane…" Mr Bingley spoke disbelievingly.

"Listen first, darling. I think Lizzy might admire your friend. Only, she and Mr Darcy…quarrelled rather harshly not long before they parted ways. I should like to see how the two act around one another when thrown in company again. Besides, it is well known that nothing makes others more eager for another wedding than a wedding."

"If they quarrelled, as you say, how can you be certain that she admires my friend—or he admires her for that matter?"

Almost as soon as he had given voice to the words, Bingley recalled the many times Darcy looked upon Miss Elizabeth, verbally challenged her, or —*he asked her to dance at Netherfield!* Bingley was now quite suspicious he had answered half of his own question. Mr Darcy might very likely admire his soon-to-be sister. *What an intriguing notion.*

"Trust a lady to know her sister, Charles. I cannot say for sure, but I am certain she is not indifferent to him."

"I have listened now as you have requested," Bingley said with significance. "Does this change your opinion on the matter of our engagement? Will you allow me to ask your father and make it open?"

Jane paused a moment, hoping she was doing the right thing for Elizabeth. "Yes, you ought to seek an audience with my father though I shall be loath to give up your company for talks of lace."

Mr Bingley beamed at her then, and she was pleased to cause him such pleasure.

"Now, Jane, now? May I go this very instant? I shan't mind a bit of discussion on lace if it means you are to become Mrs Bingley all the sooner!"

Laughing, she stood and waved him off. Jane only had to hope Mr Darcy would accept his friend's request and attend.

When Elizabeth was well enough to join the family for their meal that evening, Jane gave her father a slight nod to indicate he could make the announcement.

Jane's attention was on Elizabeth when, indeed, Mr Bennet announced that he had accepted Mr Bingley's request for Jane's hand and they were to be married. Elizabeth immediately gasped, delight infusing her features. Her congratulations were given with a sincerity, a warmth, and a delight that words could but poorly express. Every sentence of kindness was a fresh source of happiness to Jane. For her part, Elizabeth now smiled at the rapidity and ease with which an affair was finally settled that had given them so many previous months of suspense and vexation.

When queried later by her mother, Mr Bingley declared that he hoped his friend Mr Darcy might stand up with him, Jane witnessing Elizabeth's acute attention throughout the whole. But more telling still was the reply from Mr Darcy a few days later in the affirmative, expressing his wholehearted congratulations to the happy couple. It was then that Jane bore witness to a telling brightness in her sister's eyes.

～

"So I *shall* see you again, Elizabeth," Darcy said aloud to his empty bedchamber. Lifting the glass in his hands to his lips, Darcy could not help the tremor in his grasp.

CHAPTER 18

"I shall not survive this, Lizzy. An elopement begins to have much merit in my mind," Jane whined uncharacteristically as she collapsed upon her bed.

Elizabeth laughed, tumbling beside her sister, and they both lay looking at the ceiling. "You have had the misfortune, my dear sister, of choosing to marry a man both handsome and rich, the latter a favourite aspect for our mother. Did you think she would settle for anything less than the most elaborate of celebrations?"

Her sister expelled a breath and, turning to look at Elizabeth, said, "You are lucky you are to leave soon on your tour of the Lakes with our aunt and uncle Gardiner. *You* have little chance of going mad over wedding breakfasts and lace."

"There are many advantages not often looked upon when one is a spinster." Again, Elizabeth laughed, but her next words held all the sincerity for which her sister could wish. "But truly, Jane, if you need me, I shall stay."

Jane shot up on one elbow and looked at her sister with astonishment and no little disappointment. "You shall not, indeed, Lizzy! You have anticipated this tour for many months now, and I will not be the means by which you or my relations experience disappointment. No, to the Lakes you will go, and to the shops for lace I shall go."

Elizabeth smiled at her sister. "Calm yourself, Sister. While I *have* anticipated this holiday, I would forego it, as Mary might say, to '*pour into the wounded bosoms of each other the balm of sisterly consolation*' while our mother prepares for your blessed day."

Relaxing again against the pillows, Jane chuckled. "Well I shall not allow it. I have Charles now, and you shall have your tour. 'Tis only days away. Are you not excited, Lizzy?"

Elizabeth was quiet in reflection before answering her sister. If she were truthful, it had been difficult to look upon her sister's bliss and not feel an aching wish for her own. At least with her tour, her mind might be engaged in lakes and landscape and not of longing. For what are men to rocks and mountains? And the time would pass swiftly, too, towards her return for the wedding when Elizabeth would be before Mr Darcy again. Her heart sped suddenly at the thought, eagerness and anxiety swirling like a heady elixir in her blood.

"There will be so much to see, Jane. I cannot think of it without imagining how it may be a cherished memory the rest of my days."

"Then it is settled."

The two sisters spent some many minutes discussing their mother's zeal for planning this most anticipated wedding, for Mrs Bennet spared no amount of energy discussing anything else. The menu for the wedding breakfast had been adjusted no less than three times with Cook, and Jane's dress was fearfully looking to consist of more lace then style.

After a fit of giggles between the two beloved sisters, Elizabeth's eldest sister became serious and tentative in her tone. "How do you feel about seeing Mr Darcy again at the wedding, Lizzy?"

Once again, Elizabeth was thrust into reflection. Without telling her sister of the letters, she could not adequately share her feelings regarding seeing that gentleman again. And furthermore, should she be unable to secure her own happiness, it would not do to have her sister agonize over it on Elizabeth's behalf. Jane's betrothed and Mr Darcy had been long-time friends, and Elizabeth would not take that away from Mr Darcy after all that he had felt for her. If there was to be no future between them, and Jane knew the depths of Elizabeth's feelings for Darcy, then she would not hesitate to distance them from Darcy for Elizabeth's sake. Despite the hope sown from his letters, he might not have the courage to ask for her hand again. "I have decided that Mr Darcy is one of the best men of my acquaintance, and I should be happy to renew such."

"Lizzy, do you…?"

Elizabeth looked towards her sister then, knowing the question on her lips. She entreated as well as she could with her eyes and a slight shake of her head, and Jane understood and withdrew the inquiry. In this, they could comprehend each other. While Jane might suspect the state of Elizabeth's heart, it was still something more to speak of it.

The sun and moon waltzed across the heavens swiftly after this, and the small span of time before her aunt and uncle were to arrive felt mercifully short for Elizabeth. Soon she only awaited the arrival of her aunt and uncle. Her trunk was packed, the letters still safely hidden inside, for Elizabeth could not bear to part with them, nor did she feel safe without them near her person. No more letters had arrived in the post, for she was careful to check every day to assure herself. It would not do for any to be discovered.

When at last her aunt and uncle arrived, Mrs Gardiner gave her favourite niece an indulgent smile but sent her husband a slightly worried one. "Lizzy, dear, I hope you will still be pleased after we tell you our news."

Elizabeth, now concerned, looked towards her uncle just as her aunt did then, waiting for his explanation. "Only yesterday, I received notice that one of my shipments will be arriving earlier than we anticipated."

"That is good news is it not, Uncle?"

Hesitating only briefly, Mr Gardiner began again. "We shall have to curtail our holiday by a few weeks, Lizzy. And I am sorry to say we shall only go as far north as Derbyshire. We cannot go to the Lakes. Truly, I am sorry. I only just learned this, or we might have prepared you for it."

Elizabeth smiled, her heart responding naturally to the name of his county. While she knew he was in London, and the change of plans was no small disappointment, being in the place he called home, in the land he loved, was wonderful to Elizabeth. At least she would always be able to know how to picture him over the years.

Realising she had remained silent too long, Elizabeth was quick to assure her relations with undisguised sincerity that the alteration to their holiday did not distress her in the least. "I have heard much of that part of the kingdom, and you shall not see me sorry to see it."

Mrs Gardiner relaxed beside her in relief. "I cannot tell you how gladdened I am to hear you say so, Lizzy. I had worried that you might be disappointed. As it is, we shall be spending much of our time in a town I hold dear. Lambton is where I grew up, and there are many acquaintances dear to me that I should like to introduce to you."

"Then Lambton shall be fixed as the place I shall be made most happy, Aunt."

The next morning, as Elizabeth stood with her relations in preparation to board the carriage, Mrs Bennet bemoaned the loss of her daughter's aid in preparation for the wedding—not that the matron would consider any of Elizabeth's suggestions with merit, nor had she once consulted with Elizabeth regarding even one aspect of the event. Still, Mrs Bennet was in the habit of feeling herself misused and, on this occasion, particularly so.

Once they were safely ensconced in her uncle's carriage, Elizabeth turned to her travelling companions with a smile and sighed. "We shall now be required to think on nothing but such subjects as bring us pleasure."

Mr Gardiner chuckled and began then to expound upon the other sights they might visit, including such beauties as Matlock, Chatsworth, Dovedale, and the Peak. Elizabeth listened with half her attention, for the other half was reserved for *him*.

~

A knock at his study door pulled Darcy's attention from the shockingly good book he was reading. Before he could respond to the summons, the door swung open, and Colonel Fitzwilliam entered, the butler—his expression awash with offended dignity—behind him.

Startled, Darcy stood, finding himself wholly embarrassed by the book in his hands. "Richard, I see you are once again harassing my staff and displaying your deplorable manners at the same time." Darcy turned his back quickly, scanning the desk for a marker and a place to deposit the book.

As disguise of any sort was not his custom, he might have simply placed the book down without drawing any attention. But Darcy, thinking little of how unusual his actions were, lifted some documents on his desk and placed the book beneath them. Colonel Fitzwilliam noted this subterfuge but simply laughed, helping himself to the side table.

Darcy then addressed his butler. "Carroll, you will excuse my cousin. He no doubt met with some unfortunate accident as a baby that resulted in a head injury."

Mr Carroll, expertly trained as he was, maintained his staid composure, only the slight twinge of his lips gave him away. Bowing, he asked, "Will you require anything else before the dinner hour this evening, sir?"

Darcy shook his head, ignoring the guffaws of his relation. "Thank you, Carroll. I think not."

When the door closed, the two cousins broke into quiet laughter, Darcy patting his cousin on the back by way of greeting.

"Heaven forbid that my reckless louse of a brother should find his ne'er-do-well ways catch up with him and I should inherit. But I am warning you now, Darcy, should that unfortunate event happen or should I find some extremely wealthy—handsome, witty, and pleasing—heiress to wed, my first order of business will be to steal that man away from you. Carroll is my greatest source of entertainment when I visit your home, and this does include my dear cousins dwelling here."

"You may do your worst, but I assure you that you will bankrupt yourself before he will choose to leave my employ."

Colonel Fitzwilliam merely shrugged, unconcerned with the challenge, and the two laughed again.

"You are looking a mite better than last I saw you, Darcy. Certainly, you are far less dour than you were upon leaving Rosings."

Both knew to what the colonel was really referring, and though Darcy expected his cousin would broach the topic, he had not anticipated it so soon upon his arrival.

Darcy nodded, refusing to rise to the bait just yet and stepped away from his desk to pour himself a drink. Though it gratified him that Richard observed an improvement in his spirits, that did not necessarily mean Darcy wished to discuss them with his cousin. Lifting the glass to his lips, Darcy's eyes drifted to the tome on the bookshelf. He had not written her since the day he told Georgiana everything. That alone was proof he was coping better. In his distraction and self-reflection, Darcy did not notice his cousin take up the book he had buried under some papers moments before.

"*'Sense and Sensibility*, by a Lady.'" Colonel Fitzwilliam read, bursting into hilarity, his breath coming in such close succession between the laughter as to hinder his ability to speak. "Please tell me…you are not…"

Darcy snatched the volume from his cousin's hands, anger flaring up at Richard's reaction and embarrassment colouring his emotions.

"A novel!" Richard once again managed, falling into a chair with more gasping chuckles.

"It belongs to Georgiana if you must know, you buffoon."

Wiping his eyes, Colonel Fitzwilliam pressed a hand into his side to alleviate the pain in his ribs. "Sure, sure, but I can testify you were reading it, and I would suspect with some pleasure when I arrived."

Darcy frowned and, taking the book, placed it firmly again on his desk with a snap. "If you must know, as her guardian, I often examine her reading choices." When clearly Colonel Fitzwilliam would not abate his laughter, Darcy growled. "A task left entirely to me! Though I seem to remember your name also upon my father's will."

Richard raised a hand. "Pax. You shall have my promise that nobody at White's shall hear a word of this." Mirth twinkling in his eyes, he continued. "For I doubt anyone would believe me."

Darcy waited, not amused, as his once-favourite relation burst forth with a hearty laugh again, occasionally half-heartedly attempting to stem his laughter.

Shaking his head, Darcy walked with his drink to the companion chair near his cousin and sank into it. His brow was lowered, a scowl pressing his lips into a tight line while he waited. He *had* been reading Georgiana's book, but hell if he would admit to his cousin that he had been enjoying it too.

The writing style was witty and refreshing, the cheek of the author reminding him fondly of the impertinence of another lady. Since purchasing it three weeks ago, Georgiana had read the three volumes twice, so enthralled was she. He became curious—and to be honest, in need of distraction. He may have been able to withstand writing to Elizabeth, but that did not mean she was ever far from his thoughts.

Once his cousin was quiet, Darcy eyed him with a frown. "Are you quite finished now?"

A small chuckle broke his cousin's attempt at sobriety, quickly subdued, though the laughter remained in his eyes. "I believe I am."

"It *does* belong to my sister. She has spoken of little else these past weeks, and I will admit to being a little bored."

Darcy's frown deepened upon seeing his cousin's face break forth into a large smile. "Whatever your reasons, they are your own. Just assure me you have not allowed this spring's events to turn you into a simpering miss." Richard's shoulders bounced, once again belaying his mighty attempt to restrain his humour.

Despite his earlier temper, Darcy could not hold back, and the two laughed openly together. "I can promise you, Richard, I have not gone so far as to become that!"

"I am glad to hear it."

After a few minutes in which both gentlemen enjoyed their drinks, Richard turned to his cousin, all trace of humour now gone from his tone.

"You do look to be in better spirits, Darcy. I am pleased."

Darcy sighed, knowing full well that he ought to get over the inevitable discussion sooner than later. "It has not been easy, but I believe I may in time get the better of it."

"It looks to me as if you already have."

Darcy shook his head. "I am more contented with my lot, but I assure you my disappointment is still great."

"And you will still not hear anything of going after her, will you?"

Darcy did not speak for some time. A familiar wariness settled over him, effectively extinguishing any lingering effects of their previous mirth. He was at least past the abject misery he once experienced. Whilst he knew he would see her again at Bingley's wedding, having many days to both agonize and exult in the knowledge, still Darcy could not know exactly how to answer his cousin's inquiry.

Instead, he changed the direction of the topic and announced, "Bingley is to marry her sister."

Richard sat up, interest and concern warring in his features. It was clear that his astute cousin had, in a matter of moments, considered all the implications of such an event, from certain continuation of acquaintance to the occasional meeting.

"I shall more than likely see her often at any momentous events: at holidays or when Miss Bennet bears my friend a child. I have tried not to think of it, but one day I will also know of her eventual wedding too. While I may be managing not to drown now, I shall suffer greatly at that news."

Darcy's exhausted tone was incongruent with the turmoil in his expression, and his cousin silently commiserated with him. "In time, you too may find another."

Darcy lifted his eyes to meet the gaze of his cousin. Both knew such was unlikely to occur. Darcy was not a man built of many emotions; they stirred deep. Once devoted, true and faithful he would ever be—and his love, once given, was not given twice.

"I can see no other alternative but for you to woo her."

Darcy allowed a disbelieving huff and, shaking his head, said, "When next I see Miss Elizabeth Bennet, I will show her, by every civility in my power, that I am not so mean as to resent the past, and I hope to obtain her forgiveness and to lessen her ill opinion by letting her see that her reproofs have been attended to." After a moment, Darcy said, "Any other hopes are for naught."

"Unless she receives you favourably," Richard offered knowingly.

Darcy eyed his cousin, afraid to give himself away. The image of Elizabeth burst forth into his thoughts—a smile directed at *him*, her eyes lit with pleasure for *him*. It was enchanting and too unfathomable. Yet Darcy knew that he would not give her up so easily if she gave him the least bit of encouragement.

Breathing deeply, Darcy lifted a shaky hand again to his lips and finished his drink. By the time he lowered it, he had become master under good regulation once again. "So, you are prepared to spend all of your leave with us at Pemberley? Georgiana shall be eager for your company, and so shall I."

Darcy's change of topic was well understood, and Richard responded with a smile. "It has been far too long since I have had leisure to roam Pemberley's woods. Perhaps I might find that forest lake we would swim in as boys."

Laughing at the memory, Darcy shook his head. "You are welcome to it."

The clock then struck the hour, and Darcy noted the time. Standing, he extended his hand to his cousin, who accepted it with a companionable shake. "Come, it is time to change for dinner. Georgiana will be pleased you are arrived. It will be an early night for us, for tomorrow we will leave as planned for Pemberley unless you have business first to complete here in London."

Richard laughed. "As always, I am at your convenience. I have nothing in London that keeps me."

The two men had barely emerged from the study door when they perceived a small squeak from the stairwell, a rush of slippered feet, and a blur of blue fabric descending the staircase. Georgiana threw herself into her cousin's ready arms with a laugh. "Cousin Richard! You are finally here!"

Colonel Fitzwilliam's smile was broad as he set his cousin back on her feet. "Well, this is a welcome any man would find pleasing!"

"Now we may leave this place and go to Pemberley!"

Chuckling, Colonel Fitzwilliam tapped his young cousin's small chin. "Ah, I see it is not my own presence that brings you such pleasure. It is that my arrival grants you leave of London!"

Georgiana gasped, placing a hand on his arm to assure him. "No, no, Cousin. You must forgive me; I am very pleased to see you again."

"But not as pleased as you are to see London behind you tomorrow, I grant. Have no worries, my dear. Your brother has written of your boredom, and I shall do my best to see it alleviated."

With a sheepish glance at her brother, Georgiana smiled tentatively at her cousin and nodded her head.

After a pleasant evening in which both Darcy siblings were thoroughly entertained by their cousin with stories of his oft-absurd interactions with the major general, all retired for the evening in anticipation of the first leg of their journey north.

On the next to last day of their journey, Darcy left his rented rooms at the inn early in hopes of speaking with Richard. He knew his cousin's military habits had him awake far earlier than even his own. Over the past two days, his cousin had been found in the private parlour they would hire during their stay, and that morning Darcy hoped would be no different. Georgiana, he knew, would be a few more hours as, even while travelling, she slept late.

A note had been received from Darcy's steward with a question regarding a pressing matter. And while it could have waited until Darcy arrived at Pemberley with his party in only another day's time, the note's delivery gave Darcy the excuse he needed to travel on ahead.

His reasons for wishing to arrive at Pemberley alone had everything to do with the difficulty he anticipated experiencing by arriving at his beloved home without Elizabeth. When contemplating offering for her, he had often anticipated bringing her to Pemberley as his wife. Without that possibility, Darcy would rather not have an audience to the expected pain of arriving alone.

Pushing open the parlour door, Darcy stood with a smile on his face as he saw his startled cousin quickly snap closed the book he had been reading and stand abruptly, awkwardly adjusting his waistcoat.

The book laid now haphazardly on the table beside his cousin was none other than the novel Darcy had been discovered enjoying a few days before. Erupting into laughter, now at his cousin's expense, Darcy walked swiftly to the book and, lifting it to read the spine, assured himself of its title.

Richard stood stiffly, slightly pink in the face but blatantly defiant of Darcy's open humour. His expression cracked into a smile as Darcy continued to laugh.

"It is a rather good book, I must say," Richard admitted, as the smile took full precedence upon his face and he joined Darcy in laughing.

Darcy waved the book at his cousin, his satisfaction complete. "Please do not tell me that you are turning into some simpering miss!"

Richard responded in falsetto, "It's so very romantic!" his hands coming up to join at the place above his heart.

The gentlemen then sat, Richard taking the book from Darcy's hands and unabashedly flipping again to his stopping point. "The writing style is entertaining. I shall give that to the 'Lady.'"

Darcy spoke then of his approval of the plot line, and back and forth the cousins talked of the book. At one point, Darcy stopped, along with his cousin, realising together that they had been in earnest discussion of a *novel* for nearly half an hour.

"Georgiana will know nothing of this."

"Nor will my brother," Richard said emphatically.

Laughing a little, Darcy changed the topic to the intended one when he first set out to find his cousin. "Would you mind seeing Georgiana to Pemberley on your own? I hope to secure a reasonable mount and travel ahead, perhaps to arrive a day before you."

Richard nodded, unsuspicious of any other reason other than the meeting with his steward pressing Darcy ahead of their party. "Of course, I shall be happy to. Perhaps you ought to consider changing your habit of sending Salazar on ahead of the carriage, Cousin. Now you are in need of a mount, and considering last time…"

"Ha! A fair point." Laughing, Darcy stood to look out the parlour window at the early morning view. "Have you read about the fellow Willoughby yet?"

Richard looked up from the book, his brows lowered. "Yes, and I am not sure I like him."

Darcy nodded, leaving the statement as it was. It would be interesting to see how Richard viewed that character by the end of the book. He reminded Darcy of an acquaintance of theirs, one who was equally charming on the outside but utterly despicable on the inside.

CHAPTER 19

It is not the object of this work to give a description of Derbyshire, nor of any of the remarkable places through which their route thither lay: Oxford, Blenheim, Warwick, Kenilworth, Birmingham as they are sufficiently known. A small part of Derbyshire is all the present concern. But to the little town of Lambton, the scene of Mrs Gardiner's former residence and where she had hoped to see some acquaintances, Elizabeth and her relations bent their steps after having seen all the principal wonders of the county.

Elizabeth found from her aunt that Pemberley was situated within five miles of Lambton. It was not in their direct road nor more than a mile or two out of it. In discussing their route the evening before, Mrs Gardiner expressed an inclination to see the place again. Mr Gardiner declared his willingness, and Elizabeth was applied to for her approbation.

"Is the family likely to be at home?" Elizabeth asked with hardly a tremor to her voice, much to her satisfaction.

"I should not think it a bother to them if they are at home, for most of these great houses are open to tours," Mr Gardiner stated. However, as neither of her relations was apt to know, the question was then put to the maid when she came to clear away the tea setting.

Elizabeth's heart was in her throat after only discovering how close she was to Mr Darcy's estate. She listened with bated breath, releasing it only when the maid affirmed that the family was not at home at present. True disappointment flooded her senses, but endeavouring to hide it, Elizabeth smiled at her relations. She reconciled that she could do no harm should she see Pemberley. While it would not have been ideal to encounter Mr Darcy there for the first time since their departure in London, still it would have given Elizabeth a chance to gauge his behaviour towards herself. It would have allowed Elizabeth a safer venue to observe whether or not he were likely to think favourably on her—rather than before all her relations at Jane and Bingley's wedding.

Agreeing with earnest and unabashed curiosity, Elizabeth and her relations settled it that, upon the next day, they would travel to Pemberley and enquire about a tour of the estate—the very estate that, had she known better some months ago, might have been *her* home as well.

That evening in the privacy of her rented rooms, Elizabeth withdrew the letters from her trunk. She gazed at them pensively as they fell like the cards of a deck from one hand to the other and back. Her heart beat with energy the longer she thought of visiting Pemberley. Once again, the impropriety and unlikelihood of her having these letters in her possession struck Elizabeth. A moment of doubt swept through her as she considered how they came to her.

Regardless of the route they took, she knew in her heart that Mr Darcy could not have wished for it. A notion seeped into her thoughts that perhaps she ought to return them, somehow finding some place to secret them in Mr Darcy's home. She could write him a letter explaining their provenance and assuring him of her secrecy, then… What? Regard? Gratitude for the letters?

Elizabeth shook her head in frustration. He deserved more than a note in response to the outpouring of emotion given freely in his letters. Despite her justification, Elizabeth placed the letters in her reticule. While she had not changed her mind about *somehow* leaving the letters amongst his belongings, they were her only tangible connexion to Darcy. They were his heart and the closest thing she had to possessing it. She suspected she would need their presence with her as she toured his country home.

Elizabeth paused briefly at her travelling writing desk. As her hands slipped across the solid surface, her mind travelled back to her carriage ride with Darcy from Bromley to London. How differently she then saw his actions regarding his travelling case. Now Elizabeth burned with wonder: Had any of these letters once resided in that box, even at the moment she was examining it? Her feelings then now rushed to the fore as she remembered how eagerly she had investigated his personal belongings, only to become awash with shame for prying where she had no right.

Was she even now doing so in planning to tour Pemberley? Would Mr Darcy view it as a gross breach of his privacy and a wholly improper move given their past?

Elizabeth hoped not, patting her reticule for assurance. It was only a few weeks ago that she received the letters, and at that time, he had still held her in tender regard. She could only hope that, should he learn of her visit, he would not think unkindly of it.

As the carriage wheels turned, bringing her closer to Pemberley, Elizabeth did her best to appear relaxed. Then, all at once, the ground fell away, and the house came into view. Breathtaking was an apt description as Elizabeth could not breathe for a moment. It was a house perfectly suited to her, and she felt a fissure of pain run through her heart. *Of all this, I could have been mistress.* While touring the home, her pleasure increased with every room she experienced. His portrait in the hall acutely reminded her of the handsome expression of contentment she often saw directed at her.

Her relations were overflowing, too, with admiration for the home, and the housekeeper was eager to boast of her employer in the most flattering of terms. Every curved staircase, inlaid marble floor, or beautiful work of art confirmed the worth of the man who owned them—worth not measured in pounds but in true character and heritage.

After some time, and sooner than Elizabeth would have liked—for she felt as if she wished never to leave—they were relegated to the gardener for a tour of the grounds. Elizabeth anticipated her delight in the beauties of the natural landscaping to be equalled by that she experienced in his home.

It was with this delight unmistakably upon her face that she walked around a hedge in the garden and right into the broad chest of its owner. Immediately, Elizabeth stepped back and apologised, her blush as deep pink as the roses surrounding her and her wits scattered along with her few belongings. Her reticule and parasol lay at her feet, yet she stared at the items as if they were foreign to her.

Mr Darcy was at home! And from his appearance, not expecting to encounter anyone. He had removed his coat, now draped across one arm, his waistcoat was unbuttoned, his cravat missing, and his shirt collar open at the neck. His hair was slightly damp, and dark curls danced across his brow in the slight summer breeze. In a word, he was devastating. *Devastatingly handsome,* she thought. Suddenly shy, she dropped her eyes again to her belongings on the ground. As she bent to retrieve them, the gentleman did too.

Mr Darcy could not believe the sight before him was real. Yet she had collided with him, filling his senses with her heady perfume and her angelic voice. Finding his own voice, he said, "Miss Bennet! This is a surprise!"

As he returned her reticule, his fingers brushed against hers, causing her breath to hitch.

Taking courage from his friendly tone, Elizabeth peeked up at him through long lashes. When their eyes met, she felt certain that nothing had changed since he had written the last letter to her. This assurance grew like a tempest, sweeping up from her feet through her whole being and filling her eyes with exhilaration. Darcy's gaze responded immediately with a tentative light of its own.

"Mr Darcy, forgive me, but we were told the family was not at home or we never would have—"

"I am only just returned," he hastened to say. "Are the rest of your family about?" He glanced beyond her. In truth, he had to force his eyes away from her, or else he would have happily kept them glued to her for a lifetime.

"They are, sir, though not my immediate family," Elizabeth stammered. Drawing a calming breath, she continued with more confidence. "I am touring Derbyshire with my aunt and uncle."

Darcy nodded and rested his eyes on her again. The glory he felt upon seeing her there at his home left him powerless. Recalling himself once again, he sought not to squander this second chance by simply gazing forever upon her face, which seemed to work poorly at wooing her during the whole of their previous acquaintance.

Darcy cleared his throat. "Would you do me the honour of introducing them to me, Miss Bennet?"

"Of course, sir. I believe they are just beyond the walled garden." Elizabeth turned to lead the way, all the while endeavouring to contrive a reason she might extend his company long enough to allow her to demonstrate her changed feelings. Her heart's rhythm beat so furiously that it would be a miracle had the gentleman not heard it himself. Indeed, the cello played such a profound crescendo now that Elizabeth felt the vibrations through her whole chest.

Soon they reached the garden wall and found her aunt and uncle. Elizabeth was amazed at the civility with which Darcy at once engaged her relations. Smiling to herself, Elizabeth allowed her fingers to brush against the thin fabric of her reticule, reminding herself of the letters within. They had given her insight to his actions, and she could not help but be gratified that this change in him was at her hands.

After several minutes, Darcy made to excuse himself.

Elizabeth quickly said, "It is unfortunate that you go, Mr Darcy, for I am sure your perspective on the gardens would make more of an impression on us. But as we are the intruders, we will not detain you." Then, recollecting how he had written that he found her smiles and arched eyebrow irresistible, she boldly used all the arts and allurements in her power.

Darcy swallowed. *Oh, but she is lovely when she looks at me that way.* "I feel that I am not presentable for company at present, having just returned home." Indeed, he felt utterly exposed and cursed himself for stopping along the way at the forest lake that Colonel Fitzwilliam had mentioned.

Every ounce of him tempted by Elizabeth's smile, Darcy gathered his courage, and despite feeling entirely the fool in his dishabille, he continued. "If you are not pressed for time, please allow me to become presentable. It would be my pleasure to conduct the tour myself."

Elizabeth smiled brightly at him as she gave her thanks and confirmed with her aunt and uncle that they would be happy to await his return. Her smile gave him such hope as he had never before allowed himself, and he bid goodbye with a lightness he had not felt for quite some time. *Could this all be a dream?* Elizabeth was even now touring his gardens, smiling at *him*, and looking at *him* with pleasure. He hardly dared believe it. It was much as he had imagined in London before setting out for Pemberley.

His return was swift, and when he rejoined their group, impeccably dressed and his dark curls wet from his bath, Elizabeth was nearly undone. He was so handsome—and the water in his hair, glistening in the sunlight was a bit more than she could fare. Elizabeth introduced the subject of her aunt's hailing from Lambton and, with the intended effect, drew the others into conversation so she could compose herself.

They conversed as they walked the grounds and along a path around the lake. Darcy stopped them here or there to point out some prospect. He was everything amiable. For his part, Darcy was doing everything he could not to advance the encounter with Elizabeth too quickly. It was only his goal to show her that he had changed. However, not a half hour into their walk, other hopes and goals began to emerge.

In good time, Mrs Gardiner needed the better strength of her husband's arm, and her niece was left to walk with Mr Darcy. Fortunate as this was, since Elizabeth had determined to speak privately to him, she could not walk at his side without some small measure of unease. Furthermore, despite her determination, she was at a loss for any way to broach the topic of which she most wished to speak with him: the state of her heart.

While she contemplated her feelings, her brow furrowed in concentration, and Darcy clenched his jaw at the sight, worried that she was unhappy being left with him.

"Miss Bennet, I would not wish to make you uncomfortable. If you would like to join your uncle and aunt, I can make an excuse to return to the house." It was the very opposite of what he wanted, but he had since learned that attending to her desires held more happiness for him than attending to his own. If he could make her happier by leaving her side, despite his own disinclination, he would do so. They had been conversing so amiably, but then, they had been in the safety of her relations.

Elizabeth looked up at him in horror. "Oh no, sir. I am perfectly happy in your company." She fidgeted with the strings of her reticule, suddenly mortified at her forward speech, and looked down. If she had had the courage to look at him then, she would have seen his face break into a very wide grin. While fussing with her bag, she was reminded of what it contained. She had taken them with her to Pemberley because they were her connexion to its owner. Though she was loath to part from them, she knew they did not belong to her. He had probably not wished to send them, and Elizabeth now felt the time had come whereby she ought to return them.

"Mr Darcy, I am afraid that I may upset you in a moment, but I have something of yours that I believe I must return."

Darcy frowned, not comprehending to what she was referring until, with disbelief, he watched her press some letters into his hands. He stilled, his steps coming to a halt. His mind reeling at the sight, he glanced quickly back at her relations, noting they were some distance away and could not have seen the exchange. His thoughts began to spill from his lips without filter as he turned the letters in his hand.

"How? How did you get these Miss Bennet?" He could feel his cheeks colour in mortification. Beyond that, Darcy's mind was blank with the utter shock of her presentation.

"I received them in the mail, sir." Her voice was quiet, and she was afraid she had made a very poor choice and would now face the consequence of it.

"I do not understand. I did not mail them. They were never—"

"I know." A developing despair grew inside her; he did not wish for her to have them. This she had already guessed, but hearing it from his lips made her realise perhaps, regardless of his feelings, his pride would not allow him to renew his addresses to her.

Swallowing her own anguish, Elizabeth whispered, "I am sorry to have occasioned you pain this way. I did not mean to. I only wished to return them to you and to tell you…"

Darcy looked up from the letters to her face. He saw her confusion, worry, and an anguish that immediately prompted him to speak.

"Tell me what…?" he asked tenderly, unable to bear seeing her so upset.

Elizabeth took a deep breath. "To tell you that the letters were…"

Darcy could see her features transform, and he realised she was embarrassed. With a slight smile, a little more hope once again building in his chest, he pressed her. "The letters were…?"

Looking away, she whispered, "Beautiful."

Darcy had to look away as well. He was quite at a loss for words, for his lips had wished to engage her in something altogether different when he heard her soft reply—an act she surely would not welcome as considerately as she had welcomed his letters, and one that he would rather not perform for the audience of her relations. Reminded of those same relations, gaining slowly on them since they had stopped, Darcy urged Elizabeth again to walk. There was still much to say and precious little privacy if they allowed Elizabeth's aunt and uncle to reach them. *Elizabeth has received and read my letters!*

Falling short of what he wished to say, he handed back the bundle of letters.

Elizabeth looked up at him with questioning eyes.

"They are yours, Miss Bennet. They were always for you, even if I had not the courage to send them."

Her smile beamed up at him, her heart beating faster still. Elizabeth received them with pleasure and deposited them once again in her reticule. The fact that he had returned them to her spoke more than anything else did. It was now her turn to act in accordance with her own happiness.

"Thank you for them. They have become most precious to me." It was bold of her, but they were approaching the house, and she felt their time running out.

"Elizabeth…" Closing his eyes momentarily and opening them to look at her again just to make sure he was not dreaming, Darcy continued. "Elizabeth, dearest, if your feelings…if your feelings are still the same as they were in April—"

"They are changed, sir." Elizabeth quickly cut him off, more eager to secure her happiness than to bother with the dictates of good manners.

He smiled at her eager reply, his heartfelt joy openly displayed on his features, his unabashed and unabated admiration for her clear. Thus encouraged, he said, "As you may know from those letters, my wishes and hopes have not changed. If you will have me—"

"I will, sir," she said, again cutting him off.

Darcy laughed and took her hand in his, tucking it in his arm. He savoured the right and the unlooked-for ability to do so. His joy at that moment could not have been greater than hers, yet it loosed his tongue in a teasing manner she found most pleasing. "I begin to believe it is easier for me to speak on paper than in person, Elizabeth, for you will not let me finish one sentence!"

Colouring, she looked up at him coquettishly as she said, "I do apologize, sir. You were saying?"

The impertinent smile directed at him was his undoing. "You will have me? You will be my wife? Truly?"

"Truly." Her eyes began to glisten. She had hoped to encourage the acquaintance at least, allow him some means by which to know her heart. She had never anticipated that he might propose so readily and with so slight a glimpse of her feelings, but she was glad for it nonetheless.

Darcy had no words. Nothing he could say or write could describe how he felt looking down at his beloved Elizabeth and knowing that, by some small miracle from heaven, she was to be his at last. It did not seem possible. The unknown cause of the letters arriving at her doorstep nagged at his mind, yet even that mystery could not hold Darcy's attention. He cared little now whether he ever found the source of such an event, for the result of it had gained him something too wonderful.

Realising then, as they were nearly at his home again, that there was one who would be eager to make her acquaintance—given that he now had the power to grant such a wish—Darcy turned once again to his beloved. "I travelled ahead of my party today. I ought to have arrived tomorrow."

Elizabeth considered the implications of his decision to travel early. She could have missed him entirely! "Your housekeeper said you were not expected."

"I came ahead to speak to my steward. The rest will join me tomorrow. Among them is someone who will claim an acquaintance with you: Colonel Fitzwilliam." Darcy paused. Elizabeth acknowledged his words with a nod, and he continued. "There is also one other person in the party who more particularly wishes to be known to you. Will you allow me—or do I ask too much—to introduce my sister to your acquaintance during your stay at Lambton?"

"It would be a pleasure to make Miss Darcy's acquaintance," Elizabeth replied with true feeling.

Darcy was pleased, his heart full, and words escaped him once again. When they reached his home, he and Elizabeth waited in companionable silence while her relations reached them, each too preoccupied in the still surreal nature of what had just happened.

Darcy very much wished at that moment the ability to once again remove Elizabeth's bonnet as he had in the garden maze at Rosings, only this time he would not resist—nor imagine!—kissing her.

Mr and Mrs Gardiner recognised something of significance had occurred between their niece and the master of Pemberley. Upon entering the parlour, Elizabeth at once sought out her aunt while Darcy asked to speak with her uncle in private.

While Mr Gardiner could not grant Mr Darcy permission in his brother's stead, he did assure the gentleman of his own hearty approval and congratulations. It was then only a matter of a moment's work for Darcy to convince Mrs Gardiner and her husband to transfer accommodations to Pemberley for the duration of their stay in the area. And so it was that Darcy had arrived at Pemberley, though not with Elizabeth nor she as his wife but, certainly to his understanding, the next best thing. And likewise, Elizabeth found she was not required to leave the home so soon.

CHAPTER 20

THE GARDINERS, ALREADY HAVING BEEN ENGAGED FOR THE EVENING TO DINE with a previous acquaintance, were obliged to return to their lodgings for the evening but had agreed to quit the inn at Lambton for the more favourable aspect of Pemberley the following day. While the newly reacquainted and recently united Darcy and Elizabeth were unhappy for this separation so soon upon the heels of their reconciliation, it was perhaps best in the end.

While Elizabeth did find great contentment at her future home with her future husband, as the day progressed, her awareness of just how grand of a mistress she would become upon her nuptials began to unsettle her. And while Darcy was more than loath to part from Elizabeth, going so far as to suggest Mrs Gardiner invite her friends to dine at Pemberley, he really did have to meet with his steward. With Georgiana and Colonel Fitzwilliam arriving on the morrow as well, it was probably beneficial that he not postpone that interview.

When his travelling coach rolled to a stop the next morning, Darcy waited eagerly for his party. While Darcy bent to kiss his sister's cheek in greeting, the colonel noted his cousin's heightened colour as well as the lightness in his expression. "I see everything has been settled to your satisfaction."

Startled, Darcy thought perhaps that his cousin had guessed his good news already. "Then you have seen her on your way through Lambton?"

Colonel Fitzwilliam's brow lowered in confusion. "Nay, I know not of whom you speak. I was referring to the problem with your steward. You are in good spirits this morning, Darcy. I figured, if things had gone badly, we would have been welcomed to Pemberley by that great mask of doom you are apt to display when displeased."

Darcy smiled and, slapping his cousin on the shoulder, was about to answer him regarding his business with the steward when Richard cut him off.

"However, you did mention someone in Lambton?"

Georgiana gazed between her two guardians. "Yes, Brother, who is it we were to see in Lambton?"

Feeling the joy again fill his heart that had been there since securing Elizabeth's hand the day before, Darcy laughed brightly—surprising his relations immensely.

"Come inside, and I shall tell you all."

With his sister on his arm, Darcy ascended the steps, his cousin eyeing him with some speculation as he followed closely behind. Steering them directly into the parlour nearest the entrance, Darcy deposited Georgiana comfortably on a sofa and turned to address them with a brilliant smile.

"It pleases me immensely to have the privilege of introducing you later, Georgiana, to a very charming lady. Miss Elizabeth Bennet is in Lambton, travelling with her aunt and uncle."

Georgiana immediately paled. Though she could see that this lady's vicinity had given her brother much pleasure, Miss Darcy was at once preoccupied with apprehension for his future felicity as well as her own reception by Miss Bennet.

Darcy took up the seat beside his sister, her hand now grasped in his own. "Are you not pleased, Georgie? I thought you wished to be acquainted with the lady."

"Darcy, has anything occurred between you and Miss Bennet?" Colonel Fitzwilliam interjected, sensing a portion of Georgiana's concern, for it was his own. He imagined that Miss Bennet would be polite and engaging as she had been on their many encounters at Rosings even after his cousin's failed proposal. Furthermore, Colonel Fitzwilliam could easily conceive his cousin imagining more affection than was perhaps being offered by Miss Bennet. And if that were the case, then Darcy might be in for a bigger fall when the lady left the area.

Darcy smiled at his cousin. "You could say that, Cousin. Wait and see, for Miss Bennet and Mr and Mrs Gardiner are to arrive momentarily—"

A knock on the parlour door interrupted him, drawing Darcy's smile. "They must be arriving even now." Looking again at the wan face of his sister, Darcy spoke tenderly to her. "Have no fear, Georgie. I assure you Miss Bennet will be pleased with you and you with her."

Colonel Fitzwilliam, already acquainted with the lady and her kind personality, knew his cousin to be accurate, yet he still frowned. He held some little resentment for the lady. Although her motives in rejecting Darcy seemed reasonable given Darcy's account of the absurd and grossly offensive nature of his proposal, the colonel could not forget his familial fidelity. Darcy was his cousin, and charming or not, the lady had subjected him to heartbreak.

Before he could at least do his part to assure Georgiana that her brother spoke the truth, the door to the parlour opened, and Mrs Reynolds showed the guests in.

Immediately, Colonel Fitzwilliam noted the pleasure that touched Miss Bennet's cheeks upon first setting her eyes on his cousin Darcy. He did not bother to check Darcy's reaction, for it was likely to mirror that of the lady. With a charming smile, he stepped forward and greeted Miss Bennet with all the cordiality that marked their previous friendship, and the party moved further into the room towards Miss Darcy.

Darcy took up Elizabeth's arm, escorting her closer to where his sister stood near the sofa. "Miss Bennet, may I have the pleasure of introducing you to my beloved sister, Georgiana Darcy?"

"And Georgiana, this is Miss Elizabeth Bennet of Longbourn"—the ladies exchanged curtseys, the elder giving the younger a genuine smile—"who only yesterday afforded me the honour of consenting to be my wife."

The silence of the room then descended with all the delicacy of a stampede of wild animals. Darcy laughed at the amazed expressions on the faces of his relations. Elizabeth joined him, though shaking her head at her betrothed.

"You must forgive your brother, Miss Darcy, for surprising you. Furthermore, you must excuse him as no one could be more astonished by this turn of providence than we are."

Darcy chuckled, taking up her hand and bestowing a kiss upon it, furthering the shock of his relations. "But the lady is correct, Georgiana. I ought not to have been so forward in my announcement to you. I can see that I have surprised you. You must forgive me, for I am too pleased with my good fortune to have waited any longer to share it."

The colonel, recovering sooner, stepped forward to offer his congratulations, though if one looked closely, they may have seen the twitch in his eye.

Darcy, assuring them that all would be explained, bade everyone seat themselves and rang for tea. He then began to recite his sudden and unexpected encounter with Elizabeth the day before in the gardens. His pleasure at seeing her was readily shared, believed by all, and enhanced by the bloom of his betrothed's countenance.

Elizabeth explained her part, the circumstances of travelling in the county with her relations, and added her own pleasure at encountering the master of Pemberley.

Darcy listened with gratification as Elizabeth began to draw out his shy sister with calm, softly spoken words and amusing asides to her narrative, putting Georgiana at ease. When the tea service was brought in by a few maids, Elizabeth engaged her new sister-to-be on the topic of music. Amazed by Miss Darcy's genteel reticence and spurred by her shame of this further proof that she had been deceived by Mr Wickham on the subject of Miss Darcy's character, Elizabeth was most eager to set the young lady at ease.

At one point, Elizabeth excused herself to replace her tea cup and saucer on the table, and finding an opportunity to speak to his cousin's intended, Colonel Fitzwilliam quickly stood to replace his as well. In lowered tones, he said to her, "It is quite astonishing that my cousin and you should have encountered each other so unexpectedly yesterday."

Elizabeth, astute as she was, easily detected the investigative nature and doubt colouring the undertones of the colonel's words. Her reply was not at all what he expected. "Do you know, Colonel, that your cousin is quite adept at the art of letter writing?" His brows lowered, trying to understand what game Miss Elizabeth might be playing with him. "For myself, I had not known this until recently, the letter presented to me from him at Rosings being my only example."

Colonel Fitzwilliam missed the first portion of her words, his attention fixed upon the latter portion. "You have not surprised me there, Miss Bennet, for I know of the letter he wrote to you then as well as his reasons for doing so."

Elizabeth smiled, offended by neither his harsher tone nor his less congenial reception of her, for it testified to his family's love for her dear Darcy and their wish for him to be happy. That fact alone would be enough to keep her from finding any fault in the colonel's probing. "I presumed as much, or I never would have mentioned it. So you see, it was a great surprise, having only the one example—the one glimpse of insight into your excellent cousin's character—and more importantly, I might add, a great education for me when I received the next dozen letters from him."

Colonel Fitzwilliam coughed, attacked broadside by the lady's revelation. He looked around, as he attempted to gain control of himself, to see whether they had drawn undue attention. Elizabeth handed him a refreshed cup of tea with a knowing, cheeky glint in her eyes and a smile.

"You say my cousin wrote you again?" Colonel Fitzwilliam managed after a small sip from the cup.

Elizabeth laughed quietly as she nodded. "Oh yes, about a dozen more.

Your surprise could hardly have equalled mine upon receipt of them, I assure you!"

"This I cannot believe, Miss Bennet." the colonel said, gaining full control of himself. "For I know my cousin's disinclination towards anything even whispering upon the door of scandal."

The lady smiled again and, to the colonel's slight irritation, with a hint of sympathy. "No doubt you are correct, but the parchments even now in the reticule that hangs from my wrist would say otherwise."

"I am certain…but how? When?"

Elizabeth gazed across the room towards Darcy, her eyes, resting upon him in contentment, made warmer still by seeing his own gaze mirror hers though engaged in conversation with her uncle.

"That I cannot account for you, Colonel. Neither of us knows how the letters, spanning the entirety of our acquaintance, came to be posted and delivered to my doorstep—one and all." Elizabeth returned her gaze to her companion thoughtfully and added, "But delivered they were."

The military man frowned, intrigued by the mystery yet unable to question its authenticity based upon the clarity and honest expression in her eyes. A moment later, Darcy joined their twosome at the table, placing a possessive hand upon Elizabeth's lower back and relishing the right to do so.

"And what are you speaking of, Richard? I must have my share of the conversation."

The colonel opened his mouth to create some innocuous topic when he saw Elizabeth turn to Darcy with a bright smile.

"Your cousin was doubtful of my affections and worried that I may be taking advantage of your goodness."

Colonel Fitzwilliam noted the unhappy face of his cousin and began sputtering, "Miss Bennet paints me a villain. I only wished to assure myself that—"

"You need not do so, Cousin."

Elizabeth placed a delicate hand upon her betrothed's arm, immediately bringing his attention to the heat generated there. "Calm, my dear. I hope you will not be displeased, but I was simply revealing to the colonel my receipt of your letters and the display of your heart that they taught me. He could not have known that they also confirmed to me what *my* heart already felt. For I had long fallen under your spell before I ever received any hope contained within your written words."

Darcy's eyes fell to hers then and burned with emotion. Despite securing her hand the day before, he had yet to hear her express herself in such a manner and to declare her own affection. Without breaking eye contact with Elizabeth, Darcy said to his cousin, "I hope this has put to rest any doubts and that you will never again question Elizabeth's character. You will also excuse us."

Darcy—feeling all the urgency and desperation to which a man violently in love was often subjected—before all their relations, gracefully swept Elizabeth away. With a tone that bordered more on a demand than a polite request, he applied to her uncle. "Mr Gardiner, sir, your niece became quite fond of mazes while she visited my aunt's estate in Kent and has expressed a desire to see the one here at Pemberley. With your permission, I should like to show it to her now."

Mrs Gardiner delicately nudged her husband with an elbow at the side, urging him to grant the young man permission. Elizabeth had shared with her the evening before the whole of their troubled and misguided acquaintance, and Mrs Gardiner more than sympathized with the young master of Pemberley.

"You may, Mr Darcy."

Bowing swiftly, Darcy thanked the man and, without so much as a look or invitation to the rest of the party, pulled Elizabeth through the parlour doors and out to the gardens below, his lengthy stride requiring many of her shorter ones to make up the distance. His pace did not abate until he had led her deeply into the labyrinth of Pemberley's substantial maze though her laughter rang out at his behaviour.

Once Darcy had deemed them sufficiently safeguarded in the maze, he stopped abruptly, his broad shoulders flush with its hedge wall. With a hand on Elizabeth's arm, he pulled her tightly to him, abruptly silencing her laughter with the urgent press of his lips upon hers as his other arm circled her lower back.

The kiss ended nearly as rapidly as it had started though leaving its mark fully upon Elizabeth's senses. She was breathless and dazed as she looked up at Darcy, no less affected as he flashed a rather roguish smile.

"Say it again, Elizabeth."

"Hmm?" Her hand rested dreamily upon his lapel.

"Tell me again of your heart—of your affection for me. This time, to me without my cousin," Darcy beseeched in ardent tones. "Tell me quickly now for I have a desperate need to kiss you again."

Elizabeth gained a measure of her equilibrium and, presenting him with her upturned face, said, "Kiss me again, sir, and I shall."

Darcy needed no more persuasion than that and, with warmth, allowed his head to fall again to hers. Though Elizabeth had no experience with kisses, she imagined there were kisses shared among those who love each other—and then there were kisses created through only the most timeless of loves, loves so encompassing that only a few of earth's inhabitants had the privilege of experiencing them. This was one such kiss, and they were one such destined set of lovers.

When Darcy pulled back, gently breaking the connexion between them, Elizabeth's eyes fluttered open, radiating the feeling that stirred inside her, and whispered, "I love you, Fitzwilliam Darcy, with all my heart and soul."

Darcy heaved a great sigh, pulling Elizabeth to him again and burying his head in the hollow of her neck. His eyes became glossy as he felt his battered heart knit together the jaded edges where past hurts once festered.

"I am yours forevermore, Elizabeth."

Pulling back, she reached up to cup his firm jaw in her hands. Her eyes roamed his face, memorizing his expression and assuring her own heart that any pain was now in the past. After a few moments, the edges of her lips pulled up as she tipped her head to the side and said, "I begin to see that you are correct, William. I *am* quite fond of mazes."

"As am I, Elizabeth," Darcy replied with a rakish grin. Darcy laughed, releasing her for the first time since stopping in the maze. Though he was loath to do it, he knew he ought not to test Mr Gardiner's good will.

With a huff of displeasure, Darcy said, "I dislike the idea heartily, but we ought to return to the others. Mr Gardiner was kind and his wife still more so, but he will not thank me if I linger here with you much longer."

Gathering up Elizabeth's hand and placing it upon his arm, Darcy began a more leisurely amble out of the maze.

"I will admit the notion holds much appeal." Her cheerful tone made him smile, but her words made his blood heat again.

With a quiet groan, Darcy stopped and quickly dispatched a short kiss upon her lips for her beguiling impertinence. "Beware of what you say, minx, for at present I have very little holding me back from swiftly marching you back inside this maze—your uncle be damned."

With a laugh, Elizabeth blushed at his boldness. "Very well, I shall not tempt you again."

"Ha! There is little chance of that!"

~

When the couple rejoined the rest of the party, all were engaged in pleasant conversation. With the help of her cousin and the gentle encouragement of Mrs Gardiner, Miss Darcy had even ventured half a dozen words at once.

Darcy released Elizabeth's arm as she sat beside his sister then walked a pace away to the side table. Tea would not calm his fiery senses, and

Darcy needed something a little more fortifying after his walk in the maze. Smiling to himself, Darcy brought the glass to his lips, recollecting that there had been precious little walking involved.

Sensing someone behind him, Darcy turned to see the colonel step to his side. Richard poured himself a glass as well and, eyeing his cousin over the rim, spoke quietly enough for just Darcy to hear. "I am sorry for my assumption earlier. It was on your behalf that I worried."

Such an admission, so directly and unassumingly given, was enough to assure Darcy of the sincerity of his cousin's words. Darcy nodded as much as he brought his glass to his own lips.

"No harm done."

"Yes, I gathered as much from the bloom on Miss Bennet's cheeks upon her return from your *tour* of the maze."

Darcy attempted to suppress a smile, though badly, as he once again brought his drink to his lips, regarding his betrothed quietly chatting with Georgiana.

"I have to say her fine eyes were brightened by the exercise," Colonel Fitzwilliam said with a bit of mischief in his voice before walking away to resume his seat. Finding much truth in his cousin's audacious statement, Darcy smiled with satisfaction and crossed the room to stand among his guests, his hand falling gently to rest upon Elizabeth's shoulder.

CHAPTER 21

NEVER IN HIS LIFE HAD TEN DAYS PASSED SO QUICKLY YET WITH SUCH agonizing torture. Whilst Elizabeth and her relations were guests in his home, Darcy witnessed the ever-growing affection between his sister and Elizabeth develop into a thing of beauty even he could not have dreamt. Likewise, he found Mr and Mrs Gardiner endearing as he also gleaned from them more insight into his beloved and learned of their influence as she grew into the lady she was now. Their goodness, and of course their fondness for Elizabeth, would forever insure their welcome at Pemberley.

Though Mr and Mrs Gardiner had generously granted Darcy liberty on that first day to take Elizabeth unchaperoned into the maze, the subsequent days of their stay saw them much less so, much to Darcy's sorrow. To Darcy's chagrin, their dogged protectiveness of their niece proved their goodness though it could not please Darcy in this instance.

What sweet torture! Having Elizabeth in his home, so near yet so far, was agonizing and convinced him that, when their party quit the area, so, too, would his own residence at Pemberley end. For he was determined to follow them, travelling at the same time to Hertfordshire where he would officially apply to Elizabeth's father for her hand. And he hoped to God that man would be merciful in his requirements regarding the length of their engagement!

So it was settled, and when those ten days of pure bliss and utter torment came to an end, Darcy, along with his sister, boarded their own carriage behind that of the Gardiners and began the journey south to Hertfordshire

With no further concerns regarding his cousin's betrothed, Colonel Fitzwilliam packed up his own trunk as well and decided he might as well pay his own relations a visit with the rest of his leave. His borrowed carriage from Darcy took him in a different direction towards Matlock and towards his own childhood home.

Travelling was not as burdensome to Darcy as it had been in the past when surrounded by such lovely ladies, their laughter and smiles intoxicating him like heady liquor as, not long into their journey, Georgiana requested Elizabeth's company in the Darcy coach. Late the next day, the caravan of carriages rolled through the gates of Longbourn, and upon assisting the ladies down from the carriage, any heady effects evaporated, sobering Darcy immediately as the sounds of anguished cries through the parlour window reached their ears.

With no members of the household to greet them, Elizabeth looked up at Darcy with concern and then to the Gardiners, now stepping beside them. "What in heaven's name could be the matter?" she said, even as she lifted her skirts to dash into the house.

"Elizabeth," Darcy stopped her with a call. "Shall I leave and go to Netherfield? I cannot think an unexpected guest likely to be welcome."

Uncertain, Elizabeth looked to her uncle for his opinion, but seeing as he had already begun to walk rapidly towards the doors of Longbourn with his wife, she turned again to Darcy and spoke freely. "I do not know what the trouble will be, but I should very much like you with me when I find out."

Darcy nodded and replied, "I will send the other carriage on then with Georgiana and Mrs Annesley and join you forthwith."

Elizabeth hardly waited for him to finish before bestowing a grateful smile and, with a hitch of her skirts, nearly ran towards the open doors of her home. Darcy turned to his sister, who he could see was troubled by the circumstances of their arrival, and attempted to calm her.

"See now, Georgiana. I will join you at Netherfield shortly, but I must go to Elizabeth and see whether I might be of service."

Georgiana, having grown to love Elizabeth like the sister she would be, was less distressed than she appeared. She was merely concerned for the troubled look about Elizabeth's eyes and wished only that she knew what to do to alleviate it. Whatever unhappiness welcomed her new friend was of little concern to Georgiana beyond the distress it would cause Elizabeth.

With more steadiness in her voice than her brother expected, Georgiana replied, "Of course, Brother, you must go to Elizabeth and help her family. I will see you later at Netherfield."

With that, he handed his sister into the carriage and instructed the drivers to bring her to Netherfield. Once on their way, Darcy turned and speedily strode towards the house.

Stepping uneasily across the threshold, Darcy noted that no servant was about to take his coat and hat. Removing them himself, he found a side table on which to place them as he strode towards the chaos within the parlour.

The first thing that greeted him upon entering the room was an unexpected embrace from Elizabeth. Startled by her show of affection, Darcy looked about him for the reactions of the rest of the room.

While the room was quite teeming with occupants—the Bennets, the Gardiners, and even his friend Bingley—none of them seemed to have noticed his entrance or Elizabeth's generous welcome. They were all in a state of agitation, Mrs Bennet and her wails at the centre. Concern drawing his brows together, Darcy looked down at his betrothed and, gently prying her face away from his chest, found tears and obvious distress.

"Good God! What is the matter?" cried he, with more feeling than politeness. Then recollecting himself, he said, "You are very ill. Is there nothing you could take to give you present relief? A glass of wine—shall I get you one?"

Elizabeth merely shook her head, ringlets of hair cascading about her wet cheeks as she released him and, reaching for his hand, quickly led him out of the parlour and again across Longbourn's threshold. Once they reached the empty gardens, she turned to him. Dropping his hand, her arms wrapped about her stomach as she turned her anguished eyes upon him. Unsettled at such a sight, Darcy stepped forward to comfort her before he was unhappily forestalled by her uplifted hand.

"Sir, it is with regret that I must inform you that I can no longer honour my betrothal to you."

No other words uttered in the history of time could have had such an effect on Darcy. He staggered, his heart stopping as his arm automatically reached for Elizabeth. His fingers enclosed upon the air as she took another small step back again.

Her face clearly showed that she did not wish to say such heartbreaking words to him, yet she had. Knowing as he did that whatever had occurred within was the cause of this and not any kind of change of heart for Elizabeth, Darcy finally managed to gain enough composure to speak.

"Nonsense, Elizabeth. What has happened? How may I be of service?"

"There is nothing you can do. I am sorry." The despondency in her voice pulled once again at Darcy's heart.

Swiftly this time, so that she could not retreat again, Darcy reached for her and, despite her initial protests, pulled her into his embrace. It took only a second for Elizabeth to cease her attempts to retreat and instead cling to him as she began silent sobs.

Darcy led her gently to a nearby bench, not relinquishing his hold on her.

"Tell me at once what has brought this on. Let me judge how I might make it right," Darcy said as he passed her his handkerchief.

In halting speech, Elizabeth began to unburden herself of the news.

"My family received an express from Colonel Forster regarding my youngest sister. Lydia was their guest in Brighton as the militia was encamped there for the summer. She has..." Elizabeth paused, cringing at what she must tell him. "She has run off, left the protection of her hosts, and eloped!"

Darcy's brow contracted. A sinking suspicion as to the identity of the guilty officer came to his mind even as he spoke his next words.

"Please, let not this trouble you further, Elizabeth. I will find him and make certain that a marriage has taken place. Wickham is easily persuaded as it only takes one thing."

Elizabeth looked up at him then, realising the depths of his devotion to her. That he would, thinking that her sister had left with his enemy, choose to bring about a marriage for the man who had caused him more grief in his life than any other. That Darcy was yet willing to do whatever was needed to save her family and her undeserving sister, even if that meant he would become forever brother to that self-same loathsome man. Elizabeth at once realised the haste with which she decided to end their engagement. She was grateful then for his sincere wish to help her family and for how swiftly he dismissed her premature words.

Lifting up her hands to his face, Elizabeth kissed Darcy ardently. "I love you, William."

Darcy reached up to capture one of her hands at his cheek. "And I you, but I must go if I am to find the villain before too much time has gone. Do you think Mr Gardiner and your father will be able to depart soon, or will your family have need of them?"

Realising at once that she must correct his misconception, Elizabeth quickly said, "Oh, darling, it was not Wickham with whom Lydia eloped."

"What?"

"Remember, Mr Wickham is no longer an officer with the militia. However, I regret such dreadful news. It cannot be concealed from you. My youngest sister has left all her friends—has eloped, has thrown herself into the power of—of Mr Denny."

"I thought..." Darcy was confused before he recalled their conversation at Pemberley.

"I hope you will be pleased with some news." Elizabeth then told him of her

encounter with Wickham shortly after Rosings and her challenge and confrontation. The resulting departure of Wickham, complete with the selling of his commission, was to Darcy entirely too astonishing.

He had chuckled a little as he squeezed Elizabeth's hand. "My dear, dear clever girl. Though I cannot like not knowing where he has gone, somehow I do not think he will trouble you or any of the Bennets again."

"My confrontation with Wickham might have been near enough for others to hear, namely Mrs Long," Elizabeth had confessed further, a touch of a smile on her lips.

Darcy was humoured though he shook his head. "You cannot account for some people's inclination to gossip, Elizabeth."

Nodding, Darcy said, "Yes, of course."

Together they shared a sympathetic smile, and Darcy, no longer worried about Elizabeth's previous panicked declaration, pulled her to his chest once more for a brief kiss. Elizabeth laughed, amazed that she should feel so light considering the dark cloud hovering over her home and family. With the knowledge that Darcy would not break their engagement despite the scandal Lydia had created, Elizabeth was free to feel some of the burden lift from her shoulders.

"Do not ever say you wish to end our betrothal, Elizabeth. I could bear anything but that."

Setting her head against his chest, she said, "I did—do not wish to taint your good name with the scandal my family faces."

Darcy, brushing away a few of her curls, repeated himself. "I could not bear it, Elizabeth."

Gladdened as he was that Wickham was not responsible for destroying his peace, Darcy did remember, however, the serious nature of the crisis. After another moment, he said, "Come, we ought to go inside and join your family. Though I do not know the habits of Mr Denny, I will offer whatever assistance I might in ensuring that he, too, will honour his actions with marriage."

Elizabeth nodded, and as they stood, they heard another voice address them, one that was couched in such tones as to make certain both knew the extent of the speaker's displeasure.

"You will unhand my daughter at once, Mr Darcy."

"Papa—"

"Mr Bennet—"

"Elizabeth, go on into the house and join your sisters. Your mother, as you can hear, is also in need of you. As for you, Mr Darcy, you will please do me the honour of joining me forthwith in my study."

Darcy and Elizabeth exchanged a look, sorry to have their understanding thus exposed though not exactly known to Mr Bennet just yet.

However, as the three began their walk towards the house, the sounds of another carriage could be heard pulling up the gravel lane. Rounding the turnabout, an unfamiliar hired carriage came slowly to a stop. The three exiting the garden stopped in wonder at whatever visitor had chosen such an ill time to burden Longbourn with their presence.

When the door opened, the excited and unembarrassed voice of the youngest Bennet could be heard within, urging another to quickly descend and assist her out.

Mr Bennet strode forward immediately, anger clearly on his features and clenched fists at his side. Lieutenant Denny descended, his cheeks flushed with one look at the approaching gentleman. Quickly, he turned and assisted Lydia down from the carriage.

Lydia shrieked and threw herself upon her father with glee! "Papa! Is this not a great surprise? Allow me to introduce to you"—Lydia fell into a fit of giggles—"my husband, Lieutenant Denny. We have only just arrived from London!"

Astonishment caused Elizabeth's mouth to drop open as she turned to Darcy to share in this spectacle. Darcy, uncharacteristic of his usual reserve, nearly lost his composure as humour began to pull at his lips, no doubt spurred by the degree of relief he felt that the scandal, which had caused such distress to so many, had come to such a quick and unimaginative end.

"Lydia, you will cease this display. Come, what is all this about?"

With a pout, Lydia stepped nearer her husband, whose large Adam's apple bobbed with nervousness.

"Papa! Will you not congratulate me?"

Elizabeth at that point could not believe the impudence of her sister, and embarrassment again began to make her cringe that Darcy should witness her sister's impropriety so openly.

Mr Denny then, garnering as much bravery as he could, stepped forward to bow before his father-in-law. "It is a pleasure to see you again, Mr Bennet…Father."

"'Mr Bennet' will do."

With a stiff swallow, Mr Denny nodded. "Mr Bennet."

Mr Bennet took a step to the side and, with a rigid arm, indicated the newly married couple should enter the house, an invitation they quickly and eagerly accepted. Once they had begun walking, Mr Bennet turned again towards the erstwhile garden dwellers and said, "Do not think that this has made me forget our interview, Mr Darcy. But if you will, I have another pressing matter to settle."

Darcy nodded his acknowledgement, feeling some measure of pity for the elder gentleman, considering what he might have witnessed Elizabeth and him doing in his very own gardens on top of the distress his youngest daughter had caused.

Walking alongside her father, impertinence infusing her voice by the volley of emotions of the last half hour, Elizabeth quipped, "I suppose this means you will not have to search for my sister's suitor after all."

Darcy eyed her with a twinkle as they both crossed the threshold of her home. This time, when he entered the parlour, the only sound that could be heard was Lydia's own animated description of her romantic flight to London, the special license the young groom had procured through funds from his own father—a man of property in Suffolk—and by means of a large quarterly allowance, and finally, much to the breathy sighs of the room, their hurried wedding. Looking at her dear husband, who for all the world looked as if he had swallowed something that upset his constitution —probably due to the many frowns directed his way—Lydia cooed, "And so after taking our tea in London, we have returned to Hertfordshire to share our good news with my family."

While an hour past saw Mrs Bennet in the throes of despair, this saw the same matron exclaim her joy with ecstasy. Her primary objective for many years having been to secure husbands for her five daughters, their method of securing such husbands was of little concern to Mrs Bennet as long as the task was accomplished in the end. Thus, while the rest of Lydia's family viewed her impropriety with disgust and disapproval, Mrs Bennet could not have been more pleased with Lydia's forthright means of doing her duty.

The narrative once given on all the particulars of the lovers' escapade, the conversation soon made a transition towards the future of the newly married couple. Mr Denny, rightly interpreting the meaning of the sceptical looks being bestowed upon him from Mr Bennet, hastened to explain that, though he had not obtained official leave from the militia, he had only the day of their departure submitted the requisite forms—which explained Colonel Forster's neglect in mentioning it—and whilst his plans at present were to return to the regiment in Brighton, his career in His Majesty's militia was by no means his only prospect.

Being only the second son, he made the militia his choice of profession; however, he *was* the second son of a wealthy man who had set aside a small portion of his wealth for all of his children. This news could only increase his worth in Mrs Bennet's mind while the same news did little to please his father-in-law. Mr Bennet, now relieved of the strain of Lydia's possible ruin, was now more displeased by the disturbance the two lovers' reckless actions had caused his precious peace, regardless of outcome.

As time passed and Mr Bennet began to see that this troublesome affair was soon to be put behind him—allowing once again a measure of accord within his own home—and in that Lydia had always been his least favourite daughter, the gentleman's humour began to reassert itself, at least until his eyes fell upon Mr Darcy sitting beside his second-eldest daughter.

"I had always said that I should be married before all of my sisters, and so I have!" Lydia declared with glee, unaware that none but her mother joined in her merriment.

∼

When the conversation once again turned to a recitation of Lydia and Mr Denny's escapade, for Mrs Bennet was asking for a more detailed account, Darcy saw that Mr Bennet stood and left the room. Turning towards Elizabeth, he indicated he would follow and, shortly thereafter, stood before the door to her father's book room.

Knocking and entering upon the summons from within, Darcy went to stand before Elizabeth's father. Not relishing the interview before him but knowing it to be the last hurdle before anything of lasting significance with Elizabeth could be made, Darcy prepared himself for Mr Bennet's justified wrath.

Instead, Mr Bennet sighed and waved, entreating him to sit. The whole affair with Lydia had exhausted Mr Bennet, and while he could not have approved nor enjoyed walking around the bend of his home looking for Elizabeth and seeing the same ensconced in a tender embrace with a gentleman, Mr Bennet had since cooled his temper. Elizabeth was nothing if not passionate and certainly was not of the same mind as Lydia. She would never have behaved with impropriety to secure a husband but would have only allowed the liberties with Mr Darcy—Mr Bennet cringed at the memory—had she truly loved the man stoically sitting before him.

"Tell me, Mr Darcy, do you play chess?"

Not anticipating such a direction of conversation, Darcy stuttered to answer in the affirmative.

Mr Bennet nodded, removed his glasses, and cleaned them with his handkerchief.

"And are you any good?"

Hesitating, as doubt began to make Darcy worry, he eventually said, "I am."

Elizabeth's father returned his glasses to their perch on his nose and nodded again. After a few moments, he spoke, this time with obvious dismissal, for he took up a book before him at the same time. "Then you will find in Elizabeth a formidable opponent, for she is quite good."

Darcy sat there, ignored by his companion for some minutes, unsure whether Mr Bennet had just excused him or granted him his blessing in so many words.

"I came here, Mr Bennet, to seek Elizabeth's hand."

Mr Bennet looked up over the top of his glasses. His head though remained tipped towards the book. "Yes, I gathered as much by your display in my gardens."

Darcy had the good grace to colour, but he was by no means put off his designs. "Then may I assume you will give us your blessing?"

Mr Bennet sighed, removed his glasses once again—acting for all the world the put-upon individual—and looked Elizabeth's suitor straight in the eye. "I will do this much for you. I know that Elizabeth must hold you in great esteem; indeed, I would be very much surprised if the state of her affection was less than a most ardent love. She would not have acted so otherwise. This being the case, I want her happy, and you seem to have that ability. Yes, you have my blessing to marry Elizabeth."

Darcy smiled broadly, something most precious filled his breast, and he thanked Mr Bennet with profound sincerity.

Taking up his book once again, Mr Bennet added, "Yes, yes, all you young lovers are most energetic in your gratitude. But know this, Mr Darcy. You take with you my greatest treasure. And seeing as that is not likely to give me much pleasure, please do me the courtesy now of leaving me to my thoughts."

Darcy stood, feeling some sympathy for the man for he could see that the depth of affection Mr Bennet had for Elizabeth was great and, given the circumstances, could forgive him this instance of impolitic speech. If he were in the same shoes as Mr Bennet, he might also wish for a little solitude. Still, Mr Darcy owed Elizabeth's father a great deal for what he had just gifted him, and so, before leaving, Darcy extended a hand to the older gentleman.

Mr Bennet eyed the hand before him, and warring with emotions more along the lines of begrudging respect than displeasure, he accepted the proffered hand.

Before releasing Mr Bennet's hand, Darcy looked at him squarely and said, "I promise she will always know affection and happiness if it is within my power."

Mr Bennet restricted himself to a stiff nod for his dislike at the thought of losing Elizabeth even to such a man as Mr Darcy. Darcy swiftly left the older gentleman to his solitude and sought Elizabeth. It was no surprise that, when he found her, she was still among her family, imprisoned by Lydia's narrative.

In his contentment and happiness, Darcy could not find it in him to be irritated by the repetition and communicated with a smile and the passionate look in his eyes that all had been accomplished satisfactorily during his interview with her father.

After a long while, Darcy's ardent attention to Elizabeth was interrupted when Mrs Bennet addressed him abruptly.

"Mr Darcy! Heavens, when did you arrive at Longbourn?"

Mr Darcy shared a disbelieving smile with Elizabeth before he stood and, bowing to Mrs Bennet, said, "A pleasure to see you again, ma'am."

The Gardiners, unable to restrain their amusement at the scene, began to laugh along with Elizabeth. It was soon explained that Mr Darcy had accompanied them from Derbyshire. Later that evening, Mr Bennet once again announced to the assembled individuals around his dining table of his daughter's engagement, this time Elizabeth to Mr Darcy. And once again, those in company saw Mrs Bennet collapse into a fit of astonishment.

CHAPTER 22

Devoted as they were to one another, it was no wonder that Jane and Elizabeth chose to share their wedding day in a double ceremony. Their grooms, already satisfied to exchange the title "friend" for "brother," were pleased to accommodate their brides in this manner. Darcy especially was gratified that his own engagement would be shortened, considering his friend had already set a date only a few blessed weeks away.

The only source of unease for Elizabeth during these weeks of courtship had been removed from Longbourn only days after its abrupt invasion. Mr and Mrs Denny's elopement and the subsequent scandal, in addition to Lydia's neither uninhibited nor ashamed behaviour afterwards, had been a source of extreme mortification for Elizabeth. She could not see Lydia or her husband without remembering how her world had shattered almost as soon as it had righted itself at Pemberley. Nor could she look upon Lydia's impertinence without a degree of resentment for the way the news of their elopement had made Elizabeth feel that it must free Darcy from obligation to such a family. Her interview with him in the garden, where the words that would end their betrothal ripped their way from her throat, was still a sore on her heart.

Her dearest Darcy was without a doubt the best of men for his absolute refusal, and still more so, his wish to aid her family despite his initial assumption that Lydia had run off with Mr Wickham.

Though they since had discussed many topics, Elizabeth and Darcy, by unspoken mutual agreement, had not brought up that agonizing day. And since the couple responsible for the drama of that day was required to return to Brighton, the constant source of Elizabeth's discomfort was quickly removed, allowing Darcy and her once again to enjoy the bliss of their companionship without any hue of unhappiness.

When the day that was fixed to make Elizabeth and Darcy the happiest of couples was merely days away, Elizabeth struck upon a notion. With a sly smile, she set about to accomplish her task and secreted herself in her chambers, the gentlemen being engaged in sport and unlikely to call.

Retrieving her letters, Elizabeth spread them out before her. With fondness, she now perused them again. Even those born of heartbreak and anger could hold no sting in her heart, for since the reconciliation came about at Pemberley, Elizabeth and Darcy's understanding of one another had grown.

Taking up the first of his letters, Elizabeth laughed softly in amusement at his writing her so soon upon their introduction. His account of his carriage troubles and subsequent "headache" brought a smile to her lips. His kind apology for the intemperate and impolite words spoken on her behalf at the assembly was heartfelt. Elizabeth allowed herself to wonder whether, had he uttered that apology in person early on, the course of their history might have been different. With a shake of her head, Elizabeth set pen to paper to reply.

Dear Sir,

I do recall being introduced to you last evening. And I thank you for your kind explanation regarding your poor mood and manners. It is a comfort to know you find me neither tolerable nor lacking in temptation.

I shall only add that my initial favourable impression of your fine looks remains.

Regards,
Miss Elizabeth Bennet

With a chuckle, Elizabeth blew gently on the parchment and, once assured the ink was dry, set about folding and sealing the missive. With a twinkle in her eye, she addressed the missive to her beloved via the direction of Netherfield.

Taking up the next letters, Elizabeth replied to them as well. They were written while he struggled with his admiration and attraction to her as she stayed to nurse Jane at Netherfield. *"Is it not enough that you haunt my dreams? Must you now stay under the same roof?"* Elizabeth laughed aloud though her cheeks pinked with maidenly modesty. To this, Elizabeth wrote:

Mr Darcy,

I beg your forgiveness for intruding so horribly upon your place of residence in addition to your dream state. It was never my intention to disturb you so. As I have unwittingly breached this wall of privacy, you might tell my dream self that she is unwelcome, for
I cannot do anything at present about her existence.

Pausing, she recalled his expressed wish to kiss her. His later accusation that she had cast a spell on him once more brought Elizabeth's pen to her paper, even as she laughed again.

I cannot reply to your inquiry regarding what manner of spell I cast upon you, for I am unaware of any ancestors within the world of witchcraft. Do allow me to research the family Bible to find the connexion, and until then, forgive me for again so unfairly, though unwittingly, subjecting you to my unknown skills in wizardry.

Sincerely,
Elizabeth Bennet

The second letter written while she was in residence at Netherfield was another source of amusement as she replied:

Forgive me, sir, for not informing you of my whereabouts within the house. Had I known you were searching so earnestly for me, I would certainly not have put you to so much trouble. Furthermore, I shall remember not to distract you so unfairly by fiddling with the curl near my ear. How inconsiderate of me!

In a fit of giggles, blushing cheeks, and discarded first attempts, Elizabeth set about answering all of Darcy's letters. At first, her motivation was to amuse him, but as the process took her through more poignant and tender missives, her own heart began to fill the page with what she could only hope were letters equally as poignant to Darcy as his were to her.

His last letter, held in the tips of her fingers, gave Elizabeth some pause. He had written he had decided to give her up, or at least the pain she had inflicted on him, and use her inspiration to become a better man.

Humbled and warmed by his tender ardour, Elizabeth bent her head to write again.

∼

Miss Bingley's complaints and slights against the neighbourhood grated upon Darcy's ears, yet propriety required that he remain through her diatribe. *Good manners be damned!* Darcy nearly had quitted the room when a footman entered the parlour at Netherfield, interrupting her lengthy account of her fatiguing travels from London.

Her arrival that evening required the gentlemen to dine at Netherfield and reluctantly decline the dinner invitation from Longbourn that had been delivered earlier in the day while they were shooting. Looking towards Bingley, Darcy half smiled as their eyes met. Even Charles's easy nature was misused, listening to his sister's complaints when *his* Miss Bennet was a mere three miles away and without him.

Miss Bingley's appalled outburst brought both gentlemen's attention to her once again, and seeing that the footman had only delivered a silver salver of the post for her perusal as acting hostess now that she had arrived, Darcy could not account for such a sound of disgust.

"Good heavens, Darcy! Are the Bennets incapable of succinct communication?" The gentleman, with studied ennui, waited to hear her next protestation. "Your Miss Eliza will bankrupt you if she requires so much parchment to write her missives," Miss Bingley jibed.

The smile that might have disappeared at her disparaging remarks about Elizabeth's family returned in full measure as Darcy took up the letters from Miss Bingley's hand. He nearly laughed aloud as he flipped through the folded correspondence, equalling a dozen in count—exactly the number he had secretly written her throughout the course of their acquaintance.

His fingers burned with eagerness to open the letters immediately. With hardly a word, Darcy excused himself for the evening.

He had barely gone beyond the parlour doors when his friend stopped him.

"See here, Darcy, are you certain those letters from Longbourn are all for you?" Bingley said hopefully. "Surely, there is one for me among the lot."

Darcy walked back a few steps and, with an unapologetic smile, patted Bingley on the shoulder. "I am sorry, friend. Your only companionship this evening will have to be your relations. These are all addressed to me. You might consider writing Miss Bennet *first* if you wish for a reply."

"Excellent idea, Darcy!" Then as the thought struck him, he asked, "Are those letters really *all* from Miss Elizabeth?"

Darcy laughed, thinking of the possibilities that might be contained within the folded papers in his hand. With a nod, he answered Bingley. "Yes, all. And in reply to those I sent her."

Bingley's brows shot up. "Good gracious, Darcy. Was it necessary to write so many?"

"Absolutely necessary, my friend," Darcy replied with an enigmatic smile. "But you will excuse me. I have pressing business."

Charles laughed, and mumbling to himself something about *"precious business"* more likely, he entered the parlour again, only to inform his sister that he would not be rejoining her that evening, recalling a letter he ought to dispatch.

Miss Bingley nearly howled at the injustice. If it would not have caused a scandal not to attend her brother's wedding, she would have rather stayed in London. Thank goodness, she only need endure another few days, and then the unfortunate event would be over, despite all her efforts nearly a year before. As far as Darcy was concerned, she refused to think on it, for she was quite vexed enough.

∽

Taking the stairs two at a time, Darcy spun around the corner baluster and up the next flight to his chambers, nearly disgracing himself in his haste as his booted feet lost purchase of the slick and recently waxed floors.

Upon entering his suite of rooms, Darcy pulled immediately upon the folds of his cravat with one hand as he bent over the massive bed to sort through the letters with the other. They each held a small number at the corner below his name, and Darcy quickly set about putting them in numerical order.

A knock from his dressing room door sounded, and Darcy eagerly welcomed his valet. "My good man, hurry and help me with this blasted knot."

Perkins made swift work of the garment despite the mess Darcy had made of it in his fevered attempts to remove it. Soon his coat was also dispatched along with his waistcoat and boots. When finally in his shirtsleeves, he waved the man away for the evening and eagerly took up the letters. With the assurance of Elizabeth's hand, his heart pounded in anticipation.

Darcy lit a lamp near an armchair then poured himself a glass of port. Once assured of adequate illumination and refreshment, Darcy lowered himself into the chair with all the grace of a toddler awaiting a treat.

Placing the remaining eleven back on the stand, Darcy pressed a finger along the fold of the first and broke the seal, a smile already fixed upon his features. As he read Elizabeth's playful reply to his letter after the Meryton assembly, he laughed out loud, the sound echoing in the empty room.

Good heavens, but she is adorably delightful. He could just picture her chestnut curls bent over her writing desk penning such a reply to him. In his mind's eye, he also saw himself bending over her seated form and bestowing a small kiss on her nape, right on the birthmark that had tempted him at Rosings, lingering there as he inhaled her lavender scent. With a groan, Darcy closed his eyes, consoling himself in the knowledge that he did not have many more nights before he could act on such musings.

As he worked his way through Elizabeth's letters, the reminder of those moments in which he wrote the corresponding letters came easily to his mind. He vividly recalled the lonely winter nights in London after leaving Netherfield, sitting at his desk after a tedious evening out only to succumb to the need to alleviate his longing by writing to her. How differently those memories now felt looking at her replies—tangible proof now that he could secure in only two days a promise of never feeling alone again.

Her missives wove around those memories and softened their raw edges even while they began to be wrapped in the warmth of her regard. Darcy noted too that, as his own addresses to her had become more personal, so did her salutations. While she wrote each letter as if replying in real time to when they were written, Darcy felt the sweetness of her words touch his heart.

She also wrote of the things that engaged her during that cold winter's separation. How many times had Darcy sat in his London home or in any number of other locales wondering what she was doing, to whom she was talking, or what thoughts occupied her mind? To read from her script the events of her family, the wedding of Mrs Collins, and her festive holiday with the Gardiners helped to close that separation. It was almost as if they had not spent those months apart now that he had these responses.

He cringed reading the next, recalling his state when he wrote her upon his first arrived at Rosings and his initial disturbance discovering her proximity in the neighbourhood. However, her response and perspective on their time together at Rosings went some way towards calming that pulsing regret.

> *You say that my companionship during our walks has been like a salve to your longing heart. How heartily sorry I am not to have recognised it. You are a very clever man, and while our conversations frequently confused me*

(or even irritated me), I will admit to enjoyment in walking the grounds with you. I cannot say that, when next I visit Rosings, I shall be glad to have a better knowledge of the place, but I certainly shall be glad if that knowledge comes once again by means of your companionship.

Knowing as he did what had been contained in many of his next letters, and considering the state of extreme emotion, and then disappointment, he was suffering then, Darcy nearly wished he could skip those letters. But the delicate script beckoned him, his name written at her hand keeping him from the coward's path.

Again, I must apologize for my heated defence of Mr Wickham. He is not a tenth the man you are and never will be. A practiced liar is what he is, and your worth is infinitely greater, if only I had seen it sooner.

Darcy closed his eyes as her words filled a gap he had not known existed. His sister had been deceived, Elizabeth had been deceived, and his own father had been deceived. He had wondered whether he had been deficient in some part of his being for so many of those he held dear having at one time favoured Wickham over himself.

I am forever indebted to that part of you that cannot find the ability to hate me, for it is that part that kept you loving me. And it is your love, Fitzwilliam Darcy, that has freed me!

Resting back against the armchair, Darcy rubbed at his stinging eyes. All this, he ought to know now, considering her words at Pemberley, and any doubt washed away with their engagement, yet Darcy would never begrudge any opportunity Elizabeth might take to remind him of her regard for him.

With a whole and contented heart, he took up the twelfth letter, a little saddened that he was at the last.

Dearest William,

Having so little experience in the composition of love letters, I hope you will forgive me if this one does not convey to you the sincerity that resides in my heart.

This letter is meant to be in reply to the last of the letters that, so unexpectedly and mysteriously, were delivered to me. By the by, I wonder whether we shall ever discover how they came to be posted, for it is quite a delicate thing to investigate without giving away the impropriety engendered in writing them—but I digress! You see, William? I am no fine letter writer as you are. My letters shall never hold the poignancy of spirit and emotion that yours do. However, I shall attempt now to do my very best.

I could easily respond to the warmth and ardency you painted in this, your last letter. I could respond to the declarations of devotion, despite the accompaniment of hope that ought to have been there but was not. I could even say something of the most excellent man you are, even without the necessity of becoming better as you so desired and expressed in the words of that letter.

But I shall not. For you see, my own heart requires that I express to you the unmatched power your words have had over me. They have taught me the strength of your heart, the value of your love, and the gift that it is. When I first discovered them in the post, my heart nearly leapt from my chest. True, the surprise of such an unexpected delivery was to blame, but so too was the joy of connexion that I felt then. It was a connexion I had not anticipated ever being bestowed upon me again.

The last words penned by your hand on the last of those most precious pieces of paper were, "Yours forevermore, Darcy" and since I cannot claim to be any more eloquent, I simply will have to borrow your words as my own because, from this time forth, I am yours forevermore.

With all the words in my heart that I cannot write adequately,
Elizabeth Bennet

In case you have any difficulty, I shall be the one at the church dressed in pale blue, and you shall recognise me by the happiness in my eyes.

When that much-anticipated day came two mornings later, Darcy eagerly stood at the front of the church, watching for the lady dressed in pale blue. When she appeared, his heart danced, and his eyes mirrored the happiness that indeed showed there. He thought of her letters and also his own. How surprised his past self might have been to know that putting pen to paper to write Elizabeth would one day bring them together, and the very thing he had considered a weakness was his greatest asset.

The ceremony and celebration afterwards were background music to the symphony Darcy felt in his chest. He had known true happiness when he had bent over the parish registry to sign under Elizabeth's name—the last time she would ever sign it with the name "Bennet."

He had never expected to receive replies to his letters to her. And when he had received them, they were a most pleasant surprise. They also sparked within Darcy an idea that he set forth to accomplish during the two days before his wedding, requiring more than one trip into Meryton for supplies.

That evening, Darcy thanked his servants and dismissed them for the night, his voice barely able to keep its normally sedate timbre. Then turning to his new bride, Darcy sat beside her on the sofa in the cottage he had rented for their first night as man and wife.

Taking her hand, Darcy said, "I have something for you, Elizabeth."

Her eyes then met his, and it took nearly all of his strength not to get ahead of himself and embrace her. Passing her a small folded parchment, Darcy said, "I wrote you a letter."

Elizabeth laughed then, a little of the tension leaving her shoulders. "I should have known you would."

She opened the letter and read the words aloud. "'I should like to kiss you now.'"

A smile pulled at those peach temptations, and Elizabeth playfully met his gaze. She nodded. He wasted no time at all in securing the kiss requested. To his satisfaction, Elizabeth looked slightly disappointed when he pulled away.

Quickly, he pulled from his breast pocket another folded missive.

"'I should like to kiss you again.'"

A peel of laughter rang out, and this time she eagerly leaned closer to him so that he might again claim that which he had requested. Reaching into his pocket, Darcy passed her yet another note, and their heads rested together as they caught their breath after this second kiss.

"'And again,'" she read in a whisper and then, with a laugh, pulled back to look at him, her innocent hands already reaching to pat across the pockets of his waistcoat, totally unaware of this action's effect on the gentleman. "Good heavens, William, how many of these am I to expect?"

Darcy laughed then, a little huskily and, surprising her, twisted around to pull a basket from behind the sofa. With a roguish smirk, he poured the contents of it onto her lap. The silky sound of paper on paper filled the room as dozens of folded parchments tumbled from the basket like water from a fall. Elizabeth laughed with utter disbelief at his romantic and silly notions as her fingers gathered in scoops, letter after a letter.

"How many letters you must write, Mr Darcy. How odious!" Elizabeth managed to tease, even as her heart rate sped at the thought of so many kisses, her body becoming intoxicated with the idea.

"I did not want to run out," he whispered as he bent to capture her lips again.

"Then come here, you dear man!" Elizabeth said as boldness took hold of her senses and she wrapped her arms about his neck to pull him to her.

Few words, either written or spoken, were communicated for a long while after that.

EPILOGUE

Elizabeth Darcy eyed with a smile the note that sat in the sewing basket beside her. What had started as a means to communicate his feelings prior to their marriage soon became a private source of tenderness after. On occasion, her husband still wrote to her and would still post them, regardless of the fact that, in the three years since they spoke their vows, they had been separated no longer than a few hours during the day. What his servants thought of their master doing so, Elizabeth could only guess.

She did note that even Mr Carroll broke with his accustomed reserve to go so far as to smile slightly when he delivered any letters Elizabeth received if, contained within them, was one from her own husband.

His letters were usually those of love, occasionally of passion, but always of heartfelt emotion. She did not always write him back; however, she was always careful to make certain he knew exactly how pleased she was to receive his missives.

They had never figured out how the initial twelve had ever come to be posted despite subtle inquisitions of the staff. Around the time they would have been posted, Mr Carroll had said he thought that perhaps a mishap with a maid might have brought it about. But neither Elizabeth nor Darcy understood how that could be, as none were ever permitted in his study except to deliver a tray of tea or refreshments. Due to the delicacy of the topic, they had not pressed further, and when the result of the mystery was as fortunate as it was, Elizabeth and her husband had decided it mattered little in the end whether it were ever solved.

Looking towards his latest letter again, Elizabeth laughed a little as she recalled what it contained. While it was still in its essence a love letter, her husband had also written of a piece of news he had learned from his cousin Colonel Fitzwilliam.

It seemed at least the mystery surrounding the disappearance of Mr Wickham would be solved. Colonel Fitzwilliam, during one of his travels on military errands, had come across the former Miss Ellicott of Wiltshire, now owning the name of Mrs Wickham. Surprised as he was, and frankly a little concerned for the lady, Colonel Fitzwilliam conducted a small investigation of his own surrounding her union with Mr Wickham. With humour abounding, the colonel had shared the story with his cousin.

Mr Wickham, having apparently put himself out as a wealthy gentleman with connexions still wealthier due to his childhood near Pemberley, sought and caught the eye of a gentleman in Wiltshire in need of marrying off his only daughter. Unbeknownst to Wickham, that gentleman was not the wealthy landowner *he* presented himself to be, nor was his daughter the heiress Wickham believed of her. In the end, the two deceived each other, and a union was made. To the dissatisfaction of both, the truth of their empty pockets was learned too late. Mr Ellicott, being in poor health already, passed away not long afterwards, leaving his estate to his new son-in-law—though little did it profit Wickham, for it was heavily in debt. However, Colonel Fitzwilliam gleefully explained that, with prudence and a strict schedule of retrenchment, their childhood friend— now a landed gentleman—could see some little gains from his initial ruse in the short span of only ten years.

Elizabeth could not help the laughter that once again poured forth from her at recalling the details of the letter. After a few minutes, with a pleased smile, Elizabeth took up her embroidery again.

A little flutter in her belly brought her from any lingering humour-filled thoughts regarding the fate of Wickham. In fact all thought of any sort vanished as Elizabeth stilled to focus her attention on the unexpected but hoped for feeling, willing it to occur again. A second flutter caused her hand to fly to her stomach, hardly rounded at all, yet the babe growing inside so very real in her life all of a sudden. Once again, the flutter was felt, and Elizabeth's smile grew great, even as her heart's song, that rumbling cello, drew long low tones of contentment. She had hoped this feeling of quickening might have occurred soon, but since a small measure of hope was all she could hold to, she tried her best not to think too much on it. Until she knew for certain, she had not chosen to inform her husband of the good news.

They had already suffered many losses in their attempts to become parents. Each new heartbreak was a devastating nightmare that they only survived through the steadfastness of each other's devotion. Never had the changes that marked a new pregnancy lasted this long before. Always the telltale signs of loss would appear, tearing from Elizabeth the hope of motherhood once again. It was hard, too, on Darcy, for Elizabeth could recall the pain valiantly hidden in his eyes as they attended the christenings of both of Jane and Bingley's children. It hardly seemed fair, given the pain that marked their early acquaintance, that they should not always be blessed with happiness forever after.

This time, Elizabeth had been extra vigilant in her care, and with her always, a suspended hope hovered as the confinement progressed.

Her mind sent silent messages of love now to the little being inside her, a feeling of peace and contentment filling her in a way she had never felt in the times before. It was as if the babe had heard her mind's messages of love and resounded with its own message. Elizabeth could not explain it, but in that moment, she knew all would be well this time. Her gaze drifted up from where her hand pressed against her middle, and it caught again on the letter.

With a smile, Elizabeth stood and, moving from the sofa to the writing desk, took up a quill and a fresh sheet of paper. It was only correct, given their history, that she should inform Darcy of his pending fatherhood by means of a letter.

When she had finished, she pulled the bell near the desk and was soon waited upon by Mr Carroll. "I wonder if you might tell me, has my husband returned yet from his errands?"

The butler bowed and, with a nod, replied, "He has and is currently working in the study. Shall I inform him you wish to speak to him?"

Elizabeth smiled and lifted the letter in her hands. "That will not be necessary. But if you will, do deliver this letter to him."

With a barely discernible smile, the butler bowed again and took up the letter to deliver to Mr Darcy.

Elizabeth waited a few minutes, listening to the sounds outside the door. Her smile began and soon broadened as only a few minutes brought the sound of quickened boot steps falling on the hardwood passage. The speed of the steps increased, and Elizabeth imagined her husband might have broken with his usual restraint and allowed himself to run. The next sound could only be that of his boots as they slid to a stop.

Elizabeth sat upright, preparing herself for Darcy's entrance. The door did not open immediately, and Elizabeth could only guess the thoughts running through her husband's mind then. When the door swung open, his face was a mixture of incredulous delight and something indescribable. He might have even been said to be a little pale, though Elizabeth could not be certain since her eyes were fixed upon his, and the silent communion they held there for a short few seconds transfixed her.

Still Darcy said nothing. Slowly he walked towards her, and this time her heart along with the little child inside fluttered. With reverence, he bent to his knees, and soon his large hands stole up her legs to hold her about the waist. Elizabeth's eyes filled with tears as he bent his head to rest his brow against the silk of the dress covering her abdomen. She had expected excitement, a shout of joy perhaps. But she should have known her husband; a man not of many words—at least spoken—would communicate his feelings most reverently.

A tear fell from her lashes to darken the curls of his head, and her hand came up to comb through them sweetly. When he lifted his head to look at her, the sight of his own eyes watery with emotion caused Elizabeth to hiccup through a short laugh, her smile weak with the strength of her own feelings.

His eyes questioned, and she nodded. "I have felt the babe move."

Her husband then coughed, the emotion filling his eyes also choking off any words. "So you are…we are…?"

Elizabeth could only manage to nod, now too overcome to speak. Darcy stood then and pulled her firmly against him.

Finally, he found his voice and spoke softly into her ear. "My dearest, loveliest Elizabeth…"

THE END

ACKNOWLEDGMENTS

When one has a million kids as I do, it is natural to equate everything else in one's life to childhood, parenting or the like. When I first *conceived* of this book plot, the storyline was still in its *infancy*. The aid and encouragement of many convinced me to attempt to *rear* it until it was fully *grown* as a novel.

The supportive family at Quills & Quartos were essential to the upbringing and rerelease of this novel. I value their support and encouragement greatly. Every mother err author needs a friend in her corner.

Also, every child ought also to have such a devoted mentor as this book has had in my editor, Christina Boyd. I was contrary at times, petulant many times and outright obstinate too. And yet in the end the result is a well groomed, well developed novel. Thank you.

While writing this book I was also gestating madly on my millionth kid. So it cannot go without saying that my family deserves my sincere gratitude for enduring my emotional bursts, fits of insanity and manic behavior – along with the pregnancy. They are no doubt relieved this book has joined its siblings previous published, even as this baby joins the rest of family.

Lastly I must save my thanks for my darling girl, Jane Austen. I am not you. I cannot write as well as you. I am quite possibly delusional to attempt it. And yet, I thank you for your remarkable work that has inspired me to try.

ABOUT THE AUTHOR

KaraLynne began writing horrible poetry as an angst-filled youth. It was a means to express the exhilaration and devastation she felt every time her adolescent heart was newly in love with "the one" and then broken every other week. As her frontal lobe developed, she grew more discerning of both men and writing. She has been married to her own dreamboat of a best friend, Andrew, for 17 years. Together they have the migraine-inducing responsibility of raising five children to not be dirt bags (fingers crossed), pick up their socks (still a work in progress), not fight with each other (impossible task) and become generally good people (there's hope). She loves escaping into a book, her feather babies (the regal hens of Cluckingham Palace), and laughter.

She has written four books and participated in many anthologies including: Falling For Mr. Darcy; Bluebells in the Mourning; Haunting Mr. Darcy: A Spirited Courtship; Yours Forevermore, Darcy; The Darcy Monologues; Rational Creatures; & Sun-Kissed: Effusions of Summer.

For more information about new releases, sales and promotions on books by KaraLynne and other great authors, please visit www.QuillsandQuartos.com

ALSO BY KARALYNNE MACKRORY

Haunting Mr Darcy - A Spirited Courtship
2015 IPPY Bronze Medal Winner in Romance

What happens to the happily ever after when the ever after has already happened? A "spirited" courtship indeed! Jane Austen's much adored Pride and Prejudice is transfigured in this Regency adaptation. That fickle friend Fate intervenes when an unexpected event threatens the happily ever after of literature's favorite love story.

The gentlemen from Netherfield have left, winter is upon the land, and after a horrifying carriage accident, Elizabeth Bennet finds her spirit transported as if by magic into Mr. Darcy's London home. Paranormally tethered to the disagreeable man, it doesn't help that he believes she is a phantasm of his love-struck mind and not the real Elizabeth. Somehow they must learn to trust, learn to love and learn to bring Elizabeth back to her earthly form before it is too late.

Bluebells in the Mourning

Jane Austen's beloved Pride and Prejudice is readapted in this regency tale of love in the face of tragedy. Mr. Darcy is thwarted in his attempt to propose to Elizabeth Bennet at Hunsford when he encounters her minutes after she receives the sad news from Longbourn of her sister's death. His gallantry and compassion as he escorts her back to Hertfordshire begins to unravel the many threads of her discontent with him. While her family heals from their loss, Darcy must search London for answers – answers that might bring justice, but might also just mark the end of his own hopes with Elizabeth. Is it true that nothing can be lost that love cannot find?

Falling for Mr Darcy

The simple truth is proven that sometimes a gentleman never knows his heart until a lady comes along to introduce it to him. When Mr. Darcy encounters Elizabeth Bennet injured after a fall, his concern for her welfare cracks the shell of his carefully guarded heart, and a charming man emerges. Elizabeth sees an appealing side of him she never believed possible from the stoic, proud master of Pemberley. They find the simple gentlemanly act of assisting her home will test both Mr. Darcy's resolve to keep his heart safe and Elizabeth's conviction that this is the last man on earth she might have ever been prevailed upon to marry. Soon, falling for Mr. Darcy becomes a real possibility.

Printed in Great Britain
by Amazon